PREDOMINANCE

Predominance Novels
P.O. Box 426, Revere, MA 02151
Visit our Web site at www.predominancenovels.com

First Edition: June 2014

This book is a work of fiction. Names, characters, places, and incidents either are products of the author's imagination or are used fictitiously. Any resemblance to actual events or locales or persons, living or dead, is entirely coincidental.

Defaz, H. I., 1979-
Predominance: a novel / by H. I. Defaz. — 1st ed.
p. cm.
Summary: After volunteering for radical medical procedure that might just save his life, Victor Bellator becomes paranormally gifted with the power of telekinesis, but soon he learns that the same force, now-fueling his new abilities, is slowly taking away his humanity, and will soon warp him into an unfeeling being, too dangerous to be kept alive.

ISBN-10: 0692235558
ISBN-13: 978-0692235553
Library of Congress Registration Number: TXu1-891-575
10 9 8 7 6 5 4 3 2 1

Printed in the United States of America

PREDOMINANCE

H.J. Defaz

PREDOMINANCE NOVELS, BOSTON

For my Wife Yelena,
without whose support and encouragement this book
would still be just an unsettling dream from which she
awakened me one night.

CONTENTS

To every action there is always opposed an equal reaction.

Sir Isaac Newton

Chapter 1

Waking Up to Painful Memories

THE SOUND OF the storm brought me abruptly out of unconsciousness. Neurons began to fire in my brain with each thudding raindrop that hit the tin roof above me. It stunned me to realize that I could track every single one of them as they lit off. The rust and moisture that saturated the air also reached my sore senses: I could taste the bitterness, like an old coin had been shoved in my mouth. My confusion increased as my eyes flew open to the darkness of the empty shack. The right side of my face, pressed against the dusty floorboards, hurt just as much as the rest of my body did. It felt like I'd been lying there for days. Maybe I had been. I examined the wood grain of the nearest board in almost microscopic detail for a moment, and determined that it had been milled at least fifty years before using a five-tooth-per-inch, three-foot circular saw powered by a diesel engine.

I groaned as I rolled onto my back and stared up through the darkness at the ceiling, frightened by the knowledge, trying to remember how I had come to this place. But my memories were shattered, my nerves shot. It didn't occur to me at the time to wonder how my eyes were collecting enough photons to see so clearly in the dead of night, in the middle of a rainstorm.

After finding the strength to haul myself up to a sitting position, I noticed something that made my heart race even faster. My shirt had been torn to rags, and blood had distorted its original color. Concerned, I checked myself for injuries, but found nothing. The blood wasn't mine. This did not, however, put me at ease. On the contrary, it worried me even more; I winced at the bright slaughterhouse smell.

What's happening to me? The question rumbled through my head as I considered the strange connections my senses were making with my surroundings. *Sharpness* and *acuity* and *accuracy* were words too weak to describe my current level of sensory perception. Yet it wasn't until I felt a vague disturbance in the air pressure and looked over my shoulder that I realized I wasn't alone in the shack. A young woman lay unconscious or asleep on the floor. She too had bloodstains on her clothes; but although she looked like she'd gone through hell, she appeared to be unharmed. I could tell from the smell that the blood wasn't hers; it was human, but male.

Staring at her, pressing my hands to my temples in the face of the sensory onslaught, I couldn't help but notice how attractive she was. The long red curls that rested on the side of her chiseled face contrasted with her milky-white skin, which seemed almost airbrushed. *Who was she?* And more importantly, what was she doing here? I fought hard to remember, but everything remained unclear. My head was spinning and I felt exhausted, as if I'd just run a marathon carrying weights on my shoulders. I could feel the lactic acid poisoning my muscle fibers. I was also starving; I felt like I hadn't eaten in days. I was shaky, my mouth dry and bitter, and my body had already started to break down muscle tissue for energy. I knew without thinking about it that I'd already lost 1.23 pounds, and had no significant body fat left.

But none of that mattered as much as the acute increase in sensory perception I was experiencing. All my senses—sight, hearing, smell, touch, taste, balance, even the sense of where my body parts were and how I carried myself (*proprioception*, my brain supplied helpfully) had been somehow intensified. I could close my eyes and literally *feel* everything around me.

But my coordination betrayed me the moment I tried to rise to my feet; I ended up on my hands and knees instead. The bitter taste in my mouth made my lower jaw tingle with nausea, and a disgusting yellowish bile splashed out of my mouth and onto the floorboards. After my body's expulsion of the revolting stuff, I began to feel better, or at least strong enough to get up and lumber around the room. The shack was pretty much empty with the exception of a few broken crates, some old newspapers strewn on the floor, and a big old pot, which was now catching rainwater from the leaky roof.

Hoping to find a clue as to where I was, I stumbled to the only unboarded window and peered out. But the rain had been accompanied by an impenetrable bank of fog, adding to the already spooky atmosphere of the pitch-black night.

Refocusing my eyes on the cloudy window, I used it as a mirror and considered my reflection. I looked just like I felt: like crap. My face was tired and strained, and my eyes were bloodshot. Not a pretty sight, especially for someone like me. You see, my Sicilian heritage has endowed me with these big, bold, brown eyes that—although rated as attractive by some— most people would consider to be extremely intimidating. But that wasn't the case *that* night. My eyes were weary, and they looked almost as black as the night.

Come on, Victor! I encouraged myself, rubbing my eyes with the heels of my hands. "*Wake up!*" I yelled, hoping this was just another one of my nightmares. But as the echoes of my words crashed through the vault of my skull, and I ran my fingers through my thick black hair—another gift of my Sicilian heritage—I realized this nightmare was real.

The girl on the floor moaned suddenly, and turned over onto her back. I knew she had to know what was happening, yet the notion of finding out the truth suddenly slid a chill down my spine. It was as if I was subconsciously afraid to remember.

I turned back to the window and embraced myself, shivering.

And then it hit me: The pain in my head was gone! The horrible pain that had tormented me for years was *gone!*

Three years before, I'd sustained a major head injury in an automobile accident. The physical and psychological aftermath of that event had haunted me since, but probably not as much as the painful memory of how it happened.

My best friend Xavier and I had decided to drive home from school for winter break—a four-hour trip from Utica, New York to Weehawken, New Jersey. We wanted to spend the holidays with our families, who hadn't seen much of us for the previous six months, due to our hectic schedules. Xavier studied management, while I was the geek in the mathematics/physics program; and though we shared a few classes together, that wasn't the basis of our friendship. Xavier and I met not long after my father decided to sell our old house and move us out of the neighborhood I was born into. I was twelve years old at the time, and I was heartbroken. Everything that I ever knew and loved was in that neighborhood, and when we left, I knew I was never going back again.

That was the real purpose of my father's decision to move, which had not been made based on typical circumstances.

My mother left us when I was six, and my father didn't take it well. He was devastated, yet never lost hope that one day, she'd come back. But after six years of waiting, his hope became a dagger that twisted in his heart every time he thought of her. He used to say that everything reminded him of her, so I guess he figured that the only way to remove the dagger from his heart was to leave all the memories behind.

What he didn't count on was the fact that memories, unlike people, don't live in houses or neighborhoods. They live in you. And no matter where you go, you always take them with you. After we settled in our new home, a hundred miles away from our old one, I became depressed, especially when it came time to go back to school. It was then that I met Xavier. He befriended me and helped me through the most difficult transition of my life. After being my best friend through middle school, high school, and college, he became the closest thing I'd ever had to a brother.

But I digress. Xavier seemed pretty happy to be heading home to his family's Christmas party—which despite my protests, he kept inviting me to. The truth is, I don't like crowded places. I'm not claustrophobic or anything; I just like to keep to myself, and that wasn't a possibility in Xavier's house. He had a very big family. He was the third of five brothers and sisters, his parents had never divorced, and all his grandparents were still alive—not to mention his aunts and uncles and all the annoying neighbors who were going to be there too. So it wasn't really my kind of scene. Besides, I wasn't going to be alone for the holidays; I was coming home to my lonely yet lovable drunkard of a father, who was all the family I'd ever needed— which was pretty lucky, considering he was the only family I ever got.

After finally getting Xavier out of his dorm room, I helped him stuff the back of his beat-up station wagon with our bags and a whole bunch of Christmas presents, which presented a challenge when it came time to close the hatchback door. "Maybe we should strap the bags on top of the car. What do you think?" Xavier asked.

"No way! You don't have a luggage rack."

"So?"

"So without a flat surface on top of the roof, you won't have the stability to strap them down tightly enough. Not to mention that it would produce enough wind resistance to considerably increase our gas costs. Plus, it could more than double our ETA."

"Are you running your stupid numbers again?"

"No," I lied, "and numbers are not stupid!"

Xavier used to hate the fact that I related everything to mathematics. But what can I say? It was my passion and my way of making sense of the world...though I have to admit I could become quite annoying about it. But I didn't let that stop me from giving Xavier a hard time, or vice-versa. "Can you *please* forget about your stupid equations for just one day? Besides, we're supposed to be feeling the holiday spirit," he noted, getting behind the wheel after finally getting the rear door closed. "So please! Don't make me throw you out of a moving vehicle in the middle of the highway. All right?"

"Fair enough," I chuckled.

"What the hell is an ETA, anyway?"

I couldn't help but laugh as he drove away.

We knew the trip was going to be rough. A big snowstorm had already struck New York, and it was moving in our direction. We started to see the snowfall as soon as we hit I-90 East, but it didn't seem bad at first, so we didn't pay too much attention to it.

"Listen, I know I already asked, and you said no, but I really think that you and your dad should come over and spend Christmas Eve with us," Xavier offered yet again. "There's going to be plenty of food, and you guys can open some of your Christmas presents with us, and—"

"I appreciate it," I interjected. "But you know my dad… He's not what you'd call a people person. Besides, we have our own traditions for the holidays."

"Oh yeah, I know!" Xavier cast me a disapproving look. "But I don't think that listening to a Barry Manilow *drown-me-in-the-ocean-'cause-I'm-so-depressed* song while downing a bottle of Scotch is the best way to celebrate the holidays."

"Oh, come on," I countered defensively. "He's not that bad." Which was a lie.

"I'm just saying, man. I love your dad, don't get me wrong, but he gets *real* depressed around this time of year."

Though Xavier had pointed out the obvious, I couldn't help justifying my dad's behavior. "He's like an old dog, you know? He's not going to change. Besides, it's what makes him happy."

"Torturing himself while getting drunk makes him happy?" He took turns watching the road and giving me his *are-you-serious?* look.

"Can we change the subject?" I countered again.

"Whatever," he said, before giving me the silent treatment for the next few miles.

"*Lay Me Down*," I said out of the blue.

"Huh?" He frowned.

"The Barry Manilow song that my dad listens to. It's *Lay Me Down*."

"Riiiiight." He shook his head as if giving up on my stubbornness.

Nightfall caught up with us just before we reached the fork with I-87 South. I kept scanning for a clear radio station, but kept getting the same annoying static every time I turned the dial. "Will you knock it off?" Xavier complained. "Nothing's coming through, dude."

I didn't respond; I just turned the radio off and sighed. I couldn't believe how much snow had fallen in the past five minutes alone. The blizzard had turned the road into a mess of sleet and ice; yet nothing was as bad as the visibility, which was nearly zero. The windshield wipers were going at full speed, and the defroster was blasting at full power, but neither seemed to help with our visibility problem. By the time we switched highways, we were no longer able to see the vehicles around us, let alone the dividing lines on the road. A short horizon and the highway barrier were our only points of reference.

"I think we should stop," I advised Xavier, who was growing nervous behind the wheel.

"Stop where?" he yelped, "in the middle of the road?"

"I don't know. Just pull over!" I insisted.

"And then what?" he demanded. "No! We have to find an exit, a rest area, or something. Stopping in the middle of the road would be just as dangerous as continuing to drive."

Though I understood the logic in his words, I could also see the fear growing in his eyes. The blizzard made minutes feel like hours. Xavier decided to pick up the speed in order to get to the nearest exit as fast as possible. I knew that wasn't a good idea, but the storm had gotten so bad that I, too, just wanted to find a place to stop. Xavier was beginning to lose his cool, and I couldn't blame him. The wind was gusting now, causing the snow on the ground to swirl in front of the windshield.

"What the hell!" he shouted in frustration. "This is ridiculous!" In my nearly twenty years, I had never seen a storm so fierce.

"Hey, is that what I think it is?" Xavier pointed to a very dim light further ahead, hoping for an exit from this nightmare.

"I don't know. But it's definitely a sign. I just... can't see what it says. You better take the right lane and slow down. If it *is* an exit, you don't want to miss it."

"Right." He did his best to check the mirrors before changing lanes, and managed to do so successfully.

"Crap!" we both exclaimed simultaneously, realizing the light we'd seen had been nothing but a shiny billboard. I knew this was only going to upset Xavier even more.

"Damn it!" he cursed, pounding on the steering wheel.

"Relax," I said sharply, trying to calm him down. "We can't solve anything by losing our cool. Look, you've been driving for hours. Why don't you just pull over and let *me* drive for a while, all right?"

"Yeah..." He let out a defeated sigh. "Maybe you're right." He flipped on his signal and began to pull over toward the shoulder of the road. His foot had barely touched the brake pedal when the car suddenly began to skid. "Crap!" he blurted, trying to regain control of the vehicle—which in spite of his efforts just kept veering off the road. The sudden halt caused my head to whiplash forward and smack against the dashboard. Through the stars that resulted, I saw Xavier slumped over the steering wheel. We had been left skewed almost perpendicular to the highway, half-buried on the side of the road, inside a gigantic snow bank left behind by passing cars and the snowplows. The rear of Xavier's wagon was the only part of the vehicle visible, and it was sticking out onto the rightmost lane of the highway.

Xavier lifted his head. "Are you all right?" he asked groggily, dazed and squinty-eyed.

"Yeah." I hesitated. "…You?"

"Yeah," he said, raising his eyes to the enormous mountain of snow covering the hood of his car. "What the f…" Xavier's lips barely parted as he cursed in astonishment. He tried immediately to back up, stepping furiously on the gas. But the poor old wagon only wailed in response, like a bizarre animal begging to be put out of its misery. The tires spun on their axles to absolutely no avail. "Great!" he said in dismay, turning off the engine, defeated. "What the hell are we gonna do now?"

We sat there for a few minutes, listening to the annoying sound of the wind whistling into the car. I opted to spare myself the aggravation of trying to open my door; the entire passenger side had been completely blanketed by the snow. There was no way I could get out that way. "Dude, can you open *your* door?" I asked Xavier.

"Yeah, I think so." He took off his seat belt and bashed his shoulder against the door a few times, until it finally swung open. It was like cracking a window in a submarine, but instead of water, a wintry mix blew forcefully into the cab, hitting us like thousands of sharp needles in the face.

"Shut the door!" I shouted.

Xavier struggled for a few seconds against the forceful wind before finally getting the door closed. Once he did, we leaned back against our seats and breathed the same sigh of bleakness. Scowling, we turned to each other, realizing simultaneously that our heads were now all covered with snow. Xavier then broke out into his unforgettable high-pitched laughter. I guess he decided to give in to our lack of options, and just humor our misfortune. I always admired that about him—his ability to turn nuisance into humor whenever he felt at a loss. However, at that moment, I was so angry that I wanted to punch him in the face. But soon his hysterical laughter infected me, too, and I had no choice but to join in his moronic celebration.

A startling noise, however, made us stop. "What the hell was that?" I asked, spooked.

"It's the freaking wind, man!" Xavier resumed his cackling.

"No!" I disagreed, shushing Xavier. "Listen!" Xavier's smile disappeared as he saw the fear building in my eyes. "It sounds like a…" I trailed off in panic.

Yellow-white light suddenly shone bright behind us, illuminating the dark cab of the station wagon. Horror sank into my stomach as my eyes flew to the rear window and I realized that the approaching glare belonged to a pair of headlights, coming right at us at incredible speed.

We didn't even have time to blink. The inevitable collision took place in a fraction of a second. The brutal impact made me experience an immediate blackout; yet, just before the inescapable disaster sent me into the darkness, I was able to identify what hit us. The shiny and distinctive symbol included only one word: **MACK**.

The memories were incredibly sharp after all this time, preternaturally sharp, the psychological pain still fresh. I let them go, and they faded around the image of my own reflection. I felt as if I'd been transported from memories to reality in a dispersing cloud of smoke; once again I was staring at myself in the cracked window of the shack in which I had just awakened, frightened and lost. The relentless rattling on the tin roof had suddenly stopped, leaving me with nothing but the profound silence that now engulfed this place.

The cloak of fog had begun to disappear, too. Outside, majestic, building-tall pine trees began to unveil themselves before my eyes; within them, the first rays of dawn seeped from branch to branch, lingering raindrops shimmering like ornaments on their evergreen needles. The sight was almost too beautiful to be true... yet the fact that I was able to withstand the glare of the sun for the first time in three years seemed even more surreal. The light was shining straight into my eyes without inciting any pain at all. I couldn't remember the last time I was able to face direct sunlight without dark glasses and pain medications. The spectacle left me completely hypnotized, until the profound silence was finally broken by a soft voice speaking my name.

"Victor?" the mysterious young woman called. "Are you all right?"

I turn to regard her. "You know my name?" I asked, surprised.

Keeping a wary eye on me, she got up from the floor, somewhat disconcerted by my reply. Fear haunted her face, as if she were in the presence of some monster, yet her concern for me seemed genuine. After dusting herself off, she began to walk carefully toward me. The shafts of light now piercing the window intensified the natural red curls that bounced around her face, turning it an intense titian hue that was nearly blinding. Once in front of me, she deftly threw her hair back, unveiling the biggest, most fascinating green eyes I have ever seen in my life. Hesitantly, she brought her fingertips to my cheek, dabbing at a single tear that had escaped from the corner of my right eye. Her soft skin brushed like cotton on my face. "Are you all right?" she asked again in her velvet voice.

"Yeah." I cleared my throat, rubbing at the tear with the heel of my hand. *What a wuss*, I thought, *just because she's so incredible looking...* "I'm fine," I added, trying to regain my toughness in front of this beautiful woman—definitely a guy thing.

"Thank you," she said quietly.

"Um, okay," I said, confused. "For what?"

"For saving my life," she answered artlessly, timidly looking away.

I brought my fingers to my temples—a habit I developed after I acquired my tedious headaches—and tried to remember what she might be talking about. "I'm sorry," I finally said, "But I can't... well, I can't remember that. I can't remember much of anything. For days, at least, maybe longer."

She stood there in silence, scrutinizing my face.

"I'm sorry," I said, "But who are you? And what happened here last night?"

Understanding dawned in those remarkable emerald eyes. "Of course you don't remember." She shook her head in realization. "Selective memory loss is one of the major side effects of the serum."

"Serum? I don't understand."

Her eyes widened as she looked out the window and scanned the open field. "I'm sorry, Victor," she said, "but I don't think there's enough time for me to explain." She threw another glance at the window and moved swiftly towards the door. "We have to keep moving. Let's go!"

"Wait a second. I'm not going anywhere until you tell me what's going on!"

"We don't have *time* for this, Victor!" Her voice was like a whip-crack, urging me into motion.

But I was angry and confused, so I snapped back, my voice rising with anger, "Well, make time!"

She cringed, becoming almost defensive at my mood swing. "Easy, Victor… Look, your memory loss is temporary. You'll remember everything soon enough. But right now, I need you to trust me, all right? Can you do that?"

I considered for a second before yielding to her request. "All right," I said.

"Oh! And whatever happens—*please*, try to remain calm." She grabbed her jacket from the floor and rushed to the door.

"Can you at least tell me your name?" I called after her, feeling a bit more collected now.

"Sarah," she replied, "With an h." Opening the door, she beckoned me to follow.

Chapter 2
Aftermath

Is DYING REALLY so terrible?

Before the accident, I never gave it much thought. To me, it actually felt kind of peaceful, even soothing. Now, some people may consider death to be an escape from a dreadful life. But I never saw my life as dreadful. I always thought you could make your life whatever you wanted it to be, that life could be a dream. But what happens when your dream becomes a nightmare? What happens when nothing makes sense anymore, when you wake up to a reality that's no longer your own, and all you're left with is dread?

I don't remember much about the impact. The two or three times I opened my eyes during and after the car accident weren't long enough for me to process the shocking images I saw. In my first sporadic eye flutter I saw Xavier already unconscious, free-falling inside the cab, his arms floating in the air along with an empty soda can and some loose change he kept in the cup-holder. Soon afterward I felt another hit, and then it was darkness again. The second time I opened my eyes I saw snow, blowing inside the cab through a huge hole in the middle of the windshield. Xavier was no longer inside the car. Finally, I remember seeing red-and-blue flashing lights whirling above me, while some guys leaning over me shouted, *Can you hear me?*

The next time I regained consciousness—if only for a few seconds—was at the hospital. All I could see were bright lights shining above me and men wearing blue scrubs and surgical masks, talking indistinctly. I did, however, make out one sentence before I closed my eyes again: *We're losing him!*

It's amazing how many things can go through your mind in a moment like that. First, you think it's impossible. You think it's nothing but a dream, or, in my case, a nightmare, in which the theme was an episode of *ER* and I was just another guest-star with no reprieve. But then you realize you're not dreaming, and that you might just have to stay there for a while. So you think of the most irrelevant things. In my case, I tried to remember if I'd turned off the coffeemaker before I left my dorm room. Or if someone was going to tell my dad I was going to be late.

Then you understand the truth of what's really happening. And only *then* do you think about the things that really matter: Like having one last chance to tell the people you love how much you really care. Or having one last chance to say, *I'm sorry.*

This tumult in my mind soon quieted down as I began to fall into a very deep sleep, from which I thought I'd never wake again.

The agonizing aftermath began as soon as I tried to open my eyes again. Looking into the hospital room lights was like staring directly into the sun. I clenched my eyes shut and tried to speak, but my throat felt clogged. All I could hear coming out of my mouth were groans of pain and discomfort. It took just a second for my brain to sync with the rest of my body, only to realize that I was nothing but one giant wound. Every single part of my body hurt, as if an entire Little League team had taken turns beating me up with their favorite baseball bats. But nothing compared to the relentless pain I felt in my head. It hurt so bad I literally wanted to jump out of my skin.

My first reaction was to try to cover my eyes, but my arms wouldn't move; my whole body was unresponsive to my commands. I felt as I if had been glued to the bed. For me, that was the single most frightening moment of my life. But my heart resumed beating when a tingling sensation spread from the tips of my fingers through my hands and out to the rest of my body, letting me know that I *wasn't* paralyzed, just slow and uncoordinated. After some struggle, I finally managed to bring my hand to my face.

I stumbled upon some very thick bandages wrapped around my head, as well as some wires hooked to a strange machine. A long plastic tube emerged from my nose, which explained the discomfort in my throat. A natural instinct compelled me to yank all these things off, but before I could, a warm hand stopped me from hurting myself.

"Victor?" my dad called, "No, son, don't touch that. You could hurt yourself."

I tried to open my eyes again, despite the painful sensitivity to the light. When I did, I saw Dad standing at the side of my bed. His fifty-three-year-old face looked wearier than usual. He had the huge, dark circles under his eyes that he only gets when he hasn't slept well for days. But despite his obvious fatigue and sadness, he gave me the biggest smile when he realized I was conscious.

"I knew you'd wake up, son," he whispered, holding back some tears, "I knew you'd wake up—" His voice broke at the end. He pressed his head gently against my shoulder and let out a quiet sob. And though it hurt like hell to talk, I felt the need to comfort him, so I did the best I could.

"It's all right, Dad…" I croaked around the tube in my throat. "I'm okay."

"I'm going to get the doctor." My father smiled, wiping a tear off his face, and the next thing I knew he was running out the door.

The first person who came in with Dad was a nurse, who proceeded to check my vital signs, asking me how I was feeling. The first thing I mentioned was my sensitivity to the light, and how much it was worsening my headache. Even after dimming the lights it took some time for my eyes to adjust. When they did, I noticed Dr. White in the room, standing next to Dad.

It was such a relief to see him. He'd been our family doctor for as long as I could remember. He used to dress up as Santa Clause when I was a kid, and boy can he pull it off. I mean: tall, chubby, silver hair on the sides of his bald, shiny head, and of course a long white beard. I have to say that he had me fooled for the longest time. But more than that, he was a very good man.

He ordered the nurse to remove my breathing tube, which was a nauseating, painful process; thank God it took only a few moments. When I was ready, he said in a kind voice, "How are we feeling today?" while shining his penlight into my eyes.

My immediate wince, and the way I clenched my eyes shut, informed him of my extreme sensitivity to bright light. "I've been better, Doc," I admitted in my creaky voice.

"I'd say," he agreed, and continued his examination. "Look here, please."

My eyes followed his finger. "Why does it hurt when I breathe, Doc?" I gasped.

"You have a couple of fractured ribs, Victor. But they should heal in a few weeks."

"Great!" I jested. "What else did I break?"

"Your left leg is broken in two different places, and you received a severe blow to the head, which—"

"Oh!" I interjected, "That explains the headache."

Dr. White paused for a second, exchanging uneasy looks with my dad. "Do you remember what happened?" he asked quietly.

"Vaguely… Xavier and I got stuck in the snow and, um… something hit us. Something big."

"Yes," Dr. White confirmed. "It was a semi, a huge tractor-trailer. Apparently you and your friend broke down between lanes. The blizzard made it impossible for the truck driver to see what was in front of him until it was too late. According to the report, the front of the truck impacted the left rear corner of your vehicle, making it spin a few times. But it was the final impact with the side of the trailer what made your car flip over. Twice."

I laughed painfully. "That doesn't sound too good for Xavier's wagon. I'm sure he's pissed. How is he, by the way?"

Dr. White exchanged another look with my dad before lowering his eyes. "What is it?" I asked anxiously.

"Son…" My dad spoke as if there was a knot in his throat, "Xavier… didn't make it. I'm sorry."

"What?" I countered, already in denial. "No! He was okay! We were laughing just a few minutes before it happened— Doctor?" I turned to the Santa of my youth, as if asking him for a miracle.

"Apparently he wasn't wearing his seatbelt at the moment of collision." The old man sighed ruefully. "He was ejected from the vehicle and killed instantly. I'm sorry, Victor."

I lay my head back down, trying to suppress my tears, my panicky grief edging toward anger. It was easy to blame myself for what had happened, and I did. If I hadn't asked Xavier to stop and switch places with me, he wouldn't have crashed into the snowbank, or taken his seatbelt off. I closed my eyes tightly, hoping that this was nothing but a bad dream. But it wasn't. I turned my head to the side with my jaw clenched tight, and swallowed hard. Dr. White was the first to understand that I needed to be left alone for a while. "Come on, Sal," he said. "He's going to need a minute."

I didn't turn my head until I heard the door close.

Once alone, I let go of the flood of tears that pained me so much to contain, weeping in huge, wracking sobs that seemed to go on for hours. I tried to process the shocking news, hoping to find a logical explanation for what had happened. After all, that's what I did, that's who I was—a problem solver, right? In this brief eternity of insanity, I looked for answers to impossible questions, like: Why had this happened? Was there anything I could've done to avoid it? Why *him*? Why did *I* survive? What variable was I missing that I needed in order to make sense out of this horrible nightmare?

My grief and guilt created an absurd list of questions, for which I had absolutely no answers. My frustration made my heart rate spike on the monitor next to my bed as I ran the numbers in my head. But then my logic kicked in, and the sanity that I'd tried to drown with all these inane questions finally re-emerged. I realized then that this wasn't a problem I could solve with formulas or equations. This nightmare couldn't be solved, no matter what branch of math I used.

The impossible equation I'd created in my mind had no solution. My friend, my best and only friend in the world, was gone, and there was nothing—no number, equation, or variable—that could bring him back. When this world took something away, it stayed gone, a lesson I'd already learned too many times.

And then something inside my chest began to hurt.

After a few minutes, Dr. White returned to the room with my dad to ask me a bunch of silly questions that almost seemed incoherent and irrelevant to me: like which president was on the one-dollar bill, how many strikes were allowed in baseball, the name of the national anthem, the details of my class schedule. But after a few moments, I realized he was probing for signs of brain damage, of which I apparently had none. That, however, didn't ease the frown of concern on the good doctor's face.

"Okay, Doc," I prompted, annoyed and in a lot of pain. "What's wrong?"

A long moment of silence followed my question, along with another glance at my dad. A furious scowl creased my brows, and I burst like an over-inflated balloon. "Don't look at him!" I shouted. "I'm right here! And I'm asking you—what the hell is *wrong* with me?"

"Victor!" my dad scolded me.

"No, Dad!" I snapped. "I'm the one who's in pain here. And I want to know what's wrong!"

My father was startled by my shocking reaction, and so was Dr. White. I'd never behaved like that in my life. I'd never countered my father in anything before, let alone in front of other people. But there was a strange anger inside of me now that I couldn't explain or control. My dad stood there, silent and embarrassed, while I focused my impatient glare on Dr. White.

The doctor raised his hand towards my dad, as if telling him it was okay, and finally began to explain. "Victor," he said, "You've suffered a traumatic brain injury, which caused you to develop a subdural hematoma on top of your brain. And though we removed the blood clot from the surface, an unexplained intracranial pressure remains. The problem is that we have absolutely no idea what's causing it." He paused for a moment. "I don't know how to say this, Victor, but...well, we weren't expecting you to wake up. At least, not as yourself. The truth is that these types of injuries usually lead to severe brain damage, even death. You, however, in spite of your headache and sensitivity to light, seem to be in relatively good shape."

"And isn't that a good thing, Doctor?" I asked, confused.

"Well, we don't know yet, Victor. There are no precedents. So far, your condition seems to be unique. But I'd be remiss if I don't tell you what we do know." He sighed. "Your headache is a distinctive sign that the intracranial pressure is compressing your brain tissue. And if that is, indeed, the case, we have only a limited amount of time before you could suffer a massive stroke and…" He trailed off, pressing his lips into a thin line. "Do you understand what I'm trying to explain to you, Victor?"

"Yes, Doctor," I nodded, my eyes lost into space. "How much time?" I asked.

"If the pressure becomes chronic… a week, maybe less." I felt Dad's hand squeezing my shoulder as Dr. White uttered these words.

"Thank you, Doctor." My gratitude was sincere. "The truth… that's all I wanted."

"What do we do now?" my dad asked.

"We wait. The first twenty-four hours are going to be the most important. I've already ordered some diuretics to reduce the swelling, which in turn may help to reduce the intracranial pressure. I'm also going to put him on a very strong pain medication. We'll monitor his progress as we go along." Dr. White turned to meet my blank stare. "Victor, it's my job to tell you the worst-case scenario. But that doesn't mean we're not going to fight this thing 'til the end, you understand?"

"I know." I forced my lips into a smile. "Thank you, Doctor… and I'm sorry about my behavior earlier."

He gave me a warm smile in response. "Don't you worry, son. We're going to win this thing."

"Thank you, Doctor." Dad shook his hand.

"Sal." Dr. White patted him on the shoulder and left the room.

I looked up at my father. "I'll need to dictate my last will and testament, Dad. Just in case."

He took a deep, shuddering breath. "Are you...are you sure?"

I didn't dare nod just then—the pain felt like it was splitting my head open—so I just said, "Yes. Just in case."

***

The next morning I woke up feeling strangely better, my headache gone. It stayed gone as the days passed, and I started feeling like myself again. My fast and inexplicable recovery baffled the doctors, who despite my progress kept me under observation for the better part of two weeks. But after I was able to move around by myself with the help of a wheelchair, I demanded to be discharged. Dr. White complied, albeit reluctantly.

After spending the entire holiday season in the hospital, I was finally able to go home with Dad. I never thought I'd be so happy to be back in our tiny two-bedroom house in Jersey. There, I was to spend most of the next three months healing.

My rehabilitation therapy was no easy task, but my dad was there to help me—and so was Mrs. Montgomery, or Mrs. M, as I used to call her. She was a sweet lady who'd been a friend of the family for as long as I could remember. She used to babysit in our old neighborhood, and I became one of her charges right after my mother left. When she learned about my accident, she came over and offered to help. She cleaned, cooked, and did laundry; she even distracted Dad long enough to keep him from drinking. I always thought she had feelings for him, but I guess Dad was too blind to see it.

But then again, who was I to talk about love? I was twenty years old, and my only real relationship had been during my preteen years with Mrs. M's cute little niece Yvee, a blue-eyed angel with whom I used to play hide-and-seek until I left the neighborhood. And though I never saw her again, I often thought of her as my first and only love. Pathetic, I know... but what can I say? Sometimes you can't rule your own heart.

Mrs. M stayed with us for the length of my recovery, and it was great seeing her again. The truth is that she was the closest thing I ever had to a mother. I loved her, and I know my dad did, too—in his own way, of course.

After three long months of physical therapy, Mrs. M's healthy soups, and dozens of chess games with my dad, it was time for me to go back to school, and try to put this horrible nightmare behind me. But it was easier said than done. At school, everything I saw reminded me of Xavier... not to mention the fact that I found myself dealing with hundreds of condolences from people I didn't really know. This was definitely not how I've dreamed of becoming popular at school. But all of a sudden, everyone knew my name and story.

Worse, what had happened in the accident had become open debate. Everybody had their own version, which was really upsetting. One guy even had the gall to ask me if it was true that Xavier's car had exploded in midair, and that Xavier had been burnt beyond recognition. Comments like that really ticked me off... But it was more than that. I knew that something was wrong with me. For the first time in my life, I was unable to control my temper. I literally wanted to punch someone in the face, which was completely out of character for me.

Late on that first day, I walked around campus trying to clear my head, but something odd soon occurred. My hands started to shake uncontrollably, and my face began to burn, as if on fire. I didn't know what to do. I picked up my pace until I found myself running. Somehow, I ended up in the empty gymnasium, on my knees, screaming. This was the first time I pressed the heels of my hands against my temples in response to the pain— the awful pain that had returned to haunt me.

That was my first and last day back at school, and the beginning of the end of my life as I'd known it.

Dr. White gave me the same diagnosis as before, and begged me to go back to the hospital. But I decided to go back home instead. If I was going to die, it sure as hell wasn't going to be in a hospital bed. I wanted it to be in the house where I grew up, with the one person I loved.

But to everyone's surprise, including mine, I didn't die in a few days, as most doctors predicted; or in a few weeks, or even in a few months. No, soon my headaches became part of my life, along with the sudden outbursts of anger that completely changed my personality. They would come and go, but never for good. After six months of countless tests, the doctors still couldn't figure out what was keeping me alive. But they all agreed on one thing: the now-sporadic intracranial pressure would eventually produce a massive stroke that would kill me. The question was how and when.

I became pretty emotional about that at first, not wanting to die, and all. But after a few months, I grew depressed, tired, and bitter, to the point that I just wanted to get it over with. I sulked in bed for days. I didn't want to eat, drink, or even shower. I didn't even want to take my meds anymore. I shut down completely, wanting to die. My dad, however, begged to differ— and he didn't hesitate to let me know it the day he kicked my bedroom door wide open.

"Enough, Victor!" he shouted. "Get up!"

"What the…" I cursed, poking my head out of the covers. "Dad? What do you want?"

"I want you to get out of this stinking bed and start doing something productive with your life!"

"What?—No! I'm dying! Just leave me alone, okay?" I tossed the covers back over my head.

"Get up!" he insisted, this time yanking the covers off me and throwing them on the floor.

"What the hell is *wrong* with you?" I shouted back. "Why can't you just leave me alone?"

"Because I love you, that's why!" His voice filled with emotion. "And I can't believe that my son is giving up! A real man isn't always the one who wins, Victor. A real man is the one who doesn't go down without a fight—you understand? Perseverance achieves what good fortune does not reach. Haven't I taught you that? Even when your strength abandons you, you should never lose hope! Because one day, when you least expect it, the solution to all of your problems might just come knocking on your door—a sign that will lead you to your happiness!"

I started to snap back that he hadn't done such a good job of following his own philosophy, but the words died in my throat when I saw his expression. He glared at me, eyed bright. "Now, you can be skeptical about this and reject it—or you can take a leap of faith and embrace it. But whatever you do, you never—never give up!"

A knot formed in my throat, and my eyes began to tear. "I'm scared, Dad." I fought unsuccessfully to stop my voice from breaking.

He reached for my head and pressed it against his chest. "I know, son… I know. But you're not alone. I'm always going to be with you, even after I'm gone. I promise. You just wait for your sign."

I hugged Dad tightly and cried. I decided that from that day on, I was going to stop feeling sorry for myself, and that I was going to try to live the remainder of my uncertain life as normally as possible. I never went back to school, but I continued my studies from home. That made Dad very happy. Between books and endless chess games, we built a routine that lasted almost a year. And although my condition never improved, I began to hope that if I just stayed alive long enough, the cure for my condition would eventually be discovered.

But it's funny how when you try to climb out of a hole, life will sneak up on you, bash you in the head, and push you back in. That's how I felt the night I received an unexpected phone call from Dr. White, asking me to meet him at his office. I was certain he was going to give me more bad news about my condition... but I was ready. Honestly, I was more concerned about breaking the news to Dad. But to my surprise, my condition was not the subject of discussion that night. I wish it had been.

"Your Dad came to see me a few days ago, Victor," Dr. White said without preamble.

"And?" I replied, watching him as sat at his desk.

"And we ran some tests." His eyes scanned the open folder in front of him, unwilling to meet mine.

"Doctor!" I shook my head. "Please don't do that. Just give it to me straight, all right?"

His eyes rose to meet my stare, a dreadful expression of sadness overwhelming his face. "His tests came back positive for cirrhosis," he said, "and I'm afraid the damage is irreversible. I'm sorry."

I sprung up from the chair and walked aimlessly around the room, trying to put my thoughts together. But it was useless. "How long?" I asked, finally, stopping in front of the office window.

"Not long."

"Does he know?"

"Of course. And he asked me not to tell you. Legally, I shouldn't have. But I know how much you care for your father, and I thought it was wrong to keep you in the dark. He doesn't have much time left. I'm truly sorry, Victor."

I wanted to thank him, but I was afraid to try to utter the words or even to move from that window. My throat was clogged with an impossible, painful knot, and my eyes were blurred with my tears. All I could do was nod in response to his kindness.

"I'll give you a minute," the good doctor said, before leaving the room.

I saw the reflection of him closing the door in the shiny office window. The bright city lights made me switch focus, and I found myself staring blankly over the New York City skyline, a sight that always used to fill me with joy and optimism. But that night it was a background for misery and gloom. Those were the only feelings that I could fit into my heart.

I knew some people thought I idolized my father too much, and that my filial love wouldn't allow me to see him for who he really was. But that wasn't the case at all. I knew exactly who my father was: He was an obstinate man who never let go of the pain of my mother leaving us; he was very impulsive; and he chose to drown his sorrows in alcohol almost every day. My father was far from perfect, but he was my Dad. He was the man who taught me everything significant I know—the only person who never gave up on me. And yes, maybe he was never the best friend or the best husband. But who am I to judge?

One thing I know for certain. He sure as hell was a great father.

He died one rainy summer morning, and a part of me died with him. But I vowed to keep his memory alive by always remembering his teachings: To never give up, to never go down without a fight, and to know when to take a leap of faith and just believe.

Chapter 3

Run!

I FOLLOWED SARAH-WITH-AN-H out of the shack. By now the fog had completely dissipated, and the sun was rising in its full glory behind a range of beautiful green mountains. I stopped to take a second look of the majestic view. I figured I should take advantage of the fact that, for whatever reason, my eyes were now able to withstand the brilliance.

Suddenly, the same sense of hyper-awareness that I'd experienced back in the shack overwhelmed me again, as my brain began to connect to my surroundings in the most extraordinary manner. My nerve cells felt like a raw wound being caressed by sandpaper. The acuity of my senses was so intense that it *hurt*. I could feel every leaf on the surrounding trees rustling in the wind, and the roaring of rushing waters in a nearby river. The light I perceived in the subtlest shades, knowing exactly which combination of colors had produced them—right down to their Angstrom wavelengths. I could hear 37 birds within earshot, and feel the presence of hundreds more, kilometers away, chirping in the trees and gliding through the sky. But the biggest mind-boggle of all was being able to feel the rhythm of Sarah's heartbeat. It was like a soft drum playing inside my head.

Overwhelmed by the otherworldliness of it all, I reached for my head in an absurd attempt to stop it, to turn it off. But this wasn't something I could just turn down the volume on. Frightened out of my wits, I pressed the heels of my hands against my eyes and began to moan. My sense of balance and coordination betrayed me then, and I collapsed abruptly onto my knees, the rest of my body following. I writhed in pain over a moist patch of dark green grass (*Poa alpina,* a.k.a. alpine bluegrass; 5,112 Angstroms; 1.17 microliters of water per cubic centimeter) as my eyes took in the immense forest I finally realized that I was in.

"Victor?" Sarah ran to my aid. "What's wrong?"

"I don't know!" I bellowed, my voice echoing like thunder in my head. "Help!"

Sarah kneeled behind me and tried to comfort me. But the closer she got, the more I could sense from her: her heartbeat, the subtle harmonics of her voice, the smell of her sweat, the scent blood on her shirt, even her breathing was now sandblasting the insides of my head.

I just couldn't handle it.

"Step away!" I demanded, pushing her aside. But no matter how far away she was, the uproar continued inside my head. "What's happening to me?" I whispered or cried aloud; pain and confusion overwhelmed me.

"Breathe, Victor! Breathe!" Sarah urged, and added, "Your mind is wandering! Try to focus your thoughts on only *one* thing."

I did as she said, directing my attention on the farthest thing I could sense, the river. The natural soothing sound of the rushing waters, which were merely unbearable at this distance, began to calm me down. Finally it all faded. I waited a few seconds before I found the courage to open my eyes again. When I did, I saw Sarah sitting on the ground, her chest bending at the rhythm of her frantic heartbeat.

She propped herself up on her elbows and waited. "Better?" she asked cautiously.

"What's happening to me?" I demanded, my voice quaking with fear.

Sarah's lips parted, as if she was ready to tell me something, finally—but a sudden sharp crack in the distance made us cringe and turn towards the startling sound.

"Was that a gunshot?" I asked in shock.

"Oh, no!" she exclaimed. "They found us! Come on, Victor! We have to hide!"

Taking ahold of my arm, she helped me back to my feet, and led the way back toward the shack. But an unnatural, over-amplified foreboding warned me to turn back. The feeling was so overwhelming that I felt compelled to trust it. "Wait!" I stopped, pulling on Sarah's arm. "We can't go back! We have to hide in the woods."

"But, Victor—"

"Just trust me, okay?"

I took Sarah's hand and ran into the woods, acting purely out of instinct. The vibrations of dozens of footsteps shaped my foreboding into a realistic danger. I couldn't have known for sure who or how far away they were, not when I was running myself and confusing the vibrations, but what I sensed made me certain of two things: first, they were coming our way. And second, whoever they were, they were hostile.

Sarah and I dodged deep into the woods and hid behind enormous old-growth trees, trying not to breathe too loudly as we heard them approaching. I was afraid they'd be able to hear us anyway, our hearts were beating so loudly.

My eyes bulged in surprise the moment I saw them stride down the field. They looked like military personnel, yet their camouflage uniforms lacked branch identifiers. My heightened vision, however, was able to pick out a clear insignia: the letters "R.C." on their arm patches. Although I didn't know what the letters stood for, I couldn't help but think that I'd seen this acronym before...somewhere. There must've been at least thirty of the men scanning the field, and they were all packing heavy artillery: AK-47s, to be precise. I recognized the equipment from a summer I'd spent with Xavier at a shooting range a couple of years ago.

American soldiers didn't carry the Russian-made AKs. The clunky but tough and accurate machine guns were the go-to guns for terrorists and militias the world over.

Who are these people? I asked myself. *And far more important, what could they possibly want with me?* Then a shocking realization threw me completely: the insignia wore by these men was the same one on Sarah's jacket. I was just about to ask her when...

"There they are!" the shout of one of the soldiers alerted the others. "Get them!"

"Run, Victor!" Sarah shouted, and bolted for the deep woods.

I followed Sarah as fast as I could through the dense undergrowth of the forest. I was in no danger of losing her; her accelerated heartbeat was like a homing beacon inside my head, showing me the way to follow. But her heartbeat wasn't the only thing I could sense. The brigade of soldiers was getting closer, and I could hear safeties clicking off and their weapons being readied to be fired. I ran faster, trying to catch up with Sarah; she was heading towards what appeared to be an open field. But as we all know, appearances could be deceiving—as we were about to find out.

When I finally caught up with her, she stopped so abruptly that I bumped into her. Unfortunately for us, the open field turned out to be the edge of a tall cliff that plunged into a furious river—apparently the same one I'd sensed earlier. Sarah stumbled dangerously close to the edge, but my quick reflex made me catch her by the elbow and spin her around, just in time to save her from a dangerous fall.

"Thanks!" she gasped.

"Don't mention it," I replied nonchalantly, as if thirty men armed with deadly weapons weren't a few hundred yards behind, determined to kill us both.

I stepped in closer and peeked carefully over the edge of the cliff, just to confirm the breathtaking distance to the river below. I flinched at the sight. Its foaming white waters stretched as far as the eye could see in either direction, and its roaring current flowed dangerously fast. There were snags of broken tree trunks and branches clinging to the walls of the gorge, graphically displaying just how high the river could rise in rainy weather. But for me, none of that was as bloodcurdling as the height on which we were standing. It was enough to make my brain shrivel inside my skull.

"We have to jump, Victor," Sarah prompted.

I looked at her like she'd just stepped out of a flying saucer. "Are you out of your mind? It's at least a hundred feet!"

"We *have to jump!*" she insisted.

"Forget it! I won't!"

"Why? Can't you swim?" she demanded.

"No, it's not that. It's just that, that I..." I trailed off, nervously.

"What? It's just what?"

"I have acrophobia, okay?" I shouted, embarrassed, staring the ground.

Her eyebrows knitted in confusion as she asked, "You have *what*?"

"Fear of heights, all right? I have a *fear* of *heights*!"

She sighed apologetically, putting her hand on my chest. "Well, *I'm sorry*, Victor."

"You don't have to say that. You didn't know."

She gave me a dubious look, and leaned closer. "That's not why I'm apologizing, dumbass," she whispered, and I caught an unexpected sparkle of humor in her eyes just before she gave me a hard and unexpected shove. The next thing I knew I was in the air, my heart stuck in my throat.

Sarah had pushed me off the cliff. I couldn't believe it. Now I was falling straight into the waters of the violent river. I saw her jump right after me, just before I shut my eyes in terror.

When it comes to heights, I'm not exactly the epitome of toughness. I've had this horrible fear of heights for as long as I can remember—the kind of fear that can freeze you with a panic attack. Dr. White used to tell me that this was no more than an irrational fear caused by a traumatic experience that I must have had in the past.

And though I never remembered anything of the sort, I used to have recurring nightmares about falling. Dr. White considered them interesting, because in the dreams, *I* was the one who'd purposely jump into an endless abyss. But then again, dreams are dreams, and they all pass in time. What I knew would never pass was the horrendous experience of having been pushed, purposely, off a cliff by this strange woman, no matter how gorgeous she was.

This was definitely going to leave a psychological mark.

Even as I fell, waving my arms like a deranged monkey and possibly even screaming like a little girl (though I would never admit it even under torture if it were true, which it isn't), I felt my senses expanding and my body adjusting itself as I fell, heading for the least disturbed and hopefully deepest patch of water. This flail caused me to veer to the left a little, and I found that if I turned my body at this angle, I could move forward a foot or two. Without thinking I reached out and grabbed Sarah's arm, pulling her with me to the (relatively) safe spot I'd calculated, automatically compensating for the increased mass, and wind resistance.

I don't remember what was worse: the pain of hitting the water, or the fact that it was so damned cold. The moment I plunged into the river, I felt as if I were being stabbed by thousands of needles simultaneously. The impact shock caused me to lose my grip on Sarah. Once underwater, my survival instincts took over and I began to kick and pull, trying to propel myself back to the surface. But the strong current seemed determined to keep me down; and for a moment there, I really thought I was going to drown. But my senses were still expanded, and it was easy, almost instinctive, for me to avoid the rocks and find the surface.

My perseverance paid off, and I was able to break the surface with a sharp and desperate gasp. I tried to swim ashore, but my attempts proved useless. Once again, the current was too strong and was now dragging me along like a loose twig. Finally, something caught my eye downriver, giving me my only hope for survival: A huge broken log had fallen into the river, and its far end was still rooted to the shore. It didn't take a genius to see that this was my only way out, so I waited for the right moment before I surged up and clung to it, like a tick.

Pulling myself up, I turned frantically in all directions, looking for Sarah. My gaze swept the turbulent waters until I finally got a glimpse of her, at least thirty feet away from me, struggling to stay afloat.

"Victor!" she cried. "Help!—Hel..." her words were literally drowned as she went under.

"Sarah!" I called desperately, reaching in her direction. "Try to swim to me! Come on! You can do it!"

Stroke after stroke, Sarah strove against the current, but the river resisted her efforts and dragged her even farther away. "Victor!" she called hopelessly as her weary limbs finally gave up on her, leaving her at the mercy of the current.

"Sarah!" I shouted frantically, watching her get carried away.

In the next minute, I lost sight of her completely. But wait— my senses leaped out to rove my surroundings again, and suddenly I began to sense her body in the same way I had before. My hearing and other probing senses, some I couldn't define, took note of her cooling skin, her contracting muscle tissue, her delicate skeleton, her drumming heart. They were all linked, somehow, to my over-perceptive mind; it was almost as if I could touch her.

So I tried.

I kept reaching out, clutching at this enigmatic connection, my hand shaking and my heart racing. I couldn't understand what was happening to me, and yet I felt compelled to trust it. An inexplicable breeze began to swirl inside my head, or so it seemed, as if my brain were breathing on its own for the very first time. What I can only describe as a combination of *ice* and *peppermint* began to open every pore inside my head, taking me into a deep state of euphoria. Even as the breeze freshened inside my mind, I could see that the air around me was sparkling like a firefly convention. *Air and water molecules ionized by the energy flow,* a part of me noted dryly, only to have the rest of me demand: *What energy flow? What the hell are you talking about?*

Forget about it. Intoxicated, compelled not to trust my eyes anymore, I let go of my conscience self and slowly closed them, surrendering to the overwhelming feeling of power. I focused again on the energy that connected my mind with Sarah's body, and began to draw it back into my head. As strange as it sounds, I knew exactly what I was doing... I just couldn't understand why or how. It was as if my mind were reacting to a primitive instinct I never knew I had, as if I were only doing something I was always capable of—that I was always *meant* to do.

The air chilled as I pulled heat from it to power my efforts, and frost crackled across my eyebrows and hair. Shivering, I became aware of some sourceless form of energy welling up in the air around me; curious, I tapped it and it siphoned into me. As I grabbed Sarah with a spectral hand, her weight and the current wanted to pull me forward; and for a split second I felt an intense pain in my head, as if the counterforce were trying to yank my brain out of my skull. Instinctively, I used some of the energy I'd tapped to leverage me—and my brain— again the mass of the Earth, and to hold me tight to the log, like a limpet clings to a rock. I also found an opening to an amazingly deep well of power within myself, and forced it wide open.

As I opened my eyes again, I felt the energy from all these sources channeling through my hand, braided together in perfect harmony, reaching from Sarah's body to the source of it all, my beleaguered mind. Then, like a lifebuoy popping up from underwater, her head broke the surface and began to cut a path against the relentless current. I couldn't believe my eyes, but Sarah was being hauled out of the river by an invisible line connected to...well, to me.

When I finally got ahold of her physically, I let go of the energy rope, and what was left snapped back to its sources. I stood there for a long moment, astounded: I'd pulled her at least thirty feet across the water, with absolutely no physical contact and absolutely no idea of how I'd done it. Once I had her in my arms, I carried her to shore, navigating with ease along the slippery log, and laid her on the ground. After checking her pulse and breathing, I began to administer CPR. Thankfully, after just a few rescue breaths, she began to cough up water—more than a mouthful, but less than I thought she'd swallowed in the two long minutes she'd been under.

My heart resumed beating the moment I saw those emerald greens pop open again. I felt as if I'd just rescued the only human being besides myself in a desolate world. "Are you okay?" I asked, gently brushing the wet hair out of her face.

Her eyes narrowed and wandered around the clearing as she considered for a long moment. A mixture of confusion and daze knitted her brows. "...Yeah," she nodded, finally. "What happened?" Her teeth chattered.

"You don't know? R-R-Really?" I asked in dismay—my jaw was quivering, too—"B-because I was really hoping you could tell m-m-me."

She jerked upward then, as if just awakened from a bad dream. With her eyes alert now, she met my stare and reached out to touch my wet shirt. Her concern became evident. "Quick!" she commanded. "Take off your clothes!"

"What?!" I asked, dumbfounded as I watched her strip off her wet jacket. "W-w-what are you doing?"

"We've entered the first stage of hypothermia, Victor," she said, and I realized for the first time that her lips were blue. "Ou-our hearts might fail if we don't warm up soon. —Come on!" she insisted, deftly helping me out of my wet shirt. "Now close your eyes!"

"What?"

"Close your eyes!"

Sheesh, what a temper! For a second I thought she'd punch me in the face if I didn't comply, so, I shut my eyes and waited for her next command. The next thing I felt was her cold, bare skin pressed firmly against my chest. Goosebumps covered my entire body as her icy palms slid up over my shoulder blades. Her limp curls brushed the side of my face as she resumed chattering her teeth next to my ear. The whole thing was awkward enough to snap me out of my euphoric trance and to disconnect my mind completely from my surroundings—just when I wouldn't have minded being hyper-perceptive.

I felt dazed and uncoordinated, and Sarah's aggressive attitude wasn't helping the situation at all. I'd never felt more awkward in my entire life, not to mention embarrassed. I mean, I knew exactly what she was trying to accomplish—I'm not stupid. But the fact remained that Sarah was a very attractive woman—crazy, but attractive. And having her half-naked against my chest, well… It made me feel a little… nervous, to say the least.

"W-w-what do I do now?" I asked like an idiot.

"You shut up and don't move! It shouldn't take longer than a few minutes before our combined body heat brings our core temperatures back to normal." She paused. "Why aren't you hugging me?"

"You said don't move."

"Jeez, Victor! Of all the times to listen to me! You want me to freeze? Put your hands around me! And you can open your eyes now. Good God, you're acting like you've never hugged a woman before."

"Never like this! And would you mind cutting me some freaking slack here? I think you owe me that much, dammit! I still have no idea who you are, and you just pushed me over a cliff into a freaking river!"

"Oh! Um, well, I'm sorry. It's just that this is as…uncomfortable for me as it is for you."

"Somehow I find that hard to believe," I countered. "You seem in absolute control here. How do you know all this survival stuff, anyway? Are you some sort kind of polar lifeguard or something?"

"I'm a second year med-student."

"Really?"

"Yeah… Now, can I ask *you* a question?"

"Shoot."

"Never like this? Really?"

"Seriously? That's your question? You know that that's not what I meant! Sheesh! So much for cutting me some slack."

"I'm...I'm sorry," she apologized between chuckles.

"Well, I'm glad I can amuse you in the middle of a life-and-death situation!"

My scornful tone just made her laugh even louder...and I have to admit she finally forced a few chuckles out of me, too. Then I heard a stick snap upstream and went perfectly still as my senses rushed out to encompass the surrounding mile or so in all directions. It was much farther than I'd ever perceived before, but by now it almost seemed routine.

I was expecting to feel the armed men on their way to kill us, but it turned out to be some kind of furry predator akin to a weasel or ferret chasing a field mouse into some brush. Probing for the presence of the armed men, I could detect no one. Had they just given up when they reached the river, or were they scouting the banks beyond the range of my senses?

Then my hyper-perception snapped off, like someone had flipped a switch, and I was back in my body. Sarah was still giggling, and I was starting to experience an embarrassing physiological reaction that I couldn't do anything about at this time. "When you're done making fun of me, do you think maybe we should consider an alternative method of heating?" I said. "Those men are gone."

"A fire would be good," she agreed. "Let's just give it a few more minutes and then we'll break, okay? Oh! And don't forget to—"

"Close my eyes," I finished for her. "Yeah, don't worry. I won't peek."

"Thanks."

"Don't mention it."

We huddled for a few more awkward minutes before we broke apart. I have to admit that I was feeling a lot better, and so was she. The pink had returned to her lips and our skin was practically dry. I closed my eyes as I promised, while Sarah ran behind some bushes to get dressed. Then I began to look around the clearing for enough twigs and branches to start the fire Sarah had suggested, which was now more necessary than ever. The setting sun had already begun to set behind the colossal mountain, and nightfall was almost upon us. We hadn't much time.

Seeing the sun setting so fast made me wonder about the time. I'd either lost track of it, or we'd had only a few hours of sunlight the entire day. There were only a few explanations for this. But I was tired of speculating. I'd been patient enough with Sarah so far in my quest to get her to tell me what was happening. The only answer I'd gotten from her so far, besides her name, was that for some reason I was suffering from temporary amnesia—and that I should be remembering everything soon. But how soon was soon? I needed answers, and I needed them immediately.

So I decided to put my gentlemanliness aside and start pressing for the truth.

"Sarah?" I called, dropping the firewood on the ground.

"Yeah?" she yelled from behind the bushes.

"Can you come out, please? I need to talk to you." My voice was less than pleasant now.

"How are you going to start the fire?" she asked.

"Never mind that!" I called impatiently, though her question did trigger an instinctive response that made me reach into my pocket. "Can you just please come out?" I insisted. But my request was ignored for the second time. I was just about to call her again, with a much firmer tone, when the contents of my own pocket derailed me completely.

It was a small item: a vintage silver lighter with slashes, to be exact. I wasn't surprised I had it with me, even in this chaos. It was a gift from my father. He gave it to me the night before he died, and I'd been carrying it with me ever since, just like he did when he was alive. It was one of his most precious possessions. He told me he got it in the U.K. when he was very young. And though he never smoked, he wouldn't be parted from it, not even for a second. He never told me the whole story, but I think it had something to do with my mother, with how they met.

For me it held a different significance—as the symbol of an exchange made, if you will. Because that night I gave him something, too: my word. My father was never a pretentious man, but he did take great pride in being as good as his word. And as for me, being my father's son, I'd learned to be just as good as he was. Thus, my father knew very well that I'd never break a promise—*if* he got me to say the words, of course. And that night he did...

"You know, son, it's only at the final juncture that you come to appreciate things in a way you never did before. I know I have. All the things you thought mattered wither upon the things that really do, and you're left with nothing but your victories and failures. No more, no less. Because at the end, what's really important is not what you had, but what you did; what you've succeeded and failed at. That's what you really take with you."

I looked at my father, confused, not knowing what to say to this. But he went on, oblivious to my confusion: "Knowing this frightened me," he said quietly, "because I thought my failures would outrank my victories, in spite of all my efforts. But now I know I was wrong. Because when I look at you and I see the man you've become, I know I've succeeded far beyond my wildest dreams. You're my pride and joy, Victor. You're the reason why I'm no longer afraid; the reason why I can finally let go with no regrets...

"But before I go, I want you to promise me something. I need you to promise me that no matter what the damned doctors say, you'll

never give up. I want you to fight to get better, you understand? You have to live, Victor. You're destined for something greater than you can possibly imagine. I've known it ever since the moment you were born; ever since the very first time I held you in my arms. That's why I need you to promise me, son. Please."

"Yes, sir," I said, my voice a dry husk in my throat.

"Say the words, Victor."

"I promise you, Dad... I promise to find a way to get better, a way to live."

"I love you, Son."

The glare from the sunset shone warmly over the smooth surface of the lighter and wavered into my eyes, snapping me out of the memory. It's always been hard not to get caught up in that last memory of my father, whenever I stumble upon it. It's my most precious, most painful memory of all.

I flipped my father's lighter open and started the fire, putting my memories aside. Although important to me, they were of no relevance to my present situation. Instead I called up Sarah, again, and tried to focus on remembering the past forty-eight hours of my life.

"Wow!" Sarah exclaimed, getting out of the bushes, wearing nothing but her underwear. She was using her blouse to dry her hair. "Now, that's a good bonfire. How did you—"

"Look," I interjected. "Why don't you just cut the crap and tell me what the hell's going on here?"

"Oh!" she realized. "You still don't remember, huh?"

My narrowed glare gave her a clue of my snide yet unspoken response.

"I'm sorry," she apologized wearily. "It's just that most subjects regain their memories within the first 24 hours."

"Subjects?"

She sat on a log next to the fire, shaking her head as if regretting what she was about to tell me. "Look, Victor... Maybe it's best to wait and see how—"

"*Wait?!*" I snapped angrily, lunging in her direction. An uncontrollable burst of anger compelled me to grab her by the elbow and yank her back to her feet. "I'm not waiting another Goddamn minute! You're going to tell me what's going on— and you're going to tell me right now!"

Her eyes were filled with fear as she beheld the glare of this unexpected savage, a glare that soon began to burn my own eyes. "Please, Victor," she pleaded, "You're hurting me!" I looked down and realized that my grip was cutting off the circulation in her arm. "Victor! Let me go!"

My own actions shocked me to my core; I couldn't believe what I was doing. I had never assaulted anybody in my life, let alone a woman. I couldn't understand it. But it was as if I were possessed by my anger—like I was no longer the person that I had always been, but someone, or some*thing*, else. The feeling was terrifying. I released her abruptly, stepped back, and began to apologize lavishly. At first, I thought she'd run the moment I let go of her—and I wouldn't have blamed her if she had—

but she didn't. On the contrary, she stayed and tried to comfort me, which I found extremely odd, given that she'd been the one hurt by my tantrum.

Afraid I'd lose control again, I began to put some distance between us. I stumbled backwards until my back was against one of the enormous pine trees that surrounded the field. "Why is this happening to me?" I asked, frightened, and confused, my hands trembling with the lingering anger.

Sarah's brows knitted with pity. "Because they lied to you, Victor." She sighed and sat down on a log next to the fire again. "They lied to us all."

My brow creased with suspicion. "Who are 'they'?"

Sarah met my stare just long enough show me the contempt that filled her eyes as she uttered the words, "R.C. Labs."

Adding the word *Labs* to the acronym that had been haunting me from the moment I saw it was enough to trigger the flash of memories that brought me back to the very first day I was introduced to the term. And just like that, names, people, places, and even feelings began to re-emerge from oblivion.

Chapter 4
R.C. Labs

THICK, DARK DRAPES hung on every window of my cluttered apartment in Weehawken. My relentless sensitivity to light had forced me to turn the place into a mausoleum, into which not a shred of sunlight was allowed to enter. Buried under my thick covers, I laid in bed, suffering through another agonizing day, barely able to open my eyes. My headache had gotten so bad that morning that I'd even decided to turn off the phone to completely disconnect myself from the rest of the world.

Not that it mattered. There was no one out there for me anyway. For the past few weeks my only nourishment, besides instant cup-a-soups, had been painkillers and antidepressants. Dr. White prescribed them. He said that depression was bound to occur, given my condition. He always tried to make sense of things. But for me, everything was making less and less sense every day.

I was finally dozing off when I heard a knock on my door. *Crap.* "Who is it?" I shouted from bed, ready to tell whoever it was to get lost.

"FedEx, sir," a voice announced. "I have a package for Victor Bellator."

I reluctantly got out of bed—in which I had been hibernating for the past few days—and opened the door without undoing the chain. I can't imagine how I must've looked. I hadn't taken a shower or shaved in days, and I couldn't remember the last time I'd changed my clothes. But given the circumstances, I really couldn't care less.

"Good morning, Mr. Bellator," the FedEx guy greeted me.

"Good morning, Jimmy," I answered, squinty-eyed.

I knew this guy. He'd begun to deliver packages to this building about the same time I moved in. Most of the times he came knocking on my door were because he had a package from some hospital that wanted to take my case.

"Damn, Mr. Bellator. You look like crap!"

"Thanks, Jimmy," I answered apathetically. "You have something for me?"

"Yeah! It looks like another hospital letter."

I undid the chain and opened the door to sign for it. The letter was inside a thick manila envelope emblazoned with the initials *R. C.* It seemed different from any of the hospital letters that I'd gotten before; plainer, heavier.

"Well, have a nice day, Mr. B—"

"Yeah, yeah…" I didn't mean to close the door in his face, but I wasn't in the mood for chitchat. I was miserable. All I wanted to do was sleep, which was the only time I was free of my pain, both physical and emotional.

I was on my way back to hibernation when I got curious about this letter, so I went ahead and opened it. The strange letter contained information from a neural engineering research facility called R.C. Labs, short for *Reserata Cerebrum*, which is Latin for "Unlocked Brain"—or so they claimed. I have to admit, the letter caught my attention; not only for their unique name, but because I couldn't recall pleading my case to this facility. Matter of fact, I'd never heard of them before.

But unlike the hundreds of responses I'd received in the past, this one was different. The alleged research facility was said to be a state-of-the-art treatment center for rare brain injuries such as mine. Their latest procedure, according to the letter, had shown promising results for patients with my particular condition. The letter also explained that such treatment was in its experimental trial stage, and that the only way that I could take advantage of it—at no cost to me, I might add—was if I volunteered as an experimental test subject. The letter ended on a phone number that I needed to call, should I decide to accept their offer.

The simplicity of the letter only triggered my skepticism. Though it sounded good on paper, I knew it had to be too good to be true. So I walked into the kitchen, tired and annoyed, and shoved the letter in my overfilled garbage can. Without taking a second look, I turned around and lumbered back into my cluttered bedroom. I was ready to crawl back into bed when something among the trash on my bedroom floor suddenly bit my foot. "What the..." I cursed, hopping on one leg. Whatever it was, it must've been alive, I figured. So I crouched over and looked for the little critter that had bit me.

But after clearing the floor a bit, I discovered that the bug had been no other than my dad's old lighter. *What's it doing on the floor?* I pondered. I always kept it on top of my nightstand. But today it was on the floor, opened, positioned almost *strategically* to make me stumble upon it, as if set purposely to stop me from shrouding my head under the covers. I sat on the floor in misery, contemplating this piece of metal that held so many memories, a promise that I was going to leave unfulfilled; and I sobbed, powerless over my painful and impending death.

As I twiddled with it between my fingers, a tiny shaft of sunlight sneaked in through a window somehow, striking the surface of the lighter. A forceful glare shone upon my face then, making me shut my eyes and flinch away in pain. For some reason, I ended up facing the kitchen. The first thing I saw when I opened my eyes again was that letter, sticking out of the trash can like an uncanny apparition.

I slid my eyes back to the lighter with an irrational suspicion, wondering. Was this just a coincidence, or was it *Dad*, trying to tell me something? After all, it was *his* lighter. Or maybe I was just losing my mind; I didn't know. But whatever it was, it compelled me to give life one final shot.

*****

When I called the number on the letter, I expected to be greeted by one of those annoying menu options that tell you what number to press according to your particular query. But to my surprise, the phone was answered by a gentleman who not only knew who I was, but identified himself as my personal recruiter. He said his name was Mr. Smith, and that he already had my paperwork ready—whatever that meant. All I needed to do was sign the consent to become a test subject in this medical trial, and I'd be given the information needed to begin my treatment.

I thought he'd give me an appointment to have all this done. But instead he asked me to pick a place where we could meet at my earliest convenience. And though all of this was as vague and unusual as it could possibly get, I agreed to meet with him the following morning. The truth is that I was intrigued by the mystery of who these people really were—and more importantly, about the procedure that just might save my life.

Morning arrived faster than I expected, and with it came a brand new hope that I might live. After an overdue shave, shower, and change, I shielded my eyes behind a pair of extra-dark sunglasses and headed down to the little bistro in the corner—that's where I'd decided to meet the mysterious Mr. Smith. When I got there, the place was practically empty. The only people there were a couple of servers and an older gentleman in one of the booths by the window, wearing mirrored sunglasses. I wasn't sure if this was the man I was supposed to meet, but if he was, then something was definitely out of place. He wore what appeared to be a black cashmere suit, and his matching leather briefcase looked just as expensive. This guy didn't look like a hospital worker at all—an investment banker maybe, but definitely not your average middle-class employee.

I approached him slowly, thinking I was mistaken. "Excuse me? Mr. Smith?"

"Yes," he confirmed, getting up to shake my hand. "Mr. Bellator, I presume. Please, have a seat. Would you like something to drink?"

"No, thanks—and please, call me Victor." I took off my shades and sat at the table, blinking in the harsh light.

He opened his briefcase on the table and pulled out a thick file that practically screamed *contract*. "All right, Victor. I'm just going to need your signature on this consent form, and also here and here and…"

"Whoa! Wait a second!" I interrupted. "Don't you think I should know what I'm getting myself into before I sign anything? I mean, you haven't told me anything about your organization or this procedure. All I have so far is this letter with your phone number on it. And now... this. I'm sorry, but I just don't see the need for secrecy. This is my life we're talking about—right?"

He forced a smile to his lips and set his pen down on the table. "Very well," he said smoothly. "What do you think you need to know?"

I chuckled in disbelief. "Well, for starters, what's with the 'need to know' restriction? I thought this was a hospital consultation, not an interview to join the CIA." I waited for him to laugh at my snide comment, but he didn't—which made the next few seconds of silence really awkward. "Well?" I pressed.

He considered for a long moment before he began. "Well, here's the thing. R.C. Labs operates under the auspices of a much larger biotech corporation, which conducts classified research on, um..." He backpedaled. "...well, various fields in bioengineering—hence the restriction on the information we're allowed to divulge." He continued, "What I *can* tell you is that we've been in business for over 25 years, and that we hold the highest success rate in our field. Now, Victor, believe me when I tell you that R.C. Labs is about to take neuro-enhancement to a *whole* new level." He sounded, now, like he was trying to sell me something.

I rolled my eyes. "Look, I really don't care what your company does for profit, okay? What I was excited about—or rather interested in—was the procedure mentioned in your company's letter. That's what'll save my life, if anything does. Now, can you tell me something about that?"

"I'm afraid that information is above my pay-grade…" His answer made me chuckle bitterly again. "…Dr. Walker, however, will be able to answer all of your questions, once you arrive at our facility in Ketchikan."

"I'm sorry, where?"

"Ketchikan… Alaska.—If you so choose, of course." He picked up his pen and held it in front of me. I smiled grimly.

"Let me see if I've got this straight. You want me to sign this consent form, contract, or whatever it is, without knowing anything about your corporation, or the details of the procedure that I would have to undergo. *And* you want me to travel to your facility in Alaska, where I'm supposed to get my answers from a doctor I've never met before. Is that correct?"

He nodded, seeming oblivious to my sarcastic tone.

"Are you sure? Did I leave anything out?"

"All expenses paid." He smiled.

I nodded. "Oh yes, well, that's certainly a top selling point. Well, as tempting as everything sounds, Mr. Smith, I'm afraid I'm going to have to pass on your offer." Solemnly, I said, "I'm sorry we've wasted each other's time. You have yourself a good day now, sir."

As I slid out of the booth, he donned his mirrored shades and sighed. "It's progressing, isn't it?"

I froze. "What?"

"Your condition. The sensitivity to light, the headaches… the pain. It's getting steadily worse, isn't it? They've been unable to relieve the pressure, I understand?" He locked his gaze to mine, so that I could see my own wide eyes reflected in his sunglasses.

"Look, I understand your skepticism, Victor," he said soberly. "After all, you've been fighting to get better for the past three years. But what you should really be asking yourself is if this is the opportunity that you've been waiting to come and knock on your door." In the reflection from his glasses, I saw my eyebrows connect in a defensive frown. "We can help you, Victor. All you have to do is take a leap of faith." He finished with a warm smile.

Obviously, he was well practiced at this spiel, my cynical side noted. But at that moment, I couldn't help but think that my father's words had been brought back to life by this stranger. Was it coincidence? Was there even such a thing as coincidence? Or, like the lighter incident, was this an otherworldly sign, a signal trying to tell me something? Not that I ever believed in that kind of stuff, but… well, when reality becomes hopeless, I guess we tend to look for hope in the ethereal.

I pondered this as I watch the reflection of my dying self in his mirrored sunglasses. Mr. Smith held his smile as he waited patiently for my answer—as if certain of what it would be. I lowered my eyes as well as my defenses, realizing that I didn't really have anything to lose; not anymore, anyway. All I had left was a promise...and the opportunity to fulfill it. So I lifted my eyes and I found myself saying, "Where do I sign?"

***

Just a few days later, I found myself packed and on my way to the airport. As the cab sped eastbound through the Lincoln Tunnel, I took advantage of the opportunity to take an extra dose of my painkillers before I had to board the plane at JFK. My headache hadn't bothered me that morning—yet. I was really only after the strong side effect of sedation that the pills would incite in me. And though I'd never normally condone such an action, that morning was different.

You see, I *hate* flying—a fun addition to my fear of heights—and that morning I was a nervous wreck. After taking the first plane, I had to layover in Seattle and wait for *four hours* for my connecting flight. Thanks to the lack of direct flights between Ketchikan and New York, I now had to suffer the scourge of two take-offs and two landings in the same day.

I was less than pleased.

Once on the plane, I met this older couple going to the same destination. And though my reasons for visiting the Salmon Capital of the World were less than touristic, I was happy to learn a little more about it. They told me I've chosen the best time of the year to visit. Apparently, Ketchikan was normally a very cool, damp place; but during the springtime, the temperature became mildly comfortable, averaging in the lower to upper 50's, with a little less rainfall than usual. Nevertheless, they warned me not to expect to stay dry for long, since Ketchikan's annual rainfall commonly surpasses 160 inches, given that it's surrounded by the Tongass National Forest—the largest rainforest in North America. In fact, that's one of its biggest attractions.

By the time the couple was done narrating their last fishing adventure, the captain had turned off the seatbelt sign and we were in midair. I thanked them for keeping me busy during the take-off—I'd barely noticed it—and they said, "No problem," explaining that they'd noticed my anxiety from the moment they saw me board the plane. Hence the reason they'd approached me.

I thanked them again, a bit embarrassed, and leaned back on my seat. I popped another painkiller and hoped not to feel the rest of the trip.

After a terrible ordeal of switching planes, security check points, and turbulence, I finally arrived at Gravina Island, home of Ketchikan International Airport. Outside, passengers waited for an unusual-looking ferry that would take us to the mainland—a job originally intended for a bridge that was once proposed, yet never constructed. People called it the Bridge to Nowhere.

The more I learned about this place, the more I liked it.

The ferry took seven minutes to take us across the water. I must admit, I'd never seen any landscape like it before. The scenery was a canvas in which majestic mountains embraced a myriad of evergreen trees; or was it the other way around? A touch of soft mist was enough to make it impossible to tell where the summits ended and the sky began. The town's history of fishing, prospecting, bordellos, and waterfront canneries graced the horizon—the perfect finishing touch to this astonishing masterpiece.

The air was cool but crisp and pleasingly invigorating. Just being there was making me feel better already. I closed my eyes and tilted my head back, feeling the breeze combing my hair while the ferry sailed across the water—it almost felt like it was soothing my pain. When I opened my eyes, I saw two bald eagles soaring high above the water. I saw it as a sign, an omen that everything was going to be all right.

Once we docked, I decided to go and explore the picturesque town of Ketchikan. But to my surprise, transportation seemed to have been arranged for me in advance. At the curbside, a black Lincoln Town Car waited for me, complete with a uniformed driver holding a little white sign with my last name on it.

"Hi," I greeted him as I walked towards the car. "You're waiting for me?"

"Mr. Bellator?" the driver prompted. He must've been a few years older than me, but his outgoing demeanor and naive personality made me perceive him as a very young fella. But then again, my perception had been adjusted according to my experiences—which probably made me a twenty-three-going-on-fifty kind of man.

Anyway, I approached him and shook his hand. "Yeah, that's me," I replied. "And you are…?"

"Denali, sir. It's nice to meet you."

"Like the mountain?"

"That's right, sir."

"Nice to meet you, too, Denali." I gave him a friendly tap on the shoulder and brought my bag to the trunk. "But please call me Victor, all right?"

"Sure thing, Mr. Victor."

I laughed at his refreshing simplicity. "No, no—just Vic…" I backpedaled, watching the earnest look on his face. "Oh, never mind." I shook my head, smiling. "Listen, Denali. I was hoping I'd get to have a look around town before going to the clinic—maybe get something to eat, too. What do you say you drive around and pick me up in about an hour, huh?"

"I'm sorry, Mr. Victor, but I'm under strict instructions to take you straight to the mansion without delay," Denali said earnestly. He opened the back door for me, smiling like a manikin.

"Oh, hell," I mused, disappointed. "Well, I guess the tour's going to have to wait, then." I threw my backpack in the backseat, and let my body follow. "Wait—why did you call it 'the mansion'?"

"Oh, you'll see." His smile widened as he closed the door.

The drive to the clinic turned out to be longer than expected, but I didn't mind. Denali managed to keep me entertained the whole hour that it took us to get there. He was truly the epitome of Alaskan hospitality, born and bred in Sitka. But more than that, he was a good and decent man, trying to make an honest living. He told me about having to move to Ketchikan after the death of his grandfather, who'd left him everything he ever owned—including a cabin in the woods. I gave him my condolences as soon as I heard of his loss.

He wasn't happy about leaving his family behind, especially his fiancée. But he knew that after a few months of hard work, he'd be able bring everyone over and give his fiancée the wedding of her dreams. That's why his job at R.C. Labs was so important. They were paying him a small fortune to do a job that anyone could've done with their eyes close.

Talking about R.C. Labs gave me the chance to try to get more information about the place. But the funny thing was that not even Denali, who worked for them, knew exactly what the place was really about. All he could tell me was that for the last six months, he'd been picking up patients at the pier. More than a hundred, he said—which staggered me, because as far as I was concerned, my condition was unique. Or so I'd thought.

I got so caught up in the intriguing conversation that I forgot to pay attention to where I was going. The next time I looked out the window, I saw nothing but gargantuan firs that overarched the lonely road. *They must be part of the forest,* I thought—the one that I'd been hearing so much about. But what were we doing here? I would have imagined a place like R.C. Labs taking up a couple of blocks in a commercial district, not an inaccessible place like this.

I was just about to ask Denali how much farther we needed to go when he suddenly took a sharp left into a narrow and easy-to-miss gravel road. "We're almost there!" he announced, carefully guiding the car along the snakelike path. I leaned my head back against the headrest and waited, wondering about this place as my stomach plunged with anxiety. I was definitely beginning to feel the pressure of having made a decision without having all the facts at hand for the first time in my life.

Denali finally stopped next to a keypad entry-box, in front of a huge metal gate. The letters **R.C.** were engraved in the center detail of the steel beast. After punching the entry code, Denali continued down a long driveway that led us to an astonishing three-story building of a kind you definitely wouldn't expect to find in the middle of the woods.

The entire place was surrounded by dozens of enormous pines and weeping willow trees, and the astonishingly green meadow behind the building must've been as big as a football field. Not to mention the striking landscaping design that adorned the front of the building. But what really amazed and disconcerted me was the extreme security that surrounded this place. Surveillance cameras and armed personnel were posted everywhere I turned. The word *Alcatraz* flashed into my mind for a second.

Denali parked in front of the building and helped me with my bag. Once again, I told him what a pleasure it had been meeting him, and wished him luck with his wedding and all. He thanked me and returned the good luck wishes as he shook my hand.

I waved as I watched him drive away.

I turned to the main entrance with my backpack in one hand and my carry-on in the other, and saw an older gentleman in a lab coat waiting for me at the door. He must've been over sixty, yet his demeanor and posture presented a very vigorous man standing over six feet tall. His hair was gray and long, and his imposing stare lurked behind a pair of rimless glasses.

"Hello, Mr. Bellator. I'm Dr. Walker," he introduced himself, extending his hand for a shake. "How do you do?"

I quickly slung my backpack over my shoulder and shook his hand. "Very well, thank you. It's a pleasure to finally meet you, Dr. Walker—and please, call me, Victor."

"Well, Victor, I'm glad you could join us. How was your trip?"

"Eh… let's just say I'm not the best flyer." I chuckled.

"Well, you surely look like you could use some rest. Let me show you to your room." He opened the glass door and gestured for me to enter.

"Thank you." As I enter, I realized why Denali had called this place the *mansion*. The floors were paved with marble, and astonishing crystal chandeliers hung above the vestibule. Extravagant paintings decorated the elegant beige walls, further embellishing this humongous place. "Wow!" I couldn't help but exclaim as I followed Dr. Walker to what appeared to be a reception desk.

"Amy," he called to the young woman behind the desk, "this is our newest patient, Mr. Victor Bellator; he'll be staying with us on the second floor of the southeast wing. Please make sure he gets everything he needs."

"Will do, Dr. Walker." She then turned to me with a smile. "Welcome to R.C. Labs, Mr. Bellator."

"Victor, please," I corrected her with a smile. I honestly wasn't trying to flirt, but I guess she took it that way, because she responded to me with a very coquettish lopsided smile, which Dr. Walker caught sight of.

"Thank you, Amy," he acknowledged with a suppressed smile of his own, and turned back to me. "Victor? If you please…" He signaled me to follow him again.

"Of course!" I turned back again to say goodbye. "See you, Amy."

She smiled.

I followed Dr. Walker to the elevators, where he entered a code into the touchscreen panel to activate the lift. I tried to peek, but he made sure I couldn't see it. Once aboard, he pressed the number 2 among an array of buttons that didn't match the structure of the building, which seemed weird. Ten buttons didn't make sense for a three-story building, unless they had an underground parking garage I didn't know about. Anyway, once on the second floor, we emerged into a long, red-carpeted corridor with four doors along either side. Dr. Walker walked me to the one farthest from the elevator and opened the door. "I hope you find it comfortable," he said, smiling.

My jaw dropped when I walked into the room. Not only it was as elegant as the rest of the mansion, but it had all the amenities you'd find in a five-star hotel. Furthermore, my window faced the football field-sized meadow that I'd seen when we first pulled in. I was awestruck, but I tried to play it cool by joking around. "Are you sure I'm in the right place? Because I didn't sign up for a vacation."

Dr. Walker smile was unreadable. "Just try to get some rest, Victor. We have a long journey ahead of us." He turned around, closing the door.

"Wait!" I snapped. "I was hoping we could talk about the procedure and how…"

"I'll be giving a presentation this evening in the main hall," he interrupted. "You're more than welcome to join the others, and present all the questions that you may have."

"Others?"

The same unreadable smile lit the doctor's face as he spoke. "You're not as alone as you think you are, Victor." He paused. "Get some rest. I'll see you at six." He smiled again and closed the door behind him.

***

Unpacking, a quick shower, and a change of clothes were enough to make the afternoon fly by. I looked outside my window, and I saw that the bright green meadow was now covered by the shroud of the night—which startled me for a moment, because I thought that I'd missed the presentation. But after a quick glance at the digital clock on my nightstand, I realized that it was only five-thirty-five in the afternoon. Becoming conscious of this reality made me laugh at myself, because the sunset wasn't off—I was! My internal clock was all out of whack now, and it was going to take some time to adjust to this new environment.

After a few more minutes, I decided to head down to the lobby. I climbed on the elevator and found that only two buttons would function: 1 and 2. A clearance code was required to access any other level. So I pressed 1—no other choice, really.

I walked to the reception desk, where an older lady had relieved Amy, and asked her about the presentation. She pointed me in the direction of a small chamber adjacent to the main hall—apparently it had been specially prepared for tonight's presentation. When I entered this room I encountered five other people, three men and two young women, seated around an oval conference table. They obviously had no idea why we were there; their expressions showed nothing but curiosity—a familiar feeling, I must admit. I took the last empty chair and sat down. A nervous nod and a tight smile seemed to be the common greeting around the table...or at least, that's all I got. I returned their greetings the same way.

After a few minutes of uncomfortable silence, Dr. Walker made his entrance through a door no one knew was there; one of the girls started when he entered the room next to her. "Well..." he began, breaking the uncomfortable silence, "I see we're all here. I suppose the first order of business is for me to introduce myself, although I think I've met most of you already."

He smiled pleasantly. "But for the ones I haven't met: Hello, my name is Dr. Ethan Walker, and I'm the Neuro-Oncologist in charge of this research facility center—as well as the treatment protocol for each and every one of you. On behalf of everyone here at R.C. Labs, I'd like to welcome you, and to thank you for your understanding and cooperation with our security protocols. I know all of you must be equally excited and curious to learn what our new procedure is all about. But before we jump into that, why don't you just go around the table and introduce yourselves? I'd like you to have an idea of the amazing similarities that bond your extraordinary conditions. As I've said to some of you before: You're not alone as you think you are."

He paused for a second, meeting every eye in the room. "Please…" He invited the skinny blond man on my left to speak first. He was probably in his late twenties, but like most of us, his condition made his face look tired and bitter, and therefore a lot older. "Why don't you start by telling us your name and your particular condition?"

It took the guy a second to realize that Dr. Walker was taking to him. "Oh!" he said, adjusting himself in his chair. "Um… my name is Tom, and, uh… I was left with an unexplained intracranial pressure after a hang-gliding accident. The doctors said they couldn't find the cause, and that I was going to die from it, really soon… ahem, so I've been waiting." His voice weakened at the end.

"How long ago were you diagnosed, Tom?" Dr. Walker asked gently.

"Two years."

"Aftermath symptoms?" the doctor probed.

"Headaches and seizures."

"Thank you, Tom." Dr. Walker gave him a warm smile. "Would you like to be next?" he asked the guy sitting next to Tom. I looked over and noticed he was just a kid; he couldn't possibly be over eighteen. His long brown hair was tucked underneath a Red Sox baseball cap that he kept twiddling with, like a nervous tic. He looked so young that it was painful to see him there.

"My name is William," he said, shifting uneasily. "But you can call me Billie. I have the same pressure in my head that you were talking about." He glanced at Tom. "My friend hit me in the head with a baseball bat during practice—it was an accident. But after that, I started having seizures and headaches. My mom took me to the hospital, but they told me the same thing, that I was going to…" he trailed off. "Well, you know… But it's been a year since it happened and I'm still waiting."

"Can we move this along?" the blonde woman sitting next to Billie burst out, annoyed. She was definitely over-medicated. Poor excuse to act like a bitch, I thought. But she was young, too, early twenties, maybe—yet she talked like she'd been around the block a few times, if you know what I mean. "I thought we were here to find a cure, not to hear our sad little stories. And we all have one, believe me!"

"And you are, my dear?" Dr. Walker intervened.

"My name is Barbara and yes, I suffered a major head injury, too! Two and a half years ago. Different side effects, though—headaches and sensitivity to light," she said smugly.

I startled when I heard she that suffered the exact same symptoms I did. So I *wasn't* the only one. I really *wasn't* alone.

"Just that, huh?" the oldest of the group spoke. You didn't need to take a second look to realize that this man was different from the rest of us. He was in his early thirties, and yet his posture and demeanor suggested that he'd never had to endure a day's work in his entire life—other than sign a few papers behind a desk, maybe. The silk shirt and gold Rolex he wore left no doubts that he was a very wealthy man. "So the rudeness is just a natural trait?"

Barbara smirked at him; Dr. Walker gestured for him to proceed.

"My name is Damian, and I too was diagnosed with an intracranial pressure due to a severe TBI I suffered three years ago. The details of my condition I'd rather to keep to myself, if you don't mind." He stopped and leaned back in his chair, arm-crossed.

"Very well…" Dr. Walker sighed, then turned to the last woman in the group—possibly the closest one to my own age. "What about you, my dear?"

When I turned to pay attention to what she had to say, I realized she'd been staring at me. My heart skipped a beat when my eyes met her gaze; not because the extraordinary hue of her eyes resembled the clearest, brightest blue skies I've ever seen in my life, but because they reminded me of something—a feeling, something buried deep inside my heart. I couldn't put my finger on it. She looked away swiftly the second she realized I'd caught her observing me, and let her impossibly straight, long jet-black hair fall like a curtain over her angelic face, avoiding me completely.

"Hi," she began in an innocent, velvet voice, "My name is Yvette, and, uh… my story is no different than any of yours, except my major side effects are uncontrollable tremors. Um… It's, uh… been two years since it happened, and not a day goes by that I don't wish that I could find a way to put an end to it. And that's the reason I'm here." She stopped, finally tossing her hair back, allowing me to see that angelic face again.

"Victor?" Dr. Walker called, revealing my name before I did, and gestured me to proceed.

I cleared my throat before I began. "Well, that's my name. I'm Victor Bellator—headaches and light sensitivity. All I can say is that I can relate to every single one of you. It's been three years for me. Three years of pain and misery, and sometimes even wishing I was the kind of person who could end it myself… But I'm not. I am, however, the kind of person who doesn't give up. I'm here because someone once told me that one day, the answer to all of my problems would come knocking on my door." I chuckled bitterly. "And I'm really hoping this is it."

Everyone turned to Dr. Walker now.

"You are all here because you share something in common," Dr. Walker began. "The consequences of the injuries you've sustained should have killed you years ago—and yet they haven't. The circumstances that caused each of your particular brain injuries vary from case to case; however, all of you share the same final diagnosis."

He pulled down a projection screen and walked to the back of the room. Internal images of the human brain, along with text information, began to display at the command of his remote control. "You all suffer from an inexplicable intracranial pressure, or ICP—which according to most studies should produce a massive stroke in any patient in question. It is impossible under this diagnosis, however, to determine an exact timeline for this final outcome. Meanwhile, patients with ICP are prone to developing other conditions such as seizures, tremors, mood swings, sensitivity to light—and of course, excruciating headaches." A new slide flashed on the screen with every statement he made.

"How about telling us something we don't know, Doc?" Barbara said curtly.

Dr. Walker pulled a condescending smile, ignoring Barbara's comment, and continued. "After years of intense research, however, my team and I have finally discovered the source of the once-inexplicable ICPs—and that, ladies and gentlemen, is why you've been brought here to R.C. Labs." The silence in the room was now profound—dumbfounded looks were exchanged around the table. "An incredible breakthrough was made a few years ago," Dr. Walker continued, "in which we discovered that certain types of brain injuries lead to the awakening of dormant brain cells in certain patients. These brain cells, however, lack the ability to generate an action potential—in other words, they can't fire."

"Why not?" I asked, intrigued.

"Well... they never have before," Dr. Walker carried on with his explanation. "But that doesn't mean they're not trying. This conflict is producing an excessive amount of cranial pressure— and you already know what that leads to."

"All right," Damian said. "So, you've found the source of the problem. What's the solution?"

"We help them fire," Dr. Walker answered simply.

"How...?" Yvette asked, her brows creased with wonder.

"I've developed a serum," Dr. Walker explained. "It's called RC-1000. Once injected into the patient's bloodstream, it reaches the brain in a matter of seconds. From there, we monitor the attachment and penetration of the half-awakened cells by the serum. That helps us pinpoint their exact location. They will then be kindled by a predetermine amount of radiation, which in turn will generate enough action potential for them to fire."

"I'm sorry, but what does that mean?" young Billie asked, scratching his head.

Tom smiled and patted Billie's back. "It means, a cure, son— a cure!" Billie and Yvette began to smile and celebrate with Tom, while Damian, Barbara, and I remained serious and skeptical. Dr. Walker scrutinized everybody's faces.

"I'm sorry," Damian said suddenly, shaking his head. "I don't mean to rain on anybody's parade, but we haven't heard the downside of the procedure yet—and I'm sure it has one."

"Yeah, man. What's the catch?" Barbara sneered.

Dr. Walker addressed Damian and ignored Barbara. "I'm sorry, but I don't understand exactly what you mean."

Damian twined his fingers and rested his elbows on the table. "I'm no doctor, but I *do* understand that every cell in the brain has a function, even if we don't know what that function is. What are the consequences of awaking these dormant cells that have never fired before? Aren't they dormant for a reason?"

"We believe these cells have some sort of... regenerative properties. Once awakened, they might enhance your ability to heal, that's all."

"You *believe*...?" Damian repeated with a quizzical look on his face.

Dr. Walker forced a smile that soon disappeared. "I was under the impression that you ladies and gentlemen understood that this is an *experimental trial*. We don't have all the answers yet, because there are no precedents. Hence the reason you're here. And though the results are promising, I have to remind you that there are no guarantees."

"So we *are* going to be the first ones to try this serum?" I asked.

"Yes," Dr. Walker answered curtly, seeming almost offended by our skepticism. "Now, I want all of you to understand this: Although you have been carefully selected for this procedure, up until this point you can still turn it down and walk away. If you decide to stay, however, you must do so with the understanding that my instructions are to be followed diligently and without question." His eyes circled the table with a stern look. "If you are willing to accept these terms, I can schedule your procedures for as soon as tomorrow. If you're not, I urge you to speak now. Either way, I need a head count." He stood at the long end of the table with his hands behind his back and waited.

"I just want to get better," Billie said forcefully, staring blankly at the table. "I'm staying."

Tom patted Billie on the back again and turned to Dr. Walker. "I'm in."

Barbara let out a long, put-upon sigh and answered, "Sure, man... whatever!"

"I'm in, Doctor." Yvette said confidently.

Damian met Dr. Walker's stern gaze and considered for a moment. "Very well, then. Count me in."

"Victor?" Dr. Walker called.

I couldn't help but smile tentatively. "Well, I didn't travel thirty-five hundred miles just to turn back, now did I? So I guess I'm staying, too."

And just like that, we all made the irrevocably decision to put our lives in the hands of Dr. Walker... and R.C. Labs.

Chapter 5

Blast from the Past

THAT NIGHT, I lay on my fluffy, too-comfortable bed at R.C. Labs, thinking about how Dr. Walker's miracle cure might represent a new beginning for me—a new chapter in my life, one without pain, misery, or isolation, or doctors feeding me pills that didn't work. I believed that I'd found a way to fulfill my promise. I should have been happy. But the stress of it all— and something niggling at the back of my mind—kept me awake, staring at the annoyingly white ceiling.

The more I fought the feeling, the more distraught I got. I felt as if that stupid white ceiling were collapsing on me, along with the four walls that surrounded me. Soon, my distress triggered the familiar, dreadful headache, and I was brought back to my feet again. I looked for my pain medication and took it—but it wasn't enough. I needed to get out of that room or go insane. So I decided to take a walk and let the fresh air help me clear my head—after all, I was in the middle of a forest. What better air to breathe than that? But my plans were defeated as soon as I reached the lobby, where I was intercepted by two armed security guards.

"I'm sorry, sir, but nobody's allowed outside the facility at this time," one of the guards informed me, a smug tone in his voice. "Dr. Walker's orders."

His attitude triggered one of my nasty mood-swings. "*What?*" I demanded angrily.

"I'm sorry, sir, but it's for your own protection," he insisted with an arrogant grin. Dr. Walker's words flashed into mind then, reminding me that it wasn't in my best interest to break any of his rules—at least not with them watching.

"I'm sure it is," I conceded sarcastically, and stalked back to the elevators.

Back in my room, I tried to calm myself down—although I ended up punching a hole on one of the walls instead. Once they took over, those foul mood-swings were very difficult to control, and sometimes they made me do things that weren't in my character to condone. That's why I hated them so much. They turned me into a very nasty person—if only for a few minutes.

Once my tantrum was over, I decided to open the window to at least let in some fresh air. I was leaning out and taking a deep breath, trying to reorganize my thoughts, when a strange rustling sound caught my attention. I looked over to my left and noticed a huge pine tree gracing the wall next to my window. Its branches were so close together that they might as well have been a ladder. I smiled at the tempting invitation.

You see, I have this problem. If you tell me I shouldn't do something, I just might listen to you. But if you tell me that I *can't*, then you can bet your ass I *will* find a way to do it. And that's exactly how I felt when I saw that tree and thought about what the guard had said to me. I decided to fight my acrophobia—to trust the invitation of this nature-made ladder, and take the walk I had initially wanted.

After an awkward descent, from which I emerged scratched and battered, I found myself in the meadow, looking for that perfect mixture of green, yellow, and purple I'd seen when I first arrived. But the opulent moonlight shining upon the field had replaced these colors with various shades of gray, which created a somber beauty for the eye of the beholder—a beauty I'll never be able to forget.

Lost in my own thoughts, I began walking towards a light at the end of the meadow, when my attention was caught by the soft whisper of a half-familiar voice. "Stop! That's their security booth. You don't want to go there."

I followed the voice to a silhouette leaning against a stately weeping willow tree. "Unless you're *trying* to get caught, of course," the voice added.

I thought I recognized the angelic figure. "Yvette?" She stood barefoot under the tree, a pair of sandals dangling from her hand. Her hair—as black as the night—draped the right side of her face. Thick, well-defined eyebrows and impossibly fleshy red lips stood out in her exquisitely pale complexion, which seemed intensified by the moonlight.

"Yeah," she confirmed, tightening her arms around her lithe body—a black leather jacket covered the long, white nightgown she wore underneath. "You know, you're not supposed to be out here." she accused quietly.

"Neither are you," I returned, residues of anger from my mood-swing still lingering in my voice, "But I guess that didn't stop you either." I added, "What are you doing here, anyway?"

"Not much; just getting some fresh air, avoiding the guards—oh! And watching you climb down that tree over there," She snickered. "Which I do *not* recommend you do *ever* again. You really sucked at it."

Her blunt candor made me laugh. "Yeah, well, I'm not too deft when it comes to heights," I admitted. "What about you? How did you get down here?"

"Same way, just a little more gracefully." She laughed, again. "So? Are you trying to run away, or are you just looking for a way to break your neck?"

"You're not going to let that one go, are you?" I chuckled, hoping the embarrassment burning on my cheeks wasn't visible in the dark.

"I'm sorry." Her apology sounded sincere. "I didn't mean to embarrass you. You just looked kind of grumpy. I thought I should try to make you smile."

Her words made me realize that my anger was indeed gone, and that even my headache was fading. "You did," I admitted, a smile on my face. "Thank you."

"You're welcome." Her pillow lips curved into a triumphant smile of her own, yet her eyes seemed expectant, somehow. "You never answered my question, though."

"Huh?"

"Are you running away?"

"No!" I laughed, "Goodness, no. I just don't like to be told what to do, that's all. Besides, I thought a little fresh air would help me get rid of my headache. What about you?"

"Same reason." She sighed.

"Headaches?"

"No. I just don't like to be told what to do." She gave me a cocky smile and pulled a hip flask out of her inside jacket pocket. She took a big gulp from it and handed it to me. "Care to join me?"

I smiled as the smoky aroma coming out of the flask brought me back to the last time I shared a drink with my father. After years of living with him, I never needed more than a whiff to identify the smell of a good Scotch.

"Don't mind if I do," I answered willingly, reaching out for the flask.

Her hand suddenly trembled forcefully, as if a shock of electricity had run through her entire body, making her loose her grip on her flask.

I caught it and held it steady in her hand, as my eyes rose to meet her self-conscious stare. "Are those the tremors you were talking about?" I asked carefully.

"Yeah," she answered quickly, embarrassed, pulling free and hiding her hand behind her back, her eyes avoiding me now. Looking at her, I realized how uncomfortable this incident had made her feel, so I quickly changed the subject to something less solemn.

"So..." I began with a smile. "Isn't a 12-year-old single-malt Scotch just a tad too bold for a little girl like you?"

She realized I hadn't even sipped from it yet. "How did you..." she trailed off and smiled, "Very impressive. Scotch drinker?"

"My father was," I noted, taking a sip from the flask. "Now I kind of have a nose for it."

"Hmmm..."

"You didn't answer *my* question." I pressed teasingly.

"I'm not a little girl anymore, Victor." Her words held a meaning behind them that I couldn't quite perceive at the moment, though she was clearly expecting me to. "Besides, I discovered that, sometimes, this works better than those stupid pills they prescribe." She snatched the flask from my hand and took a big gulp from it—way too big.

"I know," I agreed, taking the flask back from her hand. I held an authoritative stare and tightened the cap. "But I also know the consequences of its misuse. So do me a favor and don't."

Her eyes widened with surprise to my display of authority, yet her lopsided smile suggested that she'd liked it—and that she was ready to concede to my point. "I'm not a lush, Victor," she answered, a little defensively. "But if it makes you feel better, I'll promise I'll take it easy."

"Good!" I said smugly.

She laughed.

"Where did you get this, anyway?" I asked, as I examined the leather-covered silver flask. "It's not an item I'd picture a young lady browsing for in the shopping mall." I considered for a moment. "Boyfriend's?"

She snickered. "Very smooth, Mr. Bellator."

"Please! Don't... call me that." I forced a smile. "I hate it when people call me that."

"It's your name, isn't?"

"Yeah, but..." I shook my head. "My father... he was Mr. Bellator. I'm just Victor."

"Ooookayyyy..." she drawled, not really understanding my point.

"So what's the story?" I rekindled the last subject, handing her the now-closed flask.

She frowned and took it from my hand. "It was my dad's. He left home when I was five. And that's the only thing he left behind, remember?" She waited for me to respond, but I was confounded by her remark. "You probably just forgot... It's okay." Her gaze dropped to the ground, disappointed.

"Umm..." I said intelligently, at a loss for words. "I'm sorry, I, uh..."

She stared in disbelief. "Oh my God, you don't remember me, at all, do you?" Her tone edged towards anger now. "And here I was, thinking we were having a total blast from the past, when you pretending to care was just a way to pick up a total stranger." She laughed bitterly and went for the cap on the flask again.

"Whoa, whoa, whoa! Wait a second! First of all, I meant what I said about misusing the Scotch." I put my hand over hers to stop her from opening the flask again. "And second, I've been in almost complete isolation for the past three years. The last real interaction that I can remember having with the outside world was college. And I don't remember meeting you there—and believe me, I *would* remember you." I sighed deeply and couldn't help but smile like an idiot.

She laughed mischievously, dropping her head to one side. "Are you flirting with me, Victor?" she asked, biting her lower lip in the *most* seductive way.

"I'm just saying that, um..." I trailed off, unable to get rid of the stupid grin on my face, my heart jackhammering inside my chest, and somehow found the courage to finish my sentence. "You're the most beautiful woman I've ever seen in my life."

She laughed aloud, relishing the compliment. "Now you're sounding like the Victor I know," she said, her voice taking on a yearning tone. "You used to say that to me all the time."

My eyes popped wider, filled with confusion. "What are you talking about?"

"Well, in your defense, I didn't look like this ten years ago." she admitted.

"What?"

"But I bet I can still beat you in a staring contest," she said playfully, walking to me wide-eyed, moonlight shining upon her face. Before I knew it, she engaged her impossible crystalline blue eyes with the very essence of my soul. A strong feeling of déjà vu washed over me as my eyes began to tear from her smoldering gaze. Soon this feeling brought back memories of our past contests, in which the winner was always the same. That's when my guard dropped, my eyes blinked—and I began to wonder if it could possibly be true.

"Yvee…?" I asked tentatively.

"No one's called me that since sixth grade." She shook her head in disbelief.

I just looked at her, dumbfounded, my mouth hanging open. When I could speak again I stammered, "I-I-I can't believe it. You're Yvette Montgomery—Mrs. Montgomery's little *niece*?" I phrased it as a question, but I was really trying to convince myself it was true. "Wow!" I exclaimed, appraising her from head to toe. "I mean, wow!"

"Okay, now it's getting a little awkward," she noted, folding her arms across her chest and rolling her eyes.

"I'm sorry," I apologized. "I'm just...stunned."

"Yeah, I can see that." She gave me a wide smile as she shook her head in disapproval. "Stop staring, Victor. You're embarrassing yourself." She turned around, laughing, and walked back to the weeping willow. I chuckled, blushing as I watched her sit on the grass, her back against the trunk of the tree. "You want to sit?" she invited.

I nodded like an absent-minded idiot and followed her to the tree.

"I told you to stop staring," she insisted, with a tone and look that implied the complete opposite.

I smiled and obeyed her tone, her eyes. What else could I do? She was in full command of me now.

"What happened to you, Yvee?" I asked as I lowered myself to the ground. "I always wondered after we lost track of each other."

She sighed deeply before she began. "Well... After you left the neighborhood, I went to live with my eldest aunt, Teresa, in Long Island. She was in a better financial situation than my Aunt Becky in Jersey, so they both decided that it was in my best interest to live with her instead. I missed Aunt Becky like crazy, though. And I missed the old neighborhood, too. But I guess I can't complain. I got to go to private schools, and Aunt Teresa was always supportive of my dreams of becoming a dancer. She didn't rest until she got me into the best dance conservatory in the city." She smiled proudly. "And in the end, I became what I always wanted to be: a ballerina."

"Just like your mom," I added with a smile.

Yvette's face lit up. "You remember!" Her smile as bright as the moon.

"Of course," I said softly, remembering the first time Yvee showed me a picture of her mom—a woman who shared the same amazingly black, straight hair, and that perfect contrast of pale white skin. In the picture, she was frozen in what they call the arabesque position, wearing her full ballerina outfit. I remember Yvee dancing around in her bedroom, wanting to be like her. Unfortunately, she never got the chance to meet her mother, who died giving birth to her. Stories from her aunts and dog-eared pictures of her mom's performances on the stage were all Yvette ever had of her growing up. But that never stopped her from adoring the memory of her mother.

"Anyway…" She continued. "I settled in New York, hoping to catch my big break. But all I got was rejection after rejection. Some directors wouldn't even let me audition for them, you know?"

"Why not?" I asked.

"Well," her tone turned just a tad bitter, "according to some critics, I'm just a little too well-endowed to be a professional ballerina. So they always kept my resume at the bottom of the pile. Pff!" she scoffed. "Idiots!"

"That's ridiculous!" I blustered. "You, you're perfect!" The wry look on Yvette's face made me realize that I'd actually uttered these words aloud. I wanted to crawl under a rock and die. "I mean…" I trailed off nervously. "What I'm trying to say is that, uh…"

"Shut up," she said, fighting an embarrassed smile.

I obeyed and looked at the ground, too embarrassed to say another word.

"Anyway!" she sighed, running her fingers through her untangled hair, just before she tossed it back over her shoulders. Her words began to flow in a hurry then, as if trying to put the awkward moment behind. "I didn't let that break me, you know? I kept practicing and auditioning. Until one day I got the opportunity to prove them all wrong. A big ballet company in Manhattan was seeking dancers for their new production of Swan Lake, and they called me up for an audition. I remember a lot of people telling me I was wasting my time. But I didn't listen. After two days of nonstop rehearsals, I drove myself up to the studio and waited for two hours in a room full of experienced dancers auditioning for the same role. I thought my heart was going to jump out of my chest." She sighed wistfully.

"What happened?" I urged, completely caught up in the story.

She took a deep breath and raised her eyes to the stars. "Three days after my audition, they called me up and let me know that I've been cast for the role of Odette. That was the lead role," she explained, realizing that the character's name hadn't meant much to me.

"Well, that's great!" I cheered. "I bet you brought down the house."

Her beautiful blue eyes dampened with tears. "No," she murmured. "I never got to perform."

"What? Why not?" I demanded, disappointed.

She spoke as if fighting something stuck in her throat. "I was coming out of rehearsals, two evenings before opening night, and, uh… well, a drunk driver thought it'd be fun to run through the red light while I was crossing the street. He didn't see me until it was too late." A lonely tear escaped from the corner of her eye; she wiped it off in a hurry, almost angrily. "When I woke up from my coma three days later, I was informed about my head trauma, and about my leg being broken in two places, along with a couple of ribs, and a shoulder that was now out of whack. But nothing was as painful as learning that my understudy had taken my place, and that her name was now replacing mine on all the billboards and marquees."

She growled in frustration. "She came to visit me in the hospital. I couldn't even look at her. I know it wasn't her fault, but I was just so *angry*." The line of her jaw went taut as she tried to suppress her tears. Then she went for the flask again, and took a big sip. I didn't stop her this time. "I went to visit her in the theatre after I got better, and I apologized to her. She understood."

Her eyes went thoughtful. "I decided to count my blessings and be grateful that my leg had healed so well, and that, although I didn't get to perform, I was still considered part of the company. So as soon as I felt strong enough, I went back to the theatre to try to get my life back. But I didn't last more than two weeks. I, uh, fell on stage, when one of my legs began to shake uncontrollably. I went to see a doctor, who thought I was developing Parkinson's. But then I was informed about the intracranial pressure, which was not only producing all the motor symptoms, but was eventually going to put an end to my life." She paused ruefully. "After that, I moved back to my Aunt Teresa's in Long Island, and um... I locked myself in my room for the next two years. You know the rest."

She stopped and took another sip.

After listening to her story, I was surprised to realize that sadness wasn't the only oppressive feeling in my heart. Anger was there, too; anger towards her father for not being there when she needed him the most; anger towards the stupid driver who caused the accident; anger towards this *damned* condition that was now haunting us both. But most of all, I was angry at life, which had taken umbrage against a sweet and innocent person like Yvette. She'd always been the one and only memory from my past that I had considered good and pure and perfect, and thinking that all these vile things could have happened to her just made me furious.

But I soon realized that my irrational views were only projections of another mood-swing triggered by the frustration of it all. Looking at her, I couldn't help but think: *She's just a sad, little angel whose wings have been cut off.*

"I'm sorry," I said finally, laying my hand over hers, my own jaw tight.

Another tear slid down her face as she swung her gaze to meet mine. She wiped it off, swiftly, and smiled. "It's okay—"

"It's not okay!" I snapped, "None of it is!" My fingertips flew to my temples then, as I felt my dreadful headache grinding down on me again. I groaned.

"Are you okay?"

"Yeah," I lied. "I'm fine."

She scrutinized my face for a minute.

"All right," she blurted, wiping any lingering tears from her eyes, her smile bright again. "Enough about me! It's your turn. Tell me *everything.*" She stretched the word playfully, making me laugh.

"I'm afraid we're going to need a lot more Scotch for *my* story."

"We'll make do." She handed me the flask with a crooked smile and waited.

I tried to be as thorough as she wanted me to be with my story, although some facts were too painful for me to detail: Like my dad's final days in the hospital, and his funeral. I breezed through those as fast as I could. She did stop me for a moment, though, and gave me her condolences. I thanked her and moved things along. I'm sure she noticed my avoidance of the subject. But the truth was that I had already embarrassed myself enough in front of her that night to let her watch me break into tears, too. And I had suppressed so many through the years that I knew it wouldn't be a pretty sight, so...

Anyway, I did tell her about the accident and Xavier. She stopped me there, too, and gave me a rueful "I'm so sorry." But after all the doleful things were said, I tried to lighten the mood by talking about our accomplishments rather than our frustrations. In my case, I told her about my getting my bachelor's in physics and mathematics despite of my condition, and she told me about her years in the conservatory.

The hours flew by.

There was a moment of silence, after all of our talking, in which Yvette lay her head back against the tree and raised her eyes to the night sky. I, on the other hand, took advantage of her remoteness to admire her; she looked like a perfectly chiseled marble statue. I became so enthralled by her beauty that I didn't care anymore if she caught me staring. To see her was to love her—and I think… I wanted her to know.

Her sapphire eyes widened then, with a surprise that made her lips part, just enough to let out a small sigh. "Look!" she prompted, pointing at the night sky. Her request (more than my curiosity) made my eyes stray from her face. "Isn't it amazing?" she exclaimed, as our eyes beheld the extraordinary wonder of the Northern Lights. "I was told you couldn't see them this time of the year. It must be a sign or something!" She gazed in wonder at the fluttering bands of colors that glowed across the darkness.

I wondered, too; but I was wondering if my sign wasn't sitting right beside me rather than on the threshold of space. And though I'd never seen the magnificent aurora before, my eyes chose to move back to the mortal angel to my left, taking a rain check on the natural marvel in the sky. "Have you ever seen anything so beautiful?" she asked.

"No," I breathed, my eyes fixed on her.

She threw a glance at me from the corner of her eye and noticed my staring. "You're not even looking," she accused.

"Oh yes I am."

She turned to me then, and allowed me to monopolize her absorbing eyes for the longest moment. "What?" she breathed, as a coy smile lit up her face.

"Do you really believe in signs?" I asked meaningfully.

She nodded. "Don't you?"

"My father wanted me to." I considered thoughtfully. "But I never did. Not until a couple of days ago. Something happened back in my apartment that led me to this place—and now I'm here... with you." I shook my head in disbelief. "Forget it! I'm probably just losing my mind."

"You're not," she comforted me, laying her hand over mine. "Tell me."

I deep sigh escaped my lips, as an old familiar impulse made our hands fold together. I don't think either of us noticed it until it happened. "Do you remember our last day together?" I asked, trying to resort to memories to make my point.

She let out a cheerless sigh. "We were twelve, Victor—"

"Do you remember?" I insisted.

She looked into my eyes; her gaze was overwhelming. "Of course," she said. "So many things happened that day... I couldn't forget if I tried."

"Tell me." My request sounded more like a plea.

Her brow puckered as if in disappointment. "You don't remember?"

"I do," I assured her. "But if you don't mind, I'd like to relive it through your eyes."

She tried to suppress a smile, and nodded. "Okay. Where should I start?"

"What's the first thing you remember?"

"A bike ride!" she began. "Yeah... You came and took me out for a bike ride. But you left something at home... your wallet! You wanted to get me one of those, uh, bocconottos from Rosa's Bakery, because you knew I loved them so much. So we went back to your house, but you got derailed. Your dad's car was parked in the driveway, and you weren't expecting him so early. So we went back inside through the back door, and we heard him talking with an older man in the living room. He was a realtor. He was telling your dad about the house having been sold as he'd requested, and that his offer on the new one, a hundred miles away, had been accepted.

"I remember you went pale and staggered backwards into the wall. But then you grabbed me by the hand and ran out with me into the backyard. You told me you were running away, and that you were taking me with you." She snickered sheepishly, avoiding my eyes for a moment, our hands exploring each other's as if with minds of their own. "I remember smiling and saying okay." she added, blushing.

"You wanted to leave right away. But I convinced you to wait until midnight, because I knew everybody'd be looking for us otherwise. So we readied our backpacks and hid in my Aunt Becky's cellar. I thought she'd never find us there, because of the old armoire, remember?"

I nodded in response, remembering the large, stand-alone wardrobe Mrs. Montgomery kept in the cellar. The tall, double-door, mahogany monster used to serve us well when playing hide-and-seek during the endless summers at Mrs. Montgomery's house. She could never find us, especially with all the clutter she kept around the cellar. As strange as it sounds, this piece of furniture became our secret hideout after an incident that happened when Yvette was about ten. She went missing after a stupid kid from school said something cruel about her father abandoning her. Mrs. Montgomery went crazy looking for Yvette.

But it was *me* who found her, crying in that closet. She was crouching in a corner with her arms wrapped around her knees. I remember crawling inside and hugging her. I cried, too—not only because I understood the pain of being abandoned, but because I saw my little blue-eyed angel hurting. We made a promise then that if we ever felt the need to cry again, we'd do it in there, where no one else could see us.

We cried a lot.

"Yeah." She let out a sigh and continued, "I remember you pulling me into the closet when we heard people coming into the house. We knew we were busted. But you still closed those heavy double doors on us and asked me to be quiet. Then, as we heard them descending the squeaky stairs, you cupped the back of my head and told me the strangest thing." She paused and frowned into space. "You said... *'Don't worry. Not even Space and Time can keep us apart. We're bound to find each other again.'* ...And then you promised."

Her face went blank for a moment. But then she snapped out of it and laughed quietly, tightening her hold on my hand. "You sure were a strange boy," she added. "Always adding science to everything you said, always trying to make sense of things when you knew they were senseless. It made it very difficult to read you sometimes. To this day, I have no idea what you tried to say to me in that closet." She smiled.

"Funny you should say that," I noted, "because it wasn't until tonight that I actually found the meaning of those words myself."

Her eyes flew back to mine to meet my solemn gaze, her expression skeptical. She then looked down at our entwined hands and considered for a moment.

"It's a matter of fact, I've wondered about those words for years," I added. "I've wondered if they were actually spoken or just something I thought of in the heat of the moment. But tonight you've confirmed them to be real… in more than one way."

She pondered my words for the longest time, staring blankly at the aurora, until a sudden tremor shook our folded hands, snapping us both back to reality. Her eyes hardened then and she pulled her hand away from mine, as if regretting ever holding it again. "What are we doing?" she asked, her voice as hard as a rock. "Encouraging a romantic delusion from a stupid pre-teen crush?"

Her words plunged into my stomach like a rusty knife. "Is that how you see it?" I said, my voice rough with the edge of another mood swing.

"It doesn't matter how I see it, Victor! We're letting ourselves forget that we're *sick*—that any minute could be our last. You heard what Dr. Walker said. Even with this treatment, there are no guarantees. We still might not wake up tomorrow. Why do you think I locked myself in my room for two years?

Depression? No! I didn't want to meet or get involved with anybody who was going to end up mourning me, Victor. And I'm pretty sure that's the reason you isolated yourself, too. Do you really want to rekindle something that's only going to bring us more pain? I mean, aren't you tired of attending funerals?"

Her last words got me back up on my feet.

"I'm sorry," she apologized quickly, her voice softer. "I didn't mean that. I'm such an idiot," she whispered, her eyes big and wide, like those of a sad puppy dog. "Please, don't go, Victor."

I stood there fighting my anger and debating whether or not to speak my mind; and then I realized that the answer for that question was clear. So, I began: "You know what, Yvee? I didn't have much growing up. Maybe that's the reason why all my feelings were invested in so few people—making me love them, a little too much, I guess. Xavier for instance...he was not only my friend, but the brother I never had. I loved him dearly. And yet, I never told him. Instead, I teased him and patronized him. Now I wonder if he ever knew how important he was to me.

"My dad... he was my father, my mother, my mentor, my friend, my entire family. No son could ever love a father the way I loved him. And yet he never heard me say it. He flat-lined before I could utter the words. After that, I made myself a promise: that no matter how embarrassed, self-conscious, or out of place I felt, I'd never conceal my feelings again. Because I might just not have a second chance to let them show. And you're right. We might not wake up tomorrow. But I think that only makes what I need to say all the more imperative."

I paused and paced around for a few seconds, pressing my fingertips against my aching temples. Yvette, still seated with her back against the tree, waited for me to continue, until I finally turned around and let my words gush like the waters of an open floodgate. "I loved you, Yvee. You were my neighbor, my classmate, my best friend for twelve years... You were my first kiss... You were my first love... And when I saw you again today—even though I didn't recognize you at first—my heart skipped a beat. *It literally skipped a beat.* I know how strange and even stupid that seems, but I swear to you it's the truth."

I paused for a moment, realizing how neurotic I was beginning to sound. But the throbbing pain in my head reminded me that at this juncture in my life, being neurotic was just good common sense, so I continued. "All night I've been fighting this impulse, this urge, to reach out to you and hold you. I have this irrational feeling deep inside my chest that makes me want to protect you, that makes me want to be near you. I feel a *connection* that I can neither explain nor control. I've been racking my brain, running the numbers, trying to understand what I'm feeling here. But I can't find an answer.

"All I know is that these past few hours have been the happiest I've felt in a long time—if not ever." My vision blurred with the tears I could no longer suppress, and the knot stuck in my throat was too thick to swallow. But somehow I managed to keep it all in. "My father spoke to me of a sign that would lead me to my happiness. I believe that sign brought me here. I believe that sign brought me to *you*. I wish I could've told you all this differently. Over dinner, maybe, in a beautiful restaurant, holding your hand, after dating you for some time. But *time* is a luxury we no longer have. And if I'm to die tomorrow, I want to know that I can go with no regrets. Telling you exactly what I'm feeling at this moment is the only way I can do that."

The silence that followed my words allowed me to take a breather and rearrange my thoughts. And though I knew I'd spoken from the heart, I couldn't help but fear that my blunt display of candor might be misconstrued as the cry of a psycho ex-boyfriend. So I decided to stop embarrassing myself and leave—as I probably should have from the beginning. "I'm sorry," I apologized. "I'll leave you alone, now, okay?" I turned around and took my first step out of there.

"Wait!" she called swiftly.

I stifled a sigh and turned around to face her again. She was on her feet now.

"That's it? Really? You're going to drop that bomb on me and just leave me here in the middle of the night?"

I shifted uneasily, trying to decide what to say. Finally, I shoved my hands into my pockets to steady myself, and let go of the first thing I had on my mind. "I know it sounds crazy, but I only said what I thought needed to be said… for me."

"What about me?" she asked, a thread of outrage in her tone. "Don't I have a say?"

I kept my gaze fixed on the ground, too mortified to look her in the eye again. "Well, you probably think I'm crazy. And that everything I just said is nothing but a—"

"Stop!" she protested, her voice angry now. "Don't do that! Don't presume to know what I'm thinking! It drives me crazy— it always did! Just do me a favor and just…just stay there! And don't move or speak or… I need to think."

I stood there quietly, like a reprimanded child, while she paced awkwardly in front of me. She finally stopped after what felt like hours, but in reality couldn't have been more than a few minutes. I looked up to see her leaning backwards against the tree, her eyes raised to the night sky. I could see the aurora glowing upon her face.

"When you saw me in the presentation room…" she asked cautiously, "Did you feel this… *connection* then?"

"Yes," I answered without hesitation.

She nodded softly, her face unreadable. And though her eyes seemed occupied with the aurora, her stare held complete emptiness. "Do you remember what happened in the old armoire after what you said to me?" she asked, her voice almost a whisper now.

"Of course," I answered solemnly.

Her eyes abandoned the mesmerizing aurora and locked directly onto mine. "Tell me," she demanded.

"Why? You were telling this story better than I ever could have."

"Maybe," she agreed. "But this part I'd like to relive through *your* eyes."

"All right," I agreed, retracing my thoughts back to that gloomy summer night in Jersey. "After what I said," I began, "I heard my dad's voice coming from upstairs. I knew it was over, because I knew that once he was in front of me, I'd never be able to disobey him. So I turned on my flashlight, thinking that was probably the last time I'd ever see you. It broke my heart when I saw tears running down your face. I tried to wipe them all away, but they just kept coming. I remember running my fingers through your hair, asking you to *please* don't cry. Then I promised you that no matter what, I would never forget you... because you would always be in my heart. And then I put my hand over the closet door, ready to turn myself in, but you stopped me. You pulled me close to you and said…"

I paused briefly, with an elated smile, lost in the memory. "...You said: *You never break your promises. Don't break this one. Don't forget about me. And I promise you, I will always be your girl.* And then we kissed, for the first time." I stopped then and sighed wistfully. My eyes, freed of reminiscence now, sought reaction from hers; but Yvette's eyes were lost in the vastness of the night sky again.

"You were my first kiss too," she said finally, with a faint smile on her face.

"I know." My voice held no doubt.

Her eyes slid back to me then, with a hint of regret in them, her smile gone. "Then you know I didn't mean what I said before, right? About us having a stupid pre-teen cr—"

"I know," I interjected quickly.

"Good," she breathed. "Because nothing could be farther from the truth. And I wouldn't want you to think that's how I remembered us." She paused. "I wanted to hear my own words from you, because—much like yours—they needed to be confirmed as true... just as you've done. Thank you for that," she whispered, turning back to me with a determined look on her face, her hands behind her back as she leaned backwards against the tree. "I want to tell you something that will probably just complicate things even more. But like you said, some things just *need* to be said. Especially when you don't know if tomorrow will ever come for you. So here goes."

She took a deep breath and continued. "This morning I peeked over the reception desk and, uh... I saw your name on the list. At first, I thought it was someone else with the same name. But then, when I saw you in the presentation room, I knew it was you." She smiled gently. "...My Victor. The one who use to fight bullies at school just to keep me safe... The one who made me *so* jealous when he let stupid Heather Thompson touch his beautiful, feathered hair in the fifth grade." She chuckled, but solemnity returned to her voice in a flash as she continued. "The one who'd cry with me whenever I felt sad...

The one who never got tired of telling me how beautiful he thought I was... The one I used to dream would come and wake me from my nightmares and tell me: *I've come to take you with me.*"

She paused, sniffling back some tears. "The truth is that you left a huge hole in my heart, Victor. And I'd be lying if I'd told you I didn't feel the same inexplicable urge to run to you and hug you the moment I saw you walking through that door. I did. I almost felt as if I was entitled to." She shook her head, as if trying to regain some measure of courage. But then she looked up and bored into my soul with those mesmerizing blue eyes of hers, as if determined to finish what she needed to say. "And that connection you were talking about...?" She sighed. "I feel it, too."

I stood there in shock; and though her words had brought me a flood of happiness, they had also managed to elevate the rhythm of my young ticker to a distressing jackhammering mode that I was afraid she'd be able to hear.

"So there!" she continued nervously. "Now we've expressed our feelings—exposed the truth. Now, if we die tomorrow... Well, then at least we'll do so in the knowledge that we haven't kept that knowledge from each other, right?" Her voice sounded desperately eager to justify our current behavior.

"Yes," I breathed. "But... what if we live?"

"Ha!" She blushed and hesitated sheepishly before saying, "If we live? Yeah, well, if we live..." She considered for a moment, and smiled. "Then I guess tomorrow will be the most awkward day of our entire lives."

We both broke out laughing then. Her hand flew to her face, cupping her mouth with embarrassment. She rolled her eyes at me and waved her other hand, as if blaming me for the awkward moment. For me, it was a treat to watch this blushing angel laughing in all her splendor.

"But at least we'll be able to spend that life together," I told her, and she stopped laughing abruptly, her eyes glistening green-flecked pools in the aurora light.

"So..." she said, her voice meaningful again, "can your numbers or scientific method make sense of any of this? I mean, is it normal, or even possible, for two people who haven't seen each other for a decade to stumble upon each other in such an unusual out-of-the-way environment, under circumstances like these, and feel the *exact* same thing at the *exact* same moment?"

"I don't know," I admitted.

Yvette smiled, as if pleased by my earnest response. "I like that," she whispered.

"What's that?"

"Your honesty," she said, capturing my eyes with a gentle glance, her smile so faint as to be almost unnoticeable now. "I always loved that about you. Your confidence, your loyalty, your courage, and even your stubbornness." She snickered softly. "I love the fact that you were once an Eagle Scout... And that you named a star after me for my eleventh birthday. I love that you once helped me bake my favorite pastry, although we almost burnt down the house."

We both laughed again, wishing we could return to that simple time. "I love the fact that you never left your dad," she continued, "especially when he needed you the most." Her eyes dampened then. "That shows the wonderful person you are. But what I really, *really* love the most is that you're still the same Victor I knew." She paused, piercing me with her eyes, her lips trembling. "I guess what I'm trying to say is that I... I loved you, too, Victor—I always did."

Her words made my heart skip another beat, while one of her trapped tears finally escaped from the corner of her eye. The clear droplet rolled gently down the side of her adorable heart-shaped face as her lips gave me the most genuine smile I'd ever seen.

I sighed with wonderment at my angel, lost in her beauty.

A profound silence had engulfed the entire meadow when an extraordinary thing happened. And I'm not talking about the aurora—which began to glow even brighter and greener than before—but a surreal connection that compelled our eyes to lock in an unbreakable stare, in which I felt my soul being sucked in by her eyes and hers by mine.

I'd be remiss not to clarify that what happened then was something much more profound than a mere romantic moment. A voiceless feeling began to well up in my heart, telling me that I no longer belonged to myself, but to Yvette. It was hard for me to accept what I was experiencing, given my predisposition toward logical reasoning. But I had to admit that whatever was happening to me shook my beliefs and everything I ever thought I knew to the core, leaving me with nothing but my father's transcendental beliefs—which were never my strong suit. Nevertheless, I considered the possibilities.

When our eyes were finally released from this trance, we sighed and smiled at each other with disbelief. Our mirrored reaction to the event let us both know that the experience had been shared equally —and that something inside us had been set right forever. We tried to pull ourselves together, but it took us a few minutes to actually shake our wonderment. Even when we did, we couldn't stop smiling.

"What just happened?" Yvette whispered, her expression bewildered.

"I have no idea," I said just as softly, taken aback by the strange experience. "But it was amazing," I added.

Yvette agreed with me with a vigorous nod.

I became dazed the moment I discovered that two amazingly powerful feelings lingered from this peculiar event. One was an extraordinary mixture of happiness and relief, as if a maddening emptiness in my chest had been finally refilled. The second was the familiar, yet compelling impulse to reach out for Yvette and hold her tightly in my arms—a feeling now increased tenfold by this inexplicable thing that had passed between us. Confounded by my own thoughts, I closed my eyes and fought to restrain it, thinking I was the only one having it. But soon, Yvette alerted me otherwise.

"Did you feel it, too?" she asked innocently, wide-eyed. "The relief? The entireness? The... happiness?" Her question not only gave a matching description of what I had just felt, but made me realize that we were sharing the same feelings even as we spoke. I nodded in response, too dumbfounded to use words— and kept controlling my impulse to lunge towards my dazed angel, who now seemed jittery, bouncing gently on her ballerina toes, showing an obviously forced constraint. "Do you also feel the same need to—?"

"Yes!" I confessed bluntly, before she could finish the unneeded question. It was clear now that we both shared the same overwhelming desire for physical contact, and there was no use denying it. I took a few steps, cautiously, in her direction and extended my hand to hers, my heart racing like an out-of-control engine. "Would you mind terribly if I just—?"

"No," she interjected swiftly, approving my request before my words were uttered, as if letting me know that it was no more needed than her own unfinished question.

I walked to her then, an open hand in front of me, watching her chest rise and fall faster with every step I took. She looked down at my hand the moment I stopped in front of her, and smiled. Then, she pushed herself off the tree with one graceful move and brought her hands from behind her back, our bodies just inches away now. My world stopped spinning the moment

I felt her dainty hand slowly slip into mine. For the first time in my life, everything became clear and right. I understood, somehow, that this moment was the reason why my heart had not given up on me yet.

I closed my eyes then and leaned my forehead against hers, as if tired from a lifelong journey. She seemed to feel the same way. A deep, mutual sigh of relief finally escaped our lips when our arms slid around each other in a tight and powerful embrace that lasted for the longest moment of my life. It was a moment in which we forgot about everything; who we were, where we were, and why. For that moment on, we felt no pain, sadness, or despair. All we could feel was our warmth, and a feeling neither of us knew much about: happiness. We were no longer nervous about being with each other. On the contrary, we found ourselves in a familiar place. Being with each other made us feel safe; it made us feel at home.

"I've missed you, Victor," she said, her face pressed against my chest.

"I've missed *you*," I whispered, my voice filled with emotion, "But that's over now. I promise." I softened my hug and leaned backwards to try and see her angelic face again, but her arms tightened around my waist like a grapple, making me resume my loving embrace. I smiled uncomplainingly.

"Don't," she grumbled. "Don't let go. I don't want to wake up just yet." Her voice was nearly a whisper.

"This isn't a dream, Yvee." I assured her, but my words only made her hug tighten.

"Then how do you explain what's happening to us?"

"I don't. I can't."

"Yeah, but... Is it normal?"

I chuckled, realizing the truth—our truth. "We don't need it to be normal. We only need it to be real." I curled my finger under her chin and lifted her head as I lowered mine to her eye level. "And it is. I promise."

She smiled coyly. "I should know by now that you always keep your promises."

"Will you keep yours?" I asked profoundly.

She gasped and smiled, embarrassed—her face flushed again. But then her smile softened and her eyes opened with a sincerity I've never seen before in anyone. "Yes," she said, running her fingers through my hair, her blue eyes scanning my very soul. "I'll always be your girl. I promised."

The aurora went haywire then, as if stirred by our emotions, painting its wondrous green hues upon our faces as our lips reached for each other in a slow, teasing dance. I couldn't think of anything more perfect than when her tender lips brushed timidly against mine. It was like gliding my lips over the petals of a velvety red rose after a morning drizzle. I could've died happy at that moment, and I still know that life itself couldn't possibly be any better than what I felt then. My heart had never beaten so fast—and yet, it had never been so peaceful. And I was close enough to feel hers, too—beating at the same rate as mine.

We finally consummated our kiss, opening ourselves completely to the overpowering feeling that came from us being together. Our hearts exchanged in the process. We moved apart, slowly, but just enough to lock our gaze—enough to reassure ourselves that we weren't dreaming. We held hands, completely breathless, and gazed into each other's eyes, no longer caring for answers.

Never before had I believed in the existence of soul mates—until our fingers, unintentionally, interlocked in a perfect fit, like two pieces of a puzzle that had finally been brought together. We held each other tightly then, as if we were never letting go, as if we had been waiting for this moment for our entire lives—because somehow, in this confusing, cruel, and hurtful world, we had finally found each other. She rested her head on my chest and words were no longer necessary. We had felt everything that needed to be said. We knew we hadn't lived long, and we knew we might not have much longer to live, either. But that night, we let go of our sorrows. We lived in the moment, as if it were the first and the last of our uncertain lives.

That night we lived a lifetime under the weeping willow tree.

"You're cold," I whispered finally, with a faint smile. "Maybe we should call it a night."

PREDOMINANCE

"Our night has just begun," she said softly. "Let's stay a while."

Chapter 6
The Procedure

AFTER THE INEXPLICABLE phenomenon that made us throw our inhibitions to the wind and rekindle the love we once felt for each other, Yvette and I found ourselves yearning for a future that we could only hope would come. Sitting side by side under the weeping willow, we floated off into reverie and talked about the dreams we wanted to accomplish, should Dr. Walker's miracle cure give us another chance to live. Yvette talked about finding her father, which to me sounded like a complete waste of a dream. I mean, why would you try to find someone who doesn't want to be found?—or worse, someone who'd never try to find *you*?

But I guess she believed that closure was something we all need in order to move on with our lives. She even tried to convince me, at some point, that finding my mother was something I should definitely include in my to-do list—or our

Dream List, as we liked to call it. But the sullen look on my face gave away my thoughts on the subject.

"What?" she asked. "Wouldn't you like to find her, and know why she did what she did?"

Her words made me consider that for a moment. "No," I answered finally.

"Why?"

"Because no explanation could ever justify or vindicate walking out on a six-year-old child and breaking the heart of a good man like my father. She killed him the day she left, and that's not something I'd ever be able to forget." I paused ruefully. "I don't hate her, you know? But I'm afraid that if I ever saw her or listened to her, I would begin to. And I don't want that."

She looked at me pitifully and cupped the side of my face. "You couldn't hate anyone, Victor. It's not in your nature."

I went for her hand, kissed it, and held it in mine, my eyes wide and sincere. "Thank you, Yvee. But that's something I hope I'll never have to prove." Then, taking a deep breath and heaving a rueful sigh, I deliberately strayed from the subject. "Why don't you just tell me what else you have in mind for your Dream List, huh?"

"Right." She acknowledged my avoidance and gave in. "Well, let's see... I always wanted to visit the Bolshoi Theatre in Russia," she said.

I laughed quizzically. "Okay, you're going to have to explain that one."

She laughed, too, and spun around on her bottom to face me. Her skillful legs locked into the lotus position at the end of her spin, with an ease that would make any yogini jealous. "All right," she began, with a radiant look on her face. "The Bolshoi Theatre is one of the oldest and most renowned ballet theatres in the world. Not to mention that it's a work of art, complete with Imperial décor, nineteenth-century wooden fixtures, and French-made red velvet banquettes..."

Her eyes flickered with excitement as she described this incredible Russian landmark. I listened attentively to every detail. And though the Bolshoi sounded like a remarkable tourist destination, I couldn't help but sense a more powerful reason for her wanting to visit. For me, it felt like an incomplete equation, so as soon as she finished, I probed for the missing variable.

"Well, it sounds like an amazing place," I noted. "But you still haven't told me why. Why *that* theatre? Why Russia?"

She glanced away, hesitant. "You may find my reason a little strange."

"Oh, come on!" I encouraged. "Strange? It's been the genre of my life."

She laughed aloud. "I thought *I* had a patent on that genre."

"Uh-uh. Come on, tell me," I insisted.

She considered for a moment as she raised her eyes anew to the now-fading aurora. A soft breeze made her shiver and wrap her arms around herself. So I offered my body heat to keep her warm. "Come here," I said, suggesting she sit next to me again. She gave me a coy smile and moved to cuddled under my arm. I rested my face against her hair, getting lost in her scent, and then appealed for her to continue.

After a wistful sigh, she yielded: "Ever since I can remember, I've had this recurring dream in which I see myself standing on the stage of the Bolshoi Theatre. But the auditorium is completely empty. Not one seat is occupied—and yet, I feel the compelling need to perform. The music for Odette's solo begins to play, my body begins to move, and I dance. I dance like I've never danced before. With no restrictions, no mistakes. Then, when the music finally fades down, I hear the applause of a single person. I look up, and there she is." She stopped.

"Who?" I urged.

"My mother," she answered, wiping a tear from the corner of her eye. Clearing a knot in her throat, she continued. "After years of having this dream, one day I recognized the stage in a television special I was watching with my Aunt Becky. She told me that Mom's dream was always to dance for the Bolshoi Ballet Company, and perform in that beautiful theatre. But she never did. I know that finding out that the place I'd been dreaming about for so long was real, and that it somehow had a connection with my mother, should've freaked me out. But it didn't. On the contrary, it inspired me." She mused for a long second. "Anyway, I know that not many people would understand. But I feel like it would be a tribute to her. If I could just dance to her favorite piece, even if the theatre were empty, her spirit would be all the audience I'd ever need."

She stopped then, and looked up for my reaction. "What do you think?" she asked.

"I think it's perfect," I said sincerely. "And I'm sure she'd look upon you proudly."

"Thanks." She smiled and burrowed deeper into my chest. "What about you?" she asked. "You haven't said much about your Dream List. What would *you* like to do?"

I sighed deeply. "Well, I wouldn't call it a list, really; mine only has one thing on it. But you know what? In a way, I think it resembles *your* dream—not that I would dance or anything. But my dad also had a dream that he didn't get to see realized. And I guess, at some point, it became mine, too. I always thought that he would look upon me from wherever he is, and smile proudly." I paused for a moment to glance at her meaningfully. "At least now I know I'm not the only one who thinks like this."

She studied my face for a moment. "What's the dream?" she asked.

"To sail around the world," I said wistfully. "To live the remainder of my life at sea. Anyway, after my dad died, I received a letter from the truck company involved in my accident. Their settlement was not only unexpected, but it was more than enough to realize my dad's lifelong dream. So I went down to the marina and I started looking for sailboats. I set my eyes on this beautiful Bavaria Cruiser 36 and told the sales broker that I'd be back as soon as I cashed my check."

"That's amazing, Victor!" Yvette cheered. "I bet you couldn't wait to set sail."

I pressed my lips together tightly and gave her a regretful look. "Well... I did get the check, but I didn't buy the boat."

"Why?" she asked, disappointed.

"I thought it would be a waste, you know? With me dying and all." I shrugged, dispirited.

Still in my arms, she turned around and enveloped me with her big, mesmerizing, blue eyes, her voice soft as she pleaded, "Don't say that again, please. I don't want to hear you speak like that anymore. I know life hasn't always been what we hoped. But I'm convinced now that what's happened here tonight is a beginning, not an end. I want you to believe, just like I do, that tomorrow really will be the first day of a new life—for all of us. I want you to believe that the only thing that will die here is our pain. And I want you to *promise* me that when all this is over, you *will* get that boat." She smiled encouragingly. "Okay?"

I favored her with an elated smile as I tucked her silky hair behind her ear. "I'll promise on one condition. You'd have to be my first mate for the duration of the sail."

She looked down, fighting an embarrassed smile, her face flushed tomato red. "Um-hmm." She pretended to consider— her smile seemed mischievous now. "And what does this position entail, exactly?" she asked coquettishly.

I smiled softly and said, "To be one with your boat..." gliding my fingers down her temple, over her cheek, and stopping at the corner of her enticing lips, "...and to be one with your captain," I added with a whisper, my lips reaching for hers.

"And how long would this journey last?" she asked under her breath, trembling, our lips almost touching now—

"Oh, it's bound to last forever."

Our lips met in another passionate kiss that turned our doubts into certitude, and our dreams into the desire we needed to finally see them through. And though questions remained about that night, one thing was for certain: We would never be the same. And we not only knew it, we wanted it that way.

"Okay," she breathed. "Let's set sail, my Captain."

***

Our kiss ended abruptly when a powerful beam of light shone on our faces, making us pull apart. A natural reflex brought my hand to my face, trying to block the powerful glare, which left a bunch of purple dots printed in the backs of my eyes. Soon, I realized that the beams came from the portable searchlights of the security guards.

"Hey! What are you doing out here?" one of the guards shouted, aiming the blazing light at my face. My eyes shut immediately, feeling the burn of hundreds of hot needles piercing into my skull, igniting my blasted headache all over again. "Please, don't," I growled.

The same obnoxious guard who had intercepted me at the door recognized me as soon as he heard my voice. "Oh, it's you," he said disgustedly. "Didn't I tell you patients weren't allowed outside the building? How the hell did you get out here, anyway?" he demanded, shining the blinding light full in my face.

I cursed in pain.

"Stop!" Yvette shouted, realizing my agony. "You're hurting him!"

It didn't take long for the guards to realize that the lights were the cause of my behavior. Most of them turned them off, while others flashed them down to the ground—except for the obnoxious Head of Security, who still remained skeptical.

"I'm serious!" Yvette snapped. "Turn it off!"

He finally backed down, reluctantly, aiming away the searchlight. "Take them back to their rooms, and make sure they stay there," he ordered one of his peers. "And you!" he turned to me, raising a menacing finger. "No more screwing around, you understand?"

I raised my head slowly, regaining full function, and responded, "Whatever you say, *doorman*."

He gave me a stern look and walked away, ordering one of his subordinates to take over.

The young guard left in charge rushed to help me up, with genuine concern in his eyes—a far better person than his nominal superior. I got back on my feet and let him know I was good to walk. He escorted Yvette and me back to the mansion, and insisted on seeing us back to our respective rooms.

Yvette and I couldn't believe that our night was over. I could see the wan look on her face as we began to walk in opposite directions. Her fingers, entwined with mine, held on to the last minute, until they finally slipped away. We then stopped at our respective thresholds and turned around, desperate to catch one last glimpse of each other.

"Thank you," she said. "It was a wonderful night, Victor. I'll never forget it."

"It was my pleasure," I replied gallantly.

"Come on, guys!" the guard shouted from the elevator, annoyed. "I want to hear those doors close."

We laughed, embarrassed.

"Will I see you in the lab tomorrow?" she asked, her head leaned back against the half-open door.

"You'll see me in your dreams tonight."

She smiled. "You promise?"

"I promise."

Reluctantly, our doors closed at the same time.

The next morning I woke up with a brand new desire to live. All I could think of was Yvette, and how desperately I wanted to see her again. I jumped out of bed and into the shower and got ready in a flash, excited about the big day. I almost didn't recognize myself in the mirror when I wiped off the fog to see my face; I just couldn't stop smiling, and I knew it was all because of her.

I was just about to leave the room when I heard a knock on the door. "Come in," I answered.

"Good morning, Mr. Bellator," an older woman wearing scrubs greeted me as she entered the room. "I'm Nurse Jacky, and I'm here to take you down to the lab."

"Oh... I didn't know someone was coming to get me."

She nodded with an obviously forced smile.

"I'm sorry, um... Are you taking Ms. Montgomery too?" I asked hopefully.

She glanced at her clipboard. "Hmmm... no," she answered, "It looks like she was the first one to be taken to the lab this morning."

"Oh." My disappointment was obvious. But then I thought of her being one step closer to getting her life back, and I smiled to myself.

"Ready?" Nurse Jacky asked.

I smiled nervously. "Yeah."

"Then let's go!" She gestured towards the door.

Once at the elevators, she used a special keycard to activate a hidden sub-panel that showed access to several levels underground. She gestured for me to climb on board and pushed the button for the lowest floor. For a moment there, I couldn't help but wonder about the unusual layout of this strange facility. But my thoughts derailed when the elevator doors opened again.

"Victor!" Dr. Walker greeted me with great enthusiasm. He was wearing the same white lab coat he'd worn during the presentation; and although he seemed very eager, his eyes showed the weariness of many sleepless nights. "I'm so glad you can join us!"

"Good morning, Doctor." I walked over to him and shook his hand, a quick look around made me realize that I was the only one from my group standing there. "I'm sorry," I apologized, "Am I late? I hear that some of the others were brought down here earlier."

"Yes, indeed. You all had different treatment schedules, but *you*, my friend, are just in time—come!" He beckoned me to follow as he stood proudly in the middle of this enormous two-story underground lab, which was filled with state-of-the-art computers and complete instrumentation tables. Dozens of busy lab technicians worked in an organized chaos, while shakers, incubators, and analyzers went off—all at the same time. It was enough to make you dizzy. "What you're seeing here, Victor, is history in the making. And *you* are about to become part of it."

I chuckled uneasily, trying to register the moment in my mind.

"Come on," he repeated as he walked towards a pair of strange body-size capsules at the end of the room. Their silvery metal sheathing shone brightly in the fluorescent lighting, while the thick, clear glass that sealed the tops of the cases allowed me to see their surprising contents.

"I just finished with Tom and Damian," Dr. Walker said, checking the readings on a strange machine hooked up to one of the capsules. The two older men seemed peacefully asleep inside these impressive machines. I have to admit that a slight panic knocked in my chest the moment I imagined myself inside one of those things. "But I'm sure you'll be more interested to know how your friend Ms. Montgomery's doing." Dr. Walker raised his eyes to meet my stare. "I heard the two of you made quite an impression on my security team last night."

I stammered, "Um, uh... Yeah, about that. I, uh..."

"Don't worry about it." He laughed teasingly, putting me at ease before I could finish. "Let's take a look at your friend, shall we?"

I followed him as he walked towards yet another capsule, making me realize there were more than just the two I'd seen—a lot more. "I heard she was the first one to go under," I noted as we got closer to her capsule.

"Indeed she was," he confirmed, checking the readings of her machine. "And I must say, Ms. Montgomery's brain waves are *extraordinary*." His voice was merely a whisper by then, as if he were talking to himself. "A possible breakthrough," he added just as quietly, his eyes staring blankly into space.

"Breakthrough?"

My question made him snap out his profound concentration. "Excuse me?"

I shot him a quizzical look. "Are you all right, Doc? You look tired."

"Not at all," he assured me. "We should see about getting you started, though."

"Sure. Can I just have a couple of minutes?" I asked, letting my hand rest over Yvette's capsule.

"Of course," he said, turning to the capsule immediately to his right, giving me as much privacy as one can expect in a crowded lab.

I leaned over the glass to see my Yvee. And there she was, lying completely still, lost in a peaceful dream. And although she was connected to a medusa's tangle of wires and electrodes, I've never seen anyone look so beautiful. "Yvee?" I tapped on the glass, hoping her captivating eyes would open for me—just long enough to satisfy my selfish desire to see them again.

"She can't hear you, Victor," Dr. Walker said, reminding me that he was right behind me. "She's in a medically induced coma—they all are."

I shook my head at the lack of privacy. "How long does she need to be in there?" I asked.

"It all depends on how she responds to the serum, but I'd say twenty-four to forty-eight hours—excuse me." He walked away then to welcome the rest of the group, who'd just arrived. Then, before I could swing my eyes back to Yvette, a young nurse approached me with a hospital gown neatly folded in her hands.

"Hi, Mr. Bellator," she said, "Are you ready?"

"Yeah," I answered tentatively.

She handed me the gown and asked me to follow her. "I'll show you where to change."

"I'll be right behind you." I nodded with a forced smile, signaling her to go first. She returned the same sort of smile and walked away.

I turned back to Yvette's capsule and looked at her with a love that, until the previous night, I had never thought possible. "I'll see you soon, my angel," I whispered softly, pressing my hand against her glass, hoping she'd feel my presence as well as my feelings for her.

"Mr. Bellator?" the young nurse called again, seemingly pressed for time.

"I'm coming!" I answered, giving Yvee one final gaze before I walked away.

After changing into the annoying open-backed gown, I stuffed my clothes in a plastic bag and was getting ready to go back outside when a sudden noise made me realize I'd dropped something. Quickly, my eyes swept the floor for the missing item, surprised to see that my dad's lighter had made it to the lab too—I honestly didn't remember having put it in my pocket. Thankfully, the pair of traveling pants I was wearing that day had a Velcro pocket. So I picked it up and stored it there, wondering if this incident might be another sign.

I shook my head and laughed.

I finally made it back into the lab, with one hand juggling my bag and the other swinging behind my back, trying to close the damned gown, which kept opening no matter what I did. "I really hate these things," I told the nurse, who was waiting for me outside the door.

She shook her head with a big grin on her face and took the bag from my hand. After storing it in a compartment underneath my capsule, she put her hands on my shoulders and spun me around before I could say a word. "Are you nervous?" she asked, as she tightened the strings behind my back.

I laughed, feeling an excessive amount of blood rushing to my face. "Well, truth be told, I wasn't until now."

She giggled as she finished tightened my gown.

She then grabbed a controller, with which she positioned the capsule at a forty-five-degree angle, opened the glass top, and asked me to hop inside. I have to admit I got very nervous at that point. I had no idea what was going to happen, or if this procedure was even going to work on me. After all, Dr. Walker had said that it all depended on how well a particular patient responded to the serum—and that of course, there were no guarantees. I was juggling these thoughts in my head when Dr.

Walker arrived with his medical team. My heart began to race then.

"All right, Victor," Dr. Walker said excitingly. "We're going to prep you now. These electrodes are going to keep track of your brainwaves as well as your vital signs and..." Dr. Walker kept on explaining, while the rest of the medical team began to connect my head and body to a series of electrodes, wires, and IV lines. The tumult was such that it became very difficult to follow anything Dr. Walker was saying.

Up until *then*, that is.

"You'll be awake for the first part of the procedure," I heard him say, as people moved out of my way. "The serum will be injected directly into your bloodstream. Now, this may feel strange at first. But I need you to remain calm, okay? It's all part of the procedure. Once the serum reaches your brain, you'll be put under general anesthesia. Then we'll continue to Phase Two. Your brain will be exposed to a precise series of radiation pulses in order to activate the serum, just like I explained before. Clear so far?"

"Yes, Doctor..." My voice sounded shaky and unconvincing.

"There are cameras as well as microphones installed inside the capsule, which means that we can not only see you, but we can hear you as well. You have nothing to worry about." He tried to reassure me with a warm smile, "Relax, Victor. Everything's going to be fine."

They finally put an oxygen mask over my face, and Dr. Walker asked me for a good-to-go sign, to which I responded with solid thumbs-up. The capsule then closed on me with a loud thud and Dr. Walker did an audio test, to which I nodded in confirmation. The top of the capsule, just like the one Yvette was in, was made of clear glass, which allowed me to see everything going on outside. From a drawer in a table next to the capsule, Dr. Walker brought out a metallic syringe with a clear chamber in which I saw the thick greenish substance that was about to be injected into my bloodstream.

"Administration of serum RC-1000 through IV line to Subject 1105, Bellator, Victor, commencing at 0900 hours," Dr. Walker said aloud as he administered the serum through the injection port of my IV line. I understood then that the entire procedure was being recorded. The green fluid travelled through the clear tube faster than my eyes could follow, and in a matter of seconds it was done. "Serum administration completed."

A warm, tingling sensation began to stream through the arm connected to the IV line. The sensation got warmer and warmer as it spread through every muscle, bone, and artery in my body. I tried to remain calm, remembering what Dr. Walker had said about this part being a strange experience. But *strange* was the understatement of the century. I truthfully believed something had gone wrong. Something other than my angst had increased my heartbeat, making my breathing more labored by the minute. Soon, the warm sensation turned into an unbearable burning pain that took root in my spine, reaching higher and higher toward my head. All my efforts to stay calm were defeated the moment I tried to move; my limbs didn't respond. I realized then I'd been completely paralyzed by this so-called serum.

"Dr. Walker..." I tried to scream, but a feeble whisper was all that came out of my mouth. "...something... something... is wrong."

"Relax, Victor." I could hear Dr. Walker's voice reverberating inside the capsule like the voice of God. "This is normal. Just breathe, hear me? Breathe!"

I tried, but my attempts to breathe soon became nothing but a desperate gasp for air. When the burning stream in my spine finally reached the nape of my neck, I felt as if a myriad of tiny insects had been suddenly released in my head and were now creeping and crawling their way in, burrowing deeper into my brain. The feeling was maddening.

I tried desperately to scream, but at that point I was no longer able to vocalize. Everything else had been incapacitated. I lay there, mute and paralyzed, helpless, my eyes wide open, screaming for help—yet no one would respond. The oxygen mask blasting air on my face made me feel I was underwater. I wanted desperately to run, but was unable to move. I could feel my heart pounding inside my chest, while the feeling of crawling monsters inside my brain were driving me mad; yet my reflection on the glass showed a peaceful image of me, as if I were simply falling asleep.

Then, as if in a final cry for help, my body began to shake uncontrollably and dozens of silver spots flashed across my vision, as if my brain were ready to shut down. The spots became bigger and more intense; they almost matched the irregular rhythm of my exhausted heart. "Doctor!" I heard someone shout. "He's going into cardiac arrest!"

"Stand by for defibrillation!"

"NO!" Dr. Walker's voice echoed in my head, followed by a dreadful yet familiar phrase—something I'd heard a few years before under similar circumstances.

"*We're losing him!*"

Then, like an old TV abruptly unplugged, a big flash of light sent me right into darkness…

What are dreams, if not the manipulation of our own knowledge and feelings by an unconscious mind? If that's true, then where do we draw the line? How do you use your logic, when such logic dwells in the ambivalent mind of oneself? These questions rambled in my mind as I tried to make sense of my surroundings. *How can I believe what's happening?* I thought. *It must be a dream or something.* And perhaps it was, but I swear, nothing ever felt more real…

I was hovering in the darkness of an unfamiliar place, where the emptiness of space was ubiquitous, and time seemed irrelevant. I was confused—and yet, I'd never been so content.

A far, gleaming horizon appeared against the darkness, a sight that I could only compare to diamonds and rubies sparkling on water. I was compelled to reach that distant frontier without reason or understanding. The course was set as soon as I put my mind to it.

Mind... I often wonder if the word had the same meaning as the one I knew in this seemingly foreign world—

The horizon seemed closer every time I looked, though there was no indication that *I* was the one approaching *it*, rather than the other way around. I felt neither movement nor wind resistance that would prove that I was on my way to the boundaries of this chimera. For all I knew, the horizon might have been approaching *me*. But something changed along the strange journey toward the horizon; my will and conviction weakened the closer I got to the glimmering lights. Suddenly, it became difficult to breathe. And my course, once set toward the light, began to veer downward into a dark abyss. I felt myself sinking, all my energy slipping away, as if I were drifting off into a deep sleep; one so soothing that it promised to end all my pain and suffering.

That's when I realized that I wasn't falling asleep—I was dying.

"Victor!" A faint voice wouldn't let me doze off. *"Victor!"*

I opened my eyes as soon as I recognized the distant voice. "Dad?"

"You have to be strong, son."

"Dad...? Where are you?"

'You are a survivor, Victor. You always were."

"I'm tired, Dad," I said, my voice breaking. "I'm *so* tired."

'Don't give up, son."

"Why not?"

'Because you promised."

The faint voice disappeared.

"Dad? Dad!" My own voice echoed in the darkness.

I realized then, dream or not, that this wasn't the way my father would've wanted me to go. Not without a fight. Not without giving it everything I had. I wasn't going to give up. Not then. Not ever. I let out a resilient growl and, like a bird fighting out of an oil spill, I hauled myself out of the abyss, pushing forward towards the lights.

Soon, I found myself standing in front of a giant wall made of hundreds of rather strange windows...or at least, they looked like windows to me. They weren't made of glass, though, but rather some sort of clear liquid, which was held in abeyance despite the laws of gravity. Behind every pane, there was a pulsating light, its rhythm resembling that of a heartbeat. Yet not all of them were the same. Some were white, with just a hint of blue, which gave them the appearance of diamonds shining through water. Others were red, with the same emphasis of rubies over black silk. There were as many white ones as there were reds ones. The white lights, however, seemed to be free to escape their windows as they pleased, emanating spectacular eruptions of light. The red ones, on the other hand, seemed trapped inside their windows—confined, like lifetime prisoners whose punishment was to see others go free at will.

I felt compelled to smash those windows and free the red lights from their imprisonment. But the white lights grew brighter, stronger, flashing faster with every step I took, as if warning me not to get any closer. I paid no attention. The red light was calling me now. I felt seduced by its magical glow, which led me to the biggest and brightest one of all. I stood right in front of it, close enough to touch it. I ran my fingers though its liquid pane, producing ripples like you would in a puddle of water. The red light glowed brighter as I immersed my hand in the crystal liquid, as if pleased by my admiration.

Once inside, I clenched my hand into a fist, trying to get ahold of the light. My eyes gazed into its ruby heart, while the white lights flashed brighter and faster—as if making a last, desperate attempt to stop me.

Adamant in my decision, I pulled my fist out of the window, breaking the liquid seal that imprisoned the red light, which in a chain reaction began to erupt from every window. Every eruption spewed a sudden and spectacular explosion of ruby light, each of which crashed over me like an ocean wave—over and over again.

The empowered sensation I felt with every pass of the light was intoxicating. "More!" I shouted. "I want more!" The eruptions then began to increase violently, producing a thunder-like sound which resembled the rapid fire of a machine gun. But the feeling didn't last long. Soon I began to feel that, with every passing light, a hole was being ripped right through my chest— as if this red light was now trying to break in, infecting the very essence of me.

Maybe that was why it had been imprisoned in the first place.

I tried to scream, but my voice was drowned in the uproar of light. The intensity of the violent event finally blinded me, sending me back into darkness.

***

I found myself in a state between consciousness and unconsciousness, as if I were trying to wake up from a bad dream. I heard voices; a man and a woman arguing. I was completely confused and disoriented. I felt groggy, and my eyelids were so heavy I felt that I'd never be able to open my eyes. But I tried anyway. The attempt was feeble, but enough to make me realize I was still inside the capsule. I tried again, hoping to catch a glimpse of the people arguing. When I finally wrenched open my eyes, the white lab coat gave away the identity of the man: Dr. Walker. The woman, however, was a stranger.

I tried to regain full consciousness, but all I could capture were bits and pieces of the ongoing argument...

'I won't let you do this! These are people *we're talking about here!"* the stranger shouted.

"This is my project, my research, and my decision, not yours!" Dr. Walker countered.

'I'm not going to be part of this, Doctor."

'Well, since I'm still the project leader, and chief of this facility, you can consider yourself dismissed!"

"You unethical bastard! I hope you rot in Hell!"

That was the last thing I heard before losing consciousness again.

I couldn't tell how much time had elapsed between that conversation and the next time I opened my eyes. But I was enormously confused, especially by the way I was being awakened.

I heard the voice of the unknown woman again. "Victor! Come on, wake up!" I opened my eyes as she shook me by the shoulders. She then leaned over me and, with great haste, stripped all the wires and electrodes from my head. "Come on, Victor. We have to get out of here."

"W-w-who are you?" I asked, feeble and disconcerted.

"My name is Sarah Grey, and you've been scheduled for dissection. I need to get you out of here."

"I-I-I don't… understand… Dr. Walker…"

"Dr. Walker is insane!" she cried, outraged. "He lures brain injury patients to this awful place to conduct unsanctioned experiments on them!"

"What?" I mumbled, confused, as she helped me up from the capsule.

"Here!" She handed me my bag from underneath it.

"How long... How long have I been under?" I asked clumsily, battling to put my shirt on.

"Almost three days," she replied, helping me button up.

"I'm not... I'm not feeling well," I maundered, the whole room spinning around me. My vision became spotty then; and before I knew it, I was on my knees, emptying my stomach onto the floor.

"Come on, Victor," Sarah whispered, pulling me up from the floor. She helped me back to the edge of the bed next to the capsule as I tried to pull myself together. As soon as my vision cleared from the retching, I jumped inside my pants and I put on my shoes, spurred on by the urgency in her voice—but by then it was too late.

"All right, sweetheart, that's enough." I immediately recognized the drawl of the obnoxious Head of Security as he entered the room, tapping his baton against the palm of his hand. Five more guards stood behind him.

"Listen," Sarah said, "I know you think you're doing your job. But you've no idea what's going on in here. You *have* to let us go."

"I'm sorry, Ms. Grey. But I've been instructed to take you into custody, and to take this... *freak* to the surgical unit." He beckoned to one of the guards to proceed with the orders.

"Please!" Sarah pleaded, "Just let us go."

"Why the rush, sweetheart?" The security head said suggestively. "I'm sure we're going to have *fun* together in the detention room." He rubbed his baton against Sarah's arm in an obscene manner.

"You stupid pig!" Sarah retorted, smacking the guard on the face. A ring on her finger was sharp enough to trace a long cut along his face.

The infuriated guard dabbed at his wound, and without warning slapped Sarah across the face with such force that she spun around and collapsed to the floor.

"You son of a bitch!" I yelled, with an anger I'd never felt before, and a surging energy flushed through me. I knew then that something was wrong.

"Shut the hell up, freak!" The hateful guard shouted, striking me on the ribs with his baton. I doubled over in pain, feeling an inexplicable urge to harm them all.

It was then that something clouded my judgment and began take control of my will.

Sarah trembled on the floor, surrounded by the guards. Her wide eyes flickered in fear as one of them pointed a gun at her head, while the loathsome Head of Security hit me again with his baton. The guards laughed as I writhed on the floor, folded up in pain.

"All right, Dick," one of the guards said to the HOS. "Let's wrap this up, man."

"Yeah!" he answered, all jacked up. "You two take Ms. Grey to my office. I still need to *debrief* her." He smiled savagely; and although the eyes of the other guards met in disapproval, they seemed to be compelled to follow his orders.

"Let's go, Ms. Grey. On your feet." the guard holding the gun to her head commanded.

"No." I muttered softly, still gasping for air.

"You just don't know when to quit, do you?" The HOS said disgustingly, raising his baton to strike me again.

Suddenly I felt fire rise in my eyes; a shock of electricity ran through my entire body, and my right hand rose as the guard swung his striking blow. Only this time, the baton stopped just before it hit me, inches away from my raised hand. The confused guard fought the unmovable baton as I began to rise. The rest of the guards stood with their mouths open, stunned, as they watch the baton freeze in midair. I stood up in front of the guard, tilting my head side to side and glaring murderously.

It didn't take long for HOS, as well as the rest of the guards, to realize that *I* was the cause of this unnatural event. One of the guards, standing in the back, shouted in Spanish, "Es el Diablo!" and bolted out of the lab, while the others took frightened steps backward, the one still restraining Sarah.

"Let her go!" a deep raspy growl commanded the guard holding Sarah, and it took a second for me to realize the voice had come from me. The guard's panicking eyes turned to his boss, confused and hesitant, as if asking him what to do. My focus then returned to the HOS, whose eyes seemed to defy my wishes. "Let her go!" I repeated, this time addressing *him*. But his response was a swift move toward his sidearm.

In a quick, effortless move, I switched hands in perfect synchrony. My right hand dropped to the side, letting go of the baton. Once released from my invisible grip, it dropped abruptly to the ground. My left hand rose to chest level, palm open, in front of the guard. His entire body jolted then as my hand locked into position, leaving his hand just centimeters from his holster. I demanded once again, the raspy growl that had taken over my voice sounding even angrier than before. "*Let her go!*"

The HOS gasped as my hand rose higher and higher, bringing his body along with it, until the dangling tips of his shoes barely touched the floor. I could feel the energies surging inside my body readjusting to protect my fragile brain, keeping his 200-pound bulk from crushing my gray matter to jelly.

The sudden halt in my raising hand made his entire body jolt again, like the body of a puppet being suddenly jerked up by its own strings, leaving him completely frozen. His face reflected excruciating pain, as if the entire weight of his body were being lifted by the feeble strength of his own innards. Maybe it was. Nonetheless, his obstinacy found him the strength to give one last order to the rest of the guards: "S-s-shoot, shoot them both!"

The sound of guns cocking followed his order—as did a sudden and abnormal change in my perception. My senses were incredibly well-tuned, and time crawled in what I can only describe as extreme slow motion. It was like being inside a three-dimensional picture in which everyone moved lethargically, with me having a slight advantage in speed and reaction time.

I turned my burning eyes to the guard restraining Sarah, who was now holding her in front of his body, like a human shield. Coward. His confused and terrified eyes locked with mine, while he pointed his Glock 9mm at Sarah's head, his trigger finger straight alongside the gun-frame.

I raised my free hand toward him as fast as this slow motion trance allowed me to, while still keeping hold of the HOS with the other. The remaining guards began to lift their rifles in my direction, as the guard holding Sarah reacted with a nervous jolt. I could see his finger now curling slowly into position over the trigger. Sarah's body cringed in fear, her eyes closing tightly on the dreadful thought of dying.

The event had suddenly turned into a desperate race against time, in which the lives of everyone in the room depended on who reached the trigger first. The guards pointing at me were just inches away from acquiring the perfect shooting position, while the finger of the guard holding Sarah had already began to pull the trigger.

My much faster hand, however, reached its desired position before anyone else, taking an invisible grip on the gun that pointed Sarah's head. I swung my hand fast and violently then, not only ending the slow motion trance but snatching the gun out of the guard's hand, sending it thirty feet across the room. The now-defenseless man cowered behind Sarah, his eyes fixed on the exit door for a long moment; then, throwing Sarah in my direction, he bolted for the exit, leaving his frightened peers behind.

I gestured in her direction, urging her to step behind me; trembling in fear, she did so, while I turned back to the HOS and the other guards left in the room. The mobile guards quickly snapped out of it, and tried to re-aim at us and shoot. But another swing of my hand was enough to snatch the rifles out of their hands, disarming them—and not just in the sense of being weaponless. All courage left them as they exchanged horrified glances, before they decided to run like the other two.

But their intentions were crushed the second they tried. I raised my hand again, making their bodies jolt into paralysis, just as I had with their HOS—who was now spitting blood and begging for mercy.

I heard the dreadful growl coming out of my mouth again, this time saying, "Die! Die!" as the four guards frozen under my control screamed in terrible pain.

"Please, Victor! Stop!" Sarah begged, tugging on my arm.

But I didn't listen. It felt *good* inflicting pain on these men. And though the thought terrified me, I just couldn't stop it. There was an unnatural conflict taking place in my head, in which my anger had overcome my reason. Inside I was fighting to stop; but outside, I was grinning like a madman.

The main doors suddenly opened and an entire paramilitary squad poured into the lab, carrying heavy artillery. They aimed everything they had at us, ready to open fire. But they couldn't shoot; the guards under my control were standing in the line of fire.

"Let them go!" one of the soldiers shouted, pointing an assault rifle at me. Then I heard the voice of the man in which I'd misplaced all of my hopes: Dr. Walker, who stood behind the squad. Looking me square in the eye, he gave his men a very stiff order: "Shoot them. *Shoot them all.*"

The order was executed without hesitation. Every weapon was fired mercilessly at the same time, as if we were shooting ducks and not human beings. A sudden horizontal rain of lead filled the lab, producing a war-like uproar in which I lost my concentration and dropped my prisoners. The now-released bodies of the four guards in front of us became the squad's targets: just an obstacle they needed to get rid of, in order to get through to us. They riddled them with everything they had, shredding their bodies and sending them collapsing over Sarah and me, covering us like once-human shields.

Blood was everywhere, tainting everything it touched. We should have died; how we didn't I had no idea, unless some remnant of my telekinesis somehow shielded us from the bullets that ripped the HOS and his men to shreds. Sarah and I crawled out from under the pulped remains of their bodies and took cover behind the capsule I'd woken up in. A brief ceasefire gave me the advantage I was looking for. Once again, without any physical contact, I took control of the now-lifeless bodies of the HOS and his men and launched them towards the execution squad, smashing them apart like bowling pins.

"Come on!" Sarah shouted, pulling my arm with all her strength, hauling me toward an opened hatch at the end of the room. "This is our chance!"

I followed her to the hatch as gray started to creep in around the edges of my vision. The world became fuzzy and my hearing turned bleary. All I could feel now was Sarah's arm around my waist and her panting breath whooshing in my ear. I remember the rest as if it were a dream. Brief images of the forest flashed across my eyes as I felt the cold breeze of the night blowing through my hair. The smell of pine needles, the flowing sound of a river, and the soft touch of Sarah's delicate hand—all began to take hold of my enhanced senses.

My eyes opened again to the velvet sound of Sarah's voice. "Come on, Victor. We're almost there." I saw her then, my arm around her shoulders. She was dragging my limp body inside an old, abandoned shack in the middle of the woods. I tried to stay awake, but my eyes began to close again, and Sarah's voice began to recede. The light turned to darkness and then... nothing.

Chapter 7

Camping with Sarah

FINALLY, AFTER A long battle against my own subconscious, I could remember all the strange episodes that had brought me here. Some things began to make sense then, like waking up in the abandoned shack, my memory loss, Sarah—and even hiding in the woods. Some things, however, remained a mystery. Seated next to the fire, I fed the flame for hours, staring blankly at it, pain and remorse piercing my conscience, just as that hail of bullets had pierced the bodies of those men...

Sarah, with a somber look on her face, tried to shed light on the things I couldn't remember—and also on the things I never knew. "Three months ago, I was assigned to work for Dr. Walker on the development of a new serum that was supposed to help regenerate damaged cells in the brain," Sarah explained. "The procedure was a success. Patients with a number of different types of brain damage were cured—especially those with intracranial pressure issues.

"At first, we were thrilled. We finally had all the data we needed to make the findings public. But then... something happened. Patients began to show strange electrical activity in their brains—something I've never seen before. When my mentor, Dr. Palmer, put one of the patients under observation, he realized that the serum had done more than incite a regeneration pattern; it had also awakened dormant cells, which were now apparently absorbing some sort of unknown energy from the atmosphere."

"Not just from the atmosphere," I said, remembering the other sources I'd tapped into. She looked up at me sharply, and I said, placatingly, "But we can talk about that later. Go on."

She sighed. "Well, at first we thought we were wrong. I mean, it was like nothing anyone had ever detected before. But when this energy manifested itself in a series of extraordinary abilities, we knew we'd discovered something much more profound. That's when Dr. Walker stepped in and took complete control over the project. After making some findings of his own, he concluded that this energy actually splits in two: he called it the *Dual Dominant Interaction Force.* In one form, the energy seems to be harmless to the human brain, enhancing feelings of altruism in the subject. But in its opposite form, it's harmful and addictive, even mind altering."

"What do you mean by 'mind altering'?"

"In its negative form, this energy stimulates and enhances malevolent behavior. After reaching critical levels of saturation, it takes control of the subject's volition."

"What happens then?" I asked.

She looked at me steadily. "You've seen what happens then, Victor. You lose control of your actions. Anger becomes your driving force, and you become—"

"A sociopath." I finished her sentence, feeling an awful emotional pain I've never felt before.

She met my stare and swallowed hard. "Yes. Exactly."

I closed my eyes and rubbed my forehead with a weary hand. "So why didn't he stop the project then?"

She was quiet for a long moment, then: "It's... his theory is crazy. Since this energy is driven by human emotions, Dr. Walker thinks he's found the very essence of good and evil within the human brain. And he is *adamant* about the need to harness this power, no matter how many lives he has to sacrifice in the process."

I dropped my hand, and my gaze flew back to hers. "You mean—"

"Walker's been using his patients as expendable test subjects. So far, 85% of the patients have died during the procedure. And those who have survived are being... dissected."

"You mean vivisected," I snapped. "Dissected alive. You mean *murdered*."

She bowed her head, unable to look at me.

"This is insane!" I got to my feet and began to pace aimlessly around the little clearing. "Why is he doing this?"

"The dissection—" I looked at her angrily, and she began again: "The *vivi*section serves two purposes for Dr. Walker. First, he hopes to find a way to harness this power, and he needs his... subjects... kept alive for as long as possible while he does it. And two..." She hesitated again.

"Yes?" I urged.

She said in a small voice, "He feels he has to dispose of his subjects anyway. Once this dark energy reaches critical levels, they become too dangerous to live."

Sarah fell silent then. After a full minute I asked impatiently, "Would you care to elaborate a little more on that last statement?" I asked. My fingers curled into claws, and I wanted desperately to reach for the power I could feel throbbing in the air around me.

She sighed heavily. "There's an exponential increase in telekinetic abilities once the subject's volition is altered by this negative energy. Think *Carrie* times a thousand."

"Great!" I snarled, my voice filled with sarcasm and disgust. "So I'm not only turning into a homicidal maniac, I'm turning into a *demon* too. You know, it's amazing how far some people will go for fame and fortune. How the *hell* do you sleep at night?"

Sarah stood and scowled at me. "Wait just a goddamned minute! I was never a part of this! I didn't know about it until it was too late. And when I *did* find out, I tried to stop it—and as you saw, almost got myself killed!"

"You lied to us!" I roared. "All of you *lied* to us!" As my anger raged out of control, I could hear her heartbeat step up like that of a rabbit frightened by the sight of a fox, and I could smell her fear on the breeze. The sensations washed over and overwhelmed my psyche as I did my best to control it. I kept pacing around, breathing more and more heavily; Sarah got to her feet and took a few steps back, a watchful expression on her face. I knew she was about to run, and I knew if she did, I'd reach out with my power and snatch her off her feet, just as I'd done with the security guards who had unwittingly given their lives to protect us.

"Victor, please! You need to calm down."

I kept pacing, feeling my anger escalating as it had in the lab; and just as I was about to give in to it, a loud thumping noise derailed my attention. I recognized it instantly: the blade-slap of a helicopter, headed rapidly in our direction. Without thinking I kicked dirt over the fire, and we both darted into the woods.

From our vantage point in the trees, we watched as the aircraft passed slowly over the surface of the river, a powerful searchlight sweeping its turbulent waters. Sarah immediately recognized it as one of the facility's medical transports. "They're looking for us," she whispered.

"They're searching the river," I noted, having regained control of my emotions. "They must think we didn't make it."

"Then we have a chance. We have to get as far away from here as we possibly can," she said as the helicopter made another pass and disappeared down the river. "Let's go!"

"Wait," I said, grabbing her arm. "I'm not going anywhere without Yvette."

"Who?"

"There was another patient in my group, Yvette Montgomery. She was a childhood friend. What happened to her?"

Her eyes darted around like cornered rabbits. "Victor, there's no time!"

"Sarah, please!" I begged, grasping both her elbows in a soft yet firm grip. "I need to know."

"I don't know them by name." She sighed. "But three subjects from your group died during the procedure."

"Who!—who died?" I asked, distressed, thoughtlessly shaking her entire body.

"I don't know!" she gasped, "Two men and one woman!"

"Yvette?" I breathed with dismay. "—NO!" I said sharply, countering my own thoughts. "There was an-another girl," I explained, trying to assure myself I hadn't lost the love of my life. "Yvette might still be alive. We have to get help, call the police or something!" I suggested frantically.

"You still don't get it, do you?" Sarah jerked her arms down, breaking free of my grasp. "These are *very powerful people*. Walker and his friends are politically connected, wealthy beyond anything you can imagine. It's our word against theirs, not to mention the fact that once they pinpoint our location they'll have *me* arrested and *you* back on the slab!"

Her firm statement shocked me, convincing me even more Yvette needed my help. If no one could help us, then I needed to find a way to save Yvette myself. I said to her in a low voice, "I need you to tell me if there's a way to control these abilities without turning into a monster."

Sarah frowned. "Why? You should avoid trying to use them."

"Please!" My voice wavered from a shout to a whisper as I tried to control my temper, "...Just tell me how. If you can."

Sarah took another step back, her frightened eyes fixed on mine. "Well... Apparently, the absorption of these energies is triggered by the same behavior they enhance," she said hesitantly.

"And what does that *mean?*"

"Your abilities sparked the moment you set your mind to save me in the river. And though your heart rate must've been elevated, and you were obviously in distress, your intentions triggered a part of your brain that focuses on altruism. That made the absorption of, well, positive energy possible. I know I sound like a New Age freak, but that's the easiest way to explain it."

"I don't understand. I tried to protect you in the lab, and my intentions weren't evil. What the hell happened to me then?"

"That's precisely the conflict with your condition. Even benevolent thoughts can lead to frustration and anger. Human emotions are unstable, Victor, even uncontrollable past a certain point."

"I can do it," I said confidently. "I can control my emotions. I can use these abilities to my advantage. I can use them to get Yvette out of that place."

"Are you out of your *mind?*" Sarah glared at me in the dimness; I know she could barely see me, but she was clearly visible to my enhanced senses. "There are people armed to their teeth looking for us right now, and you want to go back into the lion's den?" She stressed every word, trying to make her point as strong as possible. "Not to mention the fact that you don't even know how to control this power, if it's even possible! I mean, just trying could make you more vulnerable to the loss of volition." She paused, regaining composure. "You could die, Victor."

"If I don't try, Yvette will die for sure. And I told you, I *can* control it."

"*No you can't!*" she shouted. "Sooner or later you're going to *lose* it, and then you'll become an even bigger threat than those people chasing us." She paused ruefully, lowering her angry tone. "Then they won't be the only ones trying to take you down."

I sighed in dismay and looked at her quizzically. "Sarah, if you knew all this, why did you risk your life trying to save me? I mean, I'm as good as dead, right?" Her eyebrows knitted in self-reflection, but she kept her answer to herself. I sighed and shook my head, feeling defeated. "You should try and make a run for it, Sarah." I turned around and began to walk back to the lab.

"Wait!" she called. I stopped and turned around. "Why are you doing this?" Her voice was full of confusion and disbelief.

"Because I promised."

"I don't understand."

"I don't expect you to."

"You don't even know how to get back there! You're going to get lost!"

"Don't worry, Sarah. I have a great sense of direction." I didn't mention my heightened senses, which I knew wouldn't let me down.

Our voices got louder with every exchange. "What about the helicopter?" she cried.

"I'll hide!"

"How would you get pass their security?"

"I know a way."

"You're going to get yourself killed!"

"I don't CARE!" I thundered.

"Arghhh! Are you *always* this stubborn?" she demanded, her eyes flashing.

"You have no idea." My own tone reminded me of the obstinacy of my father.

She exhaled angrily and began to pace, massaging her forehead with the tips of her fingers. "Okay, okay," she said, the redness fading from her face. "We can't just walk through the front door, so we're going to have to figure something else out, okay?"

"We?" I asked, lifting an eyebrow. "What's this 'we', kemosabe? You've made it clear you don't want to go."

"I said 'we' and I meant it," she replied firmly. "I hate to reduce this to scorekeeping, but I still owe you one. Besides, there are still a few things you need to know before you march back in there." She donned her jacket and reluctantly led the way. "Let's go!" she called back at me.

Shaking my head, I followed.

**

I couldn't believe it when I saw the magnificent dawn again. It had taken us the entire night to put all the pieces of the puzzle back together. Now Sarah was leading the way back to R.C. Labs, still ill-tempered—not just because we were going back, but because given the fact that we had ended up on the wrong side of the river, the length of our journey back to R.C. Labs had tripled. Thankfully, Sarah seemed to have come well prepared. A large Ziploc she removed out from her inside jacket pocket contained money, credentials, a Swiss Army Knife, and a detailed map of the Tongass National Rainforest, which in the current situation was our most precious possession.

The map was leading us to a bridge downriver, the only way to get across its treacherous waters. On the other side, the map showed a one-mile trail that would lead us to a big, empty plain, which Sarah assured me was the secret location of the Lab. I had no idea what I was going to do once I got there, but one thing I knew for sure: if I were going to die, I wanted to do so for a good reason.

As with all of us, there were many moments in my life in which I wished I'd done things differently. But I refused to believe that this was going to be one of them. I refused to believe that I had lost Yvette. I dreaded the thought of dying without having the opportunity to tell her again how much she meant to me, how those few moments we spent together had filled me with the strength I needed to go on, and how one kiss from her had restored my will to live and my desire to love. I needed to tell her that if I only had five minutes left to live, I wanted to live them with her.

Being lost in my thoughts made the hike seem shorter and easier than it really was, though I have to admit the scenic views along the way were helpful. We were surrounded by majestic firs and beautiful tall greenery, and the forest floor was carpeted with amazing wildflowers. Their colors and shapes ranged from small round cotton-like puffballs to big, spiky purple thistles, each with its distinctive scent and beauty. We even passed an impressive waterfall. The cool, clear waters cascaded in four rills over mossy-green rocks and steep boulders. It was a sight that made us stop and stare—if for only a few seconds.

"Are you okay?" Sarah's question brought me back to myself. "You haven't said a word in almost an hour."

"Really?" I answered, taken aback. "I didn't notice. I was just... thinking."

"About this girl you mentioned before?"

"Yvette. Yes."

"Hmmm," she mused, throwing a glance over her shoulder. "So what's the deal? Is she your girlfriend?" She tried to sound nonchalant, but I could sense a hidden expectation in her tone.

"What do *you* care?" I countered, annoyed by her question. I didn't know why I was being so rude to her. Maybe her involvement with R.C. Labs had led me to subconsciously develop some sort of resentment toward her, or maybe I was simply fighting not to like her so much, because I was aware that she could become a threat to my emotions.

"I'm sorry," she replied, flustered by my attitude. "I didn't mean to upset you. I was just trying to make conversation."

"Well, forgive me if I'm not in the chatting mood, but my whole world has been turned upside down. And for your information, Yvette just happens to be—"

"You don't have to answer that." She turned around and cut me off on the spot. "It's none of my business anyway."

Her angry emerald eyes locked with mine for a long, insightful second, in which I experienced another episode of extreme awareness, similar to the ones I'd had in the shack and at the river. It felt like a sudden rush of electricity zapped me as my brain opened up again to that refreshing and intoxicating feeling of euphoria. A new sensation, however, crept in among the others: an unnatural, non-physical pressure created by one side of my brain over the other.

The pressure began to increase gradually, like a game of mercy being played inside my head. Terrified by the unknown consequences of having one of the two sides win, I forced myself out of the virtual contest, snatching my mind away like I'd snatch my hand out of a fire. That sent a jolt of pain through my head like a railroad spike jammed into my skull. "Aaaah!" I grabbed my head in both hands and clenched my eyes shut as I tore free of the dreadful mind-lock.

"What's wrong?" Sarah asked nervously.

"I don't know…" I answered vaguely, trying to keep the details to myself. It didn't make sense to me, trying to explain something that I couldn't even explain to myself at that point. "Look…" I began again. "I'm sorry. I'm just not feeling like… like myself, you know?" I sighed, sinking down on top of a rock the size of a small bench. I rubbed my face with dismay. "How the hell did I get myself into this mess?"

"Hey," Sarah said with a comforting tone, sitting right next to me. "It's okay. I'm sorry, too. And I didn't mean to pry. It's just that…" She paused. I uncovered my face and looked at her, not sure I wanted to hear what she had to say. "Victor," she continued, meeting my stare, "…going back to the Lab is just…crazy." She sighed. "She may not even be a—"

"NO!" I cut her off and stood up hastily. "She *is* alive."

"What if she's not, Victor?" she insisted. "Then what? You'll die, too."

"Life won't be worth living if Yvette is dead," I told her, dead serious. I raised my eyes to the clear blue sky. "Besides, I've been dying every day for three years now, Sarah, and every day I wanted to end it. She made me change my mind. She made me want to live again. If she's gone, well," I paused painfully, "if she's gone, then your boss can do whatever he wants with me."

She exhaled loudly. "Well, I guess that answered my question." She smiled timidly. "Wow. She's a lucky girl."

"Bad choice of words, considering the circumstances, don't you think?"

"On the contrary. If it was me who was trapped in that place, I would consider myself damn lucky to have someone like you stopping at nothing to get me out."

"Someone like me?" I scoffed bitterly. "You don't even know who I am, Sarah. I'm just a lonely, pathetic, sick guy, with no friends, no family, and no life. And apparently that made me the perfect candidate for this experiment. And you know what? I'm fine with that. But Yvette deserves a hell of a lot better than to spend her last moments in agony as a lab experiment." I sighed. "I don't know if what I'm doing is right or wrong. I can't tell the difference anymore. But you're right about one thing. I'll stop at nothing to get her out of there."

A long moment of silence followed my words.

"Well," Sarah began finally, "I think what you're trying to do is really—"

"Stupid?" I cut her off, turning around to meet her eyes.

"I was actually going to say brave," she corrected me, seeming offended by my attitude.

"Isn't that the same thing?" I countered sarcastically.

She studied the ground then, hiding the pained expression caused by my gibes. I realized then I was taking my anger and frustration out on her, and that I was acting like a total jerk. I couldn't blame my condition for that. "I'm sorry," I apologized sincerely. "I keep forgetting you're not the enemy." I threw an obvious glance at the R.C. emblem on her jacket.

Her hand flew to the emblem as she caught the direction of my stare. "I'm not them, Victor," she said quietly.

"I know."

"Can we not fight anymore?" she proposed with a gentle smile. I nodded in agreement. I could feel a smile curving my lips. "Friends, then?" The word struck me in a weirdest way, coming from a girl like Sarah. Not that I was trying to be sexist or anything, but I doubted that a stunning woman like her could have had many male friends without them having conflicting feelings about her.

"Sure." I laughed. "Friends."

We resumed our journey as soon as our friendship was established. Sarah kept navigating using her map, which was taking us through some really rough terrain. The hike became steeper and more difficult as we approached the bridge. In some cases we had to use our hands in order to climb over slopes along the way. All this physical activity, plus the lack of food and water, was really taking it out of us, so mid-morning we decided to stop and rest for a while. Thankfully, the hike hadn't taken us too far from the course of the river, which gave us a reachable source of fresh water.

We found a nice, clear area with a flat enough surface to settle down. Sarah dropped on the ground, exhausted. She took off her boots and massaged her toes against the cool green grass. "Ah!" she sighed, "That feels good."

"Can I see your Ziploc bag again?" I asked.

"Sure," she answered, getting it out her jacket pocket. I took it and emptied all its contents out on the grass next to her. "What are you doing?" she asked, confused.

"Just wait here, I'll be right back." I took the empty Ziploc bag and headed for the river. The bag was large enough to hold at least a liter of water, so as soon as I reached the river I filled it up to the top and sealed it. On my way back I stumbled upon some bushes full of wild berries; I quickly took off my shirt and used it to collect and bring some over to Sarah. Lucky for me, our little adventure on the river had washed most of the bloodstains out of the shirt, so I didn't feel too bad about using it.

When I got back, Sarah was arranging some wood for a campfire. She seemed to know what she was doing, so I left her alone and laid the shirt filled with berries flat on the ground. Her face lit up when she saw them, and even more when she saw the bag filled with water.

"Yes!" she exclaimed, "You're a lifesaver!" Jumping up, she sat down cross-legged right next to the rustic setting I had laid down. Her eyes closed with delight as she shoved a big handful of berries in her mouth. "Mmm!" A sigh of relief escaped her lips. I stood there watching with a smile on my face, happy to see her happy. It took her a minute to realize I was watching her getting lost in her enjoyment.

She stopped like a statue the moment she met my eyes. Her lips, stained by the red berries, curled into an embarrassing smile. "I'm sorry," she chuckled. "Would you care to join me?"

"Don't mind if I do." I smiled and sat next to her. "So, can I ask you a question?"

"Sure."

"How did someone like you get mixed up in something like this?"

"Well..." She mumbled, finishing what she had in her mouth, "I met Dr. Palmer in my first year in med school. He became my mentor and my friend. Before my first year was over, he told me about this great opportunity at this private biotech corporation. He'd been offered a job there, based on his research on brain cell regeneration, and he had the choice to bring an assistant with him, a student who would have the opportunity to learn from his research.

"The project was to be classified, and it required the intern to move indefinitely to Alaska and sign a non-disclosure agreement. Everything was on a need-to-know basis. Unfortunately for me, I was Dr. Palmer's first choice...and I just couldn't let him down, so I accepted."

"What happened to him?" I asked.

Her eyes went flat. "He vanished about a month ago. I always thought it was weird that he'd leave without saying why. But three days ago, I found a hidden message in the computer archives. In it, he warned me about Dr. Walker's intentions, and the risks of using the serum. His exact words in the message were: 'Protocol R.C.1000: Dangerous for human trials. Inevitable intrusive integration of dark energy into subject's volition, with ultimate and irreversible predominance.'

"I didn't understand what he meant at first, so, uh," she looked a little embarrassed, "I decided to break into Walker's personal records and find out what he was up to. It was then that I learned what he was doing to the patients. I confronted him, of course, but that didn't go too well. After resigning my position and saying I was leaving, he told me he couldn't let me go with that kind of information. That's when I knew my life was in danger."

She sighed, lifting her eyes to the sky again. "I knew about an emergency escape shaft in the lab and I knew it would be unguarded, so I waited until nightfall, when the Lab would be empty. When I got there, I noticed all the capsules were empty, too." –She pulled a bitter smile— "All except one. When I checked the clipboard at the foot of the capsule I saw that the patient was scheduled for vivisection. I couldn't just ignore it. So I decided to opened the capsule and save whoever was in it." She stopped then and met my gaze. "You know the rest."

"Do you regret it? Opening my capsule, I mean."

She shook her head without unlocking her eyes from mine and whispered, "No."

At that moment, we were drawn into a staring match from which neither of us seemed able to escape. Her eyes were like magnets, making me want to reach out, and take hold of her. The hyperawareness ignited in my brain again, making me able to hear the accelerated beating of her heart, as well as her out-of -control breathing *whoosh*ing in my ears. The game of mercy had resumed inside my head, and the winning force was producing an intoxicating feeling I couldn't resist. Suddenly, I felt compelled to run my fingers through her hair; I reached out, cupped the back of her head, and let my free hand slide around her waist. Then I pulled her body to mine with one firm tug that left our lips just a millimeter apart.

"Victor!" My name escaped her lips in a whisper.

The tighter the mysterious force gripped my conscience, the less volition I seemed to have. And though the other force in my head seemed to be fighting back with the same intensity as the first, it seemed an impossible battle to win. My vision began to dim, just as it had back in the Lab ...when suddenly, Yvette's image popped into my head, a perfect picture of her face—a perfect picture of love.

The two forces ceased their ferocious battle and gave me back my self-control. "Oh God, I'm sorry!" I said in shock, releasing Sarah. "I don't know what's wrong with me!" Embarrassed and confused, I made some room between us. Sarah cleared her throat and shook her head, dumbfounded by the event.

"It's all right," she finally said in a low voice, running her fingers through her hair. "It's probably just the two energies in conflict..." I could see a small wrinkle of confusion between her eyebrows. "You need to get some rest. You've been through a lot this last couple of days." She got back on her feet, giving me her back. "Ahem!" She cleared her throat loudly and added, "It's getting late. Why don't we just camp here for the night? We'll continue tomorrow. We'll leave at the crack of dawn, what do you say?"

"Yeah," I muttered, still trying to get my bearings. I reached for my lighter. "I'll make the fire," I said, trying to put the awkward moment behind us for good.

She turned back to me. "Great!" she responded with a smile, opting for the same resolution. "Why don't you start? And, uh... I'll go get some more water... for later." And just like that, she disappeared into the woods. I couldn't blame her for wanting to be alone after what had happened. I would have done the same thing if she hadn't done it first.

The sun had begun to set by then, and I could see the last flashes of light disappearing behind the humongous firs that surrounded the clearing. The sounds of the night had also begun to reemerge. Nocturnal animals like crickets and owls were tuning up for their all-night concert. I gathered some dry moss and bark in order to kindle the wood Sarah had arranged earlier, and had the fire going by the time she returned.

"Cool lighter," she said, with a more relaxed, refreshed disposition. "I didn't know you smoked."

"I don't," I replied. "It was my dad's."

"May I?" she asked.

"Sure," I said, handing it to her.

"Oh," she exclaimed, "It's beautiful!" She gave it a thorough examination. "Is he waiting for you at home?"

"No. He, uh... he passed away a couple of years ago. It was one of the reasons I took a chance with the treatment...there was no one to go back to, no one to hurt if it didn't work."

"Oh, I'm sorry, I didn't know."

"It's okay."

"How did he die?—No, wait. You don't have to tell me if you don't..."

"Cirrhosis," I answered swiftly.

"I'm really sorry, Victor."

"Yeah, me too." I smiled sadly.

"Cirrhosis? Was he an alco...? I mean, um...," she trailed off, regretfully. "I'm sorry... I, uh..." She looked at the ground as she struggled to apologize again.

"It's okay." I smiled, trying to put her at ease. "My mom, she... well, she left when I was six. And my Dad took it a little too hard, if you know what I mean. I remember him crying almost every night after she left. Until one night he brought home a big bottle of Scotch, and drank from it until he passed out. He began to do it more and more after that. I guess that was the only way he found to numb his pain, because he never cried again," I finished, staring blankly at the fire.

"I'm sorry," she repeated. She returned the lighter with a rueful look on her face. "I take it that you and your dad were really close, then?"

"Yeah."

When Sarah noticed that my eyes wouldn't leave the fire, she decided to change the subject. "We should start planning how we're going to enter the Lab tomorrow. I doubt the escape chute's going to work twice."

"Don't worry," I answered confidently. "I know a way."

Now it was my turn to change the subject. "You never told me how you know all this survival stuff. It can't all be from med school."

"Camp," she said quickly. Her answer was followed by a story about how her own father, who was a busy businessman and never had time for her, used to send her to summer camp every year after school ended. Our conversation continued for hours, consisting of stories that switched from sad to happy and back. She told me about her love of science, and I told her about my addiction to numbers. Her secret fear of spiders was challenged by my embarrassing fear of heights. We even shared our knowledge of astronomy when we finally lay down on the grass to go to sleep.

The fire sizzled between us as we named constellations. It was refreshing to discover how easy it was to talk to each other once the weirdness and awkwardness was put aside. Finally, we both began to yawn—not from boredom, but from genuine exhaustion. It had been a long day, and as much as I wanted to keep our conversation going, we knew we should get some rest.

"Time for some shut-eye," I suggested after she yawned for the second time.

She turned on her side and smiled, her head resting on her arm. "Okay," she said, as I watched her eyes close across the fire.

I turned on my side too, feeling guilty for admiring her the way I did. But the truth was that beyond her beauty and behind those captivating green eyes, there was a brave and decent woman to whom I owed my life. "Good night, Sarah," I whispered softly. "...Thank you."

Chapter 8
Testing the Ropes

THE APPALLING MEMORIES of what happened in the Lab came back to me in the form of nightmares, which awakened me near dawn with a desperate gasp that ignited my hypersenses in a defensive stance. Fortunately, the morning dew had enhanced the earthy scent of the forest: the smells of fresh air, pine needles, wood smoke, oak moss, and grass formed a naturally relaxing mixture that soon eased my nerves, tipping me back toward normal. The calming sound of the river and the peaceful string of smoke rising from the near-extinguished campfire also helped to alleviate my high-strung senses.

Looking over the dying fire I saw Sarah, lying on the ground still asleep. God, she looked beautiful! After everything we'd gone through, she still looked like a model ready for a photo shoot. Watching her lying there so peacefully made me realize she was just another victim of this heinous conspiracy. She'd never deserved to be involved in any of this, and she sure as hell she didn't deserve to be here with me right now.

I knew exactly what I was walking into, and I realized what my chances were. And though my strong resolve kept fueling my hope for success, my mind wouldn't stop running the numbers over and over again. Our likelihood of success was slight.

I realized then that dragging another innocent life into the slaughterhouse was senseless and cruel. Sarah shouldn't come with me. But I also knew that it would be difficult to convince her otherwise, so I had to come up with the right words and the right reasons to send her away.

"Good morning," she said, stretching fetchingly on the grass.

"Morning."

"Everything okay?"

"Yeah," I lied. "I was just running the numbers on my chances of getting out of there alive." She studied me. "They're good!" I lied again. "But I'm going to need someone on the outside. Someone I can trust. And that's why I need you to stay behind."

She sat up hastily and gave me a sharp look. "We both need the map," I continued. "I need it to get to the bridge and you need it to get out of these woods. So we don't have any choice but to hike together to the bridge. After that we'll part ways." I talked fast and stiffly, trying to leave no room for discussion. "I want you to go back to Ketchikan and check into the Black

Bear, a small inn I saw on the harbor on my way in. And I want you to wait for me there, all right?"

I got to my feet before she could answer. "But…" she uttered, confused, and stopped.

I kicked some dirt over our campfire and offered my hand for Sarah to help her get up. "Let's go."

We resumed our journey to the bridge, a two-hour hike during which neither of us said another word. I guess we were too busy juggling our own thoughts. But interaction resumed the moment we arrived at the edge of the bridge—where we stopped and stared in amazed disappointment.

The so-called bridge was a century-old mosaic of broken wooden boards and dry ropes, which stretched a hundred feet above the river, connecting two steep cliffs that made the Empire State Building look like a two-story house—at least to my acrophobic eyes. "You're kidding me, right?" I protested. "There is no way in *hell* you can call this a bridge!"

"Well, according to the map, this is the only way back," she reminded me. "I don't think you have much of a choice here."

I leaned out over the edge to check our landing site in the event of a collapse, and a burst of fear knocked on my chest when I saw the jagged boulders lying across the river. They almost seemed like they'd been purposely positioned under the decaying bridge, like a booby trap waiting for the first boob who attempted to cross it.

"Crap!" I exclaimed nervously, realizing that I'd made a grave mistake in looking down into the gorge. "Just my luck!"

I took a deep breath and decided to put my fears aside and deal with what had to be done. And I'm not talking about just crossing the bridge, but something I found it much harder to do. It was time to say good-bye to Sarah...and I didn't know how.

I stepped away from the bridge and turned to Sarah, who was apparently waiting for me to say something. I stood there in front of her, tongue-tied and at a loss for words—just admiring those hypnotizing eyes, which I was certain I'd never see again. Her look turned quizzical again, derailing me completely from my already confused thoughts. "What?" she demanded, sounding annoyed.

"Nothing," I said, realizing I should move this along. I was just about to express my gratitude for everything she'd done for me, when suddenly—

"Then let's go!" she snapped, jumping on the first deck-board of the bridge in one swift and sneaky move, leaving me standing behind like an idiot. "I thought we were in a hurry?" she called over her shoulder.

"What do you think you're doing?" I demanded. "I told you, you're not coming with me, Sarah!"

"The hell I'm not. This may be my only chance to get some evidence against R.C. Labs. Besides, you don't know your way around the Lab as well as I do. Without me, it'd take you longer to find her. And you know better than anyone that time can make all the difference here. And don't forget—you still need someone to keep you calm."

"Keep me calm? Are you *serious*? I've never met anybody who can get a rise out of me as easily as you can, Sarah! I'm telling you for the last time, I do *not* need your help, okay?"

"Yes, you do!"

"You're not coming!"

"Yes I am!"

"You're going to get yourself killed!"

"I don't care!"

"Argh!" I growled, kicking at the gravel. "Are you *always* this stubborn?!"

She glared at me over her shoulder and said, "You have no idea."

We scowled at each other for a long moment, until the intensity in her eyes made me realize that arguing with her was completely useless. I sighed in defeat and looked away finally, letting her know her obstinacy had triumphed over mine.

"Now," she said smugly. "Are you going to calm down and cross this bridge with me or not?"

Refusing to allow her to gloat, I just exhaled heavily while I walked to the edge of the bridge and stood right behind her. A soft breeze blew strong then enough to flutter her long red curls over my face, which I have to admit somehow dampened my escalating belligerence. Sarah peeped over her shoulder, realizing what the mischievous wind had wrought, and apologized, twisting her hair into a ponytail that she tossed over her shoulder. And though her hair was out of my face, her scent still lingered like a teasing drug, once again igniting my hypersenses.

My grip tightened around the ropes and my jaw tightened as I tried to ignore the rush of sensation and emotion her accident had triggered. Up until that point I wasn't sure which, if any, of these new feelings I should trust. For now, I decided not to trust anything I felt—including the attraction I'd begun to feel towards Sarah.

"So, how should we handle this?" I asked, trying to refocus on the task at hand. "One at a time?"

"Hmmm…" Sarah mused, looking down. "I'll go first. You just stay here."

"But…" And just like that, she begun to walk over the creaking deck-boards, sliding her tight grip over the ropes with each careful step. I just stood there breathless as I watched her reach the shallow catenary arc of the bridge. Then, as my heart seemed to rise to the back of my throat, Sarah began to purposely wobble the bridge, pulling on the ropes and stomping on the boards. A shiver shook my body when the wobble sent a vibration to the end of the rope I was holding. *What the hell are you doing?!* I shouted.

"Relax!" she shouted back. "I'm just testing its strength."

"What?! NO!" I bawled. "Don't test it, just cross it!"

"It's okay!" she yelled. "It seems strong enough to hold us both!"

"It *seems* strong enough? What the hell does that mean?"

"Just get on the damn bridge, Victor!"

"It *seems* strong enough," I muttered to myself, stepping onto the decrepit bridge. "Not the best line to inspire confidence."

Sarah was a good fifty feet ahead of me now, following the upward slope of the bridge as I struggled with my odd cocktail of emotions. My familiar fear of heights only intensified the awareness that Sarah's scent had already ignited in me; and unfortunately, this only worsened my fear of absorbing more of that "dark energy" into the newly-awakened region of my brain.

I stopped for a second and closed my eyes, trying to control my breathing, hoping that if I calmed myself down long enough, I'd be able to get rid of this worry. But my pause had the opposite effect. I stood there feeling my mind connecting to my surroundings, like creeping ivy branching out through the air, clinging to everything it touched. My heart begun to pound out of my chest when my mind reached the surface of the rocky river, somehow measuring the deadly distance between the bridge and the steep boulders below. Two hundred and seventeen feet, three point two three seven inches.

My eyes opened to the overwhelming compulsion to look down again. My jaw clenched, my hands tightened around the ropes in a grip that almost cut off my circulation as my eyes adjusted and readjusted to the terrifying height. My entire body went into complete paralysis, like a frightened cat stuck in a tree. Sarah, just twenty feet shy of reaching the other side, looked over her shoulder and realized the problem. "Come on, Victor!" she yelled. "You can do it!"

But even with Sarah's encouragement, I found myself struggling to move. My thoughts, meanwhile, were rattling along at an incredible speed. I was having trouble understanding all the images that began to overlap inside my head. All the things my mind was connected to had begun to flash before my eyes, making it very difficult to maintain coordination. I shuffled forward until I was about ten feet out.

I raised my head and fought to keep my eyes opened and fixed on Sarah as dozens of images intruded into my visual field: rocks, trees, water, Sarah, the bridge—all at the same time, dazing me. *Wait!* Suddenly the image of the bridge overcame the others, becoming clearer and more detailed with every flash. I tried to concentrate harder in order to understand what I was seeing. The strongest images belonged to the near anchor of the bridge, where the ropes had begun to stretch and give. It took a split second for the rest of my senses to join my vision, allowing me to perceive the ongoing event.

I could almost taste the dry, dusty surface of the overstrained ropes, which had begun slowly and irrevocably to tear, and hear the tiny crackles as individual fibers parted. My eyes widened abruptly as I realized the implications situation. "Sarah!" I hollered. "Go! Get to other side! *Now!*"

"What?" Sarah yelled back, unable to understand my warning, which had been drowned by distance and wind.

I cupped my hands around my mouth and tried again with everything I had. "THE ROPES ARE BREAKING! GO!!!"

This time my words didn't just reach Sarah, they startled her into action. She spun around and began to move as fast as the wobbling bridge allowed. I, on the other hand, knew that being at the middle of the bridge wasn't in my favor. The sound of the parting fibers grew stronger and faster in my head. Then one final image flashed inside my head, allowing me to see the snapping of the ropes just seconds before it would actually happen—giving me the chance to warn Sarah, who was now just a few feet away from the opposite edge of the cliff.

"SARAH!—HURRY!" I shouted, weaving my arms around the ropes on both sides, trying to ready myself for the inevitable. Sarah threw a quick glance over her shoulder that gave me the chance to shout out one final instruction: "JUMP!" Bending her knees then, she launched herself towards the edge of the cliff— just as the ropes on my side broke in one violently final *snap*.

An awful sensation of falling clutched my stomach after the sudden break. The air rushing upwards against my body reminded me of my deadly trajectory, right toward the sharp boulders below. I closed my eyes tightly as my body plummeted downward along with the remnants of the bridge, my heart beating as fast as a hummingbird's, waiting for the inevitable impact. Thankfully, the ropes I'd lashed around my arms were still attached to the anchor at Sarah's end, which changed the trajectory of my fall.

I began to swing towards the other side of the river, narrowly missing the killer boulders below. My eyes opened just in time to realize I was now heading straight for the rocky face of the cliff, which didn't look too inviting either. I closed my eyes again and cringed, waiting for the painful impact, and felt my mind throw up some kind of final desperate shield against the cliff. It lasted only a few milliseconds, and then collapsed as I struck.

I felt the deck boards break against my shoulder. The collision was such that it made me lose my grip on the ropes; fortunately, one of them ropes remained twisted around my arm, leaving me hanging by one overstressed limb.

It took me a couple of seconds to realize I wasn't dead. "Oh, boy!" I groaned softly, opening my eyes to the unappealing situation.

I heard Sarah's yell from above. "Victor? Victor!"

I looked up and I saw her leaning far over the edge, looking for me. Her hands, which were clutching the edge, knocked some dirt and gravel loose; naturally, it went into my eyes. "Stay away from the edge!" I shouted, sputtering and rubbing my eyes with the back of my free wrist.

"Oh my God!" she exclaimed. "Are you all right?"

"Yeah!" I responded wryly, still coughing out dust. "Just hangin' out!"

"Can you climb up?"

"I don't know. How does it look from up there?"

"You're not that far down. Try to use the deck-boards as a ladder."

"Right!"

"Oh, and Victor?" she called again. "Try not to look—"

"Don't say it!" I cut her off before she could remind me. I knew looking down wouldn't do me any good at this point, so I tried to focus on climbing up and forget about the nearly two hundred feet between me and the top of the cliff.

After a great deal of struggle, I finally climbed up far enough to reach Sarah's hand. She then pulled me up by the elbow and helped me over the ledge. I don't know how she managed it, but I was heartily glad she had. "Thanks!" I gasped, trying to catch my breath, thrilled to be once again on solid ground. I put a good dozen feet between myself and the edge before I stopped moving.

"Are you okay?" she asked, scanning my body for injuries— of which she found plenty. Yet her immediate concern was my left arm, which was cut from where one of the breaking foot-boards had scraped across it as I hit, and was now bleeding profusely. I also had a nasty cut across my left eyebrow, which kept dribbling blood into my eye. I brought my hand up to dab at the wound, but Sarah stopped me before I could touch it. "Don't!" she said, tearing a piece off her blouse and folding it into a wad. She then pressed it against my brow and told me to keep pressure on it. And though it hurt like hell, I tried to keep my composure and not complain too much.

"Thanks," I said, pressing the cloth against my brow. "Are you all right?" I asked, observing her distress. She nodded quickly and continued tending my wound. "Hey," I said, "Relax. I'm fine."

Her eyes met my stare, an obvious stain of guilt in them. "You're *not* fine," she said, wiping the blood off my arm. "You're banged up. You're going to need stitches."

"It'll be all right," I said encouragingly.

She stopped and looked at me with sad eyes. "I'm sorry," she whispered, as tears rose. "I shouldn't have talked you into crossing."

"It's okay," I whispered back, a soft smile in my face. "Really."

"It's *not* okay," she barked, tearing more pieces from the bottom of her blouse, which ended up looking like a crop top. "I almost lost you there," she added.

An awkward silence followed her words.

"I guess the bridge wasn't as strong as it seemed, huh?" I finally joked, breaking the uncomfortable silence. She stopped again and looked at me.

"I'm sorry," she said regretfully. "I feel *so* stupid!" She turned to my wound again and bandaged it with the pieces of cloth.

"Hey!" I stopped her, and held her hands together. I know my eyes were reflecting exactly what I wanted to say. "It's all right." My voice sincere. "*I'm* all right."

Her eyes finally softened then, and she let out a deep sigh of relief. I even saw a faint smile on her trembling lips. "Thanks for the warning," she said. "I could've fallen too."

"We're in this together, right?"

Her faint smile broadened. "Yes, we are."

"Just do me a favor and check the ropes *before* you wobble next time, okay?" I added seriously. "I'd hate to lose you too."

Her eyes lifted to meet mine. "I'll be more careful," she vowed, finishing up with my dressing. "I promise."

We laughed then, trying to put the event behind us. After Sarah finished patching up my head, we got back on our feet and resumed our dangerous journey.

***

The mansion was just a couple of miles away now; and Sarah, who was once again leading the way, had found a path that would help us save some time. The way she hiked along the path made me realize she'd probably ventured here before. But I didn't bother to ask. My complete concentration was now focused on getting out of these beautiful but treacherous woods. With every step I took, I was getting closer to a potentially fatal confrontation. But my resolve to get there before something bad happened to Yvette overpowered any fear I had. If anything, it only hastened my pace.

After hours of hiking, we finally arrived at R.C. Labs' long, graveled driveway. By then, the sky had turned gray as the sun began to set behind the trees. Fear, however, was on the rise. I watched Sarah stand in the middle of the road, staring blankly at the way back to town. My eyes, on the other hand, were locked on the edifice in the opposite direction. This place, however loathsome, still held my last and only reason to live—and I wasn't going anywhere until I got her back.

I let Sarah ponder for a few moments, hoping she'd change her mind about coming with me. I knew that if I pressured her to leave, she'd probably do the opposite just to spite me. So I just stood there waiting for her to make her own decision.

After a brief consideration, she turned back to me, head down and expressionless, and sighed. Understanding what the rational thing to do was, I waited patiently for her to say goodbye. But then a second, more optimistic sigh brought life back to her eyes and a crooked smile to her lips. Without speaking a word, she began to lead the way back to R.C. Labs. Her decision had been made, and all I could do was respect it. So I followed her lead once more.

As we trudged towards the Lab, I could feel my brain reaching out into the atmosphere, absorbing the energy that Sarah had talked about. It was impossible for me to tell which of the two forces, maleficent or beneficent, was in control at the moment. All I could feel was the delightful awareness that connected my mind with every single thing around me, living or not, especially Sarah. Through this power, I was able to perceive the forest in a way that challenged the parameters of logic. I sensed the long thoughts of the trees, the quiet whisper of the wind and the scents it carried, and even the animals jolting along restlessly in the woods, scared and confused, as though they were able to sense me too. It was an extraordinary experience that made me wonder how such a beautiful gift could ever be turned to anything evil.

My mind sifted through the vast forest, until it encountered a lone wolf 1.138 miles away. I had no idea how I was able to so accurately calculate the distance between the things I sensed and myself, assuming I wasn't just fooling myself. Yet I was compelled to believe it was accurate. So much was going through my mind at that moment that I decided not to question anything anymore; there was no point in flustering myself even further. So when the wolf reacted to my scan with a high-pitch howl, I only smiled with amazement. Sarah, on the other hand, was so startled that she stopped frozen in her tracks.

"What the *hell* was that?" she wailed, "Is that a—"

"Yes it is," I answered quickly, "But don't worry, it's over a mile away."

"How do you know that?"

"I wish I knew," I answered earnestly, watching as Sarah wrapped her arms around herself, which made me aware of how cold the evening had become. I was so strangely warm and comfortable that I wouldn't have noticed otherwise. "Come here," I said, sliding my arm over her shoulders. She buried her head underneath my chin and shivered. "You're freezing, Sarah!" I noted, as she wrapped her arm around my waist. I could feel her cold hand grazing my bare skin through my ripped shirt.

"How can you be so warm, wearing nothing but this rag?" she said, teeth chattering.

"I don't know. But under the circumstances, whatever the reason is, I'll take it."

She chuckled. "Agreed."

A sudden presentiment made me pull Sarah off the road and hide with her behind some bushes. "What now?" she complained.

I shushed her. "Someone's coming."

A pair of headlights came into view, confirming my prediction. Sarah and I crouched deeper behind the undergrowth, hoping we hadn't been seen. But when the approaching vehicle stopped not too far from where we were hiding, we knew we must have been spotted; they probably had sensors on the road. We heard the engine idle as the headlights pierced a tunnel of light right through the pitch-black road.

I ground my molars together as I heard the car door open and close; Sarah froze into a statue. Footsteps crunched on the gravel, and with an audible click, a flashlight suddenly illuminated the side of the road. In the attempt to stay out of sight, I signaled Sarah to move deeper into the woods, but the snap of a twig gave away our position, making us freeze in panic.

"Hello!" a familiar voice broke the silence, "Is anybody there?"

"Denali?" I whispered to myself. Sarah stared at me, confused.

"Hello?" he called again. This time his voice left no doubts.

I rose and began walking towards the light, palm first, trying to keep it out of my face. Though it didn't hurt anymore, I couldn't suppress three years of habit.

"Victor!" Sarah called with a frantic whisper. "What are you doing?"

"It's okay," I called over my shoulder, "Just stay put."

I kept walking towards the light until I saw the silhouette behind it. "Denali? Is that you?"

"Mr. Victor?" Denali recognized me on the spot. He lowered the light and walked toward me with a confused look on his face. "What are you doing out here? Don't you know there's a dangerous patient on the loose?"

I sighed in relief. "Denali, we need your help."

He flashed the light over the bush where Sarah was hiding, realizing I wasn't alone. He then flashed the light right back at me, his eyes slowly scrutinizing my appearance. I suppose my wounds, along with the bloodstains on my ragged clothes, were probably a lot to take in. "What the heck happened to you?" he exclaimed. "Are you all right?"

"I'm fine, but we need your help to get back inside R.C. Labs." I beckoned to Sarah to come out of the bushes.

"I'm sorry, Mr. Victor, but the entire building's in lockdown," he explained. "I was told to go home and wait until the situation was contained."

"Situation...?"

"I was told a dangerous patient had escaped from the Lab, and that no one was to enter or leave the premises until further notice." His tone sounded troubled. "I could lose my job if I go back."

"Any chance we can continue this discussion in the car?" Sarah said through chattering teeth. "Um, hi, I'm Sarah."

"Denali." He smiled and shook her hand. "Please, get inside! I'll turn up the heater for you." He eagerly opened the door for Sarah and gestured for us to get in.

Inside Denali's 2002 Buick LeSabre, Sarah found an R.C. Labs coat that she shrugged into, while I told Denali about our unbelievable ordeal. His eyes bulged in horror as he learned the truth about his employer and the gravity of the situation. After a minute of musing and hyperventilating, he finally agreed to help us. "All right," he said. "What do you want me to do?"

I thought for a second. "How big is your trunk?"

Chapter 9

Rescue

THE DARK ROAD brightened gradually the closer Denali got to the gates of R.C. Labs. His clammy hands trembled over the steering wheel and he knew his face was pale as a ghost's. His eyes narrowed in the glare of a flashlight, which beckoned him to stop alongside the security both. He bit his lower lip as one of the guards approached and tapped on his window with his flashlight. He rolled the window down, revealing his forced smile. "Hello, John," Denali greeted, showing all of his teeth.

"Denali?" The guard gave him a quizzical look. "What the hell are you doing here? Didn't they tell you to go home?"

"Yes," he answered, too quickly. "But I, uh... forgot something in the Town Car."

"What?" the guard asked, scrutinizing his face.

"W-what?" Denali stammered, losing his train of thought.

"What did you forget in the car?" The guard probed, enunciating every word as if talking to a five year old kid.

"Oh!" he snapped and followed with a nervous stammer, "M-m-my wallet. Can't do anything without it."

The guard's face was bleak and definitely not amused by Denali's unusual behavior. He pointed his flashlight inside the cab and scanned the front and back, spotting nothing but an empty soda cans and a half-eaten bag of potato chips. The guard held his quizzical look while aiming the light back onto Denali's face. Then he sighed and considered for a moment; Denali took advantage of his hesitation. "It'll only take me a minute," he pleaded. "I promise!"

The guard grunted. "Oh, all right. But, make it quick. I'm not supposed to let anybody in without Dr. Walker's approval."

"Thank you, John!"

The guard walked back to the booth and opened the gate. Denali eagerly shifted into gear and waved gratefully to the guard as he pulled into the main driveway. Once inside the premises, he drove to the back of the mansion, where the company Town Car was parked. Denali was breathing so heavily that he was just a tad away from hyperventilating again. He backed up toward the building next to the Town Car, parked, turned off the engine, and stepped out.

His vigilant eyes looked everywhere as he walked to the back of the car. He looked again and quickly popped the trunk open.

"Come on," he said, helping Sarah out of the space where we'd been successfully smuggled. "Quickly, before anyone see us."

"Do you have the keys for the Town Car?" I asked, trying not to lose momentum.

"They're tucked in the visor," he said.

"Good!" I patted his shoulder and took a deep breath. "You'd better go now. This way, they won't suspect you."

"But what about you and Miss Sarah? Are you going to be okay?"

"Yeah, we'll be fine." I tapped him on the shoulder again, trying to reassure him. "Thank you for everything, Denali—I'll never forget it. Now, go!"

Denali got back in the car and rolled down the window. "Take care, Mr. Victor. You too, Miss."

"Thank you, Denali," Sarah said with a warm smile.

Sarah and I merged with the shadows of the mansion while Denali drove away. We moved along the edge of the meadow, like stealthy thieves in the night. *I can't believe I'm back here*, I thought as I sidled against the walls of this opulent building. I was back in the place I once thought to be my salvation. Now, I knew that it was nothing but a madhouse that had cursed me for life—however long that might be. Even the meadow had lost all its beauty in my eyes.

This was now the cradle of my resentment and hatred, the birthplace of the monster I was turning into—and Dr. Walker, its father and creator, was the Reaper who'd destroyed all my dreams. Only one thing was keeping me from letting my anger and hate consume all my humanity: Yvette. The thought of seeing her again was keeping me going. The hope of holding her in my arms again was worth everything to me. I needed to tell her, before it was too late, that I now understood that the little boy she once knew had never stopped loving her... never.

All the security personnel were on high alert. Searchlights on top of the building swept the entire meadow, as if guarding the yard of a maximum security prison. Running the numbers in my head, I noticed the ten-second window in which the lights left our path in the shadows. So I told Sarah to keep her head down and wait for our opportunity to move in closer. I reached for her hand and locked my eyes on those lights, counting the seconds for our window. Then, without wasting any time, we ran as fast as we could, towards our only hope for a break-in. We stopped and crouched behind the weeping willow where I'd last seen Yvette, and waited for the light to pass. Sarah, trying to catch her breath, looked at me with a confused look on her face. "What are we doing here?" she asked with an anxious whisper.

"This is our way in," I noted, throwing a quick glance towards the second floor.

"What?" she questioned in disbelief, "Through the window? How do you know that's not going to trip every alarm in the place?"

"Trust me," I assured her. "I know."

"I hope you're right." She sighed. "All right, then, let's go!" Her command was followed by a deft move that put her on top of the first branch. I stepped back as I watched her thrust her way up the tree, as if she'd done it her whole life. "Come on!" she hissed over her shoulder, staring down at my stunned face. "Hurry up!"

"Right," I muttered, remembering my lack of dexterity when it came to heights. Though I have to admit that after climbing a two-hundred-foot cliff while hanging above a family of steep boulders, climbing a tree to a second-floor window didn't seem all that difficult. Still, Sarah had to jump to the rescue when she saw me struggling at the edge of said window.

"You know," she grunted as she pulled me inside the bedroom, "For someone with acrophobia, you certainly do a lot of *off-ground* activities."

"Not by choice," I panted.

When I'd caught my breath, I whispered Yvette's name as loudly as I could, hoping she'd be there; my hypersenses apparently saw no reason to help me at the moment. My hope vanished with the flip of a light switch. The room was empty, and apparently left the same way she'd left it before the procedure. Yvette's partially unpacked bag was still on the bed, along with her father's flask and some letters bound together by a red ribbon. Sticking out of her open purse was her passport and a return airline ticket to New York City. I quickly gathered these items and headed for the door. My room was just across the hall, and I needed to check to see if my things were still there.

Sarah and I moved fast and quietly across the empty hallway and locked ourselves inside my room. Everything was exactly as I'd left it. I grabbed my backpack in a hurry and shoved Yvette's stuff inside of it, along with my own passport, cell phone, return ticket, and some cash. I donned my jacket, followed by my backpack, and headed for the door. Before I opened it, I turned around and met Sarah's anxious stare. "We've got to go down to the Lab," I told her in a low voice.

"I know," she murmured, heaving a long, heavy sigh. "Let's go."

Sarah led the way to the elevators and opened the same panel Nurse Jacky had used to take me to the Lab. She entered a code and waited. "I managed to program a master code before I left," she explained. "Let's hope it hasn't been overridden."

After the longest five seconds of my life, green lights lit up the panel and the elevator doors hissed open. We stood there, staring at the open elevator. Sarah's face was pale as a ghost; I wondered if she was secretly hoping for the code *not* to work, so she could tell me to get the hell out of there. But I think she knew by then that I'd have just found another way to break into the Lab. "Are you ready?" I asked, my eyes fixed on the inside of the elevator.

"Are *you?*" she countered. I turned to her and meet her fearful eyes. "You...may not like what you'd find down there, Victor."

I turned back to the elevator and thought about her words, imagining the horror of finding Yvette dead. But I shook my head in vehement denial and climbed into the elevator car. "You coming?" I asked. Sarah rolled her eyes and sighed in defeat, climbing onboard. She shot me a solemn look and pushed the button for the lab.

Her face looked even paler under the elevator's florescent lighting. Her eyes flickered with a mixture of fear and determination, as though her conviction to stay alive was trying to overpower the dreadful thought of dying. I took her hand in mine as she let out a deep, shaky sigh. Her eyes flew to our entwined hands and then back to my eyes. "I'll keep you safe. I promise," I said softly.

She squeezed my hand with a faint smile on her face. "I know you'll try."

In unison, we lifted our eyes the floor indicator, trembling with every changing number, watching a countdown we couldn't stop. We were only three levels away from the Lab when another spark in my mind rattled my senses. Images began to bloom in my mind, fuzzy at first but soon clear as water. Two armed men waited for the elevator at the Lab level, and they sure as hell weren't expecting two uninvited guests coming their way.

I knew with absolute certainty that these visions were not only real, but that they were triggered by the presence of imminent danger. Knowing that reaching the Lab level would be the end of us made me react with the only solution I could think right then. I kept my eyes on the floor indictor and waited for the right moment, then reached out, quick as a snake striking.

"What are you doing?" Sarah asked, disconcerted, when I pushed the stop button.

"There are guards waiting for the elevator at the Lab level. Don't ask me how I know, I just do. You have to trust me on this, okay?"

"After what I've seen you do, no problem. But what are we going to do now?"

"If I've calculated correctly, the elevator's between two floors, right above the Lab. We only have a few minutes before they realize it's stopped, so we need to hurry."

"Hurry doing what?" she asked, and I could sense the hysteria bubbling under her words. "We're trapped!"

"Hardly," I said, pointing upward at the overhead hatch. I interlocked my fingers and held out my hands, nodding at Sarah, hoping she'd get the point. She gave me a half-angry, half-admiring look, stepped into my hands, and launched herself upward to the hatch. Lucky for us, it was unlocked and easy enough to open. Sarah climbed up on top of the elevator and I jumped up to the hatch to follow—but a slip of my hand left me dangling from the edge. Sarah came to my rescue, again, pulling me up and over as soon as she saw my struggle.

"Geez!" she protested under her breath, pulling up. "For a guy with telekinesis, I sure have to help you out a lot. How many times do I have to pull you up from a ledge?"

"Thanks!" I gasped, finally on top of the elevator.

"That's three you owe me now, buddy."

I gave her a stern look as I panted, "Let's try not to keep score, all right?"

She gave me a crooked smile and helped me shut the hatch beneath us. No need to make it obvious where we'd gone. Once it was closed, we were left in complete darkness; but my night sight was back, and we managed to find the ventilation shaft easily enough. We crept into the narrow flue and crawled towards the Lab. A moment later, a loud buzzer followed by a metallic thud behind us alerted us that the elevator had been overridden and was now on the move again. We registered the event and kept crawling toward the faint light at the end of the tunnel.

Soon we reached a slotted panel underneath us that overlooked the Lab, and watched the two guards from my vision board the elevator and leave. With the Lab now empty, we unclipped the grill and climbed down onto a capsule that sat immediately below. If I wasn't mistaken, it was Tom's; and my stomach twinged as I realized that the nice man I'd met a few days before was now probably dead. Once I hit the floor I began to check every capsule, looking for Yvette, while Sarah ran to the control panel and locked down every entrance to the Lab, sealing us safely inside.

Capsule after capsule, I found nothing. My heart was sinking fast, fearing that I'd been too late. But the last capsule brought hope back into my heart. Its mechanism was on, proving someone still lay inside, but the foggy glass shield made it impossible to determine who. So I rushed to open it with Sarah's help. Finally, I yanked the lever and stood back while the glass shield slid open. Sarah and I stepped in closer as fumes escaped the capsule, dispersing and disappearing into the air.

The shocking contents startled us both, making us stagger backwards in horror. A cold shiver crawled up my spine, lifting the hairs on the back of my neck "Oh, my God!" Sarah exclaimed in shock, turning her face from the horrific sight.

I found myself struggling to register the gruesome spectacle, yet my intensified senses left no room for doubt—the nightmare was real. Swallowing hard to keep from vomiting, I scrutinized the blood-splattered interior of the capsule, where the body of a male patient lay, lifeless, his head blown apart like a burst balloon.

His right eye, which barely remained inside what was left of its orbital socket, reflected the most disturbing look I've ever seen—as if he'd been conscious at the moment of death, and his death had been excruciatingly painful. It looked like his head had blown from the inside out, like an egg in a microwave. The identity of the poor soul was revealed the moment I checked his ID bracelet, which read: *William Delgado.*

"Oh, Billie," I groaned.

Sarah came from behind me with a clean sheet and covered the mutilated body. "Did you know him?" she asked.

"I met him the day I arrived. He was the youngest one of our group. He was just a kid, Sarah..." My eyes closed tightly as my feelings began to edge toward anger again. "I'm sorry, Billie. I'm sorry we were too late."

The thought of Yvette sharing Billie's fate transformed my anger into rage. My eyes began to burn as they had when I'd taken control of the guards during our escape. Sarah, recognizing the reaction, stepped back warily and looked at me with alarm. "Victor?" she called fearfully. "Don't—"

A soft thud made us turn our focus to the elevator, which seemed to be arriving again. "Crap!" Sarah growled. "They know we're here, Victor. We have to get out now!"

"No!" I snapped, feeling the dark force winning the game of mercy inside my head. "Let them come."

The rising tide of power was like a drug, fueling my brain with the same euphoria I'd felt back on the river. The idea of letting it control me was intoxicating—so much so that I found myself no longer fighting it.

"Victor!" Sara said desperately, shaking me by the shoulders. "Look at me. Look at me! You can't let it win, Victor. Come back! Come back, Victor!"

Part of me wanted to listen, but the other—the much stronger part—wanted revenge. Wanted to make them pay for what they had done. "Run, Sarah," I told her thickly. "You have to run. Get out..."

"NO!" she yelped as a euphoric trance began to chain my will into final submission. "Wake up!" Sarah commanded. "Wake up!"

Getting no response, Sarah decided to try a different type of persuasion: she grabbed my head firmly with both hands and mashed her lips against mine in a passionate kiss that snatched my concentration back from the powerful dark tide washing me away. Without its energy fueling me, my anger subsided and my volition returned. Finally released from its trance, I found myself completely subdued by Sarah's kiss.

When our lips finally parted I was out of breath, stunned, and confused—but still myself. Sarah let her hands glide down my face as she backed away, her eyes fixed on mine. Too stunned to ask what had happened, I stood there, dazed and dumbfounded.

"Are you back?" she asked in a shaky whisper. I could only nod in response. I was still trying to process the complexities that had just taken place, too baffled to speak. "Good!" she said sharply. "Now let's go."

I nodded again and followed her as she dashed back to the ventilation shaft. I shook my head hard, trying to shake off the groggy feeling the experience had left in me; but the daze lingered like a sedative. Sarah climbed up onto one of the capsules to reach the duct. I followed her as fast as I could, but my movements were clumsy and uncoordinated. Still, I made it into the duct...and she didn't even have to pull me in this time. Once inside, we set the slotted panel back into place and waited for company to arrive.

The doors of the elevator slid open not 30 seconds later and footsteps clacked against the tiled floor, accompanied by voices.

"Check the controls. The doors were locked from the inside," said a snappish voice—probably the new Head of Security, or the leader of Walker's little army.

"Yessir!"

A familiar voice addressed one of the guards. "What seems to be the problem?" Dr. Walker asked.

"We appear to have a glitch in the system, sir. First with the elevator and now with the lab's locking mechanism."

"I see." I heard a scuffing sound. "There's still blood visible between these tiles here, Black. I want your men back in here to clean it up after we're done."

"Yessir. We'll scour it ASAP, sir."

"We're not friggin' janitors," I heard another voice mutter close by, and held my breath. I hadn't even heard the guy approach.

Through the slotted panel, I watched Dr. Walker approach Billie's open capsule. He stood silently in front of it, scrutinizing the sheet that covered the body of the poor kid. "Put the facility on full alert," he said, disturbingly calm. "Glitches do not cover dead bodies."

"Yessir!"

After peeking under the sheet, Dr. Walker turned to address the entire squad, his voice no longer serene. "Now listen up, everyone! We all know who the intruder is. He's killed four of our guards already and should be considered extremely dangerous. So use caution. I want guards at every possible exit. He's not to leave the facility this time—understood?"

"Yessir!" a conglomerate of voices answered as one.

"Now move!"

Rapid footsteps exited the lab, leaving Dr. Walker alone with the one squad member who'd stayed behind. With the physique of a badass marine, the middle-aged soldier looked pretty intimidating, yet his eyes resembled those of a concerned father. And though the ugly scar he hid behind his goatee screamed "beware," his demeanor radiated righteousness and trustworthiness. "Dr. Walker?" he called.

"Yes, Captain Black?"

"I've dug up some information on Bellator," he said, giving Walker a dubious look. "And I must say I'm a little confused."

"How do you mean, Captain?" Dr. Walker's voice was polite.

"Well, let's see." He pulled a file from under his arm. "Bellator, Victor: 23 years old, 5'7", 160 pounds. Survivor of an automobile accident in which he suffered a major head injury three years ago. Diagnosed with an untreatable intracranial pressure. Suffers from headaches, sensitivity to light, and mood swings. Despite his condition, he continued his studies and graduated at the top of his class. His concentration was in physics and mathematics. He's been described by friends and colleagues as an upstanding, law-abiding citizen." He stopped with a heavy sigh and closed the file. "Now forgive me, Doctor. But this doesn't sound like the profile of a dangerous killer."

"I'm afraid I don't understand what you're asking me, Captain."

"I'm trying to understand how a legally disabled kid, who's never picked a fight in his entire life, came to overpower and kill four armed men, each bigger than him."

"I was under the impression you were sent here to assist me with the capture of a dangerous patient, Captain," Walker said in a bleak tone, "not to start an investigation."

"Look, Doctor, I don't know exactly what is it that you do here, and frankly I don't give a crap. But I'm responsible for the safety of my men. I need to know what I'm really going up against here."

"All you need to know, Captain, is that Victor Bellator is mentally unstable and extremely dangerous. And if you're the one who happens to stumble upon him, I'd suggest you put two bullets in his head before he can lock his eyes on you." They exchanged uneasy looks. "Now if you'll excuse me, Captain, I have patients to attend to." Dr. Walker turned away from him and walked back towards the elevator.

"Just one last thing, Doctor."

Walker turned around reluctantly. "Yes, Captain?"

"How can you be so sure this Bellator is the intruder we're looking for? I mean, he took four lives in order to escape this place. Why in the world would he come back?"

Dr. Walker smiled smugly. "Because love makes you do foolish things, Captain."

The captain pondered that while Walker gave his back to him again.

"What about this Sarah Grey?" Captain Black called out.

Walker stopped again, but this time he didn't turn. "I wouldn't worry about her, Captain. She must be dead by now." Walker finally left the room, leaving Captain Black alone in the lab, upset and confused.

After pondering Walker's words for a few minutes, a troubled look on his face, the Captain unclipped a walkie-talkie from his belt and brought it close to his mouth. He hesitated a moment before he spoke: "Attention, everyone. This is Captain Black. I've been ordered to use deadly force against the intruder." He hesitated again. "Shoot to kill. Acknowledge. Over."

'Copy that, Captain,' a *staticky* voice confirmed, followed by several others.

After Captain Black left the Lab, Sarah tapped me on the shoulder and asked me to follow her. I did so, crawling back to the elevator shaft with her. She was quiet along the way. I knew it was because of what had happened in the Lab, and I knew she wasn't going to be the one to bring it up. So despite my personal mortification, I decided to ask.

"Sarah?" I called in a whisper, trying not to make much more noise than we were already making inside the ventilation shaft.

"What?" she whispered back over her shoulder, her tone guarded.

"What happened back there?"

She stopped abruptly in front of me, making me bump into her feet. "I was hoping you wouldn't bring that up," she said bitterly.

"I'm sorry. I just want to—"

"Look," she interrupted, "I've been thinking about my theory about anger being the main trigger for your loss of volition. And I figured that if I diverted your focus from your anger, it just might stop the change from happening, okay?"

"So naturally you thought of kissing me."

She looked over her shoulder again. "Well, I thought that might get your attention." Her penetrating eyes stared at me for the longest moment, and a faint smile curled her lips before she turned back to resume her crawling.

I shook my head in disbelief and continued to follow her until we finally reached the elevator shaft. From there, we climbed up a ladder to the first floor and entered the utility room. As she headed for the door, I asked, "Where are we going?"

"I think I know where your friend is," she said, as she opened the door to peek outside. "There's an isolation unit on the east wing. That's where Walker keeps surviving patients for study. If she's still alive, that's the only place she'd be. Let's just hope we don't bump into any of those guards." She released her breath in a long sigh and said over her shoulder, "Let's go."

"Wait!" I pulled her back in. "I think it's time to put my gift to good use."

"What are you talking about?"

"In the woods I was able to sense things from a long way off, especially animals. Maybe I can do the same here if I concentrate hard enough."

"No," she argued. "I've told you what could happen if you lose control. You almost did just a few minutes ago!"

"I know. But I'm calm now. And nothing bad can happen if I'm calm, right?"

"Theoretically, yes. But what if I'm wrong?"

"Then you know what to do."

She blushed. "What if that doesn't work again?"

My eyes narrowed to slits. "I meant *run*, Sarah."

"Oh."

"Now stand back." I closed my eyes and focused my thoughts on the corridor outside the room. The spark in my head didn't take long to ignite. The invisible ramification that connected my brain with everything around me allowed me to smell, taste, hear, feel, and even mentally *see* my surroundings out to several hundred yards. The feeling was overwhelming, yet incredibly soothing at the same time. I felt no sense of rivalry within my mind, nor euphoria doping my brain; and yet, for some reason, I felt temped to taste it again. I ignored the feeling, focusing on the things I could sense around me. My mind traveled the empty corridors of the mansion, stopping at a huge metal door marked by a sign: **Block-A**. For some reason, my mind couldn't go pass that threshold. It did, however, reach outside the mansion, sensing the presence of guards swarming the perimeter.

"The halls are empty," I told Sarah, opening my eyes. "All the guards are outside covering the exits."

"Amazing," Sarah whispered in awe. "You can actually *see* them?"

I nodded diffidently, not knowing how to explain the lights, colors, and shapes that my mind was able to interpret as objects, animals, and people. Noting the confounded look on my face, Sarah dropped the subject and readied herself to go out the door. "All right, then," she said, peeking again from the threshold. "Let's go."

Her red curls bounced as she moved along the hallway, graceful as a gazelle. I followed close behind her, though not nearly as gratefully. The polished marble floor of the hallway shone like a mirror, reflecting the lighting fixtures that hung above us, as well as the images of our own bodies. After cornering into another long corridor, I was able to see with my eyes the big metal door that I'd seen in my vision: a massive stainless steel double door that shone nearly as much as the perfect marble floors. A keypad on the wall beside it prompted for an access code.

Sarah quickly punched in some numbers and waited.

"Crap!" she grunted as a cutting beep denied her access. She sighed in frustration and tried again. But the same annoying beep followed the last digit she entered. "The master code isn't working. Walker must've disabled all security clearances after what happened in the lab. We can't get in."

My first reaction was to punch the door, over and over again, while Sarah, her back against the wall, slid down to the floor in dismay. I actually dented the damned thing, but quickly realized I was hurting myself more than it. I pressed my forehead against the cold steel of the door, eyes clenched shut, feeling nothing but hopelessness. I tried to control my breathing, suppressing tears of frustration. Then I took a deep breath and tried to push myself off the door. But something odd happened: the palms of my hands stopped an inch away from touching the door, like a magnet will when driven toward another of the same polarity—yet magnetism wasn't a factor here.

Something was creating an invisible field of energy between me and the door, an energy that allowed me to feel every inch of it...as if it were a part of me. Palpating the invisible field, I realized that this wasn't the first time I'd felt it. I'd felt it in the lab during our first escape, while I was falling into the gorge, and in the river when Sarah almost drowned. Suddenly, everything was clear. This was some aspect of my telekinesis manifesting: the ability to manipulate matter without touching it, once the mind established a connection with the molecular structure of an object.

I couldn't help but see the irony in this. A skeptical physics student endowed with an ability that contradicted his knowledge, the very foundations of his faith? Xavier would've had a blast laughing at me.

Suddenly I found myself reasoning with the impossible—or at least, with what I had *thought* was impossible—and I began to analyze the variables at hand. The more I concentrated on the door, the stronger this force field seemed to become. Pressure only seemed to reinforce it. After running the numbers in my head, I found myself stepping back while pushing at the invisible field, forcing it to expand between me and the door.

"Victor?" Sarah called, clearly confused by my strange behavior.

I stopped at what I thought it was a safe distance, and planted my feet firmly on the ground. Understanding the only logical step left for me to take, I braced myself internally as well and began to push the field—not only with my hands, but with my mind as well. "Sarah, stand back!" I warned as I leaned forward, applying more pressure to the invisible field. The doors creaked loudly then, and Sarah's eyes widened. Her face held a mixture of fear and excitement as she witnessed the paranormal phenomenon.

I closed my eyes as I felt the doors shake on their hinges, and increased the pressure against the force field. The nature of the event itself challenged my concentration, which made my arms weaken and quiver. The door, however, seemed to be finally yielding to the pressure. So I steeled myself and pushed with everything I had.

My feet slid back a couple of inches over the smooth marble, an obvious display that what I was trying to move was far heavier than my meager 160 pounds. My push was followed by a loud metal groan that made me open my eyes. I watched as the extremely fine gap between the two doors began to widen, as the squealing metal bent inwardly towards the isolation ward. Sarah's face lit up with amazement as she saw the case-hardened steel stretch like putty right before her eyes. The gap between the doors was now molded into two triangular openings above and below the middle lock.

My mental strain soon became physical, and my whole body began to shake. My legs weakened and bent, as if trying to bring me down to my knees. But I held my ground. I'll admit that was ready to give up when, suddenly, the locking mechanism burst apart with a loud *spang*, and fragments of its metal parts flew down the corridor beyond as the heavy doors slammed wide open against the interior walls. I was sure the guards would come running given all the noise, but apparently they were all still outside searching the grounds.

I collapsed on my hands and knees, losing connection with my surroundings, completely drained of the energy that had fueled my powers. For a second, I thought I'd lose consciousness. Sarah came to my aid, her arms around my shoulders. "Victor, you okay?"

"Yeah." My jaw quivered. "I... I think so."

"Can you walk?"

"Yes." I pushed myself back to my feet and entered the ward. Sarah followed, casting one final awed glace at the bent doors as we passed them.

The hallway was long and narrow, with about a dozen doors on each side. I tried to concentrate on the insides of those rooms, but it was useless; my hypersenses were completely shot. I couldn't sense anything beyond my own feeble breathing and shaking jaw. A process of elimination was our only option, so we decided to open every door in the ward. Sarah took the right side and I took the left. Door after door, room after room, we found nothing. My hopes were wearing thin when I stumbled upon a locked door. "Sarah!" I whisper-shouted. "This one is locked!"

Sarah rushed over, realizing my weak condition, and decided to take matters into her own hands. With a speed that challenged my ability to follow, she faced the wooden door and threw a perfectly executed sidekick that broke the lock. The door flew open and smashed against the wall. I found myself staring at her like an idiot, a quizzical look on my face.

"What?" she muttered, meeting my eyes.

"Nothing," I said, shaking my head. "Please get to the other doors."

I entered the dark room while Sarah kept opening doors, feeling for the light switch until I found it and flipped it on. The light revealed a male patient. He was strapped down to an operating table, a strange veil covering his eyes. Seeing him so still gave me a very bad feeling. The image of poor Billie was still fresh in my mind, haunting me...yet I knew I couldn't turn away. I had to find out who it was and whether he was still alive. So I walked to the bed and took a closer look.

The restraints around his wrists and ankles were similar to the ones used in psychiatric hospitals: thick brown leather cuffs. I released the straps on his arms, which left behind angry red welts, and a shiver crept down my spine as I removed the strange veil from his face. I recognized the man on the spot—Damian.

His face was relaxed; too relaxed to be alive, I thought. I brought my ear close to his nose to check his breathing. A very faint hiss and tickle of breath reached my ear, and I saw his chest move slightly with the same rhythm. "Sarah!" I called out, remembering her medical training, and waited.

A sudden and forceful pressure on my arm made the hairs on the back of my neck stand on end. *"Shit!"* I hissed under my breath as my heart sank into my stomach. "Damian?" I said, trying to escape his grip. His eyes were still closed. "Damian?!" I said again. His head jerked backwards and his mouth opened, letting out a long, desperate gasp, as if he'd just broken the surface of a mental pool where he'd been submerged for far too long. "Damian? Can you hear me?" His eyes rolled into the back of his head. "Sarah!" I called out again. "I need your help!"

Sarah ran inside the room as Damian began to shake violently. "He's having a seizure. Let him go. Don't hold him."

"I'm not!" I explained. "He's got my arm!"

Sarah helped me loosened his grip.

The seizure ceased as quickly as it began. Sarah had me release his legs restraints, then asked me to help her roll Damian on his side. There we watched his breathing return to normal. "The seizure lasted less than thirty seconds," Sarah said confidently. "He'll be fine."

"Damian?" I said to him. His eyes fluttered rapidly before they finally opened.

"Victor?" he said feebly. "G-g-get me out of here!"

"Don't worry," I said, looking him in the eyes. "I will."

I turned to Sarah and asked her to keep an eye on him while I checked the rest of the rooms. "Meet me at the end of the corridor," I told her, and bolted out of the room.

As I ran down the corridor, I began to feel better—physically, at least. My head was no longer spinning and my body felt as if it were running on pure adrenaline. Suddenly, a spark in my head pointed me in the right direction; good, I was able to sense things again. And this feeling was by far the strongest of all. I sensed what I can only describe as the missing part of my own heart, a chaotic feeling of happiness and desperation that guided me to another locked door. I launched myself like a bull at a *muleta* and broke the door down.

This room was different than the one I'd found Damian in: well lit, with machines beeping and chiming around another capsule bed. The glass shield was foggy—just like Billie's—which made my heart pound. A small clipboard at the foot of the capsule read: *Montgomery.*

My feelings were confirmed.

Quickly, I yanked the opening lever and stepped back, hoping for the best but expecting the worse. The shield unlocked with a loud thud and began to slide open. I let the fumes disperse before I dared to look inside. When I did, I couldn't suppress my tears—she was there. Her eyes were closed and her sable hair was twisted on one side over her shoulder, as beautiful as only she could be. The pink tone in her cheeks gave me a clear indication that she was still alive.

The condition of her mind, however, was yet to be revealed. I could only hope for the best.

"Yvette," I whispered, gliding my knuckles down the curve of her cheek, admiring her perfect bone structure. The pain disappeared then—the chaos in my mind gone. The emptiness I'd felt in my chest was filled by this simple touch. I realized then that she was all I would ever need... to survive, to live, to stay.

"Victor?" she moaned. The sound of her voice allowed me to breathe a sigh of relief. "What happened?" she asked, opening her eyes. "What's wrong?"

"Nothing," I said, wiping a tear from the corner of my eye, "Nothing, now." Stroking her head, I leaned over and kissed her. Her lips were the ultimate nourishment for my famished soul.

"Ahem!" Sarah cleared her throat at the threshold behind me. "I hate to interrupt, but we're in a bit of a situation here. We need to go. Now!"

"Victor?" Yvette shot me a quizzical look. "What's going on? What's happened to you?"

Sarah interjected before I could utter a word. "I'm sorry, I don't mean to be rude, but we just don't have time for this right now. Victor." She turned to me. "I found three more patients, and they seem to be okay. But we have to get a move on if we want to get them out in one piece."

"All right," I agreed.

Yvette scowled at me, as if pressing for an explanation. "Who is she?"

"Oh, I'm sorry. Yvette, this is Sarah. Sarah, Yvette."

"Hi," they said simultaneously, with the same bleak tone.

"Are you going to tell me what's going on?" Yvette asked, confused, while Sarah glared, in a hurry to move on.

"Look," I began, taking off my jacket, "I promise I'll tell you everything as soon as we're safe. But right now I need you to trust me—can you do that?"

She didn't hesitate. "Of course."

"All right then. Put this on." I helped her into my jacket. "Can you walk?"

"I think so."

"Then let's get out of here."

We followed Sarah to the end of the corridor, where three more sickly-looking people waited with Damian. Behind them, a metal door read *Emergency Exit*. Damian seemed collected now, disturbingly calm. Next to him stood a blonde woman. She couldn't have been much older than Damian was, yet she had one of those maternal looks that inspire trust and respect. To her right, a huge black man stood, way past six foot tall, with a physique that resembled a bodybuilder's but the eyes of a man who wouldn't hurt a fly. Standing next to him was the third guy, whose ethnic roots must have been very close to mine. We shared the same height, body type, and even the same black, feathered hair. Had I ever been an actor, this guy would've been my perfect double.

They were all different, yet they all had something in common; they were all staring at the same person in the search of hope and answers. Me.

Funny, I thought. *Just a few weeks ago, my biggest responsibility was to remember to take the trash out on time.* Now I felt somehow responsible for the survival of seven people, including myself. It was enough to give anyone an anxiety attack.

"Is this our exit?" I asked Sarah.

"Yes," she said uneasily, watching a monitor above the door. "This door leads to the meadow. And to the Town Car."

I raised my eyes to the monitor, and discovered what had troubled Sarah. The monitor showed the other side of the exit door, where three armed guards stood with their itchy trigger fingers ready to fulfill Captain Black's orders. Apparently someone had discovered the ruins of the ward door. Though oblivious to our presence on the other side of the exit door, they certainly expected someone to try to come out this way—and seemed eager for that to happen.

"What are we going to do?" the blonde woman said in despair.

"We find another way," Damian suggested.

"There isn't one," I countered, running the numbers in my head. "Okay, listen up. We're going to have to work together if we want to make it out of here alive, you understand?" Everybody nodded. "All right, then. I'm going to need you three," I pointed at the men, "to each handle one of them guards while the girls run to the car. Once in the car," I turned to the girls, "I'll need you to pull in and pick us up, all right?"

The men exchanged confused looks and pondered for a second.

"Are we all good to go?" I asked.

"Wait!" my stunt double snapped. "What are *you* going to do?"

I took a deep breath and said, "I'm going to open the door and disarm the guards for you."

Silence followed my words.

I stood in front of the door, with all their eyes on me, and lifted my open palms. I closed my eyes and concentrated as my senses roved outward, feeling my mind connecting to the objects I needed to move. The door and the guards' weapons were the only things in my mind now. I knew that in order for this to work, it needed to happen in one abrupt move. Anything less than that would alert the guards and ruin our element of surprise. And though the truth was that I was dealing with something beyond my own comprehension, there was something strangely familiar about it—something that compelled me to believe I could do it.

After establishing a solid connection with the objects that I wanted to manipulate, I began to concentrate on that invisible force field that linked me to them. I could feel the energy draining into me from the atmosphere as my hands were pushed back towards my chest, and the force field became bigger, stronger. Again, the mental strain became physical, and my arms and legs began to quiver. I opened my eyes with the strong determination to succeed, and launched my hands forward in one violent thrust.

The metal door exploded out of its frame and landed at the far end of the meadow, but not before striking the guards in its path, wreaking havoc on their fragile bodies.

"GO!" Sarah shouted to rest of the group, who'd frozen in astonishment after witnessing the incredible spectacle. I collapsed to my knees, drained and exhausted, while Damian and the other two men went after the now-disarmed guards.

"Victor!" Yvette ran to my aid as an alarm buzzed stridently throughout the mansion. It wasn't until I heard her voice that I realized Sarah had also stayed behind. She was kneeling in front of me with a concerned look on her face.

"How are you? Can you get up and go on?" she asked fretfully.

Panting, I raised my eyes and scowled at them. "What the hell are you still doing here? Go! Get the car!"

"I'm not leaving without you," Yvette countered with a strong grip on my arm.

"Victor?" Sarah seemed to be asking me what to do.

"Go," I repeated, meeting Sarah's gaze. "Get the others. We don't have much time."

"All right," she conceded, turning her eyes to Yvette. "You got him?"

"Yeah," she said, exchanging looks with Sarah, who then turned and darted out the doorless exit.

Yvette helped me back to my feet and walked me out into the cold night, where Damian and the other two guys had overpowered the three injured guards. But our problems were far from over. Surely the alarm, triggered by the loss of the emergency door, had alerted the rest of the squad. It was just a matter of time before they caught up with us now. I gathered in the rest of the group and was asking them to stick together when I looked up and saw a pair of headlights headed our way.

It was the Town Car. Sarah had done it—we were one step closer to leaving this horrible place! But my premature celebration of victory was thwarted when a sudden spark in my head alerted me of the danger also coming our way. A jeep filled with paramilitary forces was cornering around the building, and they knew exactly where we were now. Sarah stopped right in front of us at the same time the loaded jeep stopped at a safe confrontational distance, both autos facing each other. A brilliant searchlight from the jeep pinned us before we could move any farther.

"Freeze!" a warning was shouted through a bullhorn. *"Don't move! We have been authorized to use deadly force against you. Surrender now!"*

Damian raised his hands and stepped forward, as if surrendering to the squad, his face hard as stone. "On my signal, run to the car," he said in a low voice as he walked past me. Not knowing what his plan was, all I could do was take Yvette's hand and wait. "I surrender!" he yelled to the jeep.

"Stay where you are," the soldier on the bullhorn commanded.

Damian looked at me over his shoulder and gave a quick nod. I tightened my grip on Yvette's hand and told her to get ready.

What happened next occurred in a matter of seconds.

"Now!" Damian shouted, as he clenched his surrendering hands into powerful fists. With this action, all the lights on the jeep exploded in perfect synchrony—even the headlights—leaving the soldiers stunned and confused in the darkness. I didn't stop to ask what had happened; I just ran as fast as I could to the car, the rest of the group following. I opened the back passenger door and shoved Yvette into the car, then held the door open as the rest of the guys got in too.

That's when my hypersenses expanded suddenly, allowing me to hear the words of one of the soldiers a hundred feet from us. *"I've got a clear shot on Bellator, sir."*

"Take it."

My mind ignited the same slow motion trance I'd experienced back in the lab during my first escape, and I was able to track the bullet the moment it was fired. I wish now that I'd erected a shield against it, but I hesitated when I realized its trajectory couldn't possibly hit me. At first, I thought the shooter had just missed his target... but too late, I realized I was wrong.

The shot wasn't going to miss. It was going to hit dead center, just as the trained sniper had intended when he pulled the trigger. The sniper, however, had fired at the wrong man: my stunt double, the man who had the misfortune of sharing my general build and features. The bullet slammed through his head before he could reach for the door. Blood, gray matter, and bone fragments splattered over the roof of the car. My slow-motion trance, which had made the event all the more painful to watch, ended as soon as his lifeless body hit the ground.

I was aghast. Another life wasted!

A hail of bullets reached out for us after that first deadly shot, producing the kind of uproar I'd heard only in war movies. This time I threw up a barrier that turned the bullets to dust as they struck; I could feel the impacts as they shattered themselves against it. I jumped into the passenger seat and shouted out to Sarah to punch it. She shoved her foot on the accelerator and turned the car around, leaving the jeep behind us. Some of the bullets managed to reach us as my shield weakened with distance, blowing out the rear window as we got away. The granulated glass showered down over Yvette, Damian and the two others in the back seat, and even Sarah and I got peppered with a few fragments. She cringed but kept racing towards the gate, which we knew would be closed and guarded.

Her eyes widened when she saw the assault team standing in front of the gate, which also began to shoot at us with everything they had. Tapping the energy pervading the atmosphere, I wrapped us in a 360° shield.

"I can't ram the gate with this car!" Sarah said frantically. "Victor?!"

I raised my hand and tried to link my mind to the gate, but it was too far away. Plus, I was too weak from my latest round of paranormal activity. It was all I could do to maintain the shield keeping us alive. We were doomed. "I can't!" I bawled in frustration.

Sarah began to decelerate.

"Don't stop," Damian ordered, leaning forward between the front seats, his open palm aimed at the approaching gate. "Go faster!" he shouted to Sarah, who floored it at his command. As Damian's hand began to vibrate between us, we watched the soldiers tossed into the air like toys, one by one. With no more bullets flying our way, I dropped the shield, groaning with relief as Sarah maneuvered the car straight toward the iron gate and braced for impact. But the gate began to vibrate at the same rhythm as Damian's hand and, just feet away from collision, burst wide open. We darted through, and Damian swiftly turned and aimed his hand back toward the gate. It swung violently shut on the pursuing jeep. The impact made the driver lose control of the jeep, which swerved and tipped over off the road.

"That'll buy us some time," Damian said smugly as Sarah and I exchanged uneasy glances, understanding there was now another paranormal threat out in the world besides me.

Chapter 10
Piano Key

THE TOWN CAR'S engine objected strenuously as Sarah pushed the bullet-holed car to its limits. The tires squealed when she finally cornered onto the main road. The car flew along the empty highway. A distinctive glare coming from the distant horizon made me look up: the sun was rising, welcoming me to another day I'd survived to see. I turned to Sarah, who was taking turns watching me and the road. As soon as our eyes met, she flashed me a wide, victorious smile.

I smiled too. We didn't need words to understand each other's feelings at that point. After everything we'd gone through, we'd made it. We had actually made it!

Our celebration was cut short when the blonde woman in the back seat began to scream hysterically. I turned to find the brawny black guy barely conscious, with his hands covering his midsection. Blood flowed between his fingers. "Easy, buddy," I said, reaching for his hands. He groaned. "I'm sorry, buddy, but I need to look." I moved his hands away carefully and saw blood oozing out of a nasty gunshot wound on the left upper side of his torso. "He's been shot," I said, turning to Sarah.

The blonde lady began to scream again, only this time she didn't stop. Sarah cursed and hit the wheel.

"Hey, hey, hey!" Damian turned to the screaming lady. "What's your name?"

"Laura," she cried, hyperventilating.

"Laura?" Damian glared at her. "Shut the hell up!"

It was crude, but it worked. Laura stopped screaming and began to sob quietly, staring at Damian with accusing eyes. Damian turned back to me. After another quick look at the big man's wound, he shook his head with bleak eyes. I gave him a disapproving look and turned back to the injured man. "Hey, what's your name, buddy?"

"R-r-roger," he said feebly, "M-my name's Roger."

"Okay, Roger. You're going to be all right. We're going to help you, okay? I just need you to keep pressure on this for a little while longer, can you do that?"

He grunted as I put his hands back on the wound, nodding. "Yeah."

My eyes slid to Yvette, who was in complete shock. "Hey," I said softly, stroking her head. "Are you okay?" She nodded, reached for my hand, and pressed it against her cheek—she was trembling. It was only when I leaned towards the back that I realized how much wind was entering the car through the hole where the rear windshield had been. "We need to stop to regroup," I called to Sarah over my shoulder.

"And where do you suggest we do that?" was her tart reply.

I kissed Yvette's hand and sat back on the passenger seat, but not before I locked eyes with Damian again. He seemed to be scrutinizing everyone in the car, especially me. I dug through the glove compartment, and luckily I found exactly what we needed: an address. I asked Sarah for the map that had taken us out of the woods and studied it. It didn't take me long to get my bearings and locate the place I'd decided to go.

"Keep driving south," I told Sarah. "I think I've found a place we can go."

"Whoa!" Damian broke in. "I'm not going anywhere until I get my wife."

"Your wife?" I asked, taken aback.

"Walker said my wife would pay the price if I didn't cooperate. That's the only reason I agreed to be his guinea pig for the last three days. I'm afraid when he finds out I'm one of the people who'd escaped..." he paused, "...that he'll send someone for her."

"Wait," Sarah jumped in, "Walker's been studying you for *three days?*"

Damian ignored Sarah's question and turned back to me. "I need to get to my wife." His statement had the tone of a command—no, it was more like a warning, as if he were hinting that he'd stop at nothing and yield to no one in order to get what he wanted. Having watched what he was capable of, I knew I'd be a fool to piss this man off. Besides, how could I judge him for his adamant determination? Just an hour ago I was operating under the same sort of compulsion, so I knew exactly what he was going through. Yet I couldn't stop thinking about the safety of the rest of us.

Damian was borderline distraught and growing more impatient by the minute. It was like watching a time bomb getting ready to blow. I considered for a minute, throwing glances at every person in the car, especially my Yvee, and then tried to handle the situation. "Where is she?" I asked Damian.

"We rented a cabin twenty minutes south of Ketchikan. Walker made me call her after I woke up from the procedure." His jaw went taut with regret. "I told her everything was okay. I told her to wait for me."

"Does Walker know the location of this cabin?"

Damian's face drooped, anger overflowing in his eyes. "Yes," he rasped.

"Are you aware of the details of your new condition, and the side effects of the procedure?"

"The good and evil bullshit?" Damian's voice was hard. "Yes. I am."

A profound silence engulfed the car as I ran the numbers in my head. In the rearview mirror I saw Yvette, Laura, and Roger exchanging confused looks.

"Stop the car," I said to Sarah after a long moment.

"What?" She frowned confused.

"Stop the car," I repeated. "Now." She gave me a puzzled look and began to pull over. "Check on Roger, will you?" The car stopped on the gravelly shoulder lane and I opened my door in a hurry. "Damian?" I called as I got out of the car.

Damian exited the car and followed me several feet away from the vehicle.

"Look," I said as I turned around to face him, "If you truly know your condition, then you know your exasperation can only lead to disaster. You need to calm down, understand?"

"How can you ask me to do that when I know what those people can do to my wife? When *you* know that—"

"I know!" I burst out angrily. "But for her sake and yours, you need to learn to control your feelings!" I took a deep breath and lowered my voice. "Sarah told me the details of our...condition. Once we lose our volition, it's over. We'll become a threat to the people we love—and we'll be taken down like rabid dogs. By R.C. Labs, by the police, by the military, or anyone else who learns of our existence."

"I won't let that happen. I've seen what I can do. I can take on a whole army if necessary—"

"Oh yeah? At what cost?"

"I can control it!"

"No, you can't." I sighed ruefully. "Not alone. Believe me, I know."

"What are you saying?"

I took a second to respond. "I was scheduled for termination—vivisection—when Sarah got me out of the lab. You and I shared the same procedure, yet for some reason Walker intended to keep *you* alive. That means you have something he wants...and I'm sure he wants it back. By now he knows you've escaped, and he knows where you're going next. But knowing the level of control you have over your powers, I doubt he'd be stupid enough to come at you head-on. He'll wait for an opportunity to catch you off guard. And the only way to do *that* is by making you believe there's no danger."

I paused. "Going back to your cabin is a death trap." Damian looked thoughtful. "Unless," I continued, "we can find a way to create a diversion that'll allow us to go in and out undetected. Of course, that doesn't lower the risk factor. We can still spring the trap and get caught in another confrontation."

"We?"

"I'm coming with you, Damian. I'm going to help you get her back."

He scoffed. "You don't even know us. Why would you do that? Why would you risk your life?"

My response was plain and simple. "Because it's the right thing to do. Just like getting these people to safety is the right thing to do." I looked into his eyes and saw reason coming back to his troubled mind. "Let me get them out of harm's way, and I promise you I'll go with you."

Damian considered for a moment. "Time's of the essence," he said finally. "We have to move fast." He stuck out his hand. I reached out and bound my promise to help him with a strong shake.

***

Back in the car, Sarah informed me that Roger's wound had looked a lot worse than it actually was, and that he was going to be okay. All she needed was a medical kit to patch him up—which was great news, considering the circumstances. In the few minutes I'd spent talking to Damian, she had also managed to bring the others up to speed on what was happening. She did, however, manage to keep the fact that Damian and I were on the verge of turning into vicious, unstoppable monsters out of the conversation. Later she told me that was something I should tell Yvette myself, and I agreed. Sarah's abridged explanation had been enough to leave Yvette, Laura, and Roger in complete shock, so I figured I should let that settle before I jammed anything else in.

Back on the road, I let the severity of my thoughts disconnect me from reality. Once or twice, I think, Sarah tried to talk to me, but I was too far away to hear her. I had no idea how I was going to ask Yvette to wait for me again, or tell Sarah I'd decided to go on another suicide mission—without her this time. Knowing how stubborn she was, I knew I'd have to talk her out of coming with me. By now Sarah had begun to think of herself as my official sidekick and I… well, I had begun to care about her. A lot. She was not only my friend, but the woman who'd saved my life more than once. I didn't have a shred of doubt about my feelings for Yvette; I loved her more than life itself. But I really hoped I'd never have to explain to her, or to anybody else for that matter, my feelings towards Sarah… because that was something I couldn't explain myself.

Sarah followed my directions into a small gravel path off the highway. At the end of the road stood a log cabin. The place was rustic in nature, yet it held a beauty I'd only seen in paintings. A peaceful pond, just a short stroll away from the entrance, reflected a dull image of the old cabin; tall, majestic firs kept it well hidden from prying eyes. The name *Johnson* was stenciled on the rusty mailbox outside the porch.

I asked Sarah to stop the car and stay put while I knocked on the door. I tried to be subtle, but the squeaky floorboards on the porch gave away my presence before I got the chance to knock. My knuckles were left hanging in the air when the solid wooden door flew open and a rifle barrel stopped an inch away from my face.

"Whoa! Whoa! It's me!" I waved my hands frantically in front of the cocked weapon.

"Mr. Victor?" Denali lowered his rifle as soon as he recognized me.

"Yeah. It's me." I exhaled heavily and tried to recover from the shock. "Geez! You scared the shit out of me!"

"You scared *me*. I wasn't exactly expecting company after what happened last night." He paused and uncocked his rifle. "How did you manage to find me, anyway?"

I pulled a wallet from my pocket and handed it to him. "You actually *did* leave your wallet in the Town Car. I found it in the glove compartment." He took it and thanked me with a confused look on his face. "Look, Denali, I'm sorry I've dragged you into this. But you're the only other person I know within three thousand miles that I feel I can trust."

"Are those your friends?" he asked, throwing a quick look toward the car, where Sarah stood impatiently by the open door.

"Yes," I said quickly. "And one of us is wounded. Can you help us?"

He looked at me for a long second and smiled. "Sure, Mr. Victor," he agreed, inviting me in. "I have plenty of food and water. You and your friends help yourselves."

"Thank you, Denali." I heaved a deep sigh of relief and patted him on the shoulder. Then I turned to beckon the others to the house. I did the introductions as they came inside. Yvette quickly noticed that Sarah wasn't introduced, but rather greeted by Denali as a known acquaintance. "Do you have something for them to wear?" I asked Denali, pointing out that everyone—except for Sarah and me, of course—was wearing hospital gowns.

"Sure," he said, watching Yvette walk into the house barefoot. "This, um, this was my grandmother's cabin," he added. "I'm s-sure there are still some dresses in the closet that you can wear. Some shoes too. You're welcome to take a look," he said, pointing at a built-in closet in the living room. Yvette thanked him and walked to the closet, where she began to dig through a couple of boxes labeled "Granny's Stuff."

Damian helped Laura bring Roger to the couch, and Sarah began to treat his wound with a first-aid kit Denali fetched for her. Meanwhile, I brought Denali up to speed with everything that had happened during our daring escape from the lab. The poor man didn't take it so well. His face paled, and for a moment I thought he was going to throw up.

As soon as Sarah finished with Roger, she came over to me, took my face in both hands, and tilted my head to the side. "I need to clean the cut on your head," she said, and began to unwrap the piece of cloth that covered my wound. "Don't move," she commanded as she wiped the dry blood from my forehead with a piece of gauze soaked in alcohol. The sting made me flinch. "Oh, come on! Don't be such a baby."

I scowled at the grin on her face. Out of the corner of my eye, I caught Damian staring at us. He'd found some clothes in Denali's closet and was now leaning against the door frame with his arms folded, watching Sarah replace my dressing. "Done!" Sarah finally said, placing the last piece of tape over the wrap.

"Now all you have to do is kiss it to make it better," Damian said sarcastically.

Sarah narrowed her eyes at him and then turned back to me. She took my face in both hands again, pressed her lips against my bandages, and smacked a kiss that was heard throughout the entire cabin. "There!" she said with a smile on her face.

Damian sneered.

Looking in his direction, I noticed that Yvette had been standing behind him this whole time, her eyes moving back and forth between Sarah and me. She stalked hastily to the front door and opened it. "Yvette?" I called after her. She stopped at the threshold and waited, her eyes looking at the floor. "Where are you going?" I asked.

Her eyes rose with a glare that pierced right through me, practically making a hole in my chest. "I need to get some air," she said icily and stormed out of the cabin, slamming the door behind her. Damian gave me a trenchant look, and walked over to Denali.

"I'll be back," I told Sarah, and ran after Yvette. I didn't have to be a genius to understand what had upset her; I only hoped I could set things straight. I looked around from the porch and found Yvette standing by the pond, her eyes facing the water. As I walked over there, I examined her pick from Granny's Stuff. She was wearing a tea-length flowered dress that ended exactly at the beginning of a pair of three-quarter length boots. The dress was old, yet it fit perfectly, as if tailored intentionally to accentuate the curves of her body. The boots were made of suede with an embroidered pattern on the sides, which gave them a Pocahontas look.

The cherry on top of the ice cream was the black-and-white Yankees jacket I'd given her when we escaped from the lab, which she'd decided to wear over the dress. And although the whole outfit was a complete mismatch, I couldn't help noticing how well she pulled it off. Her beauty was so compelling that she could've been wearing candy wrappers for a dress and still would have made it look like a fashion statement.

"Yvee?" I called, trying to sound comforting—but, for some reason, I sounded guilty instead. "Are you all right?" I asked.

She spun around and faced me; anger filled her eyes. "No, Victor! I'm not all right! I thought I understood what was happening, but I don't! I'm more confused now than ever before—and it's killing me!" She paused and took a deep, calming breath. "Please, Victor... just tell me the truth."

It took a long moment for me to figure out what truth she was talking about. I really didn't want to try to answer an unasked question, especially one where I'd be at a loss myself. "Well," I finally began. "I still don't have all the answers, Yvee. All I know is that the procedure wasn't what we thought—"

"I'm not talking about the procedure!" she cut me off sharply. "I'm talking about you and Carrot-Top over there!"

Though her words didn't catch me entirely by surprise, they still startled me. "Sarah?" I said innocently. "She's my friend, Yvee... She saved my life. Several times."

She sighed in defeat, her voice calm now. "Yeah... I know." She paused regretfully. "I'm sorry. I don't know why I'm acting like a psycho... *am* I acting like a psycho?" she asked distressfully, too cutely for me not to laugh.

"No," I said, reaching out to her. Her eyes followed my hands as they entwine with hers, then rose to meet my gaze. A coating of tears glazed her amazing baby blues now. My smile disappeared as I got lost inside her eyes, which sent an inexplicable shock of energy throughout my entire body. A message was decoded in my brain in a fraction of a second, as if the wave of energy I'd felt from her had been nothing more than an unspoken question my mind had been able to sense through our touch. "*Do you still love me?*" my mind interpreted, as her eyes probed the depths of mine.

"With all my heart," I said aloud, tightening our clasped hands.

My words startled Yvette, yet a soft smile lit up her face. "What?" she asked.

I shook my head, as if coming out of a trance. "I'm sorry. I thought you asked me something."

"I didn't say anything," she mused. "But I felt it... Just like I felt your answer before it came out of your lips." She exhaled heavily, confused. "This is weird. Should we be worried?"

"About reading each other's feelings?" I smiled. "I wouldn't change it for the world."

She grinned and cupped the side of my face. Her eyes closed as if concentrating on what she was able to feel now. "Wow," she exclaimed softly. "Is this real?"

"What do you feel?" I asked.

She opened her eyes. "I feel... *you.*" She smiled and blushed. "Do you really love me this much?"

"Of course." My voice was merely a whisper, yet it held all the power of the truth.

"Then say it," she said, just as quietly.

I took her face in my hands and lowered my head to her eye level, searching for her soul in that perfect, clear ocean inside her eyes, and said, "I really do love you this much, Yvette Hermione Montgomery."

"Oh my God! I'd hoped you'd forgotten that awful name by now." Her voice was light, but her face relaxed as her lips curved into the most pleasant smile I've ever seen, as if some terrible pain had just been soothed by my words. It was then that I realized those three simple words had become our very own salvation—three words that when played in unison become the most beautiful and powerful sound of all. Like a piano key: a high-octave note buried deep inside our hearts, a key that when finally played could ignite the most intense and profound feeling known to humanity. A feeling that can make any and all logic and reason disappear; a feeling that once felt can dictate the course of the rest of your life.

I had just played this key inside Yvette's heart.

When her eyes opened again, they opened as if to a brand new world. No traces of fear or sadness haunted her face now. She was happy, and so was I. This inexplicable connection that our touch had created between us had allowed our minds to read our feelings like open books. Yet understanding that I now knew how much she felt for me didn't stop Yvette from striking that high note inside my heart as well. She cupped the back of my head and, pulling my face close to hers, said, "I love you too, Victor."

At that moment, nothing else mattered—nothing. The entire world's population could have circled around us, and we still would have felt as if we were the only ones in it. Our lips could no longer resist the urge to reach out for each other, so we closed our eyes and let our love take over. Soon we found ourselves lost in a kiss that ignited that powerful spark in my head again, allowing my hypersenses to expand so that I felt everything in extremes: the beating of her heart, the warmth of her body, the susurrus of her breathing, the taste of her lips...it was driving me absolutely mad. But this time, my mind was not only sensing and reading, it was also being sensed and read by Yvette's, creating a connection beyond our comprehension. The ecstasy we felt through this connection was such that neither of us wanted to let go from the kiss. The need for oxygen, however, soon made us break apart, if only to catch our breath.

What we witnessed then made us realize my mind had gone a little farther than just connecting with Yvette's mind and senses.

Stones from the shore of the pond were hovering around us, like planets orbiting a powerful binary star. It was like watching the abstract power of our love, laid bare by this otherwise intangible event. Alas, the connection with them broke as we realized that, and they pattered to the ground. Yvette laughed in astonishment. "Wow!" she panted, still trying to catch her breath. Her awe-filled eyes locked with mine. "Did you do that?"

"I guess I did," I admitted. "I'm still trying to control this...this thing I have, you know? But it sometimes gets out of hand." I stopped as my voice began to sound cagy and studied Yvette for a moment, wondering about the connection that had allowed her to sense my feelings. Was it just a projection of my new mental abilities, or had Yvette's mind also been altered by the procedure? The mere thought of it frightened me.

"What is it?" she asked, as she noticed my scrutiny.

"Nothing," I said feebly, then: "No. I won't lie. It's just that... My brain was changed by Walker's procedure, Yvee. Yours could have been altered too. Maybe not in the same way as mine or Damian's—I mean, according to Sarah, this is the rarest of side effects—but it could still carry some consequences. That's why

I need you to tell me if you feel anything strange at all, anything that you feel is out of the ordinary."

"Well," she began with a smile, "there's one thing... Look!" she said, placing her hands firmly over mine, her eyes fixed on them. At first I couldn't see what she was trying to show me, but then she finally said it: "My tremors are gone!" she exclaimed, tears in her eyes. I smiled, realizing what a big deal this was. I'd felt the same way when I realized my headaches were gone.

Of course, I would never have agreed to let Walker cure them had I known the price I was about to pay, but...

"This is great!" I celebrated with her.

"What about your headaches?" she asked excited.

"They're gone, too." My response was short; I didn't want to get into details for the fear of ruining our happy moment.

"You know what this means?" Her question was rhetorical. "We have another chance..." she paused, as if waiting for me to finish the sentence. Her eyes were enough for me to go back in time and remember our conversation under the weeping willow.

"To live?" I asked softly.

"To live," she confirmed with a smile.

Two worries invaded my mind at that moment. One was the possibility of the change wrought by the dark energy, a transformation that would only lead to my demise. The other was the thought of having found the love of my life, only to lose her again.

I pushed the worries into the back of my mind and locked them away, hoping I'd never see them again.

But neither our celebration nor our happy moment lasted long. A brand new chapter in our ordeal was about to start, and there was nothing we could do to stop it. I was still holding Yvette when a distressed call yanked us back to reality. "Mr. Victor?" Denali yelled.

"What's wrong?" I shouted over my shoulder.

"I dunno! You better come and take a look!"

My eyes followed him as he ran back into the cabin, scared and confused. I tried to keep calm; somehow, I knew I had to. I could sense that something terrible was about to happen. I asked Yvette to come with me; she held my hand with both hands and walked with me along the path. I couldn't help but notice someone staring at us from the window, following us with her eyes as we walked back to the cabin. It was Sarah; her eyes seemed glossy and sad, yet fixed on us.

I needed no clairvoyance to realize that she had been watching us all along. I had to admit that her surveillance made me feel uneasy... And after learning how Yvette felt about Sarah, I knew that Yvette wouldn't like it either. So I kept my eyes away from the window, thinking that if I didn't look in that direction, maybe Yvette wouldn't look either. But once again, I underestimated the female power of perception. When I turned back to Yvette, I noticed she was already glaring into the window. It was then that I realized that Yvette had probably noticed Sarah presence even before *I* did.

It seemed odd that none of my newly acquired powers were a match for feminine intuition.

Yvette wrapped her arm around my waist, sending a distinctive and intentional signal of possession. Her eyes wouldn't turn away from that window—they almost seemed defiant. I took hold of her, mirroring her gesture, and picked up the pace, trying to end this awkward moment. Sarah took one last look at us and turned away from the window, thank God. I couldn't help wondering what was going through her head at that moment.

When Yvette and I walked into the cabin, we found everyone on their feet, standing around the big couch where Roger had laid down to rest. "What's going on?" I asked, cutting between them. The fact that nobody answered me straightaway should have tipped me to the severity of the situation. Sarah, who was now kneeling next to the couch, held a belt folded into a wad and was trying to slide it between Roger's teeth as a protection. He was having a seizure-like episode and was grinding his teeth. She was able to successfully slide the belt into place right before he began to shake with uncontrollable spasms. I didn't have to be an expert to realize that this wasn't a normal seizure. Roger's body was rejecting whatever had been deployed inside his brain; the question was, would he live through it?

His back suddenly arched, his eyes rolling to the back of his head. The whole experience was terrifying and painful to watch. One final spasm shuddered through his body as we all just stood there, watching, powerless to help him. Once the convulsions stopped, Sarah asked Damian to help her roll the nearly three-hundred-pound man onto his side while she fixed a pillow under his head. "Roger?" Sarah called, trying to get a response from him. But he was out. "He's not responding," she said.

"Oh my God!" Laura exclaimed. "Is he going to die?"

"No!" Sarah said quickly, but then she shook her head and turned back to me. "...I don't know. His vitals are normal. But for some reason he's fallen into a comatose state. It's the first time I've seen something like this. We have no choice but to wait it out."

A strange mixture of pain and anger filled me as I watched Roger lie there, completely helpless. I felt pain because no one should have to go through such suffering, and anger because I knew the responsible ones hadn't paid yet and maybe never would. The feelings overwhelmed me, and I began to feel my eyes burning with my anger.

"Victor!" Sarah chided me, realizing my feelings were getting too intense for me to control. "Maybe you need to step outside for a moment."

I exhaled sharply, understanding Sarah's concern, and turned and headed for the door. "Victor?" Yvette tried to intercept me at the door, her brows knitted in confusion.

"I'm fine," I lied unconvincingly. "I just need some fresh air."
I forced a smile and opened the door.

"Okay," she breathed. "If you say so."

I faked another smile and walked away.

I wasn't trying to lie to Yvette by keeping her in the dark about my condition. I honestly thought I had it under control—and that somehow I could find a way to reverse the change. I suppose my logic was blinded by hope. Whatever the case, I didn't want her to know that the man she loved was turning into a monster. Not until I was absolutely sure there was no turning back.

I walked back to the pond, wringing my hands, trying to keep them from shaking. For a second, I felt that dreadful contest within my mind, where my anger tried to overpower my will and become my reason. I closed my eyes and, once again, I began to work to calm my mind. But to my frightened surprise, abating my anger was becoming increasingly difficult—and I was beginning to feel my evil extreme battering at my defenses. After a few minutes of mental battle, I was able to regain complete control over my thoughts and feelings. However, the struggle had left me weak and irritable—the perfect state for the dark energy to strike again.

A twig snapped behind me. "I asked you to stay in the cabin, Yvette," I said wearily, rubbing my eyes with the heel of my hands.

"It's not Yvette." Sarah's counter made me turn; her voice seemed changed, somehow, unlike the friendly tone I used to hear from her. "Are you okay?"

"Yeah… just, uh… just a little shaken up, that's all." I forced a smile.

"Really?" She sounded upset. "You're going to lie to me, too?"

"I'm not lying to anybody, Sarah."

"Victor, Yvette just asked me what the hell happened with you in that room," she scolded. "She's completely oblivious about your condition."

"What did you tell her?" I asked frantically.

"I didn't know *what* to say!" Her response put me at ease; I sighed. "Victor, you need to tell her."

"There's nothing to tell." I turned my eyes to the pond; I couldn't lie to her face. "I can control it, and if I can control it, I can reverse it." I tried to sound as convincing as I could, but I'm sure my body language was giving me away. I've never been a good liar.

"Can you?"

I turned to look at her; her eyes, like her words, were filled with disbelief. I had to look away again. "Look, Victor," she began. "I know you think you're protecting her. But you can't protect anybody by keeping the truth from them. That only complicates things even more. And in the end, you're only going to hurt her."

"I'll—"

"Look, *you're not alone.* I'm going to help you exhaust every single possibility in an effort to stop the change, and even reverse it if we can. But you need to be open to the idea that we may not succeed. And if that's the case, don't you think that she'd love you more if you'd let her be there for you and help you try? I know *I* would—I mean..." she trailed off. "She deserves to know, Victor."

I turned back to her, shaken by her acumen. She was making too much sense for me to ignore. "You're right. She deserves to know."

Sarah sighed, relieved that she had gotten through me. She gave me a quick smile and turned back to the cabin.

"Sarah?" I called, realizing that something she said had intrigued me. She turned. The wind blew her ginger curls out of her face; her eyes opened wide, waiting for my words. "Are you *really* willing to exhaust every single possibility for me?"

"Of course." She seemed surprised that I'd asked.

"Why?"

"Saving your life is becoming a bad habit, I guess." She let out a soft chuckle. "Besides, we're friends, right?" She turned to walk back to the cabin.

"Sarah?" I called again.

She stopped and turned to me once again, lifting her eyebrows. "Yes?"

"Thank you."

I had never meant those words as much as I did at that moment. And though she gave me no reply, I know she felt the sentiment in my voice. She just smiled her dimpled smile and walked away.

Chapter 11
Mayhem

I STAYED BEHIND, facing the pond, wondering how to break the news to Yvette without freaking her out. After a few minutes of brain-wracking, I realized there was no way she *wouldn't* freak out, so I decided to just steel myself and tell her.

By then, gray clouds had begun to streak the sky, blown in by the sporadic breeze that had been chasing us all morning. I closed my eyes and let the first drop of rain hit my face, amused by the fact that I could feel it before it actually reached my skin.

I ran back inside as soon as I felt the deluge coming down above me, and hit the door just as the rain began to pour. I was determined to talk to Yvette immediately. I cleaned my shoes on the ancient welcome mat that lay at the front door and walked in, but Sarah intercepted me before I could find Yvette. "I think you need to talk to Damian," she said, frightened. "He's really freaking me out."

"Okay," I answered, confused. A quick glance into the living room made me realize what Sarah was talking about. Damian was loading weapons with Denali. They were standing next to a gun cabinet I'd failed to notice when we first arrived. It seemed that Denali was either a gun collector, or one of those people who prepares for Armageddon. Whatever the case, he was *packed*. "What the hell's going on?" I asked.

"I've wasted enough time here," Damian responded aggressively, never taking his eyes from the double-barrel shotgun he was loading. "I have to get to my wife."

"Whoa! Whoa! Wait a second!" I exclaimed. "You can't just go to your cabin waving guns around."

"Why the hell not?" He tucked a pistol in the back pocket of the camouflage army pants he was wearing.

"Well, for starters, the place is probably already guarded. We talked about this! These people have orders to shoot us on sight."

"Not *us*, Victor." Damian stared at me as he said these words. He turned to Denali and gave him the kind of look a boss would give to a servant. Head down, Denali walked away. Damian leaned over next to me and whispered, his voice ominous, "I know why they killed that kid back at the Lab. They thought it was *you*." He moved back, his face stony. He no longer whispered. "Dr. Walker wants *you* dead, Victor. Not us. Back in the Lab, we were just bait in order to attract *you*."

"And what makes you think that?" I tried to sound as indifferent as possible. I was getting the vibe that Damian didn't like me very much, and to be honest, I was beginning to feel the same way about him. It was nothing personal; on the contrary, it was something I couldn't control. If there's an innate nature in cats and dogs that makes them hate each other, then Damian and I were definitely developing something of the sort.

"I can *sense* it, Victor." He gave me a portentous smile. "The same way you can." His face reflected nothing but arrogance, as if he were trying to show off what he was capable of now. This wasn't the same man I'd spoken to on the highway.

"Then you should be able to sense the danger I sense about this." My words came out as fast as I thought them. "If you go in in an offensive mode, you'll lose. You and your wife will be killed."

The cocky grin suddenly disappeared from his face and his eyes turned hesitant, as if trying to decide whether or not to believe me. The truth was that I couldn't sense any danger in that peaceful place, let alone his wife, who was at least ten miles away. But I needed to do something to make him listen. I wasn't trying to scare him, but to save him from making a big mistake. His plan was a terrible idea, and I didn't need special powers to see that—just common sense and a tad of reality check.

"You can sense that?" he asked, dead serious.

"Yes," I replied earnestly, trying to fill my voice with conviction. "You're going to get us all killed with your commando strategies if you're not careful."

"So, do you have a better idea?"

"As a matter of fact, I do."

For the next hour we discussed a plan that involved a note that Damian was going to write, directing his wife to meet him at a restaurant on the outskirts of town—a public place full of people. Denali was to deliver the note, driving an old pickup truck he kept in the garage. The old Toyota Tacoma belonged to his dad, who used to run his own landscaping business, *Johnson & Sons.* Fortunately, the logo was still visible on both sides of the black sand pearl truck, which would definitely work to our advantage. Denali even had his dad's old overalls, which he was going to wear in order to create the perfect disguise.

Meanwhile, Damian and I were to drive Denali's sedan to the restaurant and wait for his wife to arrive. But Damian insisted on going to the cabin, too—and he wouldn't have it any other way. He maintained that he could hide in the truck bed while Denali delivered the message. He said that he would know if anything was wrong just by gauging her reaction. I personally thought that he just wanted to see her, which I felt was an unnecessary risk. But then again, who was I to judge? I'd just hiked a rainforest for three days with absolutely no provisions, just to break into a highly guarded facility and dodge bullets on my way out, all so I could rescue the woman I loved.

Eventually Damian won the argument, and we agreed to hide in the truck bed while the note was delivered. Yes—we. I told Damian that I'd hide there with him in case he needed my help. And despite the fact that he was acting oddly hostile towards everybody, I had never turned my back on a promise. Dad had always taught me that a man's word is his bond, and I wasn't going to betray his teachings—or his memory, for that matter. My decision to go on this trip wasn't well received by Yvette, who sat in the middle of the living room, listening to us argue.

"What?" Yvette jumped up from the sofa when I proposed this. "Why? Why do *you* have to go?"

I quickly pulled her aside to talk to her—although I don't know why I did that, as the living room was a fifteen by fifteen box without much privacy. Nonetheless, I tried to keep my voice down. "I *have* to go, Yvee. I promised Damian I would. I'm sorry, but I can't back out on my word."

Yvette's blue eyes turned as angry as they could be, and for a moment I thought they were going to pop out of their sockets. "Then I'm going with you!" she said angrily. Everyone in the room heard her.

"I don't think that's a good idea," Sarah said from behind me—a comment that only fed Yvette's anger.

Yvette looked slowly around my shoulder and met Sarah's stare. "I couldn't care less what you think, *Sarah*." She enunciated her name slowly and defiantly. Sarah's eyes widened;

then she shook her head, got up from the sofa, and left for the kitchen—but not without throwing a nasty scowl at Yvette on her way through.

Yvette swung her angry eyes back at me and continued. "I just got you back, Victor." Her angry tone was now edging toward sadness. "I don't want to lose you again." Her words registered in my brain as a dreadful possibility, and suddenly I began to have an uneasy feeling about the whole thing. Damian saw the conflict in my eyes.

"Victor," he said quickly, "We don't have time for this!"

Looking around my shoulder, Yvette turned angry again, scowling at Damian; she seemed ready to counter his comment with a snide response. But something else happened: she suddenly swayed back and forth, as if about to lose her balance. She shook her head and shut her eyes tightly, fighting against an obvious wave of weakness. "Yvette?" I blurted, "Are you all right?"

She took hold of my arms and opened her eyes. She looked confused, disoriented. "Victor?" Her voice sounded frightened.

I fastened my hands around her arms, trying to stabilize her, but her limp body collapsed in my arms. I quickly carried her over to the love seat and called for help. Sarah came running from the kitchen as I knelt on the floor next to the sofa. I brushed the hair away from Yvette's face and waited for her to react, but nothing happened. She was completely out. Sarah knelt next to me on the floor and checked Yvette's vitals. "What happened?" she asked softly.

"I don't know. We were talking, and the next minute she collapsed."

"Her pulse is strong," Sarah said, pressing her thumb on Yvette's wrist. Then she held an eyelid wide open. "Her pupillary response is normal, and so is her breathing." She cursed in dismay and turned to meet my stare. "She's fallen into the same comatose state as Roger."

"What will happen to her?" I asked, suddenly feeling disheartened.

"I don't know. It's hard to tell. The reaction from the serum varies from patient to patient. It also depends on the amount of radiation used, and the specific area of the brain targeted. And I know nothing of her particular procedure—or Roger's, for that matter." Sarah got up from the floor and looked at me with rueful eyes. "But if I had to theorize, I'd say this is the result of a completely different procedure than the one you and Damian went though. Dr. Walker might have been experimenting on different groups of dormant cells with them. The side effects are unpredictable."

My mind pointed in thousand different directions at that moment. I didn't know what to do, think, or feel; I just wanted so badly for this nightmare to be over. I felt like I couldn't solve a problem without having another one bash me over the head—it was pure mayhem. "What about Laura?" I asked, taking advantage of the fact that she had stepped out of the living room.

Sarah rubbed her forehead and lowered her voice. "She seems to be okay… for now. Still, the timing doesn't add up with her. I doubt her procedure was the same as Yvette and Roger's."

"What can we do?" My voice was dispirited now.

"Like I said, we have no choice but to wait."

"Well, I guess she *did* manage to make you stay after all," Damian burst out angrily.

"You're an asshole!" Sarah shouted, fed up with Damian's attitude.

I, on the other hand, ignored him, knowing how fast my anger could escalate if I didn't control it. I just stayed by Yvette and ran my fingers through her hair.

"Look," Damian began again, his voice remorseful now. "I'm sorry. I really am. But I can't wait another minute. My wife needs me too. And I know that if anybody could understand that it's you, Victor." He interpreted my silence as my reply and sighed. "All right, then. Let's go, Denali."

"Wait!" I snapped and got back to my feet. "I'm coming with you!" I kissed Yvette on the forehead and turned to Sarah, who was scowling at me.

"What are you *doing*?" she demanded.

"The right thing," I answered firmly. "And please, don't!" I stopped her before she could utter a word, knowing exactly what she'd try to do. She frowned, as if angry at the fact that I'd anticipated her thoughts. "I need you to stay here, Sarah. Take care of them. Please, take care of—"

"Don't worry," she interjected. "I'll look after her... I promise." She threw her arms around my neck and hugged me.

"Thank you, Sarah."

"Promise me you'll be careful," she whispered in my ear before she kissed me on the cheek.

"I will," I promised. "I'll be back."

**

The day, which had started beautifully with my reunion with Yvette, had turned once again bitter and uncertain. Yvette was now in a comatose state similar to Roger's, and we had absolutely no idea why. Damian, on the other hand, was frightening me more by the minute. I wasn't sure if his odd behavior was triggered solely by his fretfulness over getting his wife back, or if the change was already spreading through him, like an unstoppable cancer. What if this dark energy was infecting his volition progressively, rather than in one single snap of anger, as I was dreading would happen to me? What if Damian was already changing in front of my eyes?

These questions rambled inside my mind as I thought of my own fate, and about what the right thing to do would be if we couldn't stop our change. I mean, if the desire to do evil was the only power that would drive us after the change, then our supernatural abilities would become a major threat to society—a hazard that would need to be contained, even destroyed. Maybe Dr. Walker was right: we would simply be too dangerous to be allowed to live. *Maybe I should start thinking about a back-up plan*, I thought... something I should do in case the change became inevitable.

All these questions bombarded my brain, just like the heavy rain that blasted the plastic cover that concealed us in the back of the truck. A little sliding window in the back of the cabin kept us in contact with Denali, who despite my suggestions was driving with a couple of rifles on the passenger's seat. Damian's idea, of course, obediently followed by Denali. I couldn't help but be curious about that.

After closing the sliding window that separated us from the cabin, I finally asked Damian what the deal was between the two of them. He had to explain a little more about himself in order for me to understand Denali's new disposition. That's when I learned that Damian was a renowned and *wealthy* lawyer in California. His firm was one of the top ten in the country, and he just happened to be their most recently appointed partner. "Did you know that Denali's engaged to be married?" Damian asked. "And that his fiancée wants a dream wedding?"

"Yes," I answered, trying to follow his explanation.

"Well," he continued, "Let's just say that my wedding gift will cover that and more."

"I see." My tone was ironic. Everything made sense now; I just hoped poor Denali wouldn't get stiffed in this deal. It was nothing personal toward Damian, it's just that I've never trusted lawyers, especially the ones with a lot of money. There's a reason why they have so much, and it's *not* because they're generous.

Before long, Denali slid the window open and warned us we were getting close. Damian and I stuck our heads underneath the plastic cover and got ready.

By the time we arrived at Damian's cabin, the rain had stopped, leaving behind nothing but a steady dripping and the sound of the wind rustling the giant firs surrounding the place. Denali eased to a stop at the right side of the house and waited. The place was similar to Denali's, only twenty years newer and with no adjacent water of any type. Naturally, Damian wanted to jump out of the truck as soon as we parked, but I convinced him not to. We needed to stick to the plan if we wanted to have a prayer of coming out of this alive.

After a while, Denali got out of the truck wearing his dad's overalls, which also had a very visible logo that read *Johnson & Sons*. A perfect disguise, if you ask me. But then again, our plan wasn't based purely on diversion, but also on strategy and timing—and we didn't have much of neither. I only had a few variables running in my head, and they didn't look very good.

Denali walked cautiously to the front door. The eerie near-silence made me nervous. I tried to focus my senses on my surroundings, hoping to trigger that special radar I'd used before, but I could see nothing—not because I didn't sense any imminent danger, but because something was blocking me. Somehow, Damian was radiating a strong energy that was keeping me from making full use of my powers. I could only assume that this was the dark energy Sarah had told me about, trying to keep my brain from absorbing the energy that had sparked my powers before—but why, I could only speculate.

Denali stood on the porch, sweat dripping from his forehead. His eyes scanned the area just before he reached the door. He was trying to keep it together, but it was obvious he was on the edge of a nervous breakdown. In the past few days, the poor guy had turned from limo driver to human smuggler to spy. I couldn't help feeling guilty for putting him through all of this—he was a really good man.

Denali finally knocked on the door and waited. After a few seconds with no response he knocked again, but nothing. Suddenly, my mind overcame Damian's jamming and began to branch out and scan the deceptively calm forest. "Wait," I whispered. "Something's not right." My words alarmed Damian, making him want to jump out of the truck again. "Wait!" I insisted, taking hold of his arm. "Can't you feel it?" He shook his head; I guess his troubled mind couldn't focus on anything beyond his wife. Yet the truth of the matter was that I couldn't sense her anywhere near the cabin.

"Tell me!" Damian demanded.

"Your wife isn't in the cabin." I explained quickly.

Damian's forehead creased with a mixture of anger and confusion. A cloudy image flashed into my head then, making me flinch. At first I couldn't distinguish what it was; it took me several attempts before I could completely unveil it. When I did, I saw Captain Black leading an assault squad through the woods. Some of them were already aiming their weapons at the cabin, ready to open fire at the first sight of their target. I didn't need to see any more to understand we had just walked into an ambush. "It's a trap," I snapped. "We have to pull back before it's too late!"

"NO!" Damian countered. "If my wife's not here, they must know where she is!"

"And what the hell are you going to do? Ask them politely?"

"We can take them, Victor." His voice hardened. "You and me. Together!"

"No!" I objected, understanding all too well the consequences of using our abilities in a state of anger. "It's too risky! If we lose control, we'll lose ourselves. Besides, I didn't come here to start a war I can't win, Damian!"

"You've seen what we can do with this power!" Damian insisted, looking right into my eyes. That's when I first noticed that his eyes seemed to have changed color. They were now a light brown that, at first glance, seemed to be the result of the refraction of the sunlight through the plastic cover that concealed us. "What makes you think that we can't win?" he added confidently.

"The fact that I'm not willing to kill anybody, Damian." I waited to see his reaction. "Are you?"

His eyes dropped as he let out an apparent sigh of despair. For a second I thought that I'd gotten through to him... But when his gaze slid back to mine I realized that his sigh of despair carried a painful yet unyielding decision. "Then I'm afraid this is where we part company, my friend."

His words hit me like a truck. I knew what would follow, and the consequences of it all. But what rankled the most was knowing that there was nothing I could do to stop it. Still, realizing the repercussions his decision would have for all of us, I gave it one final try as Damian tossed the plastic cover to the side and readied himself to jump out. "Please," I begged, taking hold of his arm. "Don't do this."

He glared at the hand that held him down and said, "If you're not with me, then you just another snag in my way." His eyes cursed at me as he shook my hand off his arm.

"Damian!" I called after him as he jumped out of the truck bed and ran to the cabin.

Another sharp perception shocked my brain, allowing me to hear voices coming from the woods; yet my distress limited my ability to pinpoint their exact locations.

'I've got a visual on one of them, sir."

"Bellator?"

'No sir. The other one."

'Wait for me to arrive at the site. I'm on my way."

'No time, sir. I have a clean shot... I'm taking it."

'I said wait, *goddamn it!"*

Though Captain Black seemed strangely opposed to opening fire, some of the soldiers aiming at the cabin had their own agendas—possibly retaliation for Damian's display of power back in the Lab, which I'm sure left some of them seriously injured, if not worse. Still, the advantage I had of knowing their next move gave me the opportunity to warn Damian and Denali before it was too late.

"Get down!" I yelled at the top of my lungs.

Damian's reaction to my warning was far quicker than Denali's, yet they both hit the dirt before the first bullets reached their position. Fuming at having missed, the squad opened fire with everything they had. The peace of the forest was shattered by an incredible uproar of gunfire in which Damian was the main target and poor Denali had become, once again, the unfortunate collateral.

The first round of bullets forced Damian to seek cover behind a huge stack of logs next to the cabin. Denali, on the other hand, dodging bullets, crawled and crept off the side of porch and headed back toward the truck. Knowing my presence would only worsen the situation, I kept my head down and away from their scopes. During a momentary lull, Denali was able to reach the truck, while Damian seemed to be cornered between the shed and the tall stack of wood. Meanwhile, I was trying desperately to scheme a way out of this mess—when another vision showed me the shooters advancing towards the cabin. Denali, still on the ground, opened the truck door, slid out one of his shotguns, and cocked it.

"Denali," I called and shook my head at him, knowing that shooting back would only draw their fire. Denali saw me and stopped, nodding.

"Shoot!" Damian's voice resurfaced from behind the stack of wood.

"NO!" I countered, looking at Denali. His face was scared and confused.

"We have a deal, damn it!" Damian insisted furiously. "Now, shoot!"

Denali, seemingly scare of him, obeyed the foolish command, and began to shoot at the squad from behind the opened truck door. One of the approaching shooters returned fire, just as I had expected, blasting out the window above Denali's head. He ducked down behind the door, cringing; I could see his eyes bulging with fear as his trembling hands reloaded his weapon. "Shoot! Shoot!!" Damian kept pressing, his voice filled with rage.

Denali cocked his shotgun and moved around the door to shoot. And though I could see the imminent danger in my head, there wasn't enough time for me to warn him, and the spark of my hypersenses hadn't awakened my ability to shield him. The shooter, who was a trained professional, had taken advantage and moved in closer while Denali reloaded the shotgun. He was now only twenty feet away and ready to shoot at his new target.

The slow motion trance I'd experience before suddenly took control of my senses, putting me in the first row of a horrifying spectacle. Denali's eyes widened in surprise when he realized the close proximity of the shooter. I saw him trying to lift the barrel of his shotgun at the same time the shooter was pulling his trigger. The last desperate warning I tried to shout out to Denali was drowned in the blast of gunfire, and the slow motion trance only made the horrifying event even more painful to watch.

The shooter opened fire before Denali could even aim his weapon. The next thing I saw was Denali being brutally riddled by the rapid fire of the Mac-10 the shooter held in his hands. Not even the slow motion trance allowed me to keep count of all the bullets that pierced his body. All I was able to see was the blood splattering from every wound inflicted, along with the expression of agony on Denali's face as he fell slowly to the ground.

"NOOOOOO!!!" I screamed at the top of my lungs, popping up from beneath the plastic cover. The shooter, who didn't let go of the trigger until his magazine was exhausted, recognized me the second he saw me. My slow motion trance ended the second my feet touched the ground. I held Denali's mangled body in my arms while the shooter hastened toward me.

Denali gargled blood for a long second before his eyes closed forever. A lone tear escaped the corner of one eye, and in that moment I hated Damian more than I had ever hated anyone in my life.

New heights of pain and anger roared through me. I tried to control my rage, but it was useless; I could feel it soothing my pain, taking control. My eyes began to burn again, this time with the same intensity they had back in the Lab during my first escape. I directed my blazing gaze toward the shooter, who was now just a few feet away from me. *'I've got Bellator,"* he said, pressing his earpiece. The empty magazine he'd used to kill Denali dropped to the ground as he reached for a new one behind his belt.

Everything I saw from that moment on I saw as a spectator only, sitting behind my eyes, with absolutely no control of the actions my body took—or of the secondary reasoning I felt gearing up in the back of my head. My hand rose before the shooter, who was just about to fire his weapon. I glared at him and clenched my fist tightly, so hard my arm trembled with the strain. The shooter dropped his gun then and brought his hands to his throat, as if trying to remove invisible hands from around his neck. With his face reflecting nothing but pure horror and desperation, he began to gasp like a fish out of water. I could feel the connection that my mind had established between my hand and his windpipe. And though my anger was in control of me now, I still understood the consequences of what I was planning to do, and how easy it would be. All I had to do was squeeze a little tighter, and my friend would be avenged.

But something blocked me, resuming the game of mercy in my head once again. Suddenly, I found myself stuck in the middle of a mental conflict. Part of me condoned the change I was undergoing and even saw it as just, while the other part dreaded and hated it. *Should I fight it?* I asked myself. *Why? It's going to happen anyway.* And if I let it go now, I might just be able to avenge all the innocents who had suffered at the hands of Dr. Walker and R.C. Labs. As these thoughts stoked my anger, my fist tightened. The shooter's eyes turned bloodshot as tiny vessels burst in the whites.

It was then that Damian's voice caught my attention—a growl, similar to the one I'd used to address the guard during my first escape from R.C. Labs. "Ready to kill yet?" he asked as he emerged from behind the woodpile, his eyes an opaque sulfurous hue—a color that no longer seemed human, but rather a representation of pure evil.

As my glare returned to the shooter, I caught my reflection in the truck's wing-mirror—and saw that my eyes had changed too. A dark and unnatural cloud of gray had erased all the humanity from the honest brown eyes I'd inherited from my father, and a streak of my dark hair had turned dead white, as if part of the innocence of my youth had been taken away by the unnatural anger I felt.

"NO!" I snarled to myself, refusing to accept what was happening to me.

The imploring look on the shooter's face sparked a hint of mercy that made me stall—if for only a moment. Then I thought of Yvette, and the promise I'd made to my father flashed into my mind. Their voices began to echo inside my head…

"I love you, Victor."

"You have to live, son. You're destined for something greater than you can possibly imagine. I've known it ever since the moment you were born; since the very first time I held you in my arms…"

My fist released the soldier then, allowing him to gasp in a huge lungful of much-needed breath. He dropped to his knees as soon as the connection was broken. I lowered my hand and breathed slowly myself, feeling the burning sensation in my eyes slowly subside. The soldier was frozen in fear, yet he kept glancing at the machine gun in front of him, undecided about what to do. I looked into his uncertain eyes and uttered one word that helped him make his decision. "Run!"

He looked at me, frightened and confused, then opted to follow my suggestion and got back on his feet again, his eyes wider than any I'd ever seen in a human being.

Damian, who was watching from the corner, didn't seem too happy about my decision. "What are you *doing?*" he shouted.

"Finish him off!" Another look from me was enough for the shooter to flee like a whipped dog. A quick glance into the wing-mirror proved that my eyes had returned to normal. I slowly laid Denali's lifeless body on the ground while Damian kept screaming at me, like a kid throwing a tantrum. "What's wrong with you? He's getting away! "

"Damian!" I shouted back. "Get in the truck! We can still make it out of here!"

"*NO!*" he roared. "It's *their* time to run!" His eyes follow the shooter, who was about to rendezvous with five more soldiers coming our way. He turned to the stack of logs next to him; each was about three feet long and a foot in diameter, and weighed at least thirty pounds. He raised his hand before the nearest log and shut his eyes. The log began to vibrate on top of the others; Damian's hand vibrated too. I got up from the ground slowly, watching a disturbing expression distort his face. "Damian?" I called. "What are you doing?"

His answer was to jerk his hand upward, levitating the log before him. As I ran the numbers in my head, I saw his intentions. The log was aimed at the soldiers, who had stopped roughly a hundred feet away. He opened his sulfurous eyes; maintaining his evil smile, he swung his hand forward, mimicking a baseball pitcher's delivery. The log flew in a beeline toward the soldiers at an incredible rate of speed. It reached them in a fraction of a second, impacting one man dead center in the chest. Blood splattered out of his mouth as the strike hurled him back ten feet, into the trunk of a tall fir tree. The other soldiers hurried to check on him, but it was obvious he was dead.

One of the soldiers pressed his earpiece. *"Man down!"* he shouted.

I heard the voice of Captain Black then: *"Weapons free! Fire at will!"*

The crackle of gunfire started again, chewing into the front of the cabin. I took cover behind the truck, while Damian cackled behind the wood stack, pleased with the battle he'd started—though in his defense, we hadn't started this war. It was never my intention to engage, but now I was running out of options.

A brief lull allowed me to peek from behind the car door and study the opposition. The squad consisted of ten men, and they were all moving forward carefully. They spread strategically through the woods, but I could still sense their presence, even behind the thickest cover. I could only assume Damian could do the same.

Damian smiled and raised his hand again, taking control of more than one log this time—a half-dozen more. One by one, the logs sped through the air like wooden gigantic bullets, striking the soldiers one at a time. Gunshots, screams, and blood were all I heard and saw for the next sixty seconds—the longest minute of my life. Damian paused for a moment as he took his time pinpointing the last three soldiers standing, among them

Denali's murderer. Raising their hands, those three dropped their weapons and bolted for the woods.

But Damian didn't accept their surrender any more than they would have accepted his. With one swing of his hand, he took control of exactly three logs and aimed them at the retreating soldiers. I took advantage of the opportunity, darted from behind the truck, and jumped Damian from behind. The logs crashed to the ground like puppets with cut strings as soon as I restrained his arms. "Enough!" I yelled, holding his hands down.

His face went dead and his sulfurous eyes pierced into mine, bearing nothing but contempt. He then escaped my grip as easily as an adult would break the grip of a child. It was obvious he was somehow manipulating his telekinesis to boost his physical strength. I stood stunned in front of him as he squared off to confront me.

He brought the palm of his hand to the center of my chest and growled, "I told you to stay the *hell* out of my way!" Next thing I knew, I was flying backward through the air toward the side of the truck. All I remember before I impacted it was feeling the power of a crushing wave exploding between my chest and Damian's hand as he finished his little speech, tossing me away like a piece of crumpled tin foil.

Damian turned back to the fleeing soldiers, but they were no longer in sight. They must have regrouped somewhere in the woods with Captain Black before retreating. I was glad to feel the jolting hum of danger finally subside in my mind. Damian, on the other hand, was miffed at having missed the opportunity to kill again. I slowly got up from the ground, shaking my head at the big dent my back had left in the truck's fender—not because I cared about the vehicle, which was already destroyed, but because I realized Damian could have really have hurt me if he'd wanted to. I was lucky he hadn't.

"Are you done?" I asked sarcastically, rubbing my knuckles against my lower back. He turned to me and gave me that piercing glare again. I ignored his unnaturally yellow eyes and tried to talk some sense into him. "Did you forget the reason we came here?" I demanded, hoping he'd fight the evil trance and beat it back, just as I had.

My words shook him up, making him stand down from his aggressive position. Snapping out of his stupor, he ran inside the cabin. I followed him inside, just to discover the cabin was exactly as I'd sensed it to be—empty. Damian, however, didn't rest until he checked every room and closet in the place. "Sonya! Sonya!" he kept calling, without getting any response. As I walked into the living room, I noticed that there were no signs of a struggle anywhere, yet I couldn't shake the feeling that something terrible had happened in this place besides the massacre I'd just witnessed outside.

I looked around the elegant living room, searching for anything unusual. The only thing that caught my eye was a framed picture on the glass coffee table. I stepped in closer and picked it up. Damian was in the picture, hugging a beautiful woman from behind, his chin over her shoulder. They were both laughing. Obviously this was Sonya, Damian's wife. She was very pretty; short dark hair, hazel eyes, olive skin... In the picture she was wearing the same thick silver wedding band Damian wore on his ring finger. Her look was the one of a woman in love.

"She's not here!" I heard Damian shout frantically. "She's not here, Victor!" He dashed into the living room, his yellow eyes almost sad now.

"Is this her?" I asked, handing him the framed picture. He reached for it and looked at it for the longest moment. I watched as his eyes, now filled with tears, gradually faded from that sinister, ugly yellow to their original dark brown. I realized then that neither of us had yet reached the point of no return— that somehow, there was still hope for us both. Damian staggered, picture in hand, and collapsed miserably on his knees, as if all the evil energy that had driven his will through the battle had been yanked right out of his body.

"Help me," he said, his voice breaking, as he reached out to me. "Victor, please. Please!"

I couldn't believe that the defenseless man pleading before me was the same unstoppable monster who'd just killed seven people outside. I *refused* to believe he was. So I grabbed his hand and helped him up. "I promised I would," I reminded him. "We'll find her."

A phone rang then, breaking the ominous silence in the room. Damian rushed to an alcove beside the door and pressed the speaker button on the phone there. "Hello?" he answered, his voice hopeful.

"Damian?" a terrified woman's voice asked.

"Sonya?" Damian yelled desperately. "Sonya!"

"Well, hello, Damian," Dr. Walker's voice said smoothly, stunning us both. "I hear you've been having fun with your new gifts."

"Where is she?" Damian snarled.

"She's safe," Walker said calmly. "For now, that is. Keeping her that way is up to you."

Damian's brows knitted in confusion. "What the hell do you want from me?"

"My most precious asset, of course."

"All right," Damian bargained, "I'll turn myself in. Just let my wife go."

"Aw! Isn't that the romantic gesture?" Walker mocked. "But I'm afraid you're mistaken, Counselor. You see, you were no more than a tiny piece of the puzzle, and I've already taken everything I need from you. One of the subjects you have befriended, however, has something I want; something I never had the chance to… dissect." His tone took a more serious turn. "Bring me what I want, and I promise to let your wife go free."

Damian looked at me, probably mirroring my thoughts about who the subject was. "Why should I trust you?" he demanded. "You've already tried to kill me twice."

"I think you're missing the point, Damian," Walker said. "You're not in any position to disagree with me, son. But if it makes you feel better, I'll let you in on a little secret: My men did not withdraw. I called them off. After all, I can't risk destroying the most important piece of the puzzle. So you can rest assured, there will be no more shooting. So… do we have a deal?"

Damian met my gaze and waited, as if he knew it was up to me to finish the deal. After all, it was obvious to both of us that the last piece of the puzzle—the one scheduled for vivisection—had always been me. And though I knew what this meant for me, I couldn't let anyone else get hurt on my account. So I did what I thought was the right thing to do. "All right, Dr. Walker, we have a deal," I spoke up, giving myself away.

"Victor?" he asked with a hint of surprise.

"Yes, Doctor, it's me. I thought you might want to deal with me directly."

"Oh, yes." His voice sounded bitter now. "I knew I'd eventually have to deal with you to get what I wanted. The question is, are we going to have a problem?"

"No, Doctor," I responded. "I promise to turn myself in, without a struggle, as long as Damian's wife is unharmed. *After* she's released, and with the condition you leave the rest of our group alone." Damian's face lit up at my words. "Now you tell me, Doctor. Do we have a deal?"

Dr. Walker laughed. "Oh my, you certainly live up to the hype, Mr. Eagle Scout. That's by far the most noble and heroic gesture I've ever heard in my life!" Damian and I exchanged confused looks as Walker cackled over the speakerphone. "There's only one problem," Walker continued. "Who ever said I wanted *you*?"

His words felt like a bucket of ice water dashed in my face. Again, Damian lost his cool and began to rant at the speakerphone like a crazy man. "Who, then?!" he demanded. "Who do you want?! Tell me! "

Walker waited a beat before he spoke again, and then he ran me through with an answer that created an immediate conflict between Damian and me—an answer that left me completely at my wit's end. "I want Yvette Montgomery."

Chapter 12

Roger's Foresight

DEAD SILENCE FOLLOWED Dr. Walker's demand. Damian and I exchanged uneasy looks, our own personal conflicts showing in our faces. Walker, of course, had been suspicious of my relationship with Yvette. Otherwise, why would I risk my life by going back to rescue her? His ploy was simple and easy to read: he knew that Damian would do anything to get his wife back, and my silence had just confirmed my position on protecting Yvette. He was counting on it. Now Damian would have to eliminate any obstacles between Walker's prize and his wife's freedom. Walker was looking to kill not two, but *three* birds with one stone.

"Oh my!" Walker suddenly exclaimed. "It seems the two of you have a lot to talk about all of a sudden. Only, I wouldn't waste too much time talking if I were you, Damian. Because your wife could end up paying the price for your noncompliance." His voice hardened. "Midnight. R.C. Labs. Ms. Montgomery for your wife. Or I'll see to it personally that she takes Ms. Montgomery's place on the table. Oh, and before I forget: if you'd be so kind, Victor, please tell that double-crossing bitch Sarah Grey that I haven't forgotten about her. As soon as I'm finished with you gentlemen, I'm going to concentrate all of my efforts on finding her."

A loud click followed Walker's last word, leaving us with nothing but decisions to make.

"Son of a *bitch*!" Damian hurled the speakerphone against the living room wall and began to hyperventilate. I knew we couldn't have that. I couldn't afford to lose Damian to another tantrum. In order to make this work to our advantage, I needed to keep him calm—and on our side. I couldn't risk having another confrontation with him. Not after witnessing the unstoppable power of the dark energy he already had inside him. But on the other hand, there was no way in hell I was going to let him take Yvette. I needed to think of something, and fast. So I ran my numbers again.

"Damian," I said quietly, "please calm down. Remember the change. We can't afford to fall apart now. That's exactly what Walker wants: for us to lose our cool and turn on each other. You understand?"

He stopped and leaned against the couch, his eyes clenched shut as if in pain. "I can't lose my wife, Victor."

"You won't. But you have to stay focused, all right? If we work together, maybe we can turn Walker's expectations to our advantage." I paused. "No one else needs to get hurt, Damian."

Damian's eyes flew open, his look quizzical, as if trying to decide whether or not to trust me. "All right," he said finally. "What's your plan?"

"We need to go back to Denali's cabin and regroup. Sarah knows the ins and outs of that building like the back of her hand. She might be able to figure a way to outsmart Walker before he realizes what hit him. We did it once. We can do it again."

"All right," Damian agreed wearily. "Let's do it."

***

As we laid Denali's body in the truck bed, I couldn't help thinking about the conversation we'd had when he first picked me up from the airport. All of his dreams of getting married and starting a family were gone now. His unconditional goodness, his integrity, his decency... lost forever. And although part of me blamed Damian, I couldn't help thinking that it was *me* who had brought them together. It was *me* who came knocking on his door asking for help.

"I'm sorry," I said, looking at his ruined body. "I never meant for any of this to happen." My voice almost breaking. "But I promise you, I'll find a way to make them pay. I'll seek justice for you, my friend. I promise."

Damian just watched and listened, saying nothing. I sighed and pulled the plastic cover over Denali's body.

How much more blood will have to be shed? I wondered despairingly. *How many more lives will have to be sacrificed before I see the end of this nightmare?* I didn't know what to think, feel, or do. My head was nothing but a tangle of conflicting thoughts, and keeping myself from feeling anger at this point was no longer a choice, but a challenge. Soon these conflicting thoughts became a vicious circle, a merry-go-round that wouldn't stop spinning inside my head. At one point, I even thought that bringing Damian back to Denali's cabin would be a mistake.

The truth was that I didn't know how much I could trust him. After all, he was a practical man. He negotiated with other people's lives for a living...and unfortunately, in this case Yvette was his bargaining chip. But I was running out of options. I needed to go back. I needed to know how Yvette was, and whether she had awakened from her sudden collapse. Besides, trying to keep Damian away would only have proven my distrust, and *that* could've caused Damian to react in an unfavorable manner.

Sarah was sitting on the porch in an old rocker when I parked the bullet-holed truck in front of the cabin. She run to the truck and opened the door for me. "What happened?" she asked breathlessly. "Where's Denali?"

"It was an ambush. Denali was shot." Sarah's hand flew to her mouth. "He's dead, Sarah."

"Oh, my God!" she exclaimed in a whisper. But then her eyes flew to my head, where my new shock of hair hung over my brow. "Are you all right?" she asked, running her fingers through the silvery patch. "What happened to you?"

"I'm fine," I said, reaching for her hand. "Don't worry about it." Once again, why try to explain something I couldn't explain myself? "How's Yvette?" I asked, walking hastily towards the cabin. Damian followed close behind.

"She's still out, but I think I've figured out what's happening to her and Roger. My mentor once told me that the reason patients couldn't survive the procedure was because dormant, immature cells were being awakened inside mature brains. In some patients, these cells, once awakened, aren't able to catch up with the current maturity state of their brains. My theory is that the immature cells awakened in Yvette and Roger found a way to accelerate their maturity process: by wrapping themselves into a mental cocoon, forcing the brain into a hibernation state."

"So, what happens when this mental cocoon opens?" I asked, intrigued.

Sarah sighed. "I don't know."

"Wait a second," Damian burst out. "How come *we* didn't go through any of this?"

"Well," Sarah began, "Like I said, it's obvious their procedure was different than yours. Walker was probably trying to target a new set of inactive neurons. After the first incidents with patients who developed telekinesis, Walker began to avoid targeting the same set of neurons in every patient. Why he targeted the same ones in the two of you is beyond me. He knew the consequences, and the side effects the two of you would suffer."

"All right," Damian began. "So how long will it take for her to wake up?"

Sarah frowned, confused by Damian's sudden interest on Yvette's condition. "I don't know," she said slowly. "Hours. Days, maybe. It's uncertain at this point."

"Can she be moved?" he asked keenly.

Sarah scowled at him, confused.

"Hey!" I snapped at him. "I know what you're getting at, but no one is moving her *anywhere*, is that clear?"

Damian scowled at me, his arms crossed.

"All right, what the hell is going on?" Sarah demanded.

It took me a few minutes to bring Sarah up to speed with our new situation. It was only noon, which meant we still had twelve hours to figure out what to do. So I decided to give Denali at least the honor of a burial—nothing remotely close to what he deserved, of course, but a burial nonetheless. Sarah and Damian helped me move the body to the back yard and dig the pit where we finally rested his body. In his shirt pocket, next to his heart, I slid a picture of his fiancée that I'd found in his wallet—as well as a note explaining the circumstances of his death and the people responsible for it. I'd promised to seek justice for him, but at that moment, I wasn't sure if I was going to live past midnight.

As Sarah stuck a crude wooden cross at the head of Denali's grave, I asked her if she had any idea what Walker could possibly want with Yvette. But she seemed as lost on that point as I was. She did ponder the question for a long moment, and then lifted her head as if with a theory. But something drew her eyes in surprise and made her gasp, "Oh, my God! …Look!"

I turned to follow her stare and saw Yvette walking towards the pond. The hem of her dress fluttered in the wind; her glossy black hair flowed in the same direction. I dropped the shovel I held and ran to her, calling her name. She failed to respond, so I walked around and faced her. Her sapphire eyes were wide open, staring blankly at the forest. "Yvette!" I said again, gently nudging her shoulders.

"Victor?" She blinked.

"Are you all right?" I asked.

"I… think so," she hesitated, as if waking up from a dream. "Where'd she go?"

"Who?" I asked.

"Denali's grandmother," she said, looking around the pond. "She looked sad."

"There's no one else here, Yvee. Maybe you were dreaming. Sleepwalking."

She shook her head, confused.

I stroked her hair and smiled. "It's all right. Let's go back to the cabin."

"Wait!" she said, realizing my clothes were recently bloodstained; and she gasped when she saw the new silvery patch in my hair. "What happened? Did you end up going with Damian?"

"Yeah," I said regretfully. "But I'm back, as I promised... And I'm fine. Don't you worry about me," I said, gliding my knuckles gently down her cheek. "I'm just so glad you're awake. Don't you ever scare me like that again, all right?"

"You scared me too," she said, choking back a sob, her fingers grabbing my new silver hair, pulling my head towards hers.

"I know," I said. "I'm sorry."

We kissed then, hungrily, as if we'd thought we were never going to kiss again. My senses went haywire at the touch of her lips, overwhelmed by all the love I felt for this amazing angel, hoping she could feel the same. Getting lost in this mixture of love, passion, and extrasensory perception, I experienced the most extraordinary ecstasy a human being can achieve. Eyes closed, I wondered if we'd made the stones levitate again. If they did, they probably dropped at the same time Sarah's desperate call startled us both. "Victor!"

Roger had awakened too, and his behavior had frightened everyone in the cabin. He was screaming incoherently, like someone on the verge of a nervous breakdown. His anxiety only worsened the moment he saw me. He showed an irrational fear towards me, as if my presence alone was enough to hurt him. I couldn't understand what was happening to him... yet something beyond my enhanced senses warned me his fear was based on something he had seen during his "mental cocooning." I realized it was imperative for me to understand what had incited this fear.

So despite Roger's trepidation, I asked everyone to step outside so I could have a minute alone with him. I grabbed a folding chair from the kitchen, opened it, and sat right in front of him. He hugged a blanket that rested on his lap and stared at me with frightened eyes. I leaned forward, my elbows resting on my legs. I interlocked my fingers and forced a quick smile, hoping Roger would calm down. But my close proximity only made him cringe.

"You want to tell me what's going on?" I asked genially. But his only answer was the piercing silence of a pair of penetrating black eyes. "Listen," I continued, my voice careful. "I know that what you're going through is enough to make you very angry. Believe me, we're all in the same boat here. But maybe that's a good thing, because it also means that we're not alone. We can help each other, Roger."

I waited again for a reaction, but nothing; so I continued to probe. "Look, whatever's bothering you, it obviously has something to do with me. So why don't you just tell me what it is? Maybe I can find a way to make it right." His silence continued. "Roger, I can't help you if you don't talk to me."

He still refused to answer.

Discouraged, I hung my head and sighed. "What have I done for you to fear me like this?"

"It's not what you've done," he finally muttered. "It's what you'll do." His words made me pop my head back up. "What you'll become."

"What do you mean, what I'll become?" I asked, flustered.

He leaned forward on the edge of the sofa and whispered, "I've seen it… In my head. You change, Victor. And you do terrible things."

"What are you talking about?" I asked, frightened.

"Behind my eyes, there are days beyond tomorrow," he said mystically. "Memories of what will be. Things that I'll never live to see."

His words were a cold draft that pierced right through my bones. "You're telling me that you can see the future now?"

A rueful smile pulled up the corners of his lips slightly. "What we call *the future* is no more than a destination based on our choices, Victor. And normally, there are as many futures as the numbers you keep running in your head. But in your case, there's only one, no matter what choice you make."

"And what destination is that?" I asked.

"The path to evil."

"No," I said firmly. "I won't let that happened. I won't let this dark force turn me into something I'm not. And if your clairvoyance can't see the power of my convictions, then I'd have to say that your visions are nothing but a delirium from your comatose state."

I sprang aggressively from my chair and turn around, distraught and confused by Roger's alleged foresight. Through the window I saw Damian, Sarah, Laura, and Yvette standing next to the bullet-riddled truck, talking. My eyes selfishly focused on my angel alone, as I thought of all the promises I might not be able to fulfill—with her and for her—should this dreadful prophecy come true. Then I realized my biggest fear wasn't turning into a monster, but having this monster hurt the angel that had brought me back to life—the angel that I had loved my entire life.

I shut my eyes tightly, forcing my heart to shut up, so I could let my analytical mind tell me the right thing to do in order to keep my Yvee and everyone else safe from the monster I might soon be. Then I thought that if Roger had seen my future, he might have seen Yvette's as well. So, I turned around to ask him... but my question was lost in the terror of what I saw next.

"Roger?" I gasped, watching him pull a gun from underneath the cover on his lap. A .32 Colt pistol that he had somehow liberated from Denali's gun cabinet, to be precise. "What are you doing?"

"I'm sorry, Victor. I just can't let it happen."

The blood drained from my face. "Why don't you just calm down and give me the gun, all right? Nothing bad is going to happen. I promise."

He laughed bitterly. "You should stop making promises you can't fulfill, Victor. It'll only bring you more pain."

"You can trust me, Roger. I haven't backed out on a promise yet. Ever."

"You haven't seen what I've seen! The horror, the suffering... the pain... And my *knowing* it only makes things worse. You see, they get ahold of me, Victor, and they use what I know to decide who lives and who dies. I can't let that happen, Victor." He whispered again, "I can't let that happen," bringing the pistol to his temple.

"Roger!" I pleaded desperately. "Please don't do this. I can help you!"

Tears ran down his cheeks now. "There's no help for us once we cross over to the dark side. You'll soon see that for yourself... goodbye, Victor."

"Roger, NOOO!" The spark in my brain ignited and I reached out for him—too late. Even my powers can't outrace a bullet that exits the chamber faster than the speed of sound.

I jerked at the dull crack of the gunshot, as if I were the one shot, and it left a ringing in my ears that blocked all sound from my surroundings. Fortunately, my eyes closed reflexively when he shot himself, so I didn't have to see the worst of it. A bloodstain spread over the fabric of the couch as I watched Roger's head dangle over his shoulder, and his big body keel over onto its side. I stood there in shock, trembling before the horrifying scene. I couldn't move, speak, or hear. Damian, who was the first to enter the room, had to push me out of the way to get to Roger's body. He leaned over the big man and checked his pulse, just to confirm that Roger was gone...although the ruin that had been his head should been enough for that.

I could see Damian's lips moving as he shook me by the shoulders, as if asking me for answers. But I heard nothing; the ringing in my ears continued to deafen me. Then I felt the touch of Yvette, which sparked my senses again. This shook me out of my deafness as if out of a nightmare.

"Victor?" I finally heard her voice, as if from a mile away. "What happened?"

"He…. he killed himself," I answered past a knot in my throat.

"Why?" Sarah asked, horrified.

I took a minute to answer. "He was clairvoyant. He chose not to be a part of what he saw in his visions. "

"And what was that?" Damian asked.

I sighed. "A horrific future that he's taken to his grave." I paused and walked toward Denali's bedroom. "I guess we're all just going to have to wait and see what it was… what it'll be."

After telling everybody that I needed some time alone, I stepped into Denali's bedroom. I stopped and leaned forward over the dresser, looking blankly into the mirror. After a few minutes I began to scrutinize my own face, trying to find the monster behind my eyes. But soon my appearance derailed my intentions and got me to thinking. If we were to escape this godforsaken place, we needed to attract as little attention as possible. A man in rags, covered in blood, just wasn't going to do. I was the only one in our group who still looked like I'd just walked out of a slaughterhouse.

I decided to strip out of my tatters and bandages and jump into the shower. Strangely, the cut on my brow had healed almost completely, yet I chose not to even question why. As I saw the murky water running down the drain, I thought of all the blood that had been shed in vain. A sudden burst of anger caused me to drive my fist through the shower wall, carving a hole into the white fiberglass, which in return cut my knuckles in several places. I saw my bright new blood run down and spiral into the drain with the clear water.

The pain, along with the act itself, reminded me to keep calm. The frequency of these outbursts, as well as the intensity of them, was an obvious sign that I was running out of time. The more I felt this dark energy growing inside me, the more difficult it became to reject it. The truth was, my anger was the only thing soothing my pain now—or at least, that's how this dark energy was making me feel. Yet the thought of losing Yvette kept me from choosing this seductive escape.

Quickly, I drenched my head under the gushing hot water and tried to regain complete control of my feelings. But something was wrong. Fighting my anger wasn't easy, but it was doable. Pain, on the other hand, proved to be a different proposition. I shut off the water and stepped out of the shower. Steam engulfed the entire bathroom. I wrapped a towel around my waist and panted distressfully over the sink, fighting a smothering sensation of hurt and anger that I was finding difficult to shake. The mirror was too clouded to show my reflection, so I wiped my hand over it to clear the fog. An electrifying shiver stroked my spine when I saw the reflection of my own eyes.

The unnatural gray that had tainted my eyes at Damian's cabin had returned, along with the same evil expression that screamed out for hate and revenge. I could've sworn I even saw a disturbing smile jeering at me from the mirror. The shock forced me to shut my eyes tightly as I staggered backwards against the wall. By the time I'd built the courage to open my eyes again, the steam had covered the mirror with another coating of fog, which I frantically began to wipe way. I never thought I'd be so happy to see the stupid expression of my good old self again.

Did I imagine it? I wondered. Maybe it was just another trick of my rapidly evolving dark side, trying to make me lose my grip on reality. I couldn't know for sure. But whatever it was, it was growing stronger, and becoming more difficult to control.

I stepped into the bedroom, trying to shake the frightful experience. The change of temperature in the room helped me to do that. It was cold—freezing! I couldn't understand how this place could have hot water but no heating system. It must have been at least thirty-five degrees outside, and all we had for warmth was an old fireplace in the living room. I threw another towel over my shoulders and began to look around the room, searching for something fresh to change into.

The closet door in the room caught my attention; it contained a laundry basket overflowing with clean, unfolded laundry. Digging through it, I found a pair of jeans and a white T-shirt, which I slipped into right away. A nice jacket and a pair of boots that I found at the back of the closet complemented my new outfit—I guess I was lucky that everything fit as if it had been meant for me. The jacket was a brown leather bomber; the label read *Trapper Alaska*, and it had one of those removable faux-fur collars that reminded me of those black-and-white war movies I used to watch with my father when I was a kid. The initials *D.J.* had been laser-engraved on the front of the jacket. It took me two seconds to realize what they stood for: *Denali Johnson*, of course.

Then there were the boots: Durango. Brown leather, rubber soles, with harnesses around the ankles. I have to admit, it felt great to look decent again. After combing my damp bicolor hair,

I decided to go back and rejoin the others, who had taken it upon themselves to bury Roger's body in the backyard next to Denali's.

"Hey!" Yvette came to me with a smile and hugged me. "You look great," she said, running her fingers through my silvery patch of hair again. "I'm beginning to like this. It's definitely you."

I looked into her innocent eyes and I couldn't help feeling guilty for keeping the truth from her all this time. I was just trying to protect her, but my time was running out and she deserved to know the truth. So I steeled myself and decided to finally reveal my secret. "Yvee," I began. "There's something I need to tell you—"

"It's all right," she said swiftly. "You don't have to. I know."

"How…" I trailed off, confused. But then my eyes flew to Sarah—Damian stood silently behind her, studying our every move like a hawk.

"I'm sorry," Sarah said. "I thought you were never going to tell her—and like I said before, she deserves to know."

"So much for doctor-patient confidentiality."

"I'm not a doctor, and you're not my patient. If it makes you feel better, there's a reason why I decided to reveal your condition. While you guys went to Damian's cabin, I managed to contact my mentor in Sitka. He's finally resurfaced, and says he's fine. He told me he's willing to try to find a way to help you and Damian, though he said no promises. I'm confident he can find a way to reverse the change." She smiled hopefully. "Your guys are going to be all right."

A sigh escaped my lips and, once again, I was dumbstruck. I guess I was having trouble believing the good news. My eyes slid back to Yvette, who was caressing my cheek with the palm of her hand. "It's all right, baby," she comforted me. "You're going to be okay."

I reached for her hand and kissed it, finally heaving a deep sigh of relief that I ended with an elated chuckle. "That's— that's great news," I said, trying not to cry. "Thank you, Sarah."

"Hey, I wouldn't be much of a heroine if I didn't help my sidekick get better, would I?"

That cracked me up. "So now I'm the sidekick, huh?"

"You always were, buddy." She laughed with me and then met Yvette's stare. "Is it okay if I hug this gigantic pain in my ass?"

"By my guest," Yvette conceded with a smile, and pushed me gently in Sarah's direction.

Sarah leaned the shovel she had in her hands against a wall and walked to me with a serious look on her face. Her arms wrapped around me tightly, as if she'd been wanting to do this for a long time. Her lips graced my ear when she whispered, "You deserve to be happy, Victor. And I won't leave until I see that through. I promise." She let go of me and met my eyes candidly. "We're still in this together, right?"

I nodded, overcome with sentiment.

"Ahem!" Yvette cleared her throat and addressed me. "Victor, I want you to go with Sarah and meet this doctor in Sitka." She paused ruefully. "And I want you to promise me you'll respect my decision."

I let go of Sarah and turned to Yvette, confused. "What are you talking about? What decision?"

"I know about Damian's wife, and I won't allow anyone to get hurt on my account. I've promised Damian I'll do the swap, without any tricks. That way he can have his wife back. And I'm sure that once you get better, you'll come back for me again. Sarah has information that you guys can take to the police. I'll just hold on until they arrive. I can do it."

"Are you *crazy?*" I asked, stunned. "Whose idea was this?" My eyes flew to Damian and Sarah.

"No one asked me to do this, Victor," Yvette continued firmly. "I decided this on my own. I just can't stand to see anyone else get hurt. And I need you to please just respect my decision, all right?"

"No!" I barked. "And I don't care how much you'll hate me for it when I don't. I will *never* let you do this, not in a million years!"

"Victor?" Damian finally spoke.

"And you'd better stay the hell away from this, Damian," I said defiantly.

He smirked challengingly. "I guess I always knew it would come to this." He dropped the shovel in his hands and strode towards me, as if ready to engage, his eyes faintly glowing the same sulfuric yellow I'd seen back at his cabin.

My eyes began to burn too.

"Wait!" Sarah shouted, jumping between us. "I think I have an idea about how to use this swap to our advantage. Damian!" She turned to him. "We're going to get your wife out of there—and we're all going to help you, all right? But we have to work together, you understand? And Victor." She turned to me. "I know you're not going to like this. But in order for this to work, Yvette needs to be involved." She lowered her voice. "Victor, we can still beat this... together."

Damian and I kept glaring at each other.

"I'm in!" Yvette snapped, making eye contact with Sarah, who smiled and nodded.

"Well, that's one," Sarah said. "Damian?" she asked, turning to him.

"All right," he said, backing off both literally and figuratively.

"Victor?" Sarah turned to me now.

I took a deep breath and sighed—reluctantly. "All right," I said finally. "And what about Laura?"

"She's in pretty bad shape," Sarah explained. "I spoke with her earlier, and we decided it's better for her to just go home. Besides, we're going to need someone on the mainland to tell people what happened here, in case none of us makes it. She's got my flash drive with all the information I extracted from

Walker's personal files. She knows what to do with it if she doesn't hear from us within the next forty-eight hours."

"All right, then," I said grudgingly. "What's your plan?"

The night was upon us, although the clock only read fifteen minutes to six. Normal for this time of the year, Sarah had said. Ketchikan nights weren't that much longer than the days during the springtime, yet nightfall finds you a lot early than usual. The cold front that had swatted us for the last couple of days was finally giving us a break, allowing us to enjoy a more comfortable night. A little outdoor thermometer in the porch pointed its needle at the lower fifties. It was the perfect setting to just stand on the porch and enjoy that naturally purified air that can only be found in a place like this.

Unfortunately, I was incapable of enjoying anything at the moment. I was beyond distraught. I couldn't focus or reason anymore... And yet, I couldn't stop thinking about what was going to happen that night. I needed some time alone to reflect on the conflicting ideas that were muddling up my mind, so I thought I'd stay on the porch for a little while and try to reorganize my thoughts.

I closed my eyes and allowed my mind to connect with my surroundings. It was an amazing feeling, having even partial control over this extraordinary power. This ethereal connection with nature was incredibly comforting. The trees, the calm waters of the pond, the air, even the sound of the crickets among the undergrowth were somehow soothing to my tumultuous mind.

I was finally beginning to feel better when the sudden presence of a strange and almost negative energy rattled my concentration.

"Hey," Damian called from behind me. "You all right?"

"Yeah." My tone was cold. "What's up?"

"Everyone will be ready in about thirty minutes," he said, uncharacteristically friendly. "The girls are just packing some necessities for the trip."

"Yeah, well… I'll be ready."

"Listen," he began. "I know we haven't seen eye-to-eye since we met. But I want you to know, that doesn't mean I don't appreciate what you're doing." He walked toward the newel post I was leaning against. "I guess what I'm trying to say is, um…" he trailed off, but managed to continue: "I'm sorry." He turned to me and offered his hand for a shake.

I stared at his hand for a moment before I met his shockingly sincere haze and sighed, letting go of my defensive attitude towards him. I pushed myself off the post and shook his hand firmly. "Apology accepted."

"Great!" he said, with a big smile on his face. "So…" he stretched, resting his arms on the porch railing, his eyes peering into the dark night, "How bad do you think it's going to get?"

"Bad." My tone was ominous.

"Come on!" He slapped my arm in a cheerful manner. "We have to have optimism and faith, right?"

I chuckled sardonically. "You don't understand," I said. "You're talking to the ultimate geek. Optimism and faith don't fit into any of the equations in my head. When I see a problem, I run the numbers and opt for the variable with the highest probability."

"Ouch!" he jeered. "That sounds cold. Did you run the numbers when you stormed into the Lab, looking for Yvette?" He sounded just like a trial lawyer then, trying to turn my words against me. He was good indeed.

"No," I confessed. "I didn't have anything to lose then."

He turned to me, leaning on his side, his elbow against the rail. "But all that changed the moment you found her, didn't it?" His eyes scrutinized my reaction, making me feel like I was sitting on the witness stand. I turned my eyes to the night sky, ignoring his rhetorical question, knowing that my face reflected the answer. "Yeah," he said, turning to the night again, "maybe one day I'll be able to run the numbers, too." He turned around and walked away, stopping right at the door. "But not tonight," he added, turning his eyes back to me. "Not as long as she needs me."

"I know," I admitted. "That's why I'm still here. Because I know how irrational love can make us. In my case, it was worth every dumb decision I made." I shared a hopeful smile with him.

"We're going to get her back, Damian." My tone turned serious again. "I promised."

He nodded, a wistful smile on his face. "You're a good man, Victor. It's a pity our paths crossed here and not under more favorable circumstances. You're someone I'd be proud to call my friend."

I smiled. "Likewise."

Coming back to Denali's cabin was no longer part of the plan, so we packed as many provisions as we possibly could. Sarah brought some canned food, water, and medical supplies, while Yvette packed the camping gear she'd found in the cabin's garret. Damian, on the other hand—despite my firm disapproval—insisted on bringing as many guns as he could. In the spirit of keeping the peace, I let him bring them. After all, if everything went according to plan, we'd be in and out of that place long before anyone needed to discharge a firearm.

"Victor!" Sarah called. "We're ready."

I took a final look at Denali's place, swallowing the Gordian knot my guilt had created in my throat, and said, "Thank you, Denali." Then I slung my backpack over my shoulder and turned around. I jumped into the truck bed with Damian, letting Laura and Yvette ride in the front with Sarah, who we had picked as our designated getaway driver. I tapped on the window and gave her a good-to-go signal. She shifted into gear and took off.

None of us had the strength to look back.

Our first stop was the ferry terminal, where we dropped off Laura. Strangely, she had been the only one who had survived the procedure without any adverse side effects. And not only that, but her original condition seemed to have been cured as well. Perhaps we saved her just in time, which gave me an incredible feeling of accomplishment. At least one of us was going to make it out of this damned place alive and well.

Laura was nervous, but happy to finally be leaving. Sarah gave her a few last-minute instructions, along with some money she could use to get home. Yvette gave her a tight hug and wished her well. "Take care," she said, still sitting in the cab of the truck.

"You too, sweetheart," Laura whispered maternally, and got out of the truck. She walked toward the terminal, looking back and waving over her shoulder every two seconds. But then she stopped and pondered for the longest moment, her eyes to the ground. She looked up as if with a sudden insight and turned, calling my name.

I jumped out of the truck bed and ran to her. "What's wrong?" I asked, watching her smile for the first time.

"You get to see her again!" she blurted.

"What?"

"You don't need to be sad," she said, holding my hands, her eyes filled with hope. "You get to see her again," she repeated, as if convinced of her own words. "Don't let your sadness turn you into something you're not."

"I-I don't understand," I muttered.

She leaned toward me and whispered in my ear, "You even get to see her dance." She quickly moved away, letting go of my hands, smiled, and ran towards the terminal. "Remember," she called over her shoulder, "Don't be sad!"

I returned to the truck, staring blankly into space, trying to find some meaning to Laura's words. But I found myself musing to no avail. "What did she say?" Damian asked as I jumped back into the truck.

"Beats me," I muttered, sitting on the bare truck bed, pondering on whether Laura had really survived the procedure without any consequences—or if she'd been the smartest one of all, keeping her new talents a secret. And if so, to whom was she referring? Yvee, or someone else?

I guess I'll find out, I told myself.

Chapter 13

Tragedy at the Warehouse

THE ROAD AHEAD was as dark as the ominous future that had awaited us at R.C. Labs. But in our own ways, we all seemed determined to do our best to achieve what we believed to be our last mission against the man we'd once thought was our last chance for survival. I reiterated to Damian that my goal was to get his wife out of there by using the element of surprise—via wits rather than force. I reminded him that the success of this operation depended on our ability to maintain cool heads, no matter what happened.

I understood that this was easier said than done, but the last thing we needed at this point was another bloodbath like the one at Damian's cabin. Damian didn't argue with me, but he didn't agree to anything either. He just sat there in silence, leaning against the cab with his arms wrapped around his knees.

Eventually I realized that he wasn't even paying any attention to me; he was listening to a conversation taking place in the cab.

I'd been so busy with my own thoughts that I'd forgotten completely about Yvette and Sarah being alone together in the cab... and they were apparently having a very engaging conversation. Sitting with my back against the tailgate didn't allow *me* to hear anything. Damian, on the other hand, seemed amused by their repartee. At one point, he even pressed his ear against the sliding glass to try for clearer reception.

"What the hell are you doing?" I asked him, annoyed.

"Shhh!" he hissed, finger to lip. His brows puckered in surprise then, as if he'd just heard something of great interest. "Wow!" he exclaimed, finally leaning away from the glass. "You just missed a very interesting chat."

I narrowed my eyes in disapproval, giving him nothing but silence. "What?" he demanded; an annoying grin on his face. "Aren't you going to ask me what I heard?"

My silence continued. "Oh! I see," he realized, letting out a sarcastic snort. "A goody-goody Boy Scout like you probably thinks eavesdropping is an evil thing, right?"

I smiled at his taunt. "Information from third parties can often be... misleading," I said, feeling it was my turn to taunt. "Even a sleazy shyster like you should know that."

He broke into laughter. "You really don't like lawyers, do you?"

"Nobody likes lawyers, Damian. Let's just say that I've seen how you guys take advantage of easily misconstrued information in order to manipulate the system—without even caring what's right or wrong." I flashed him a sarcastic smile.

"Right..." he drawled, a wry tone in his voice, "The good ol' debate about what's right and wrong." He mused for a long second. "It's useless, you know?"

"What is?" I asked, intrigued.

"Trying to separate the two," he said.

"Not in my book."

He chuckled, a mixture of sadness and irony on his face. "You'd be surprised to see how easy it is to vindicate a wrongdoing when you know it could save someone you love, Victor. And if it does... then how can *that* be wrong?"

I sat quietly as he elucidated his own justification of evil. "Motivation and purpose," he declared. "They both cling to our own personal viewpoints, which in turn determines what's right and what's wrong... what's good and evil." He smiled at me, as if he'd just won a debate. And although I know I could have argued this radical conclusion, instead I found myself pondering its disturbing logic.

"So," he said, returning to our previous conversation, "Do you want me to tell you what I heard or not?"

I smiled. "Well, let me ask you this... Is it something that I'll be able to find out for myself if you don't tell me?"

A mischievous smile curved his lips as and nodded his head. "Yeah, probably."

"Then I'd rather wait."

"Suit yourself," he chuckled, leaning back against the cab.

We both remained quiet for the rest of the ride.

***

Sarah's plan consisted of using an unpaved road she knew connected the Lab's warehouse to one of the main highways. The road had never been finished, so it lacked surveillance and security. No cameras or guards would learn of our presence once we'd reached it. It was the perfect infiltration point, as well as the perfect getaway. Once inside, Damian would approach the entrance to the warehouse, where a single camera was used to check the outside of the overhead door. There, he would deliberately give away his presence, which we hoped would bring Dr. Walker out to negotiate, giving his keen desire to acquire Yvette.

There were two strategic points in our plan: a utility shed between the warehouse and the road, where Sarah would have the truck running and ready to go, and a lamppost thirty feet away from the overhead door—the only source of light in that part of the facility. Yvette was to wait behind the shed for Damian's signal. Once his wife was sent out for the trade, he would call Yvette, who would walk towards the warehouse to complete the swap. When the moment was right, I was to smash the light on that lamppost using my telekinesis, leaving the meadow in darkness, which we hoped would cause enough commotion for us to move in closer. Sarah then would drive the truck to the 'swap spot' and have everyone jump into the truck bed before bolting for our exit.

If you think this was a crazy plan… you're right. It was.

It got darker as we approached the unfinished road, with no more markers or lights guiding our way. We heard nothing but the crunch of the gravel being compressed by the tires of our truck. Sarah drove as quickly as she could with the headlights turned off, while Damian readied two guns to take with him. One was a loaded .38 Smith & Wesson Special, which he tucked behind his back. The other was a Glock 9mm, which for some reason he unloaded completely. He even checked the chamber twice just to make sure it was empty. Both weapons were concealed by the mid-length jacket he was wearing. I was just about to ask him about the unloaded gun when Yvette slid the rear window wide open. "Get ready, guys. We're almost there."

"I'm ready," Damian assured us, stone-faced. He zipped up his jacket, and got ready to jump out. I too readied myself, giving Yvette a quick nod. I felt like my heart was about to jump out of chest, but I tried to project a steady serenity. After all, I was the one asking everybody to keep a cool head.

Sarah pulled over to the edge of the road, amid some trees. We were now about 300 feet away from the warehouse entrance—and yet we seemed completely invisible to them. Every element in the surroundings was playing an essential role in creating the perfect camouflage. The full trees shrouded us, and our black truck merged perfectly with the dense darkness of the night. The lamp I was supposed to burst with my telekinesis illuminated the portion of the meadow where we were planning to fake the swap; and just as we expected, there wasn't a guard in sight. The coast was clear for Damian to make his surprise entrance. Not knowing how Damian had reached the warehouse without tripping all the alarms in the place was going to be our first jab to their senses.

I jumped out of the truck and shook Damian's hand. "Good luck," I said quietly.

"You too." His brows knitted in a heartfelt expression as he put his free hand firmly on my shoulder. Words seemed to come hard for him. "Victor..." he began with some difficulty.

"Hey," I stopped him. "Tell me over a beer when this is all over, all right?" I tapped him on the shoulder and smiled.

He did the same, then turned and walked swiftly into the meadow.

Yvette quickly took his place in front of me to wish me luck. Her eyes seemed relaxed, as if she had nothing to worry about. My eyes, I'm sure, were expressing the complete opposite. But a soft touch of our hands was enough to erase any doubts about what we felt at that moment. The same strange shock of energy that had allowed us to share our feelings before struck us again when we felt each other's touch.

Yvette's beautiful blue eyes opened even wider, as if she'd just been shocked by my doubts about this crazy stunt. I held her hands up in front of me and smiled, trying—unsuccessfully—to hide my fears. "Don't worry," I said. "This *will* work. And everything will be just..." My voice betrayed my lack of confidence at the end.

"Shhh," she stopped me, pressing her finger against my lips. "You don't need to pretend with me, Victor. I know what you're feeling." She shook her head and laughed. The expression on her face held a mixture of amazement and confusion that—somehow—seemed to make her happy. "I don't know how," she said, tightening her grip on my hands. "But I can *feel* you... And it's okay to be scared. I am too." Her voice seemed to become more profound with every word that followed. "You don't need to feel responsible for what happened to Denali, or for what may happen tonight. You've done nothing but care. And that's what matters, Victor. I'm sure your Dad would be very proud... I know I am." Her beautiful lips sealed her heartfelt speech with the most captivating smile I've ever seen.

I suppressed my tears and pressed her hands firmly against my chest. "Can you feel past my fear?" I asked. "Can you?"

She closed her eyes and sighed, trying to indulge my unusual request. Her bee-stung lips curled again, this time with a victorious grin. "Yes!" she said. Her eyes opened, glazed with a coating of tears that didn't leave her eyes. *"And I love you, too."* Her voice was almost breaking by then.

"I won't let anything happen to you." I said adamantly. "I promise."

"A*hem!*" Sarah cleared her throat behind us. "We better get into position," she advised.

"Right," Yvette answered quickly, throwing a glance over my shoulder. She turned back to me and ran her fingers through my hair and kissed me like only she knew how. *My God!* I exclaimed in my head. *Is it really possible to love someone so much? Is it right?* My heart literarily hurt at the thought of losing her. The truth was that loving her so much scared me. Yvette Montgomery had become my reason for existence—my reason to fight that evil growing inside of me. I knew that as long as I had her, my heart would never give up on goodness, on life, on her love.

We finally let go of each other with a reluctant look on our faces and turned away. Yvette walked cautiously towards another small shed in the middle of the meadow, while I went back to the truck where Sarah waited behind the wheel, her expression unreadable. I shut the door and watched Yvette hide behind the shed, her back against the wall. A familiar touch pulled my concentration away from her, if for only a few seconds. "Relax," Sarah whispered, her hand over mine. "She'll be fine, Victor. She's stronger than you think." Her comment somehow soothed my edginess.

"I know," I replied, really meaning to say: *Thank you.* My tone made it sound like I had, and she nodded as if she understood. I turned my eyes back to Damian, who was taking his time walking through the meadow, as if picking his way through a minefield. Yvette was waiting for him, peeking out from behind the shed.

Suddenly, I realized I hadn't let go of Sarah's hand, and that we had unconsciously begun to fidgeting with each other's fingers. I stopped, embarrassed, without letting go. For some reason, I thought it would be rude for me to withdraw my hand first. Awkwardly enough, Sarah kept fiddling with my fingers, her eyes fixed straight ahead. "Sarah?" I called in a whisper, but she didn't react. "Are you okay?"

Her eyes suddenly blinked and her fingers stopped. She looked down at our hands and withdrew hers gently but quickly. "I'm sorry," she said, her face tomato-red. "I guess I'm a lot more nervous than I thought."

"Hey!" This time I reached for her hand, taking a firm hold on it. My eyes searched her emerald greens. "You don't have to be." I chuckled softly. "I don't know how we wound up together in this mess, or why, but I'm honored that life has given me the opportunity to meet the bravest woman in the world." She rolled her eyes, unconvinced. "Hey, you know I wouldn't dare hike another forest, or climb another mountain, without having you there to pull me back up, right?"

She burst out laughing. "We do make a great team, don't we?" she said, a fond glint in her eyes.

"Yes we do," I agreed. And though I smiled, my voice was sincere.

She turned her eyes back to Damian, who was just a few steps away from the security camera's field of view. "All right, then!" she exclaimed, squeezing the truck's steering wheel tightly with both hands. "Let's do this! Are you ready to bust that lamp?"

"Yes, I am," I assured her, igniting that spark that connected my mind with my surroundings. The ethereal ramification grew rapidly, reaching farther and farther, until it allowed me to feel every inch of the aluminum fixture that encased the tempered glass of the lonely lamppost in the meadow. The light that emanated from it had a warm color, a deep yellow hue that blanketed a small portion of the meadow, giving it an eerie, somber look—a perfect match for my current frame of mind. This light also exposed the overhead door that marked the entrance to the warehouse. Damian finally stopped fifty feet away from the door, close enough to be detected by the security camera. All part of the plan, of course.

"Walker!" he yelled at the top of his lungs. "*Walker!*"

Security didn't take long to notice the unexpected trespasser. The big silver rollup door began to rise just a few moments after

Damian let out his angry shouts. Two guards came out of the warehouse, pointing their rifles at Damian, who immediately raised his hands. The profound silence of the night, along with my amplified sense of hearing, allowed me to make out Damian's exchange with the guards. "How the hell did you get in here?" one of them demanded, approaching him cautiously.

"Easily!" Damian said, showing his hands. "I'm not armed... But I'll only surrender to Dr. Walker himself. Got it?"

The guards stopped in their tracks and looked at each other.

The voice of our nemesis emerged from the shadows of the warehouse. "It's all right, gentlemen. I'm sure we don't have anything to worry about." Dr. Walker strolled out of the shadows and into the light. "I doubt that Mr. Black would put his wife's life in danger by trying to pull a fast one on us." He smiled, stopping at the threshold of the enormous overhead door, two more guards behind him. "Well, well, well. It's good to see you again, Damian. How are those seizures of yours? Gone, I suppose. Along with those vicious headaches, am I right?" Damian stood quietly for a second, staring at him. "What? Don't I get a thank you?"

"Where is she?" Damian demanded.

"Of course." Walker taunted. "The counselor wants to get straight to business, yes?" Dr. Walker signaled the guards to stand down. Damian lowered his hands. "Then I should ask you the same question, Damian. Where's the girl?" Walker's tone changed drastically with his last question, from jeering to grave.

Damian took a couple of steps forward. "I want to see my wife first!"

"How about this?" Dr. Walker countered. "You show me you really have Ms. Montgomery, and I'll let you see your wife. Deal?"

Damian hesitated for a moment, then looked back over his shoulder and signaled Yvette.

"No, no, no!" I whispered aloud. "That's not part of the plan!" Damian should've waited until his wife was in sight.

"What's happening?" Sarah asked, sounding worried. She could see them at this distance, but was unable to hear them like I could. She might as well been watching a silent movie, until my undivided attention to what was happening made her understand that it wasn't the same for me.

Yvette began to move slowly from behind the shed. Her body language showed all the uneasiness that she must have felt. Damian gestured for her to hurry. Soon, Yvette was standing under the somber yellow light I was supposed to destroy. Damian grabbed her by the elbow and pulled her closer to him.

"Good!" Walker smiled, pleased. "You brought her with you. That makes things a lot easier for me, Damian. Thank you."

"All right," Damian said, "she's here. Now, show me my wife."

Walker signaled one of the guards behind him, who ran inside the warehouse and disappeared around a corner—but not before flipping a light switch that turned on a fluorescent light above Walker's head. The gloomy white glow gave us a dull view of the interior. The two-story warehouse contained countless crates with the logo *R. C. Labs* stamped on them; they were stacked all over and under frameworks of steel grating. On the right stood a large cylinder rack, stacked with oxygen tanks. I also noticed a fairly large collection of steel reinforcement bars, the kind that are tied in place prior to pouring a concrete floor. They were stacked in a rack behind Walker. *Probably leftovers from the road work*, I thought. I couldn't make out what was on the left side of the massive storeroom; the weak fluorescent light couldn't get past one of the huge crate-filled frameworks, which cast a large shadow over the room.

Walker turned back to Yvette and Damian and spoke. "At last! The final piece of the puzzle… How are you, my dear?" His eyes fixed on my Yvee, who was imprisoned by Damian's grip. "I'm *so* glad to have you back unharmed. It was rather unwise, the way Victor took you out of here. He could've gotten you killed."

"What do *you* care?" Yvette snapped angrily. "You've been trying to kill us all ever since we arrived!"

"Oh, no," he argued. "Not *you*, young lady!"

"Oh, really?" she jeered. "And what's so special about me?"

"You have yet to understand your importance, Yvette," Walker said, almost gently. "Your new powers are the key to unraveling the greatest mystery of all. You and you alone can help me find the answers I've been looking for."

"Powers?" Yvette scoffed in disbelief. "I didn't *get* any powers, you crazy old bastard! Victor and Damian are the ones whose lives you've ruined!"

"Ruined?" Walker protested. "Hardly! I merely awakened their minds to a larger world, a world in which power is not measured by limits but by desire."

"Bullshit! What about the side effects? The dark energy that's turning them into something they're not?"

"Is it really?" Walker asked, "Or are they simply being suborned by their own personal desires? Regardless of what you think you know, this *evil*, as you call it, cannot enter their minds without an *invitation*. It's like a drug, you see? One you *choose* to take. One that you become more dependent upon the more you use it. And yet, it's still a matter of choice. The real problem here is that it's in our nature, as human beings, to crave power. The more we feel it, the more we want it. And Damian here has tasted this power, haven't you, Damian?"

Walker's gaze slid over to the lawyer, who seemed increasingly uneasy. "Yes…" Walker murmured, with an ominous smile on his face. "You *have* felt it!" His voice almost hissing, he continued, "The limitless power of this mysterious force that now dwells inside your mind… It makes you want to exceed all boundaries, doesn't it? All those petty social constructs like morality, guilt, and regret… It makes you feel *free*, doesn't it, counselor? I suspect you're craving your next taste even as we speak."

Damian couldn't hide his feelings—the confusion on his face, the anger in his eyes, the anxiety in his breathing, all connected by an overpowering fear that was beginning to get the best of him.

"It's a trick!" I whispered hopelessly, knowing that my words couldn't reach his ears. "Don't fall for it, Damian! Just stay calm."

Walker turned his attention back to Yvette. "I'll bet Victor is craving it too." He smiled at her...and something, possibly her expression or just the way she moved, gave him pause. He narrowed his eyes and began to scan the meadow, as if looking for something—or someone. "Which reminds me... Where *is* that troublesome boyfriend of yours?"

"I took care of him!" Damian answered, shaking Yvette roughly by the arm. I knew it was just part of their role-playing. Walker needed to think that I was gone in order for this to work, and Damian was just telling Yvette to go along with it without actually saying it. She groaned, straining against his grasp. I didn't know my little ballerina could be such a good actress, but from what I could see of his expression and detect of his vitals, Walker was buying the whole thing!

"Well, I have to say I'm impressed, Damian," Walker complimented him. "But you don't have to trouble yourself with *her* anymore." He signaled the two guards in front of them to take Yvette.

"Back off!" Damian raised his hand in front of the guards. "The girl isn't going anywhere until I see my wife." The two guards stopped again and swung their heads back toward Dr. Walker. He nodded immediately for them to stand down. "What are you going to do, Damian? Kill *more* of my men?" he sneered.

"Don't tempt me! You have no idea what I'm capable of."

"On the contrary, counselor, I know *exactly* what you're capable of. Don't forget that it was *I* who made you what you are now." Walker held Damian's eyes with a defiant glare.

"Stop!" Yvette cried, trying to calm the stressful situation. She knew as well as I did that if Damian lost his temper the whole plan would go down the drain, and many lives might be compromised. "No one is going to die because of me. I won't allow it!" She wrenched herself free of Damian's grip, but stayed by his side.

"Yvette!" Damian scolded her.

"I'm here, Dr. Walker!" Yvette gestured with opened arms. "I'm not going anywhere! Just let Damian's wife go and I'll come quietly... No one needs to get hurt."

"I'm glad you feel that way, my dear." Walker agreed, turning toward the dark side of the warehouse, where the guard who had left before was bringing someone out in a wheelchair. It was too dark to make out who, but we all assumed it was Damian's wife. The guard wheeled her toward Dr. Walker, who was standing before the shadow-casting steel framework. A cold shiver ran though my spine at that moment. I couldn't understand why, but all my senses grew cold and erratic, as if something awful were about to take place... and I knew there was nothing I could do to stop it.

And yet none of my newly acquired senses could have warned me or prepared me enough for what happened next.

Walker pushed the wheelchair out of the shadows and into the light, revealing a hooded woman handcuffed to the chair's armrests. She was barefoot and wearing a hospital gown similar to the one I'd worn during the procedure. Damian went ballistic the moment he saw her. Although he couldn't see her face under the black hood, he recognized the wedding band on the woman's ring finger. This was indeed Damian's wife. "Sonya!" he called. "It's me, baby. I'm right here. Everything's going to be okay now."

But Sonya didn't respond.

Walker stepped hastily from behind the wheelchair. "All right," he barked, "enough of this! It's time to hand over the girl, Damian." Once more, Walker signaled the two guards to seize Yvette. They re-aimed their weapons and began their approach.

"All right, you!" one of them shouted. "Step away from the girl!"

"Back off!" Damian threw him a furious scowl, raising his hand toward the guards, but they didn't stop. No longer able to contain his anger, Damian finally unleashed his rage upon them. "I said *back off!*" he shouted, making a thrusting motion with his fist that send the two guards flying fifteen feet across the meadow, to land back first against a concrete wall. They dropped unconscious to the ground, cut and bleeding. The two behind Dr. Walker reacted immediately, raising their weapons and stepping in front of their boss, acting as human shields. They were just a second away from opening fire on Damian when a sharp order from Walker made them stop on the spot. "Hold your fire! I need the girl alive."

Damian pulled Yvette violently in front of him, imprisoning her in his tight grip. He then pulled the concealed Glock 9mm from his waistband and held it against Yvette's head, ordering her not to move.

"What the hell are you doing?!" Yvette cried out, stunned and scared.

"My wife!" Damian demanded, "Or I'll blow your precious little science project's head off! And I believe you *know* that I don't lack the conviction to do so!"

"What the hell is he doing?" Sarah echoed Yvette, distressed as she watched the confusing scenario unfold.

"Bluffing," I said quickly, remembering how Damian had purposely emptied that particular gun prior our arrival. I understood then why Damian hadn't said anything to anybody. He wanted this to look as real as possible, in order to intimidate Walker, and trick him into giving up his wife first. Damian now had a bargaining chip.

"Get ready to move this truck," I alerted Sarah. "Floor it the moment I tell you to."

Sarah propped her hand over the shifter and waited, her eyes fixed on the meadow.

"Why don't you just put the gun down, Damian?" Walker stepped forward from behind the guards. "Like the girl said, there's no need for anyone to get hurt."

"Sonya!" Damian called, purposely ignoring Walker's attempt to persuade him. "Are you hurt, baby? Come on, talk to me!" He was becoming extremely anxious, and so was I. "What's wrong?" His angry eyes swung toward to Dr. Walker. "Come on! Take the hood off her."

Walker hesitated. "NOW!" Damian demanded furiously, pressing the gun harder against Yvette's temple.

Walker stood next to Damian's wife and began to remove the hood. Damian waited anxiously to finally see the face of his beloved. Besides my own experience with Yvette, I've never known anyone as passionately in love as Damian. But his passion morphed into horror the moment the black hood was finally removed.

Sonya's head hung loosely to one side, exposing a large surgical scar on the side of her partially shaved head. The incision curved in a 'U' shape cicatrix that stretched from her left temple all the way up to her hairline. Her eyes, although opened, were fixed on nothing, and drool streaked her chin.

Damian's face paled at the sight of this travesty of the person he loved the most. His guard dropped, along with the 9mm he had pointed at Yvette's head. "Sonya?" he breathed in complete dismay, too shocked to respond or react. He dropped to his knees and began to sob. "What have you done to her, you bastard?" he cried.

"Oh, that, "Walker said unctuously, "I forgot to tell you. Your wife insisted on knowing what had happened to you, so I figured the only way that she'd truly understand was by letting her experience it for herself. Unfortunately, her brain absorbed too much dark energy, making her, well… far too difficult to control. I was forced to intervene surgically." Walker gently stroked Sonya's head while Damian sobbed. "The procedure I performed on her makes her more obedient. She now responds only to my commands. Would you like to see?"

"You bastard!" Damian cursed between sobs, disheartened by the pain he was feeling—a pain that I was able to sense despite the space that separated us, like a thorn jabbing into my brain.

"Victor, what do we do?" Sarah whispered. I heard her, but I couldn't answer. I couldn't even swallow the knot that had suddenly built in my throat.

Dr. Walker leaned over the wheelchair, his lips inches away from Sonya's ear. "Sonya?" he called. "Won't you say hello to Damian?" Damian looked up and realized that Sonya was indeed responding to the sound of Dr. Walker's voice. She slowly lifted her head and began to look for him with bulging eyes. Another sharp shiver ran down my spine when I realized that her eyes didn't resemble the sparkling hazel that I remembered from her photograph, but the unnatural gray that had been haunting me in every mirror ever since I felt the evil change come upon me. Sonya had turned completely to the side of evil, and she was now under Walker's control—a combination far too grave for me to ignore. I needed to do something, and fast. I kept running the numbers in my head, but with every alternative I sought only one answer: Yvette. I needed to get her out of there.

I was about to tell Sarah to step on the gas when a sharp sense of danger spiked in my hyperawareness, making me turn once again to the gloomily-lit meadow. My eyes began to scan the field, looking for the source of what had alerted my hypersenses, but it was Yvette's warning cry to Damian that pointed me in the right direction: "Damian, look out!" she shouted at the top of her lungs.

One of the guards Damian had thrown against the wall had just come to, and he was pointing his sidearm at the lawyer. I saw Yvette trying to get Damian off his knees and out of the way when I heard the gun fire. Yvette and Damian both fell abruptly to the grass.

"That's it!" Sarah snapped, revving the engine. Her shimmering green eyes turned to me, looking for concurrence.

"GO!" I shouted. Sarah stomped her foot on the gas pedal as I thrust my hand into the air, connecting my mind to the lamp's tempered glass, which vaporized with one swift clench of my fist. The fluorescent above Walker's head went as well. A myriad of electrical sparks showered down upon the field, like a drizzle of fire that gave the meadow one final burst of light before plunging it into darkness.

Sarah raced the lightless truck across the field, heading straight toward the spot where Yvette and Damian had fallen. The truck kept bobbling up and down over the uneven surface of the meadow, making it difficult to maintain control, yet Sarah managed to keep it going in an unwavering beeline without missing her target destination—when suddenly, the bumpy ride came to halt... Or so I thought. Then I realized we hadn't stopped at all: I had merely entered that slow-motion trance in which I was able to see, with fine detail, everything transpiring in my surroundings.

The trance that occurred only in the deadliest of situations.

First I saw Damian, getting up from the field. His eyes were no longer teary, his stare no longer sad. He had turned all his pain to anger, his sadness to vengeance. If there was a threshold between us and our inevitable transformation, Damian had certainly reached his own personal borderline. He stood up and pointed his grabbing hands toward the guard who'd shot at him. The guard got to his feet to try to fire again, but his efforts were truncated before he could even lift his gun.

Watching what happened next, through my slow-motion trance, made it seem all the more gruesome. Damian took control of the guard, who was standing fifteen feet away from him, and tilted the man's head ninety degrees to the side. He began to flex his finger in the air, as if kneading an invisible piece of soft clay. This began to gradually increase the angle of the guard's tilted head—or at least, that's how I perceived it through my trance. The guard screamed in pain and desperation as he tried frantically to stop his neck from straining any further. But all his efforts were futile. His neck finally snapped, causing his desperate hands to drop and dangle at his sides, like a puppet whose strings had been suddenly cut.

The body began to fall as Damian turned his wrath toward Dr. Walker, who cowered behind his two personal guards as soon as he realized Damian had zeroed in on him. His eyes glowing bright yellow, Damian ran toward the warehouse, leaving Yvette lying defenseless on the ground. It wasn't until then that I realized she'd been wounded by the bullet intended for Damian. My slow-motion trance ended abruptly at the realization, returning my perception to its natural speed.

The next thing I saw was the dashboard, hitting me straight in the face. A blaze of blue and purple stars flashed across my eyes before I could open them again. When I did, I realized it had been the sudden drop of the truck's front end into a yawning pothole that had brought our race to an abrupt and unexpected end. I turned my disoriented head toward the driver seat, looking for Sarah. A trickle of blood dripped from her brow—apparently from bumping against the steering wheel—

yet she seemed all right, just dazed. My eyes darted back to the warehouse and I saw Damian running decisively towards his enemy. He barged into the warehouse, thrusting his open palm forward into the air, like a football player ready to strike an opponent standing in his way.

The guards who shielded Dr. Walker raised their rifles and took aim. Damian switched his focus to the guards; with one upward movement of his hand, he lifted one of them from the ground and tossed him aside, as easily as a normal man would toss away a crumpled piece of paper. The discarded guard crashed noisily against the cylinder rack, knocking loose several oxygen tanks, which fell and rolled across the cement floor. The guard slid to the floor, unconscious and no longer presenting a threat.

His partner, however, took advantage of this two-second-window of opportunity to lock onto his target. Damian tried to raise his hand again toward the second guard, but it was too late. The guard opened fire, wounding Damian severely. The left side of his body was pierced by multiple high caliber bullets; I saw crimson blotches bloom on his leg, arm, and shoulder. He collapsed to the floor, groaning in pain, yet he still found the strength to drag his wounded body to the threshold of the overhead door and lean up against the wall.

I got out of the truck as fast as I could and ran to Yvette. She was lying on the grass, her hands keeping pressure tightly on her left thigh, face as white as paper. "Yvee!" I kneeled on the ground next to her.

"I'll be all right," she gasped. "You need to help Damian. He'll die if you don't."

"I need to get you out of here!"

"Victor!" she countered fiercely, "We can't leave him!"

"I have her!" Sarah appeared out of nowhere, placing Yvette's arm around her neck. "Let's go," she said sternly, helping Yvette to her feet as she groaned in pain.

I looked back to the warehouse and saw Dr. Walker screaming into a walkie-talkie, calling for reinforcements. It was just a matter of seconds before the whole place would be swarming with soldiers. I knew there was no time to think; if we were to survive this, I had to move quickly. I let my instincts take over and tapped into my power, trying to pull energy out of the air and myself so I could limit the potential draw on the dark energy. Suddenly, my breath came in puffs of white frost as I ordered Sarah, "Get back to the truck and get it out of that hole! I'm going to get Damian!"

I turned and ran toward the warehouse, reaching out with my shield, trying to erect it around Damian's half-dead body. The guard who'd shot Damian was standing over him; he'd reloaded his weapon, and was ready to finish the job he'd started. Walker screamed at him to shoot—when suddenly something unexpected happened.

One of the steel reinforcement bars that lay next to Damian's wife flew out of the stacked pile like a guided missile, piercing the guard's back and running him through; it stopped abruptly when it hit the weak wall I'd managed to erect around Damian. Mortally wounded, the guard dropped his rifle and clutched futilely at the half-inch-thick beam that protruded from his chest, before collapsing dead to the floor.

The shock of the scene made me stop in my tracks, close enough to be seen by the creator of my evil side.

"Victor!" Walker exclaimed, thinking that I was the one who had avenged Damian. But the truth is that I could never have brought myself to do something like that. Even Damian, who had already taken lives before, seemed as stunned as I was about the rebar piercing the guard; obviously, he hadn't done it. But if neither of us had done it, then who...?

That's when my eyes swung over to Sonya, and I realized that Damian had been avenged by his own wife. Walker's control hadn't been as complete as he'd thought. Sonya had developed the same telekinesis abilities Damian and I now possessed, and had used them against Walker to save her husband's life. Realizing this, Dr. Walker spun and ran towards the exit door up the stairs in the back of the warehouse.

"*WALKER!!!*" Damian shouted at the top of his lungs, his volume amazing for a man obviously mortally wounded. Walker stopped just a few steps away from the door, turned around, and threw a hateful scowl at him, as if saying: *This isn't over yet!*

But it wasn't over for Damian and Sonya, either. "If we die, you die, you son of a bitch!" Damian yelled furiously, pulling out the loaded .38 Smith & Wesson Special that he'd kept tucked in the back of his waist. Damian pulled the trigger several times as Walker wrestled with the doorknob. His final shot hit a spot on the door close to Walker's face. I'm not sure what it was; it could've been fragments from the shattered door or the bullet itself, but something bounced up and hit Dr. Walker in the face. His hand jerked up to cover his eye as blood began flowing profusely. Screaming like a girl, he managed to yank the door open and disappeared through it.

Damian's hand dropped to the ground, along with the empty revolver, the barrel still smoking. "Sonya..." he called, stretching his hand toward his wife. But they were at least fifteen feet apart.

Sonya's blank stare slid over to Damian. And though reflecting pure evil, her eyes still flickered with a faint spark of humanity. "K-K-Kill me..." she whispered feebly.

"No," Damian choked out between sobs. "I can't."

A shout stopped me before I could take another step forward: "Freeze!" a soldier ordered me from behind. Hands up, I turned slowly and saw him standing there with his rifle aimed at me, ready to shoot. I took a quick look around, and saw that least a dozen soldiers were surrounding the meadow. Two of them were covering Sarah and Yvette, who'd never had the chance to make it back to the truck.

I folded my hands on my head in surrender—when the situation suddenly turned for the worse. Another steel bar flew right past me, only inches from my head, and flashed through the soldier standing behind me. Eyes wide, I spun and watched him fall dead to the ground, even as more of these steel bars began to zoom through the cold, dark meadow, piercing and killing every single soldier in sight. One of the last surviving soldiers zeroed in on the origin of the silent missiles and began to shoot wildly into the warehouse. Meanwhile, I dropped to the ground and yelled to Sarah and Yvette to do the same, while Damian dragged his limp body behind a wall, looking for cover.

One of the first shots fired hit one of the stray oxygen tanks rolling across the floor. Unfortunately, this tank was too close to one of the platforms-supporting beams—the one casting the shadow over Damian's wife. When the bullet hit the tank it exploded, not only dismounting the supporting beam from its foundation but also imprisoning poor Sonya in a mess of broken crates and metal that twisted around the wheelchair to which she was handcuffed. The entire platform of steel grating then began to collapse with a slow but awful inevitability, brought down by all the enormous crates that it held on its second level. Ton of wood and metal were an instant away from crushing Sonya when I did the unthinkable: I jumped back to my feet in the middle of the hell of gunfire and ricocheting rebar and connected my mind swiftly to the platform to stop its collapse.

As I connected to the beam, like I'd done before with other objects, I felt an immediate strain on every muscle in my body, immediately realizing that the weight of the crates was beyond anything I could control. Pain exploded in my head as I counterbalanced the massive weight, which brought me to my knees. Yet somehow I managed to stop it just in time to save Sonya, who despite our dire situation wouldn't stop attacking the soldiers. The soldiers, on the other hand, kept shooting blindly into the warehouse, missing her every time. The same broken crates that were now imprisoning her were also acting as a barricade against their attack.

A sudden, sharp prick in my shoulder almost made me lose concentration. Whatever it was, it hurt like hell—like a mosquito on steroids, which instead of sucking on my blood had injected me with hot lava. I wondered if one of my veins had burst. But I didn't have time to worry about it; I hung on grimly until one of the soldiers shot into a crate labeled FLAMMABLE in the back of the warehouse.

A small explosion followed the shot, along with a chemical fire that began to spread, quickly, through the entire place.

"Damian!" I called desperately. "I can't hold it any longer! You have to get Sonya out of there—now!" Damian began to drag himself toward Sonya, leaving a thick, dark red trail behind him as he crawled across the floor.

A disturbing silence made me realize that the gunfire had stopped, finally, and that Sonya was no longer launching lethal steel stakes at everything that moved. She had killed them all...and yet her blank gray eyes wouldn't stop scanning the gloomy field, looking for more of them to kill. I followed her eyes until they stopped and narrowed, as if locking on a new target. I looked over my shoulder and realized her glare had focused on Sarah and Yvette, who laid side side-by-side on the ground, arms clutched over their heads. But why would she feel any hostility against them? She didn't even know them.

But I guess she didn't have to. The answer was right in front of my face—or should I say, on Sarah's shoulder. The insignia '*R.C.*' displayed on her arm patch had caught Sonya's attention as well as her desire to kill, and she was now ready to continue the job.

Damian stopped dragging himself across the floor when he saw three more of the steel construction bars being levitated out of the stacked pile. He turned his eyes to the meadow, frightened and confused. "She's aiming at the girls!" I yelled to Damian. "If she launches those bars, I won't be able to stop them without letting go of the platform!"

"NO!" Damian shouted, "Don't you let go!" Damian turned to Sonya then and tried to reason with her. "Honey... Baby, please! Listen to me. They're not the enemy. Listen to me... Sonya!" But all his pleas were unheard. Damian failed to realize that the person sitting in that wheelchair was no longer his wife. She was just the outer image, the shell, of the person who he once loved—a shell filled with nothing but evil, revenge, and a death wish.

"Yvette! Sarah!" I called over my shoulder. "Don't move from where you are!" I figured I had a better chance of stopping those bars if I knew exactly where they were. In those few seconds I realized I had to make a choice... And then suddenly, Roger's words rumbled inside my head:

'What you call the future is no more than a destination based on your choices. There are as many as the numbers you keep running in your head. Yet in your case, there's only one, no matter what choice you make.'

"Sonya!" I called out desperately. "Please! Don't do it!"

But she just scowled and launched those bars with the full force of her hatred.

Like a splash of cold water inside my brain, my slow-motion trance kicked in once again, allowing me time to try to find equilibrium within this chaos. But deceleration or not, what happened next happened too fast to control or stop.

The three bars approached in a triangle formation—an effective way to cover any miscalculation Sonya might make. This shot was not going to miss Sarah. On the contrary, it was going to kill her, and anyone around her, in this case my already-wounded Yvee. No time to run the numbers on this one; there was only one thing I could do, hoping it would work as well in real life as it did in my head...

I let go of the platform as soon as I saw the bars pass by me. A desperate yell from Damian reached my ears, but I paid no attention. I spun around, aggressively, with the intention of making a full 360° turn in order to get back to Sonya and stop the platform once again. I followed those bars with a glare as soon as I began my spin, my hands clutching the air, trying to gain control over the deadly steel. Sarah and Yvette cringed in slow motion, closing their eyes and tightening their hold on each other, as if they were waiting hopelessly for the end. I yanked my hands toward me as soon as I felt my mind's final connection to those bars, which came to a sudden stop in midair, radiating their lost kinetic energy as heat—just a couple of feet away from the faces of the two people who mattered the most to me in the world. Then I let go of the bars, which dropped straight to the ground in a noisy clatter of steel-on-steel, and continued my spin back to my point of origin—Sonya.

I could see Damian trying desperately to stop the falling platform using his powers. But he was too weak, and the platform far too heavy. I thrust my hands in the air as I completed my 360° spin and aimed at the platform again. My mind connected to the giant beam even faster than expected... But wait! Something was wrong! An overlooked variable from the equation I'd never had the time to run in my head had made it impossible for me to stop the platform. The 1.23 seconds that it took me to complete the spin had been time enough for the platform to build momentum, making the entire structure feel twice as heavy as it had before. I fought with all my strength to keep the platform from falling, my head, and upper body pounding with pain, until something suddenly *snapped* inside my right shoulder. The excruciating pain wrenched a scream of agony from me, and even then, I tried to hold it up the platform—but it was too late.

The platform finally gave in to gravity, coming down hard. Sonya was crushed instantly by the colossal collapse, before the eyes of her beloved husband. *'NOOO!!!"* a painful, bereft cry burst out of the deepest corners of Damian's soul. "SONYA!"

I got to my feet, my vision blurry, and began to stagger towards the warehouse. I found myself clutching my shoulder, which I suddenly realized was bleeding profusely. The injected-lava sensation that I'd had felt earlier had been a wayward bullet lodging itself in my deltoid. As I got closer to the warehouse, I saw that the chemical fire had spread beyond containment. It was only a few feet away from reaching the cylinder rack, the one filled with oxygen tanks.

"Damian!" I called, reaching the threshold of the overhead door. "I'm sorry... *I'm so sorry*—"

"Get away from me!" he growled furiously. A steady stream of tears flowed down his ravaged face. "Get away!"

"Damian, I can't even begin to imagine what you must be feeling right now," I said weakly. "But we can still make it out of here. Let me help you. Please!"

"Sonya…" Damian sobbed over the wreckage, pressing his head against the rubble that had buried his wife. "Sonya! Sonya! *Sonya!* "He continued his disheartening call, knowing too well that he would never hear an answer again.

"Come on, Damian." I knelt next to him, and tried to get him back on his feet. But he wouldn't let go of a piece of metal that stuck out of the debris. "Come on. You have to let go."

"Let go?" He captured my eyes with a livid glare. "Like you did?"

His words made a horrible feeling of guilt overrun my heart, making my voice betray my growing conviction of the truth. "S-s-she tried to kill Sarah and Yvette, Damian… I had to stop it. Believe me. I tried to save her."

"Save her?!" A push of his hand mixed with some of his telekinesis sent me five feet away from him, making me land almost flat on my back. "You… you killed her!"

His face began to shudder, along with the rest of his body, his eyes bulging with hatred, as if they were going to pop out of their sockets. His breathing became frantic, a desperate wheezing that made his eyes roll to the back of head. Then I saw what I thought to be the first tangible manifestation of evil incarnate. A gaseous cloud of red vapor spawned out of thin air, like an unearthly apparition summoned by Damian's wrath. I watched this bizarre energy whirl around his head for a second or two, before it began to force itself in through Damian's eyes.

I didn't know what else to do but watch. I was perplexed, stunned by the unnatural event. Then I realized that this visible force was not trespassing any boundaries; on the contrary, it was being absorbed willingly by Damian himself. The more he absorbed it, the more his eyes changed toward the sulfurous yellow I'd seen before. Soon, the mysterious red vapor was gone, inhaled completely by Damian's brain.

"Damian?" I called warily, watching as his breathing returned to normal. His eyes were solid yellow now, so yellow they glowed, an enhanced version of the wicked hue that had driven him to kill more than a dozen men back at his cabin.

And now they were glaring right at me.

"She's dead because of you," he rasped. "Because of *them*," he added, looking over my shoulder, locking his hateful glare on Yvette and Sarah.

"Damian, you need to calm down!" I warned, getting back on my feet.

Despite his wounds, Damian found some way to stand, regaining his feet even before me. "You are going to die," he said, raising his hand toward me, curving his fingers as he had when he snapped the guard's neck, "And so are they."

Invisible iron bands curled around my throat, cutting off my air supply as I instinctively reached for my neck. But my choker was incorporeal; there was no way to fight it with my hands, so I decided that my only chance was to fight fire with fire. "Stop!" I managed to gasp, thrusting my hands forward toward

Damian. It felt like someone had put a hot poker in my shoulder and twisted, but my effort caused him not only to release me but staggered him backwards a few feet. After I dragged in a deep, sweet breath of oxygen, I declared, "I am *not* going to fight you!"

"Then you *are* going to die!" he said, thrusting his hands forward again. He left me no choice but to do the same.

As our wills collided, an incredible, almost tangible energy field filled the space between us, warping reality, but stopping our attacks from reaching each other. I held my ground as well as he did, even as I felt him pushing harder and harder. My arms began to quiver. Damian's changeover was complete, and he was more powerful than ever. I had no idea how long I could hold out against him, or even if I could. I knew for certain, though, that if I were to let go, I was as good as dead. So I tried to hold it up as long as I could. "Damian! I am *not* your enemy," I gasped. "Stop!"

"You *killed* her!"

"Damian, please!" This was my last plea before I noticed that the fire inside the warehouse had reached the cylinder rack and was cradling the oxygen tanks. At that moment I felt as if the force field between us was at the same state as those oxygen tanks—ready to give.

A sudden and powerful explosion sent me flying into the air, extinguishing my consciousness like a sharp exhalation extinguishes a match. I never knew what went off first: the burning oxygen tanks on the cylinder rack, or the burning desire for vengeance that Damian had unleashed upon me. But what I did know was that I couldn't blame him for hating me, and as I went down in the dark I wished desperately that I'd had a few more seconds before the explosion—not to understand what really set it off, but to have the opportunity to say *I'm sorry* one last time.

Chapter 14
Spit and Image

A COLD SHIVER forced opened my eyes, followed by a desperate gasp that echoed inside my head, as if my brain had suddenly taken over the role of my lungs. I tried to understand where I was, but it was too dark to recognize the place. All I could make out was the corner where I was crouching—cold and frightened, with no memory of how I'd gotten there. Groping blindly in the dark, I forced my eyes to adjust to the shadows. But it wasn't until my hands stumbled upon the fourth corner of this dark place that I realized I was trapped inside a room—a room with neither windows nor doors. A room filled with nothing but silence.

Terror flooded me then, because I got the feeling that I wasn't alone in this place, that *something* was sharing these tight quarters with me, and that for some reason, it didn't like me much. I groped my way back into a corner and crouched warily against the wall, hoping that this feeling was nothing but paranoia... But soon, the echo of a half-familiar voice proved it to be otherwise.

"Do you *really* think ignoring me is going to make me go away?" The tone of the voice made me shudder, not because it alerted me of its presence but because it frightened me to think that I knew who it belonged to. "You don't look so good," the voice added. "In fact, you look *exhausted.* Maybe it's time for you to let go of your stubbornness, and embrace the truth."

"What... *Who* are you?" I asked tentatively.

"That is a question, I'm afraid, that only you have the answer for." The *thing* reply to my query in a casual manner, yet it gave me no real answer. I sat quietly in a corner while my eyes scanned the shadows, looking for the source of the voice. But despite the fact that my hypersenses were in full flood, I found nothing.

"You seem confused to be here," the voice noted, as it began to take on solidity in the opposite corner of the room, a silhouette mirroring my crouching position on the floor. "I guess that's the difference between you and me. You look for answers that aren't there, whereas I don't bother."

"What is this place?" I asked warily, as my eyes finally adapted to the darkness. My tormentor was still just a dark shape across the room. "How did we get in here?"

"See?" The man in the corner laughed, his face still shuttered by the shadows. "My point exactly. Though honestly, the nature of your inquiring mind is not your *real* problem. I think it's your choice of inquiries that throws you off."

"What the hell does that mean?" I snapped, frustrated by his cryptic talk.

"It means you're not asking the *right questions!*" he retorted angrily, leaning towards me in the darkness, as if offended by my insolence.

"I'm sorry," I apologized quickly. "I meant no disrespect."

"Of course you didn't," he scoffed, leaning back against the wall. "You're spineless, weak. You've always been weak." His tone became angrier and more contemptuous with every word he uttered. "Your weakness disgusts me!"

I ignored his snide comments and tried to go back to the previous subject, realizing that it wasn't in my best interests to upset the only person who might know what was happening here. "What did you mean by saying I'm not asking the right questions?"

"Hmm…" he sighed, "Well, isn't it obvious? The real question is not *how did we get here?* But *how do we get out?*"

"Okay, then, how do we get out?"

"Funny you should ask," he remarked flippantly. His leather-soled boots made a loud thud on the floor as he got to his feet in a single jump. He took a few steps and stopped in the middle of the room, peering over his head. I didn't see the point; it was too dark to find the ceiling, if there even was one. "There's only one way to get out," he said, "but you may not like it."

"Tell me."

He made me wait for a few seconds; his loud breathing was the only thing that disturbed the dead silence that engulfed this prison cell. Then he turned to me and blurted out his terrible truth: "One of us needs to die."

"What?!" I demanded, jolted to the core. "What kind of answer is that? Why?"

"You keep asking the wrong questions, *Victor*." He spat my name as if it were an obscenity.

"Stop toying with me," I said steadily, "and just tell me who you are."

"I've told you," he said, his voice beginning to distort into a malevolent growl, "*That* is a question that only *you* have the answer for." The change in his voice made the hairs on the back of my neck stand on end. I leaned backwards and began to climb up, cautiously, against the wall, until I was finally back on my feet.

"Tell me, then," I said. "Are you here to…?"

"…kill you?" He finished the question I was dreading so much to ask. "Not exactly. You see? It's complicated… I can't kill *you* any more than you can kill *me*." His voice suddenly returned to normal. "But one of us can persuade the other to forfeit his life."

"That's ridiculous!" I countered. "Why would I persuade anybody to do something like that?"

"*Argh!*" he complained, turning violently toward one of the walls, where he landed a powerful punch that echoed through the entire room. I felt a sharp pain in my head, as if he had punched *me* and not the wall. "You're asking the wrong questions!"

"All right, relax!" I said calmly. "Let's pretend I'm stupid. I'm definitely ignorant, so teach me. Tell me, then: What's the right question?"

He turned back to me, and although I still couldn't see his face, I could feel a powerful scowl being thrown in my direction. "You want me to formulate your own questions?" he asked, with an audible stain of disgust in his voice. "That's so typical of you, *Victor*. But I'm afraid that this time, you're going to have to run the numbers all by yourself."

His words made me realize that this person—whoever he was—knew a hell of a lot more about me than just my name. I decided to do what he said and analyze the problem at hand. So—I ran the numbers. "You want out," I noted swiftly, "But you're stuck. You need me dead, but you can't kill me... thus, the real question is: what would be strong enough to persuade *me* to give up on my own life?"

"Finally!" he remarked jeeringly. "And do you know what that is?"

"No. Why don't you tell me?"

"Love," he said quickly, as if afraid of the word.

"Love?"

"Yes, *love*," he reaffirmed, "That irrational emotion that leads to personal attachment towards another human being; an emotion that, in your case, is the only thing that would persuade you to give up your own life." He paused just long enough to catch his breath and continued. "And I know you well enough to know that you *would* sacrifice yourself in order to save someone you love."

"Of course I would," I said matter-of-factly. "So now we're talking about a trade?"

"In a way," he responded thoughtfully.

A long uncomfortable silence followed his words, forcing me to probe for more information. "Well, would you care to elaborate?" I pressed.

"Something is coming, Victor," he said, "Something unforeseen, something that'll put the last two people you care about in this world in grave danger."

"If that's true, you just gave me a reason to persuade *you* to give up your life."

"So *you* can get out?" he asked with a mocking chuckle.

"I need to protect them."

"That's just it!" he said, leaning against the darkest corner of the room, making it even harder for me to try and see his face. "You can't!"

"What the *hell* do you know about what I can or can't do?" I snapped angrily. "You don't even know me! You're nothing but a hack who knows my name, that's all!"

"I'm afraid I'm a lot more than that, Victor," he countered. "And I *do* know your limitations when it comes to your delusional views of morality—which have only gotten people killed so far. I also know that this so-called conscience of yours is your greatest weakness, which will eventually not only be your undoing, but will result in the deaths of everyone around you."

His words were like jet fuel tossed onto the flames of my blazing fury. But my strong desire to know the truth forced me to maintain my composure and allay my craving to run across the room and swing my fists into his face. He laughed as he said, quietly, "I, on the other hand, do not bind myself to petty ideals of altruism, thereby giving me an advantage over people like you... Not to mention that my powers have grown far beyond yours."

"Powers?" I breathed in shock.

"What you really should be asking yourself right now is, *what's the right thing to do?*" He began to pace around the room as he delivered his disturbing argument. "If you set me free, I will not only keep Sarah and Yvette safe from the danger that is upon them, but I will also avenge the deaths of the people who have fallen in vain, from your father to Denali and Sonya. Even Damian, not to mention all the nameless others whose bones are rotting in unmarked graves scattered over R.C. Labs' grounds."

He stopped in the middle of the room and sighed. "If you don't let me live, I'm afraid you'll be condemning the girls to death, along with everything they've fought for. And you, my friend, will be back in this cell with *me*. I'm not threatening you; I would never hurt either one of those girls." He paused. "There! I've given you the facts. Now it's up to you to choose the variable with the highest probability. You or me, Victor?"

"You're insane!" I exclaimed in shock. "Even if I choose to believe that an imminent danger is stalking Yvette and Sarah, I would never trust someone like you to protect them!"

"Did you just say *someone like you?*" He seemed amused for some reason.

"Yes! It's obvious you hate me. You've made that point perfectly clear. Why would you care what happens to the people *I* care about?"

A long-suffering sigh escaped his lips before he began to speak again. "I don't hate you, Victor," he said quietly. His voice was almost sad now. "How could I? In fact, I've often wished I could be more like you... just like I know you've wished to be more like me sometimes." He paused again. "But that will never happen. It can't."

A cold shiver ran throughout my entire body. "Who *are* you?" I demanded, though I was beginning to suspect the truth.

He ignored my terrified question and continued. "Our nature is to be opposites, sharing nothing but one thing. Do you know what that is, Victor?"

A morbid feeling compelled me to probe. "No," I whispered. "Tell me."

"Affinity," he hissed sharply. "We share the same inclinations towards the same things."

"What are you saying?" I asked puzzled.

"I'm saying that I love them, too, Victor. And just like you, I feel the conflict of loving them both at the same time." His words made my heart stop, sending an icy shudder racing up and down my spine, as if my subconscious were truly beginning to understand the meaning of his twisted words. "I suppose that's another difference that sets us apart," he added in a ponderous tone. "I'm not afraid to admit my emotional dissonance, which in my case only supports my claim. And my strong commitment to keeping both of them safe, no matter what extremes I have to take."

Though I was beginning to dread the answer, I kept asking the same question. "Who are you?" But he kept ignoring me, as if my question had never left my lips, let alone reached his ears.

"And as for *trust*," he continued, "Sometimes all we can do is take a leap of faith... Isn't that right, *Victor*?"

'Who are you?' I demanded, edgier than ever before. *'Tell me!'*

A powerful quake shook the room, knocking us both off our feet. And it continued to shake us with such magnitude that it made it impossible for either of us to get off the floor. I could hear the walls cracking, like a walnut under the pressure of a powerful fist. With every splintering sound I felt an agonizing pain that stabbed through my head like an ice pick—or one of

Sonya's steel rebars. I applied pressure to my temples with the heels of my hands, like I used to do not so long ago when my headaches got the best of me.

I felt crack after painful crack. I thought my head was about to explode—until the quake finally stopped.

I opened my eyes and slowly lifted my head, to see that strange shafts of bright light were beginning to stream through the cracks in the fissured walls. I was relieved to see the light—relieved to discover that this dreadful darkness didn't continue beyond this room. The light was white and powerful, almost...cleansing. Yet the cracks where the light were entering were too narrow to illuminate the entire room, which—as strange as it may sound—made me feel safe.

I no longer wanted to see the face of the man I had to relinquish my life to.

"What... What just happened?" I asked, still shaken by the episode.

"We're running out of time," my mysterious cellmate replied, pacing nervously back and forth in the only corner still untouched by the light. "You have to let me *out*."

Then, driven by his trepidation, he strayed away from the shadows and walked right through one of light beams, which in its narrowed form created, from temple to temple, an unveiling eye-mask that allowed me to see, if only for one second, the intensity of his glare. A sharp knock of fear suddenly pounded my chest when I realized that I'd seen those eyes before. The color was pure gray, the same malevolent gray that had tainted my eyes when my anger and revenge had almost taken control over my volition. I stumbled backwards in fear and asked the same dreadful question, one last time: "Who *are* you?"

He lunged at me like a raging bull, wrapping his hands around my throat. "Let me out!" he demanded. "*Let me out!*" His hands tightened by the second.

I tried desperately to escape his grip, but he was strong— much stronger than I was at the moment. The ground began to shake again, this time crumbling down one of the walls behind me, flooding the room with a powerful white glare that finally shone upon the face of my oppressor. For a long moment, I couldn't believe, or understand, what I was seeing. This maddening reality couldn't possibly be real. The man with whom I've been speaking all this time, the man who had tried to convince me to forfeit my life for his sake, the man now choking me with all of his intense hatred...

...was me.

He was my own spit and image—and yet he wasn't. His unnatural gray eyes were filled with an anger and hatred I could almost taste, like a disgusting bile that was trying to invade all of my senses. His feathered hair was silver, the same dead silver that streaked my hair in an uneven patch above my forehead...and his inclination toward evil made him the perfect opposite of me.

Fortunately, his eyes were overwhelmed by the same light that had exposed his identity, making him turn away from the intensity of the glare. I took advantage the second he turned his head away, yanking his hands off my throat and delivering a powerful kick to his solar plexus that sent him sailing ten feet across the room and gave me the opportunity to turn and run toward the light.

"This isn't over, Victor!" he screamed furiously at the top of his lungs. "You can't run from me forever! Sooner or later, you're going to have to let me out! It's inevitable!"

I kept running toward the light, until I was no longer running, but floating bodiless in the comforting white glow: not in body, but in my own subconscious mind. I waited there patiently, until a familiar voice that echoed in the distance brought me back to reality...

Chapter 15
Laws of Physics

"VICTOR, COME ON, wake up!" Sarah sounded distressed. She kept speaking, and her voice grew stronger by the second—unlike the white light, which was diminishing into a soft yellowish glow that began to warm my eyelids. I tried to open my eyes once I realized I was reconnected to my corporeal self, but my eyelids just fluttered, as if refusing to wake up from a nightmare—a very *vivid* nightmare. When I finally did open my eyes, I saw a distraught green-eyed face break out in a smile of relief.

"Sarah?" I croaked feebly.

"Yes, I'm here!" she answered.

"Where... Where's Yvette? Is she all right?"

Sarah sighed, as if relieved to hear my voice. "She's lost a lot of blood," she said, "But she's going to be all right." Her eyes flew to my far left.

It wasn't until then that I realized I was lying on a bed, apparently in a motel room. Sarah was sitting on the edge of my mattress, while Yvette lay on the adjacent bed. She was asleep; I later learned that Sarah had administered morphine for pain, enough to knock her out for a good, long while.

"She was very lucky," Sarah said. "The bullet went through and through without hitting any bones or major arteries. I just had to stitch her up and gave her some pain medicine." She paused for a second, changing her tone. "You, on the other hand, had me worried to death!" She chuckled with a mixture of anxiety and relief. I narrowed my eyes in confusion. "You don't remember, do you?"

I shook my head silently.

"I had to extract a bullet from your shoulder, which caused an infection. You've been fighting it for two days." I was shocked to hear that I'd been out for so long. "Do you remember the explosion?" she asked.

"Vaguely," I said, still disoriented.

"When the oxygen tanks went off, the explosion launched you far out into the meadow. By the time I got to you, your heart had stopped. Yvette and I worked on you for the longest time before we brought you back." She cleared her throat. "For a moment there, we thought we'd lost you."

"Damian," I asked fretfully. "What happened to Damian?"

Sarah lowered her head. "He didn't make it, Victor. He was too close to the oxygen tanks when they went up."

I closed my eyes tightly, feeling an overwhelming sense of guilt. "I failed him," I said miserably.

"He was trying to kill you, Victor."

"I failed him," I repeated, holding back tears.

Sarah stroked my head. "Just try and get some rest, okay?"

"No," I disagreed, remembering what had just happened inside my brain. "We don't have much time. We have to get to your mentor, before my side effects become irreversible."

"All right," she conceded, a confused look on her face. "He gave me his address. But I'm afraid we can't get there by car, and we've already run out of money."

"Don't worry about money," I answered confidently, thinking about the settlement money I'd never used. "I have enough to go around."

After reaching for my backpack and dragging it over, I gave Sarah a credit card and asked her to arrange transportation to wherever we needed to go. She agreed and left, reassuring me she wouldn't take too long. Just a few minutes after she left, Yvette began to wake up. She turned and moaned in pain before opening her eyes. "Victor?" she called in a hoarse whisper.

"I'm here!" I answered eagerly, although it took me a minute to get out of my own bed—the pain in my shoulder was excruciating. I lumbered across the room until I reached the side of her bed, then sat on the edge of her mattress and ran my fingers through her hair. My touch elicited a soft moan that made her close her eyes and curved those sweet lips into a soft, pleasing smile, as if my mere touch had somehow abated her pain. But the fact was, a touch shared between us could do a lot more than that, as she reminded me the moment she opened her eyes.

"I love you, too," she said softly.

"Hey!" I complained playfully. "I'm supposed to say it first, you know?"

Her voice suddenly overloaded with emotion. "You did."

Despite her obvious pain, she grabbed me by the shirt and pulled me toward her bee-stung lips. My blood rushed faster through my veins, accelerating by the escalating rhythm of my enamored heart, just as it had the very first time under the weeping willow tree back at the Lab. The taste of her lips was definitely the nourishment my heart had hungered for all along—an aphrodisiac that was driving me absolutely crazy. And though we knew there were a thousand problems hovering around us, we decided to forget the world and get lost in our kiss.

My God! I really thought I could go on kissing her forever. And I could have if her caressing hand hadn't strayed from playing with my hair, to wander down to my neck and then go straight to my wounded shoulder, triggering a sudden jolt of pain that made me stop and groan like a baby.

"I'm sorry!" she apologized, biting her bottom lip—which I swear only drove me crazier. I cupped the back of her head then and mashed those fleshy lips against mine, as a highly uncharacteristic lust suddenly took control over me, plunging me into a deep ocean of ecstasy, in which I'd rather drown with her than resurface without her. I slowly began to caress her bare arm, brushing her soft, milky-white skin with the backs of my fingers, until my hand reached and cupped her delicate elbow. My mind then began to branch out, reaching an incredible resonance with Yvette's heart, which seemed to match the accelerated beat of my own. I listened to this hypnotic rhythm as I continued my search for Yvette's hand. I wanted to interlock our fingers like we'd done back in the meadow. So I kept gliding my fingertips along Yvette's forearm, raising tiny goose bumps on her skin along the way.

This was, without a doubt, the most erotic moment of my life up to that point. But more than that, it was a moment of tenderness and complete surrender, in which I realized once again that this woman was not only the love of my life, but from now on my sole reason for existence.

I finally found her hand resting on top of her bare thigh, which, I have to confess, only made me stray from her hand. Call it instinct, heat-of-the-moment, or simply naughtiness. But the truth is that I just couldn't restrain myself from gliding the palm of my hand over the side of her bare leg—so gently that I was barely touching it. Unfortunately, an oversight on my part was about to ruin the moment. It happened when, despite my gentle touch, my hand stumbled upon a thick dressing around Yvette's wounded leg.

Yvette's reaction was instinctive. "Oww!" she wailed, cringing in pain and dropping the hand she'd buried in my hair right onto my wounded shoulder again. I joined her painful cry, grabbing my throbbing arm. We both winced and complained for the next few seconds, and then we laughed in unison. "I'm sorry!" she apologized again.

"No, I'm sorry..." I trailed off, trying to snap out of the euphoric stupor I was in.

"I guess it's not safe for us to be this close right now, huh?" she said, blushing.

"I think you're right!" I laughed, stroking her head again.

**

After our intense yet painful romantic encounter, Yvette and I decided to behave ourselves and just talk over a cup of coffee, which Yvette managed to make with one of those funny one-cup coffeemakers often found in motel rooms.

We sat at a small round table near the window, where I decided to tell her about my horrific experience after the explosion. I emphasized that it could have been nothing but a nightmare, or a delusion caused by the explosion—hence the reason why I left out a few points from the conversation, like the fact that my evil counterpart had accused me of having feelings for Sarah. However, I did tell Yvette about the danger my dark twin had warned me about.

We spoke for hours, about many things: Denali, Damian, Dr. Walker, and even Sarah. But mostly, we talked about *us* and our plans. Yvette was firmly convinced I was going to be okay, and that our real story was yet to be written. And though I didn't share her blind optimism, I was beginning to feel like there was, indeed, a light at the end of the tunnel. I decided to put away my negative thoughts and began to embrace a more positive frame of mind.

I remember sensing Sarah's presence even before she even got out of the cab that had brought her back to the motel... and I have to admit that my mind not only alerted me of her approach, but jolted in happiness at the thought of having her near. This irrepressible feeling made me ponder again the words of my evil reflection. *Could it be true?* I asked myself. Could my gratefulness toward Sarah have developed into something more? If so, what was it—what was this feeling that brought guilt to my heart the moment I felt her? I knew it was more than friendship, but I couldn't allow it to be any more than that.

I turned my eyes to Yvette, and realized that whatever this feeling was, it would never be able to compete with the love I felt for her. The thought of hurting her, if only with my thoughts, crushed my heart into a million pieces. Yet the truth couldn't be concealed by denial, and the truth was that Sarah's presence *did* bring a warm feeling to my heart. "Sarah's back," I informed Yvette nonchalantly. She looked toward the door as the key turned in the lock and Sarah entered.

"Hey, guys!" Sarah said as she came in, setting a pair of crutches against the wall. Then she turned back outside and picked up a bunch of shopping bags that she juggled through the door and set on my neatly-made bed.

"What's all this?" Yvette asked, a smile on her face.

"These are for you." Sarah handed Yvette the pair of crutches. "I also got us new clothes"—her hands dug through the bags—"some toiletries, new bandages, pain medicine, an arm sling for Victor—oh! And, of course, some food!" She grabbed one of the bags and put it on the table. "I hope you guys like Chinese."

The smell that emerged with the steam was intoxicating. "Mmm!" Yvette beamed as she dug through the takeout boxes.

"What about transportation?" I asked, concerned.

Sarah pulled up a chair and put it in between Yvette and me, then grabbed an eggroll before she began. "It's all arranged," she said, taking a big bite. "We're taking a six o'clock charter to Juneau tomorrow morning." She paused to chew. "When we arrive, I'll call Sidney, my mentor. He'll tell us where to go from there."

"A charter?" I asked. "You mean a plane!? Can't we just take the ferry?"

"No," she said, annoyed. "It's a ten-hour ferry ride."

"And?" I urged.

"And the plane only takes one, Victor!" she answered, confused. "Besides, the tickets are already paid for. And they're non-refundable."

Yvette grabbed my hand, noticing my sudden anxiety. "What's wrong, Baby?"

"Nothing," I lied unconvincingly.

She closed her eyes then and tightened her grip on my hand, as if reading me with nothing but her touch...which was exactly what she was doing. "Aw, Victor," she said wistfully, opening her eyes, an empathetic smile on those precious lips. "You needn't be worried about how high planes travel."

"Is this what this is all about?" Sarah jumped in with an amused smile. "Your acrophobia? Don't tell me you're afraid of flying, too."

I scowled, trying to hide my embarrassment.

"You know about his fear of heights?" Yvette asked, almost suspiciously.

Sarah let out a loud snort. "Yeah! Can you believe, with an army on our tail, he froze like a statue at the edge of a cliff? I had to push him off into the river!"

'*What?!*" Yvette exclaimed, then joined Sarah in a fit of giggling.

I crossed my arms and took turns scowling at them. "Well," I said sarcastically, "I'm *so* glad my phobias amuse you both."

They laughed even harder.

After a few moments, Yvette caught her breath and said, "I'm sorry, Baby," trying unsuccessfully to suppress her laughter. "It's just *cute*, you know? You're so brave about everything else, and then...this. We're not laughing *at* you," she assured me, doing her best to look serious now.

"We're not?" Sarah asked, with a seriousness that only lasted for a second. She then broke out laughing again. Her contagious laugher infected Yvette, who soon joined her, even louder than before.

"That's it!" I snapped, getting up from the chair and striding angrily towards the bathroom. "I'm taking a long shower, a few of these pain pills"—I picked up the bottle of Demerol Sarah had brought—"and going straight to bed!"

Yvette blew me an apologetic kiss before I closed the door, which made Sarah stop laughing as she cleared her throat. "You shouldn't get those bandages wet," Sarah called casually. "Let me know if you need some help in there."

"I think he can manage," Yvette said quickly. "Can't you, Baby?" Her blazing blue eyes pierced right through me, as if in warning.

"Sure," I nodded with a smirk on my face, and closed the door behind me.

"I should take a look at your leg, then. Is that okay?" I heard Sarah ask Yvette.

"Sure. Thank you."

After the shower, it didn't take long for the powerful narcotic to take effect. After a few minutes I was in bed, drowsy and ready to pass out. I remember hearing the introduction to the news broadcast Sarah was watching on TV as Yvette climbed into my bed and buried her head in my chest... And then nothing.

***

An annoying buzz went off next to my ear, snatching me away from the first deep and undisturbed sleep I'd had in ages. I opened my eyes a slit, looked through my eyelashes, and noticed the glow of the alarm clock on top of the nightstand. The big, green digital numbers read 4:00 am. What a lousy time to set the alarm for!

As I tried to stretch, cursing the room's previous tenant, I realized Yvette was still cuddling under my left arm, with our entwined fingers firmly pressed against her chest—a sweet entanglement I wished I never had to break. Curiosity made me throw a quick look over to the adjacent bed, where I was hoping to find Sarah. But she wasn't there. There was no water running in the bathroom either, nor lights on over the coffee table.

An irrational anxiety filled me, a fear that something might have happened to her—so I closed my eyes and commanded my hypersenses to find her. My mind began to scan the place, starting with the melodic sound of Yvette's heartbeat. Beyond our room I sensed another couple next door, sleeping. I sensed the wind whirling outside the building too. I saw cars, lights, newspapers being blown by the wind in the parking lot. Soon I reached the front desk, and there she was, her heartbeat pounding as strong as always. I detected neither anguish nor anxiety in her breathing. It was fair to assume that no danger was present. She was merely checking out... what a relief!

A confused scowl startled me when I returned to myself and opened my eyes. Yvette had awakened and she had been studying me, apparently, since I'd begun my mental scan. The incriminating glare she was giving me now made her magnificent eyes almost glow in the half-lit room. "What are you doing?" she asked accusingly, as the annoying buzzing suddenly stopped—

"Nothing!" I lied unwittingly. Her question had caught me off guard.

She let go of my hand and scrutinized my face. "You promised you'd never lie to me, remember?" she reminded me, sitting up straight. Her eyes were almost sad now. "Don't start now, especially knowing I can feel what you feel with one touch."

"I'm sorry," I said quickly. "It's just that I don't want to freak you out with the things I can do now." I paused, watching her brows knit into another scowl, as if letting me know my apology wasn't going to compensate for the answer she was expecting. "Okay," I began, letting out a defeated sigh. "When I concentrate hard enough, my mind can connect with the things in my surroundings. That's how I can use my telekinesis. But it can also help me locate nearby objects or even people that are not in my visual field. So when I woke up and I—"

"When you didn't see Sarah, you scanned the whole place, looking for her," she interjected with an unexpected tone of understanding in her voice.

"Yes," I confessed. "I needed to make sure she was okay." Yvette's glare had disappeared, as if she'd felt the sincerity in my voice. "She's okay, by the way," I added. "She's just checking us out of the motel."

She sighed, as if embarrassed. "I'm sorry," she apologized. "I just, uh… I can't see specifics, you know? I can only *feel* things when I touch you… your fears, your worries… your love." Her voice hardened. "But just now I felt your yearning for her." She sniffed and shook her head. "And, I don't know, I guess I got a little jealous," she admitted, embarrassed, looking down at her fidgeting fingers.

I held her face in my hands, as if admiring a porcelain doll, and lowered my head to her eye level. Looking into her eyes, I landed a soft kiss on her lips and said, "How can you be jealous of anybody when you can feel how much I love you?" My lips barely parted from hers as I uttered the words. "I mean, you can *literally* feel it, can't you?"

She chuckled. "Yes," she answered quickly. "I guess I'm just scared."

"Of what?" I asked.

The earnest tone of her voice was as overwhelming as the wistful look in her eyes. "Of losing you," she whispered.

I held her firmly in my arms and matched her wistful eyes with the solemnity of mine, allowing my whole heart to show in every word that followed. "Yvee," I began. "Finding you... Finding that little girl I fell in love with as a boy, and see her transformed into a beautiful woman who has stolen my heart and soul as a man, can't be coincidence. It can only be fate. Loving you has given meaning to my life. And feeling your love has given me the absolute desire to live it." I paused, watching as her eyes dampened with tears. "I guess what I'm trying to say is that you couldn't lose me if you tried."

She threw her arms around my neck then and pressed her lips firmly against mine, sparking that mixture of tenderness and passion that only she could incite in me.

The sound of the door closing made us break apart. Apparently my connection with Yvette was powerful enough to monopolize all of my enhanced senses, which had allowed Sarah to sneak past my special radar and enter the room undetected. "Oops, sorry!" she said. "I didn't mean to interrupt... I thought you guys were asleep." Her reaction was sincere and almost nonchalant. "Anyway, I just checked us out, and I arranged for a cab to pick us up in an hour to take us to the airfield. So we'd better get ready." Her gaze slid over to Yvette. "I can help you get dressed...fix your hair maybe?"

Yvette smiled sincerely, as if a weight had been lifted off her shoulders. "Sure! That'll be great. Thank you."

Sarah helped her with her crutches and walked with her to the bathroom. I sighed with relief, feeling like everything was finally falling into place.

***

When the cab finally arrived I was ready, just waiting for the girls to come out of the bathroom. I stood by the door, wearing the boots and jacket I had inherit from Denali over a brand-new T-shirt and a pair of blue jeans. After letting the girls know the cab was there, I went ahead and loaded our stuff into the trunk and waited for them outside.

My jaw dropped when they walked out of the room. They had both fixed their hair and put on makeup; for a moment I thought I was looking at two models ready for a photo-shoot. And though they were wearing similar outfits, it was remarkable to see what a distinct and unique look each of them could display.

The contrast of Yvette's milky-white skin with her jet-black hair made her chiseled face stand out from the long and perfectly straight tresses that framed it. Sarah's naturally dark red curls, on the other hand, seemed almost alive, bouncing with every movement she made. But what dazzled me the most was how they had both enhanced what I'm sure they knew were their most striking features, which in both cases I can only compare with precious jewels: their emerald and sapphire eyes. Even the cab driver couldn't keep a quick "Wow!" from escaping his lips.

I opened the back door of the cab and complimented them both. I guess I thought a general compliment, as opposed to an individual one, would keep me from inciting jealousy between them. After all, they were finally getting along, and I wasn't going to be the one to tarnish their new friendship.

Once at Ketchikan Harbor, I caught sight of the single-engine floatplane that waited for us. Our destination: Juneau, where we were to meet Sarah's mentor, Dr. Sidney Palmer, the father of the R.C.-1000 serum and perhaps the only man on the planet who knew how to stop its horrific side effects—or so we hoped.

We were soon in the air, and after an hour of soaring over the impressive Alaskan landscape we finally began our landing in Juneau. The majestic mountains on the horizon not only caught my eye, but forced me to subdue my fear of heights and look out the window. The peaks were cloaked with forests of green fir trees, which shaped this natural work of art with an imperfect beauty. The summits appeared to reach the undisturbed sky, touching its overwhelming blue, while the mirror-like bay below reflected the exact twin of the exquisite scenery in its still waters, creating a greater view that was impossible to grasp with a single glance.

We docked in the harbor, near the Merchant's Wharf Mall in downtown Juneau. A woman on the dock seemed to be awaiting our arrival. She wore an elegant pantsuit and glasses. Her brown, medium-length hair fluttered in the wind as the plane engine began to whine down. She was very attractive, probably in her late twenties or early thirties, yet her light brown eyes revealed a wisdom you usually saw only in older people.

"Hello, my name is Dr. Yelena Ivanova," she introduced herself, with a handshake for each of us. "Welcome to Juneau."

"It's a pleasure to meet you, Doctor. I'm Victor Bellator. And these lovely ladies are Yvette Montgomery and Sarah Grey."

Dr. Ivanova nodded and turned back to me. "Dr. Palmer is very excited to meet you all. If you will please follow me, I will take you to him."

We grabbed our bags and followed her to her car. Calmly, Dr. Ivanova drove to the outskirts of town, where Dr. Palmer's hidden cabin was located. She was a careful and precise driver, and kept her eyes strictly on the road as she explained to us that this cabin/laboratory wasn't marked on any map, and that it was imperative that we keep its location a secret. We all agreed to do so, of course.

A man stood on the porch watching as we parked at the end of the driveway. He was slightly overweight and not much taller than me. The deep lines that creased his face reflected more than half a century of life, just as his doleful eyes reflected the intelligence and wisdom that one can only collect by perseverance and sacrifice. "Sidney!" Sarah called excitedly, leaping out of the car. She ran toward him, taking the stairs to the porch two at a time, and hugged him like a daughter would hug her beloved father.

Meanwhile, I helped Yvette out of the car and walked with her and Dr. Ivanova to the porch. Sarah made the introductions. "Sidney, this is Victor Bellator, and this is Yvette Montgomery—the last two survivors of the latest R.C.-1000 procedure. Guys, this is my mentor and friend Dr. Sidney Palmer."

"It's a pleasure to meet you. Dr. Palmer," I said, my hand extended for a handshake. "Sarah has nothing but the best to say about you."

He shook my hand. "Well, it's a pleasure to meet *you*, Victor... Yvette." He turned to her and shook her hand too. "Why don't we all go inside? We have a lot to talk about."

We spent the next three hours in the good doctor's office, talking in detail about what had happened to bring us there: My accident, Yvette's, our meeting with Dr. Walker, the procedure, my new abilities, what had happened to Damian and his wife, Dr. Walker's interest on Yvette, and even my inner-mind episode with my evil counterpart.

Dr. Palmer sat at his desk and listened patiently to every word we had to say. I was awed at how well he was taking the whole thing. Very little surprised him. After getting him up to speed, it was my turn to ask questions; I wanted to know the truth of it all. "First, I need to know why, Doctor? Why me? Why Yvette?"

Dr. Palmer interlocked his fingers over his desk and let out a heavy sigh before he began. "You and the others were carefully selected by Dr. Walker himself. Through R.C. Labs, he's gained access to medical records throughout the country, so that he can select ideal candidates for the R.C.-1000 procedure. Requirements were narrowed to patients with TBI—an unknown source of intracranial pressure—and most of all, plausible deniability of involvement—patients without strong community or family attachments."

"In other words," Dr. Ivanova added, "people no one would miss if they were never seen again."

"How did our particular condition fit in all this?" Yvette asked.

Dr. Palmer explained, "Some studies have shown that some patients with TBI have developed prodigious abilities after sustaining their injuries, such as enhanced sensory perception or photographic memories. Unfortunately, in the majority of these cases, the patients' higher cognitive functions were compromised by the same injuries, creating severe mental disabilities."

"Savant syndrome." My understanding of the subject escaped my lips in a near-whisper.

"Precisely!" Dr. Palmer smiled, seemingly pleased to have an educated audience—though compared to him, was little more than a layman. "I have to admit," he continued, "that I did become somewhat obsessed by the idea of finding the source of these hidden abilities in the brain, which compelled me to research every single case I could find. Then I realized I was on the wrong track; I was analyzing old data. So I began a new protocol of correlational research between patients with savant syndrome and recent victims of TBI. I discovered that three of the patients I was studying had suffered with a similar—if not the same—type of injury. And I'm talking about the same external force, type of impact, trauma, even location in the brain." He stopped abruptly and got up from his chair, seemingly troubled by his own confession. He walked towards a liquor cabinet and poured himself a drink.

"What happened to them?" My voice held a sense of urgency.

He walked back to his chair and sighed. "The first patient died a week after his accident. The second became permanently disabled, losing control of his motor and cognitive functions. He did, however, gain the inexplicable capability of predicting the weather—with extreme accuracy, I might add. At first, we thought that it was a coincidence, until he foresaw the exact time and location of a lighting strike. That really caught our attention." A rueful sigh escaped his lips. "Unfortunately, he used his own predictive abilities to end his life."

An awful silence followed his words as Dr. Palmer sipped his drink.

"What happened to the third patient?" Yvette asked.

Dr. Palmer took another sip of Scotch and explained. "The third patient not only survived his accident, but recovered from all his injuries except one... An unexplained intracranial pressure, which according to most doctors would eventually trigger a venous thrombosis and kill him." His words were now bringing up painful memories of my own diagnosis. "When I met this patient, he was suffering from severe headaches, uncontrollable tremors, and painful seizures. He had lost his family in the accident, and according to him, he had nothing left to lose."

Dr. Palmer shook his head with an expression of pity. "After running numerous tests, I came to realize that there was unusual neural activity in an isolated part of his brain. A concentration of once-dormant brain cells was now trying to fire. But something was somehow blocking them from doing so. I quickly compared his data with the second patient's, and discovered that these cells belonged to the same group that had been excited in our weatherman. This led me to believe that the cells that *did* fire up on the second patient were not only the ones responsible for his unexplained ability, but also the ones responsible for impairing certain regions of the prefrontal cortex, affecting his higher cognitive functions. This, in turn, led me to theorize that the third patient was in the middle of a neurological conflict between these rebellious new cells trying to fire up and his prefrontal cortex, which was sending signals to stop them."

"Do you really think that this… neurological conflict was the cause of the intracranial pressure?" Sarah asked.

"It was indeed!" Dr. Palmer exclaimed, "Which, of course, left the third patient which extremely limited options."

"What do you mean, Doctor?" I asked.

"Had the condition been left untreated, the intracranial pressure would have killed him eventually, just like it did the first patient." Dr. Palmer paused and glanced at Yvette and me. His logic troubled my resolve—because I understood then what our ultimate fate would had been if Walker hadn't gone through with the procedure that had cursed me. "So besides dying," Yvette asked, "What other options did he have?"

"A medically induced coma," Dr. Palmer responded, pouring himself another drink. "This would stop the prefrontal cortex from sending inhibiting messages to the newly-firing cells, allowing them to awake fully."

"But wouldn't that have left the prefrontal cortex vulnerable and exposed to these freak cells?" Sarah speculated. "I mean, according to your theory, these cells were the ones responsible for the failure of the second patient's higher cognitive functions, right?"

"Yes," he replied, "but you have to understand that I was just giving him options."

"With all due respect, Doctor," I interjected, "I don't think that waking up with a mental impairment should be a viable option for anyone. No matter how extraordinary you think their new abilities may be."

Dr. Palmer set his drink down and leaned over his desk, scowling at me. "Some people don't have any option at all, Victor. And I wanted to save his life." His voice seemed sincere.

"Did you?"

Palmer leaned back against his leather chair and let out another profound sigh. "After many failed attempts to stop these newly awakened cells from firing, I realized that this was Mother Nature at its best—a kind of self-defense mechanism. The human brain would rather destroy itself with intracranial pressure than allow these cells to fire. And these cells, which were never meant to be awakened in the first place, could never fire under full brain cognition. It was like the perfectly bioengineered booby-trap," he mused, his gaze wandering to the ceiling.

"What happened then, Sidney?" Sarah asked respectfully.

Dr. Palmer's eyes returned to us, as his face creased in a regretful frown. "I did what most of us scientists do. I tampered with nature in order to save a life. I created a serum with neurotransmitter-blocking properties in order to stop the prefrontal cortex from sending inhibiting messages to the newly awakened cells, which tricked them into believing there was no longer full brain cognition, stopping them from inducing further damage to the prefrontal cortex."

"Then what?" I prompted.

"Then, the secondary properties of the serum would locate the cells, and help them fire up when exposed to a controlled dose of radiation." He drank again. "Patient Number Three volunteered for this procedure. He was a very strong man, yet the procedure proved punitive to his brain. He slipped into a coma that lasted for three days. I was beginning to think I'd lost him. But when he woke up, with full motor and cognitive response, and with no remaining intracranial pressure, I thought I've done the impossible." A proud smile suddenly lit his face. "But the real surprise occurred two days after the procedure, when he tried to reach for his TV remote control—and the remote just flew straight to his hand. I mean, we were expecting an increase in cognition, yes. A new ability to play music, perhaps, or to sketch paintings or be able to resolve complex algorithms. Never in a million years would I have expected telekinesis." He chuckled and shook his head.

"The facts of his new condition reached the Department of Defense. And they, of course, insisted that I continue with my research. My project was fully funded and transferred to Ketchikan, Alaska. I believe they felt more comfortable with the isolation. That's when I came looking for Sarah. I knew I needed someone I could trust. I've known her since she was just a little girl; her father and I were like brothers. And when he

died, I promised I'd take care of her… like my own daughter."
He met Sarah's eyes and gave her a lovable smile. She
responded in the same way. "Besides, she's the most dedicated
student I have ever had the honor to teach. That's why I'm so
terribly sorry I have dragged her into this." Dr. Palmer's lowered
his head, staring at his desktop.

"You didn't know, Sidney." Sarah tried to comfort him.

"Wait a second!" I snapped. "Did you say Department of
Defense?"

"Yes."

"Well, that explains a lot," Yvette noted. "How they found
us. How they knew so much about us. And the military
personnel that have been after us."

"And the reason we can't go to the police." Sarah reminded
us.

"What happened to your patient, Doctor?" Yvette asked.

"He was transferred to R.C. Labs… where he was later
destroyed."

"What? Why?" Yvette asked in shock.

"He became aggressive, violent. The more he used his
abilities, the more he got lost in his rage—which eventually
made him too dangerous to be kept alive."

"So they put him down like a rabid dog." I took a deep
breath, and finally got to the point that had brought me to him.
"The change. What triggers it?"

"After this... unfortunate incident, I went back to the drawing board, thinking I'd made a mistake, and that the serum was creating this so-called side effect. But after a thorough analysis and more than a dozen procedures, we came to the conclusion that it wasn't the serum itself. The newly awakened cells weren't responsible for the abilities acquired by the subjects. They were merely conductors used to obtain the energy needed for all these preset abilities to work."

"Preset?"

"Yes," he said swiftly. "It seems that a countless number of paranormal abilities are buried inside the subconscious mind; however, they're useless without the appropriate energy to make them work. These freak cells, as Sarah has so eloquently put it, were disabled by nature or... by some higher power," —he frowned in disbelief— "to deny us access to such energy."

He paused and studied our astonished faces, then said abruptly, "You seem like an educated man, Victor. What's your field of study?"

"Physics," I said. "And mathematics."

"Then you just might be able to understand this better than anyone else. Do you remember the First Law of Thermodynamics?"

"Of course," I said taken aback. "Energy can neither be created nor destroyed. It can, however, change its form." The words flowed as easy as reciting my ABCs.

"Very good. Now, if this is true, then, we have an unlimited supply of energy all around us, just waiting to be transformed into whatever type of energy we need. Solar energy, kinetic energy, potential energy, possibly even zero-point energy from the vacuum, if that proves out."

"So what you're saying is that my brain is extracting energy from the atmosphere and using it to activate these abilities." It was more a statement than a question.

"Well...from somewhere, possible the atmosphere, possibly the zero-point energy I just mentioned. But yes, that's basically it."

"As fascinating as it sounds, sir, that still doesn't explain why Damian changed into a monster before he died. Or why my own anger is getting harder to control."

"No, it doesn't." Dr. Ivanova stepped in. "But in order for you to understand why a change occurs in the first place, you need to understand more about the energy that you are tapping into."

"Indeed," Dr. Palmer agreed. "Dr. Ivanova was actually the one who discovered the reason for the change, and she's been working with me in finding a way to avert it. You'll want to listen carefully to what she has to say. Please, Lena, go ahead."

She sat slightly on the edge of the desk and crossed her arms. "Would you mind reciting another physics law for us?" she asked politely.

"Sure." My brows knitted in confusion again.

"Newton's Third Law, please."

I exhaled heavily. "For every action there is an equal and opposite reaction."

"Yes, indeed." Dr. Ivanova's smile didn't reach her eyes. "Now, we have reason to believe that this volatile energy we've been talking about has an opposite counterpart—a dark energy responsible for the change in some patients after the procedure." Sarah, Yvette, and I were hanging on her every word. "We are just beginning to understand that there is a conflict between the newly awakened cells and the prefrontal cortex. As you have just learned, the activated cells draw this energy pervading our surroundings, whatever its source, directly into the brain. They do not discriminate between the types. But we have come to realize that the prefrontal cortex does. This part of the brain chooses which of these two energies is absorbed."

"How?" I asked.

"Through the emotions in play at the time," she replied.

I sighed, trying to register all this new information. "Okay, that makes sense. Walker has his ideas about the two types of energy, and we've already figured out that it was anger that was triggering these evil thoughts that have been threatening to overcome my volition. That's why I've been trying to control my impulses."

"And you've done an incredible job, Victor," Dr. Palmer assured me. "So far, you've been the only one with a will strong enough to delay the change this far."

"Delay?" I prompted. "What are you saying?" Dr. Palmer and Dr. Ivanova exchanged uneasy glances. "Is there a cure?" I demanded.

"Well," Dr. Ivanova began, "there is. And there isn't."

"What the hell does *that* mean?" I said angrily.

"Victor!" Sarah scolded me.

"It's quite all right, Sarah," Dr. Palmer said soothingly. "I completely understand his reaction." He turned to meet my glare. "Victor, you have to understand that we still don't fully comprehend the nature of these two forms of energy. However, we *do* have some good news... Lena?" He signaled for Dr. Ivanova to proceed.

"I have designed a new serum protocol that can inhibit the absorption of this dark energy into your brain—which, according to my calculations, should stop the change from occurring." Her words alleviated my tension, if only for a second. "Your new abilities, however, could still be triggered by what we choose to call white energy. That, Victor, is the good news."

"So, by implication, there's bad news as well?"

Dr. Ivanova took her time answering. Just as I was about to demand what she meant, she replied, "The bad news is that every time you used this dark energy to stimulate your abilities before, you poisoned your brain with it, making it susceptible to the change—predisposed, almost. And my new protocol can only inhibit the subconscious absorption of this dark energy, not its conscience absorption."

"I'm sorry, I don't follow." I shook my head in confusion. "What are you saying?"

Dr. Palmer took over then. "What Lena's trying to say is that if you concentrate hard enough, and if you're angry enough, you can still call upon the change voluntarily."

"Why in the world would I do that?" I countered in disbelief.

"In our last study," Dr. Ivanova continued her explanation, "we discovered that this dark energy is addictive, and its psychological and physical dependence more than *triples* that of heroin or crack cocaine. We also discovered that, for reasons still unknown, this dark energy can also increase the power of your abilities exponentially. You can see the problem here, I think." She paused and met my eyes expectantly. "This dark energy not only makes you dependent on its use, but it poisons your prefrontal cortex, altering your cognitive behavior, personality expression, decision-making, and even your social behavior. And since this cognitive distortion works with extreme negative thoughts, it can easily turn you into a psychopath."

"I understand the facts," I conceded. "What I still don't understand is why you'd think I would willingly choose that?"

Dr. Ivanova scrutinized my face. "Because you have had a taste of it," she said quietly. "And you *will* want more."

Chapter 16
Not a Goodbye

IN A SHOCKING confession, Dr. Palmer then admitted the real reason why he had allowed us to come to him. His intentions had never been to help us, but rather to meet the latest "abomination," as he put it, created by R.C. Labs. He left decorum far behind when he said that word, and I bristled at the implied insult.

But who was I to judge him? I myself was disgusted by the whole thing. All I could do was sit there and listen while he explained his total contempt for Dr. Walker and R.C. Labs. They had taken his idea of helping people and turned it into a Machiavellian plan to weaponize his patients' new powers, without considering the consequences of their actions. The reason that he'd left R.C. Labs—besides their unethical procedures and their lack of respect for human life—was because he'd finally realized that what they were dealing with was beyond the realm of science. He said, and I quote: "It frightened me." Then he concluded his thoughts with the most horrifying confession of all: the ultimate reason he had brought R.C. Labs' latest abomination to his lab was to kill it.

To kill *me*.

Our eyes met as he choked out these words, and although my reaction should have been different, I remained calm. I had my new abilities to thank for that. The truth was that I didn't sense any danger from either him or Ivanova; on the contrary, I felt safer than I had in days. Yvette, on the other hand, tightened her grip on my hand, interlocking her fingers tightly with mine. Her head pressed firmly against my shoulder as she glared steadily at Dr. Palmer.

I leaned my head over hers and waited patiently for his next move.

He just stared at us for the longest time, until Sarah sprang from her seat, frowning. His eyes met Sarah's glare and then slid back to us. "Lena?" he called upon Dr. Ivanova.

"Yes, Doctor."

"Ready the lab for immediate administration of the blocking protocol." A warm smile suddenly lit up his face. "I'd like to have our patient up and running as soon as possible."

"Of course, Doctor." Dr. Ivanova gave us a wholehearted smile before exiting the office.

Yvette could no longer suppress her tears, and began crying silently against my shoulder. Sarah, seemingly fighting a similar reaction, patted my back and gave me her beautiful dimpled smile.

Dr. Palmer got up from his chair and headed toward the door. Yvette got up grabbed him by the arms before he'd reach the threshold. "Thank you," she whispered. Her eyes were wide and glazed with tears, but I think it was the sincerity in them that nearly overwhelmed Dr. Palmer.

Dr. Palmer took Yvette's hand, his lips pressed into a line, and gave her a paternal pat on the shoulder. He reminded me of my Dad when he did that. "It's been a distinct pleasure meeting you both," he said in an unsteady voice. "I'm sure you'll be the ones to go the distance." He turned his eyes back to me. "Victor? I'll see you in the lab." He smiled once more and exited the office.

After an emotional moment with the girls, I finally found the strength to get up from my chair and head for the Lab. Sarah and Yvette held hands as they watched me go.

***

By the time I reached the lab, Dr. Palmer was ready, Ivanova standing next to him. Both wore long white coats and surgical masks, and there was a gurney just a few feet away from them, set at a forty-five degree inclination. Dr. Palmer asked me to lie down while they secured my wrists and ankles to the rails around the edges. Once I was locked down, Dr. Ivanova inserted an I.V. line in my arm, while Palmer loaded an injection gun with the blocking protocol. "This may knock you out for quite a while," he warned.

"Don't worry, doctor. I'm getting used to that."

I felt the warm serum enter my vein almost as soon as Dr. Palmer punctured the injection port of the I.V. line. Dr. Ivanova kept smiling at me as she placed electrodes on my chest. Seconds later, I was able to both hear and see my heartbeat, spiking on a monitor next to the bed. "You have to relax." Dr. Ivanova said firmly, pressing a button that began to move the bed into a horizontal position.

I stared at the ceiling with my heart filled with hopes and my head filled with fears. Soon, I began to experience drowsiness, and the room began to spin. The voices of my doctors became just a dull echo in my head. But I did, somehow, make out Palmer's last words before my consciousness faded: "Good luck, Victor."

Then, nothing.

***

I awoke in a cozy, comfortable bedroom. The surface beneath me was soft and fluffy, yet every muscle in my body hurt as if I'd been sleeping on a bed of sharp rocks. My head was spinning and my mouth bone-dry—yet my spirits had never been higher.

I was alive! And that was all that mattered to me at that moment.

As soon as the spinning in my head stopped, I tried to get my bearings. I sat up on the edge of the bed and tried to reorganize my thoughts and feelings. I remembered everything: R.C. Labs, Dr. Walker, Denali, Damian... And although I felt sadness about a great many things, none of them triggered the horrible thoughts and feelings I'd felt before. Hatred and revenge were no longer overwhelming desires; neither was the awful need to deliberately harm others. All of it was gone—erased from my mind. An uncontrollable mixture of tears and laughter soon took control over me, and I began to celebrate the triumphal recovery of my father's son. The good, forgiving man he'd once raised and was proud of was back, ready to reclaim his life.

In all my excitement, I also realized my arm splint was gone—and so were the bandages around my shoulder. My wound was almost healed, which made me wonder just how long I'd been out. The next thing I noticed was the I.V. line attached to my arm. I almost yanked it out when I tried to stand up. The line was connected to a half-empty bag of saline that had been hydrating my body.

At first I decided to wait for one of the good doctors to come in, but voices heard at a distance compelled me to jump out of the bed. After withdrawing the long plastic needle from my vein—clearly a stupid idea, as I had to quickly apply pressure to stop the bleeding I caused—I walked to the window and looked out. The most beautiful sunny day greeted me then. The sky was perfectly blue, not a cloud in sight. Majestic firs that spread as far as the eye could see surrounded a small meadow at the back of the cabin. That's where I found the sources of the two angelic voices I'd heard.

In a playful setting, Sarah was teaching Yvette how to fight. She was executing a 360° spinning kick, and Yvette was shadowing her movements. I was surprised to see my Yvee fully recovered and prancing around like that. Her beautifully sculpted body flowed effortlessly around the field as she spun over and over again, throwing her leg high into the air. Her version of the spinning kick seemed more like a choreographic ballet performance than a fighting strike, which was no surprise, given her background. Sarah's athletic body, on the other hand, made her kicks look like a sword cutting through the air.

The result would be a very dangerous hit indeed—yet it was indescribably sexy. They both made mistakes at one point or another, for which they pushed and taunted each other playfully. I laughed as I watched them kid around and laugh together, as if all our adversities were nothing but a horrible nightmare left in the past. My best friend in the world, and the love of my life—the only two people for whom I would and had put my life on the line—were now friends, happy and safe. I couldn't ask for more.

"Oh. You're up!" Dr. Ivanova chirped as she walked into the room. "You shouldn't have done that!" she chided, as she took hold of my arm and taped a piece of cotton gauze over my bleeding vein. I smiled at her and turned back to the window. She glanced outside. "Enjoying the view?"

"Yes, I am." My eyes were fixed on my two fighting angels rather than on the scenery.

"How are you feeling?" she asked with a warm smile.

I slowly turned to her, returning the same earnest expression. "Never better!" I grinned. "Seriously, I feel better than I have in years. Maybe my whole life."

"Very good!" After checking my vitals, Dr. Ivanova asked me to dress and prepare to come downstairs, where Dr. Palmer was waiting for me. Apparently, I had awoken right on schedule, and he was eager to follow up on his work.

"How long have I been out?" I asked.

"About three days." Dr. Ivanova noticed my disconcertion as I reached for my shoulder. "Don't worry," she said, "Dr. Palmer will explain everything soon." She gave me another warm smile and closed the door behind her.

I did as she asked, and got ready to meet with my favorite doctor in the world. As I entered his lab, I found him sitting in front of a computer, tapping away at some kind of spreadsheet program, entering new data that had him frowning in concentration. He noticed my arrival as soon as I closed the door behind me. "Victor!" he called excited. "Come on in!"

"Well, Doc, I'm not a scientist, but I'd say the protocol worked. I feel great!"

Dr. Palmer grinned at me happily, in a way that took ten years off his face. "Let's take a look, shall we?" He gestured for me to sit down, then taped a bunch of electrodes across my forehead, and asked me to relax. He went back to the computer, called up another program, and his fingers began racing over the keyboard.

"Doctor?" I asked. "I've been meaning to ask you about Yvette..." His eyes strayed from the monitor and met mine. "I know her procedure was different than mine, but I have no idea what it was. Will she have any side effects from it at all? I mean, Dr. Walker was absolutely adamant about getting her back. There has to be a reason."

He sighed, rubbing the bridge of his nose with the tip of his forefinger. "Well," he said, "Yvette seems to be fine now. She does heal incredibly fast, I have to say. That's a positive side effect you both share. I ran a few tests on her while you were under, and they all came back normal otherwise. The coma-like state into which she fell was perfectly normal—you simply took her out of her capsule a little too early, a little too fast. In regards to Walker's adamancy about getting her back, well..." he trailed off, scratching his head. "He probably thought that because Yvette had survived the G-Protocol, she was going to..." He hesitated for the second time, and backpedaled. "Um, let's forget it. There's nothing to worry about."

"Wait! G-protocol?" I asked, puzzled. But then I ran the numbers in my head. "You know the reason why he wants her, don't you?" I asked, almost accusingly.

He stopped typing and met my quizzical glare. "Yes. Yes, I do. When we studied the cluster of activated cells in our first groups of subjects, we realize that one particular group never fired—no matter the patient, serum, or radiation dose. Later, Walker discovered that these cells had the same characteristics as those of sensory neurons, which normally convert external stimuli into internal electrical impulses, allowing us to perceive the world around us. He theorized that if we could find a way to fire up these metasensory neurons, as he calls them, we would be able to *perceive*—or even communicate—with the source of it all." He stopped speaking and went back to his keyboard.

"What do *you* believe?" I probed.

Dr. Palmer pondered that for a few seconds as he typed, then: "I believe that if there's a larger world beyond the one we're allowed to perceive by nature, then there's probably a powerful reason why we're not allowed to perceive it."

"So, where does this…G-Protocol fit in all this?"

"Walker took my original design and created one that would target only those particular cells. He called it the G-Protocol— I suppose the G is short for 'God.' Unfortunately, every patient who underwent this new protocol died on the table. We couldn't figure out why. That's when I left."

"And you believe that this G-protocol was used on Yvette?" I asked warily.

"Oh, I know it was," he replied confidently. "One of the tests I performed found traces of the G-Protocol still lingering around those metasensory cells. I suspect it was used on poor Roger as well."

"Was the G-Protocol able to awaken the Meta cells?"

Dr. Palmer frowned. "Well, as of now they show no unusual activity. For all we know, they may never fire." His voice tuned into a more cheerful tone. "Look... the best we can do is stick to the facts: She survived the procedure, her intracranial pressure is gone, her ability to absorb this volatile energy you've tapped into was never triggered—which means she won't have to worry about developing any paranormal ability—and she's not suffering from any obvious side effects. For all we know, Yvette just might be the lucky one."

"What about her ability to interpret my feelings with nothing but a touch?" I reminded him.

"She told me she can only do it with you," he answered quickly. "For all we know, it could be *your* brain that's sending messages into hers. You're the one who needs to be on the lookout, Victor. Your brain is just discovering the things that it's capable of."

"What about her leg?"

"You got me there." He seemed almost embarrassed. "As I said, you both heal fast, and we can only speculate on how you do it. But then again, it's to your benefit."

I thought about that as he resumed his typing, and decided there seemed to be no harm in it. "Well, we're done here!" he said cheerfully. "Everything looks great. Your subconscious receptors for dark energy seemed to be completely blocked," he explained as he peeled the electrodes off my head. "There's only one more test we need to do. But I'd rather do it in a less confined place, if you don't mind."

"Sure," I replied, happy to leave the lab. I'd had enough of labs for a lifetime.

***

When we entered the living room, everyone was there, jittery with excitement; I felt like I was walking into a surprise welcoming party. Yvette was the first one to greet me up close and personal. She wrapped her arms around my neck and kissed me thoroughly. I could only press my forehead against hers and hug her as tightly as I could. That was heaven for me.

"How are you feeling?" Sarah called with a smile, not so far behind Yvette. "Ready to jump off another cliff?"

"I didn't jump. I was pushed." I winked to take the sting out of my works. "But I'm ready to face my fears." Yvette let go of me with a smile and gestured me toward Sarah, as if giving me permission. Sarah opened her arms and hugged me. I pressed my chin over her shoulder and closed my eyes tightly. "Thank you, Sarah… Thank you."

"Hey!" Dr. Ivanova said jokingly. "Don't I get a hug?"

I was surprised to see her so extroverted now, but happy to be allowed to thank her properly. "Thank you, Doctor." I shook her hand before I gave her a tight hug, patting her on the back.

"Enough with the doctor business!" she complained playfully, looking me straight in the eyes. "You can call me Lena now. Okay?"

"Okay," I laughed. "Thank you, Lena."

"Well, are you going to give us a demonstration, or what?" she requested.

"Demonstration?" My brows knitted in confusion.

"Yes." Dr. Palmer stepped in, holding a big box filled with random household items. "That's the last test we need to perform. We need to make sure that your abilities weren't compromised by the new protocol. So, if you please?" He set the box on the floor in front of me. "I'd like you to use your telekinesis to move any of these items."

"Okay." I stretched, smiling in disbelief. "Now I see why you didn't want to do this in your lab. Afraid I'd break something important, huh?"

He chuckled. "Well, I don't know how much control you have over your abilities now," he admitted.

"Well, let's see…" I stepped back, taking a deep breath. I closed my eyes for the few seconds that it took my mind to connect with the entire living room—and I'm talking about *way* past the box Dr. Palmer had set on the floor. I'm talking furniture, decorations, picture frames, chandeliers, walls, framing, insulation (I needed to warn him about the termites) and especially the people standing around me. I could hear their accelerated heartbeats along with their excited breathing, while all their eyes fixed on me. I didn't want to show off, but the temptation was too great.

First, I began by rattling every piece of furniture in the room. Lena gasped; knowing Yvette and Sarah had seen *much* worse than that, I wasn't expecting much of a reaction from them, though I did hear some giggling. I continued my demonstration by creating a spinning tornado with the gadgets inside Dr. Palmer's box: a pair of sunglasses, a calculator, a tape recorder, a camera, several heavy books, and even a smoothing iron. They were all whirling in a small cyclone in the middle of the living room when I opened my eyes, just to see the astonishment on Dr. Palmer's face. His mouth was partially opened, his body frozen. Lena's hands covered her mouth, while Sarah and Yvette were just giggling.

The love of my life then blew me a kiss, and I thought of the perfect way to finish my spectacle. After commanding the spinning gadgets back into the box, I pointed my hands at the center table. A big white vase on top of the table held the most beautiful bouquet of sunflowers. I focused my thoughts on the biggest and tallest one of all; the handsome bloom then rose from amongst the others and began to spin on its own stem. I levitated the spinning favor toward my beautiful ballerina, who shied and covered her flushed cheeks like an embarrassed little girl. The sunflower left a trail of yellow petals in the air as it traveled across the living room, until it finally stopped in front of my blushing beauty. She let go of her cheeks and took hold of the spinning flower, mouthing the words, "I love you."

Lena was the first one to break the silence. "You have an amazing gift, Victor," she said in a small voice. "Please don't lose sight of the responsibility that comes with it." She walked to me and put her hands over my shoulders. "I know you'll find the wisdom to always put it to good use."

"Thank you, Lena. I owe you so much."

Her eyes searched mine. "Only your friendship," she corrected me, setting the record straight with a smile.

"What will you do now?" Dr. Palmer asked.

"Live." Yvette answered for the two of us as she walked toward me, holding her flower close to her chest. "Live the life we thought was taken from us," she added, as her gaze captured mine. Then she said, "I'm sorry, I didn't mean to answer for you," as the palm of her right hand glided over the side of my face.

I smiled and reached for her hand. "There's no *me* anymore, Yvee. Only *us*. And you're right. That's exactly what we're going to do."

"You're all welcome to stay for as long as you'd like, of course," Dr. Palmer offered.

"Thank you, Doctor. But I think Yvee and I want to go someplace where nothing will remind us of this nightmare—no offense."

"None taken," the good doctor said, laughing. "I do, however, think we should keep in contact. When do you think you'll be leaving?"

"Tomorrow," I said decisively.

"No!" Sarah snapped. "I mean…" she trailed off, trying to cover up for her outburst, before continuing, "It may still be dangerous for you out there, you know?" Her tone was persuasive. "Maybe it's better if you stay here for a while and then—"

Lena's phone went off then, interrupting Sarah's argument. Yvette took advantage of the short pause to find concurrence with Dr. Palmer. "I really think Victor and I should disappear for a while, at least until we can figure out a way to let the authorities know what happened here. What do you think, Doctor?"

Dr. Palmer mused, "I agree. If you have the means to do so, I'll definitely say go for it."

The sound of a door being slammed made us stop and look around. An inexplicable feeling of guilt knocked inside my chest when I realized Sarah was gone.

***

The following morning arrived in the blink of an eye, and it was suddenly time to say goodbye. After having one final conversation with my new friends Lena and Sidney, I arranged transportation for Yvette and me to our next destination: Port Angeles, Washington. From there, my plan was to get to Long Beach, California, where I had a big surprise arranged for Yvette. Before leaving, Yvette and I expressed our intense gratitude to the good doctors for taking us in and helping us in our most desperate hour of need, and for giving us another chance to live our life together.

Yvette waited for me on the porch as I exchanged contact information with Dr. Palmer. I promised him I'd keep in touch, and that I'd return when the time was right. As I walked down the porch steps, I noticed Lena had already pulled up in her car, ready to give us a ride to the dock—but there was something else I needed to do before I could even think on getting into that car, probably one of the hardest things I'd had to do in a long time: I needed to say goodbye to Sarah.

And I didn't know how.

I found her standing in the meadow facing the mountains, her back to the house. Yvette had decided to come with me to say goodbye. She made a face when she grabbed my hand to walk to the meadow, and I often wonder now if she felt what I was going through at that moment.

"Hey!" Yvette snuck up on Sarah playfully, grabbing her shoulders.

"Hey." Sarah turned around with a smile that didn't reach her eyes. "You're all ready to go, I see." Her voice was cheerless.

"Yeah," Yvette began, leading her a few steps away from me, where they both lowered their voices, as if trying for privacy... but of course, my enhanced hearing wouldn't have it. I was forced to hear everything they said. "But we couldn't go without saying goodbye." Yvette's voice grew sad as she held Sarah's hands, her blue eyes wide and sincere. "Sarah," she continued, "thank you for everything... especially for being so honest with me in the truck." She sighed wistfully. "I honestly wish we could've met under different circumstances. You are definitely someone I'm proud to be friends with. And I'm *so* sorry I was such a bitch when we first met."

Sarah snickered. "Don't mention it. I would've probably acted the same way if I were in your position." They both laughed. "What I said in the truck, though..." She paused, throwing an uneasy glance in my direction, "Still our little secret, right?"

"Of course," Yvette promised, her face serious.

"Then, I guess we're still friends, huh?" They laughed again. "Just do me a favor," Sarah asked, raising her voice until she knew I could hear what she was saying. "Take good care of this clumsy lug for me! He always finds a way to get himself in trouble!"

Yvette chuckled. "You know I will."

"Do you mind if I...?" Sarah's request was almost inaudible even to my sensitive ears.

"Go ahead," Yvette agreed in the same tone, obviously understanding what she wanted. They gave each other a tight hug and then Yvette turned to me. "I'll meet you in the car, all right?" She gave me a quick kiss and left.

"Thanks," I said, and turned to Sarah, who'd shoved her hands in her jacket pockets and begun to shift uneasily. "So..." I stretched awkwardly. "What was *that* about?"

"Girl stuff," she answered sharply.

"Okay," I conceded, clearing my throat. "So, I guess this is it! For now."

She nodded with an ambiguous smile. "I guess so." Her emerald green eyes were wide, expectant.

"Are you going to be all right? I asked. "Staying here, I mean."

She snorted. "Don't worry about me! I'm not the one who's decided to 'disappear for a while,' remember?" Her voice held a hint of anger.

"You're not going to make this easy for me, are you?"

"Make *what* easy, Victor?" She chuckled sardonically. "You're the one making a big deal out of this. You should just go, all right?" She turned around and faced the mountains again.

"I don't understand why you're so angry with me."

"I'm not angry with you, Victor." Her voice softened into a whisper I could barely hear. "I'm angry with myself."

"What?" I reached for her shoulder.

"Nothing," she retorted. "Can you please just go?" She pushed me away angrily. "You're the one who's making this harder!"

"Wait a second! Why the hell are we fighting?" I asked. "This could very well be the last time we ever see each other, and—"

"Don't!" She shushed me, her fingertips to my lips. "Please, don't say that." She shut her eyes tightly and, breathing heavily, said, "I'm sorry."

Gently, I removed her fingers from my lips and held her in my arms, her head pressed firmly against my chest. "What's wrong? I asked, my voice soft and soothing. "Come on. What's *really* bothering you?"

She sighed deeply, hugging me tighter than before, before she pulled back just enough to make eye contact with me. Piecing me with the intensity of her gaze, she stated, "You're going to think I'm crazy."

"Try me."

"You know how people say that life is too short?" she asked. I nodded in response. "Well, that used to scare the hell out of me, because I always thought I'd never have the courage to do anything even remotely significant with my life... until I met you. The truth is that my stupid obsession to always be the best has kept me from having a life of my own. I mean, friends, parties, boyfriends—all that was out of the question if I expected to go the best medical school, or if I wanted to win the next karate tournament. My father never believed in second places you know? And when he died, I guess I just buried myself deeper into my secluded life, just to disconnect myself from the pain."

She fought her voice, obviously trying to keep it from breaking. "And then I met *you*. And my whole life turned into this incredible adventure, where I got the opportunity to experience things I had never thought possible. Like trusting someone the way I trust you. I felt like I'd finally found someone I could tell anything to." Her eyes began to glaze with tears. "And now he's leaving... And here's the crazy part. You haven't even climbed into that car, and I'm missing you already."

I stood there speechless.

"I promised myself I wouldn't do this," she continued. "But I know how good you are at keeping promises, so..." Her eyes rose to meet mine. "I want you to promise me something."

"Anything," I vowed.

"Don't forget about me—our friendship, I mean." Though she trailed off a bit, her request was solemn.

I held her gently in my arms and gazed into those emerald greens of hers. "Sarah, I couldn't forget you if I tried. You're the best friend I've have ever had. The partner in crime I always wanted!"

The last part made us both laugh. But my voice was solemn as I continued, "You saved my life in more ways that you can possibly imagine. And my promise to you goes far beyond the fact that I will never forget you. My promise to you is that this is not a goodbye… And that we'll see each other again, soon. I can feel that. And no matter what happens, I'll always be there when you need me, all right?"

"Okay." She smiled, dabbing at her tears.

"You know what?" I reached into my pocket. "I want you to have this." I placed my father's lighter in the palm of her hand and curled her fingers around it.

She opened her hand and realized what it was. "Victor! I can't take this."

"I want you to," I insisted. "This lighter was always a reminder of my Dad's best and worse qualities, you know? His bravery, his stubbornness, his incorruptibility, his impulsive character, his integrity, and his annoying talent of always making me laugh, even when I was mad at him." I pushed down a knot in my throat. "But most of all, to me it represents his absolute loyalty. These are qualities I never thought I'd find in another human being, until I met you." Her eyes dampened again. "Maybe when you look at it, you'll remember mine."

She threw her arms around me and hugged me again. "Thank you." Then I felt her lips gliding over the side of my face as she began to pull away...but not before she landed a kiss on my cheek, the corner of her lips barely touching mine.

She then took a step back, still holding my hand. "Take care yourself, okay?" she said, taking yet another step back, and then another, and another, until our hands were just a tug away from letting go.

"You, too," I replied wistfully.

Then I turned away, feeling the tips of our fingers slipping apart.

Chapter 17

Our Boat of Dreams

LENA'S BLACK SEDAN idled on the driveway as I walked towards it, fighting the compulsion to look back—something that I knew would only make me feel worse. Her eyes followed my arrival as she waited patiently, arm crossed, leaning back against the driver's door. For the looks of it, she's watched my entire farewell with Sarah, yet she seemed indifferent to the event. Yvette, on the other hand, waited motionless in the backseat of the car, facing the big gray dashboard.

She didn't blink even when I opened the door. My first impression was that she had gotten upset by the whole thing, but her apparent disconnection with reality quickly made me realize it was something else. "For a moment I thought you weren't coming," she said in a whisper.

"I'm sorry," I apologized. "I just needed a few minutes to—"

"To say goodbye," she interjected. "I know… your dad told me." She added, knitting her brows without losing her blank stare, her voice almost inaudible: "He told me not to worry, that your love dwells in my heart."

"What?" I asked, befuddled.

Her eyes suddenly came back to life and swung over to meet my stunned face. "What?" she asked, as if completely oblivious of what she'd just said.

"What...what did you just say?" I pressed.

"Nothing." Her face was relaxed, sincere.

"No, you just said something about my father. You said he told you something."

Looking annoyed, she said, "No I didn't. Did I?" Her tone was defensive now.

We exchange confused looks for a few seconds, until Lena broke the unnerving silence. "Should we go?" she asked.

My eyes returned to Yvette, whose face radiated nothing but excitement now. "Are you ready?" she asked, biting her lower lip, which to me was enough to put aside the awkward moment and return us to our happy reality: We were cured, free, happy, and nothing was standing in the way of us spending the rest of our lives together.

I let my happiness finally show on my face, as I got in the car and wrapped my arm around the love of my life and responded with the conviction that only the sight of her could elicit in me. "I'm ready!"

Lena dropped us off at the dock and wished us well. We kept waving goodbye as our plane left the port. I've never seen Yvette so happy. She was literally romping around and bouncing on her seat, hugging me and kissing me, like we were off to our honeymoon.

I have to admit that being with her like that not only took my mind off my fear of flying, but actually made me feel *safe*—as if nothing in the world could ever go wrong as long as we were together. It's said that angels can fly. Well, then, I guess that's why I felt so safe. After all, I was flying with one. That's how I saw her from that day forward: as my angel, my soulmate, and my sole reason for existence—all these things and more.

Although flying no longer seemed to be an issue for me, thanks to my Yvee, I decided to rent a car as soon as we reached Port Angeles. I thought it was the best way to travel undetected, and it gave me the opportunity to test the fake I.D. Dr. Palmer had given me before we left—an Alaska state driver's license, to be precise. All my other identifying papers had already been shredded and the pieces scattered across six dumpsters in two towns. Yet I knew that even if I were to use this I.D. on a commercial flight, Yvette would still have to present hers, and that would have helped pinpoint our location if anyone were still trying to track us down. You need only one driver's license to rent a car.

Besides, Yvette seemed to love the idea of a road trip as soon as I mentioned it. She told me she'd always wanted to drive cross-country, but she'd never had the chance to do so—and that a couple of days on the open road with me sounded like a dream come true. So we went ahead and rented this awesome candy-apple red Ford Mustang convertible at her suggestion. Plus, the counter agent told us that traveling in a convertible was the perfect way to enjoy the scenic roads of the Pacific North and Southwest. And so we did!

Our journey began down U.S. Highway101, alongside the remarkable Olympic National Forest, which kind of reminded me of Ketchikan. Maybe the similarities between the rainforests were to blame for the immediate flashback I experienced, or perhaps just the slightest trace of green was now enough to incite memories of my days in the unforgettable Tongass National Rainforest—memories I knew I would be tattooed on my heart for the rest of my days.

Anyway, I had my reasons for taking this particular route. I knew that the *One-oh-One* stretched along the shoreline; and although I knew it would take us longer to get to our destination, I figured the scenery along the way would make it worth our while. Besides, since I'd never seen the Pacific Ocean live and in person, and neither had Yvette, I figured that this was the perfect opportunity to enjoy it all, from beginning to end—so to speak.

We reached the coastline just in time to watch the sun set. Yvette seemed almost hypnotized by it, watching every single second almost without blinking. And who could blame her? The whole spectacle seemed like something out of a movie. Living on the East Coast, I'd seen many sunrises by the beach, but never a sunset. Never like this. I had to keep reminding myself to keep my eyes on the road, which of course didn't stop me from glancing over every five seconds. It was absolutely amazing to watch that ball of fire being swallowed by the seemingly endless ocean.

But not even the extraordinary shades of yellow, red, and orange that overlapped the distant horizon were enough to keep my eyes from straying towards Yvette. She almost seemed caressed by the sun's dying glow. I could see it glide over her beautiful pale skin while limning every strand of her long, silky black hair as it fluttered perfectly in the wind. I almost felt jealous... But then I laughed at my silliness. Not because I conceded to my idiocy of being jealous of the sun, but because I couldn't blame the celestial body for trying to reach such an enticing creature.

"What?" Yvette asked me, a wide smile revealing her ivory teeth.

"Nothing," I smiled, feeling my happiness overflowing my heart. "I was just wondering how I could ever top a moment like this."

Her eyes turned back to the sunset. "It *is* beautiful, isn't it?"

I chuckled. "I wasn't talking about the sun." My words made her turn back to me, her eyes flickering with emotion. She leaned over me and kissed me passionately, making us both forget for a split-second that we were traveling at a very high rate of speed.

"Whoa!" she exclaimed, realizing the danger and pulling away. "I'm sorry." Her apology suppressed an embarrassed smile, as she moved reluctantly away from me. "But *you* need to drive." She added, "And *I*... I need to behave myself." She finished her sentence with a long, deep sigh.

I just couldn't help laughing at how adorable she looked, huddling embarrassed on the passenger seat, covering her face with both hands. She glanced over me, and noticed that despite her safety advice I had not stopped gazing at her. "Hey!" she complained playfully. "Eyes on the road, Mister!"

I turned my eyes back to the road, my grin relentless. "Yes ma'am."

My answer made her laugh again.

Soon the eerie shadows of the twilight shrouded the majesty of the forest, while a rising full moon gradually relit the dark sky the sun had left behind. The monotonous hum of the car's engine was the only disruption to what was otherwise a profound silence. I watched Yvette fight to keep her weary eyes open as she admired the moonlit ocean, but the tranquility soon overcame her senses.

I watched her drift away with her head pressed against the rolled-up window. Half-smiling, I reached back and snagged my jacket from the back seat to cover her body from the shoulders down. She curled up even tighter when I tucked her in, snuggling her face against the jacket's fur collar as if searching for my scent.

She looked so peaceful then, so fragile, so vulnerable, and so unbelievably beautiful that the very sight of her elicited a thought that made my heart ache: How could I ever be able to live without her? The answer in my head was quick and clear... I couldn't. "Sleep, baby," I whispered, running my fingers through her silky hair. "Tomorrow will be a brand new day." I put the car's top up and kept driving through the night.

***

To my surprise, I never got tired of driving. It was weird; I mean, I knew that if I were to lie down and rest, I most certainly would've been able to get some sleep. Yet the more I concentrated on the task at hand, the more I felt that I didn't need to.

By the time I saw the distant dawn, I'd driven for over ten hours straight, and yet I felt as fresh as a daisy. Part of it was that the normally tedious stress of driving at night had been entirely overcome by my supernatural abilities. I mean, how could I possibly worry when I could sense any approaching vehicle, animal, road debris, and even bugs in a one-mile radius, minutes before any of them came in sight? It was like driving with radar in my head, and I have to admit I liked it.

Yvette woke up just in time to see a beautiful stretch of the Oregon coast. The sun was up and shining, and blue skies extended as far as the eye could see in all directions. The off-shore views were so amazing and breathtaking that Yvette insisted on stopping to get a camera—which we did, of course. She enjoyed taking pictures of the natural rock formations along the coastline. The off-shore islands, the sea caves, the beaches—you name it, she photographed it. She even held the camera at arm's length to fit us both into the frame and snapped a few photos of us together. God, she was happy… And for me, her happiness was all the nourishment my heart could ever need. We were, indeed, living our dream.

We made a few more stops along the way; mostly for sightseeing, food, and entertainment. But I think one of the biggest treats of all was to drive across the Golden Gate Bridge in San Francisco. It was an extraordinary experience. Yvette leaned back against my shoulder, held the camera at arm's length, and snapped a picture of us as we drove over the bridge. Despite the simplicity of the photo, it perfectly captured the reflection of our happiness together, our happiness at being in love. I came to love that picture more than any other in my life.

After two days on the road, we finally arrived at our destination, Long Beach, and it was time to tell Yvette about the surprise I've prepared for her. Mitch Goodman, the yacht salesman I'd met back in Jersey, was now living in Los Angeles—and he was going to meet us at the Long Beach Shoreline Marina to close the deal on the Bavaria Cruiser-36 I had fallen in love with a couple of years ago. She wasn't a brand new model, but Mitch assured me that she was in perfect condition and that her sole owner had taken very good care of her. After reminding Yvette about our little bucket-list pact, I told her that I'd thought this was the perfect way to start crossing those wishes off the list. Her reaction was exactly what I expected.

"I can't believe it! Is it really happening?" she asked, her voice shaking with emotion. "Is it?"

I found a parking spot at the gorgeous Hyatt Regency—the hotel closest to the Marina—and shut off the engine. Yvette was still waiting for my answer, so I turned to her and cupped the side of her face in the palm of my hand. "It's real. It *is* happening." My voice was firm and sincere. "You were right, Yvee... You always were: Our *real* story is yet to be written. We'll soon forget the nightmare we've been through. I promise!"

Although her eyes dampened with tears, her smile was broad and genuine—and her reply was a passionate kiss that kept us in the car for a long, long time.

We were so eager to move things along that we decided to call Mitch right after we checked into the hotel—which, by the way, was absolutely gorgeous. The Harbor View King, as they called it, was a very large, modern room, filled with everything you could possibly need. The plush down duvets that fitted the king-size bed were so inviting that I couldn't help but jump in and get sucked in by them the moment we walked in. Yvette ran to the four horizontal-pane windows at the end of the room and gushed about how amazing the view was; the room overlooked the harbor and the city skyline. "It's breathtaking!" she said, beckoning me to come and take a look. But given the fact that we were on the fifteenth floor of a seventeen-floor building, I decided to just take her word for it. Flying was one thing...but looking down from a tall inanimate object still gave me the creeps.

"It's all right, Yvee. I believe you," I chuckled, and picked up the phone to call Mitch.

Luckily for us, he was just finishing up with a boat auction at the Marina. He told me he couldn't wait to close this deal. Of course, what broker wouldn't be happy to close a cash deal and get his commission right away? Anyhow, he gave me the boat's dock and slip information and asked me to meet him in twenty minutes. "Just face the docks from the Pelican Pier Pavilion," he said. "You can't miss me… Oh! And don't forget to bring your checkbook!" he joked—although I knew he really meant it.

"You got it, Mitch!" I agreed happily. "I'll see you in a few!"

I gave Yvette the good news and asked her to come with me. She couldn't hide her excitement. She gave her hair a quick brush and put on some lipstick, which I honestly thought was a waste of time and make-up. Her relentlessly straight hair would never stray from falling into anything but the perfect place, no matter how strenuous the surrounding elements were. And her lips... well, I guess I just thought it was unmerciful to make them look any more alluring than they already were.

We headed down to the lobby as soon as she said the word. Once there, we asked the front desk agent where we could find this Pelican Pier Pavilion. "Rainbow Harbor," said the tall blonde behind the desk, showing us the direction to take right outside the door. "Just follow the signs for Shoreline Village," she added politely. "It's just a short stroll from the hotel."

"Thank you," Yvette said before I could even open my mouth to do so myself. She grabbed my hand and, before I knew it, she was leading the way toward the shore.

When we got there, we thought we'd accidentally taken a wrong turn into a harbor-front carnival. There were games, rides, restaurants, shops, arcades—you name it. The colors were so bright and ubiquitous they were almost overwhelming, and everywhere you turned there was something fun and exciting to do. It was like a great big party, thrown unintentionally just for us. As we walked along the promenade, Yvette looked at me and smiled. She was probably thinking the same thing.

Yvette and I held hands and walked happily through the crowd until we got to the Pelican Pier Pavilion. From there we began to scan the docks, looking for Mitch, whom we soon saw waving eagerly from the foredeck of a beautiful white Bavaria Cruiser-36. The boat was securely anchored at one of the slips of the P Dock.

"Is that him?" Yvette asked.

"Yes," I answered. "And *that*, my love, is our boat of dreams."

We both laughed and ran toward the boat, impatient to meet our new friend Mitch, who proceeded to give us the grand tour of our soon-to-be love nest.

The interior was solid oak, with chestnut floors and a faux leather-covered paneled ceiling. She was nicer than I could have possibly imagined; no picture or catalogue could ever have done this beauty the justice she deserved. Yvette was in awe. She kept giving me this cheerful smile as she slid her fingertips over the smooth surfaces of the bright, shiny wood. I remember how her eyes kept gazing around avidly as she walked through every compartment of our new boat. She was in heaven, and so was I.

"You cook?" she asked, grinning, as she saw the interest I directed towards the three-burner stove and oven that I found in the galley.

"I'm Italian-American, baby!" I said proudly.

She laughed and hugged me from behind. "I won't fight you there," she said, pulling my face towards her bee-stung lips, landing a soft kiss on my cheek.

"Ahem!" Mitch said as he suddenly walked in. "So, should we get down to business?"

Yvette and I exchanged a glance and responded simultaneously, "Absolutely!"

***

Our motivated broker led us back onto the main deck and opened his leather briefcase on a small pedestal table, whereupon he proceeded to lay out a number of papers for me to sign. I asked him for a pen and signed them all with little more than a cursory glance at each page. Everything was in order; my enhanced senses now apparently included photographic memory and comprehension. When I'd completed the last flourish, I pulled out my checkbook and cut the check for the asking price, which was less than expected— yet more than I've ever spent on anything in my life. But what the hell. You only live once.

After jamming all the paperwork back into his briefcase except for my copies, he took a set of keys attached to a red floating keychain from a special pocket in his jacket and held it up in his hand. "Before I give you the keys, I should tell you about a minor hiccup," he said. "The sale won't be final until we have the seller's signature on the contract. But don't you worry! He'll be here tomorrow afternoon to sign the paperwork. He only insisted on meeting the lucky couple buying his baby, that's all. He said he's got sentimental reasons…" he added. "But he *did* say to give you the keys and to tell you to make yourself at home. He'll meet you at the Hyatt tomorrow at 3PM, all right?"

My face was less than happy.

"I guess it's all right." Yvette said. "I don't mind staying an extra day in Long Beach—do you, baby?"

"Uh…" I hesitated for a second. "No," I finally answered, knowing that we didn't have much of a choice. "I guess not."

"Can we use the boat?" Yvette asked guardedly.

"Of course!" Mitch answered quickly. "You can sleep here tonight if you want! Go ahead and check out of the Hotel. That'll save you some money. And tomorrow you'll be off to…" Mitch waited for me to finish the last part of his sentence.

"An undisclosed location," I answered with a wry smile.

"Of course," he added, catching my drift. He gave me the keys and shook both our hands. "Very well, then. I guess I'll see you tomorrow to get that signature. Other than that… Congratulations!" He smile warmly and left the boat, turning back once to wave before he stepped onto the dock.

Yvette waited for Mitch to disappear around the corner before she started jumping up and down. She wrapped her arms around my neck and began to kiss me, like she had back on the highway. "Should I go check out?" I tried to ask between her kisses.

"Unh-unh!" she refused, and began to pull me though the companionway and into the cabins below.

"Should I go get our stuff?" I kept chuckling between her kisses; my insistence obviously a playful front.

"Unh-unh!" she refused again, this time bumping her head on the overhead hatch. "Ow!" She laughed, embarrassed, rubbing her head.

I did my best not to laugh, but I'm sure she could see it in my eyes. "Maybe I should go get you some bandages?" My smile broadened.

"Shut up!" she laughed, running her fingers through my hair.

Her playful smile suddenly disappeared, replaced by a penetrating stare that disarmed me completely. I'll never forget how she leaned forward and pressed her trembling lips against mine, or how her body began to quiver in my arms then. The light in her eyes not only reminded me of that little girl who had once vowed to love me no matter what, but of the woman who'd fallen in love with me unconditionally. The woman *I* had fallen in love with, with all my heart—the woman who was now telling me, "We've made it! We're *together*. And we've made it!" The woman who was telling me, "I love you. I love you. *I love you…*" The woman I loved, the woman I had loved since childhood, the woman I would love for the rest of my life. Maybe even after.

We held each other and let our love take over completely. No more restraints, boundaries, or limitations. Our love needed not know of such things; they were things our love couldn't understand anyway, much less abide by. God, I loved her! *Forgive me,* I pleaded to God, *Forgive me for loving her so much.*

Needless to say our powers kicked in, allowing us to read and feel each other in an otherworldly way. But not even this ethereal feeling was a fair match for the feeling of our love, which had proven to be more powerful than any mere supernatural force. An exchange was made that night, one that allowed us to become one in body and in soul. Her heart for mine, and mine for hers. An exchange only possible for soulmates like us.

I thanked the all-merciful God for allowing us to experience that lifetime of love in one night. I still do.

***

A loud thud woke me from a dreamless sleep in the darkest depths of the night. At first I thought it was just the beginning of a nightmare that my brain had averted just in time; but then I realized the noise had not only awakened me, it had prompted my senses into full alert. Confused and disoriented, I tried to get up—but something derailed me. Yvette lay on my bare chest, her long tresses of shiny black hair covering most of her face. Gently, I tucked some of the errant strands behind her ear so I could see her angelic features again. A not-so-faint smile touched the corners of her lips. I could only assume a blissful dream was now in progress, soothing her battered mind.

The last thing I wanted to do was disturb such serenity, but something was compelling me to get up and check on that noise. I just couldn't stop my senses from going haywire, as if they were trying to alert me of some sort of danger in the midst. Though my senses were reaching toward whatever had alerted me, I couldn't quite grasp what was wrong. It was almost as if something were blocking me.

As I finally decided to unbundle from Yvette's tight embrace, I heard a similar thump strike the side of the bed. The sound was not the same, however, and neither was the reaction of my senses towards it; but it made me scan the floor nonetheless. When the thump happened again, I was able to pinpoint its exact location. I chuckled in disbelief at my silliness; I had forgotten we were no longer on stable ground. The subtle sway of the ocean was rocking the boat back and forth, and a loose Coke bottle had been wondering around the floor, knocking against everything on its path.

I smiled silently as I aimed my hand towards the empty glass bottle, stopping it right before it hit another compartment wall. It levitated at my command, moving across the cabin and finally landing right into the trashcan next to the bed. *You have to pull yourself together, Victor,* I told myself, letting out a deep sigh of relief, somewhat upset. I couldn't understand how a simple noise could have caused me to become unglued like that. A soft moan from Yvette made me turn back to her. I pressed her head back against my chest, and decided to forget about the incident and go back to sleep.

The cry of the greedy seagulls fighting over their morning meal woke me up again. Sunshine filtered through the portholes, creating beautiful shafts of light that pierced the stateroom. Apparently, the relentless rocking of the boat had worked better than any sleeping pill. We had slept like babies all through the night—with the exception of my silly confrontation with an empty soda bottle, of course.

One of the greatest moments of my life occurred when Yvette finally awoke in my arms. And although the sun had already illuminated the inside of the boat, it was Yvette's dazzling smile that really brightened my day. "Morning," she said artlessly, a twinkle in her eyes.

"Morning," I answered, trying to tame the stupid grin on my face. "Did you sleep well?"

"Wonderfully." She twirled, stretching on the bed, her face alight with a huge smile. "I had the most wonderful dream," she added, sticking her toes out of the covers, "and you were in it!"

I smiled. "Well, I got news for you, Ms. Montgomery... It was no dream."

She laughed, embarrassed, throwing the covers over her head. "I'm not talking about that!"

"No?" I prompted.

"No!" she said, laughing, peeking out from under the covers. She threw a quick glance at me and then turned on her stomach, crossing her ankles in the air. "I'm talking about afterwards."

"Really?" I purposely tried to sound jealous. "Well, that's not fair! How come you get to dream and I don't?"

Her face turned serious, profound almost. "Maybe it's better if you don't," she said. "You always have nightmares."

My grin died as my brows knitted in confusion. "What makes you say that?"

"I don't know." Her eyes suddenly seemed lost in space, just as they had in Lena's car. "I don't even know why I said that. It just came out," she added, with her eyes alive again. "But is it true?"

"Yeah…" I confirmed suspiciously.

"How did I know that?" Her face was thoughtful for a long moment. "…Anyway!" She shook her head, returning to her last, happy thought. "You want me to tell you my dream?"

"Sure," I said, still shaken by her unexpected comment.

"Do you remember that recurring dream I've told you about?" she asked, and I nodded. "Well, I had it again," she began with a spellbound look on her face. "But this time was different… My Mother was no longer alone in the audience; your father was seated next to her. And I could see other people, too, faces I recognized even though I've never seen them before. And then, as the music was about to end, the main doors flew open and I saw *you* enter the theatre. But your face was changed.

Your eyes were no longer... soft. But I didn't care. I just kept dancing, even more motivated than before because now I knew I was dancing for you. Then you threw an invisible lasso around my waist and pulled me towards you. I flew above the audience and into your arms, and then we kissed and hugged just like we did last night."

"That's quite a dream you had," I said, enthralled by her words. "I can't believe you still remember what my father looked like."

"Yeah..." she whispered, holding that blank stare again, "But he looks happier now."

"What do you mean?"

She shook her head again, suddenly looking dumbfounded. "I don't know."

Before I could respond, an urgent knocking at the main hatch ended our conversation. I jumped out of bed, slipped into my clothes, and hurried to see who it was. As I opened the hatch, I found Mitch standing on the deck. He seemed nervous; even his rehearsed salesman smile couldn't make up for the sweaty forehead he kept dabbing at with his handkerchief. It wasn't that hot out. "Are you all right?" I asked, concerned.

"Yeah!" he said emphatically. "I'm great! I'm just here to let you know the owner's arrived, um... well, a little earlier that anticipated. And he wants to finish the transaction as soon as possible." His voice became edgier with every word. "He says he'll meet you in the hotel lobby in twenty minutes to sign the rest of the paperwork, and he also reminded me that the radio on the bridge needs to be replaced. So I just called a technician, who's coming around the same time. It shouldn't take that long, but it'll be better if someone stays in the boat during the switch." His eyes flew to Yvette, who was now standing next to me, grinning.

"Sure!" Yvette said after a pause, then turned to me. "I'll stay. Why don't you just go ahead and close the deal? Hopefully, everything will be fixed by the time you get back."

"Great!" Mitch said, relieved. "So, I'll see you in the lobby in twenty minutes?"

"Yeah," I agreed dubiously. "Tell Mr....?"

"—B!" Mitch said quickly. "Mr. B."

"Tell Mr. B that I'll be there."

Mitch gave me another insincere smile and left. When my hypersenses reached for him, wondering what the hell was going on, I couldn't read him at all. I was a bit concerned about that, until Yvette distracted me with a passionate kiss.

She gave me another before I left the boat, and I almost decided not to go. "That's a reminder not to take *too* long!" she warned in a whisper, her gaze boring into mine. Looking into those heavenly blue eyes was enough to make me understand how empty and incomplete my life would be without her now, because my heart was in them. My life, my love, my very soul were in them.

That's when I realized I shouldn't go anywhere; that nothing was more important than staying here with her. I was just about to say the hell with it when Yvette reminded me I still needed to pick up our bags from the hotel and check out. Sighing, I realized that I had no choice but to go back to the hotel. *Might as well finish this deal,* I thought. So I kissed my Yvee one last time and left.

"I love you!" Yvette called from the open hatch as I jumped onto the pier.

I turned around and smiled, watching my angel wave goodbye. "I love *you!*" I shouted out loud. "I'll be right back!"

Famous last words.

Chapter 18
Predominance

When I got to the hotel lobby it was completely empty, with the exception of the same tall blonde receptionist who had helped us with directions before. She was standing behind the huge mahogany front desk with a bulky envelope in her hand. She smiled at me as soon as she saw me walk in. "Good morning!" she chirped as I approached the desk.

"Good morning." I answered politely. "I'm supposed to meet a 'Mr. B.' here in the lobby. Do you know if he's around?"

"Oh!" she realized. "Then you must be Mr. Bellator."

My blood rushed faster through my veins at the sound of my name. All my recent transactions, including the purchase of the boat, had been made under my new alias. Not even Mitch, to whom I had spoken in the past, had ever gotten my real name. Whoever I was to meet knew exactly who I was. "Mr. B. left this for you," the receptionist added, handing me the sealed envelope she'd been holding. As I took it, I realized that a couple of hard, heavy objects had been stuffed inside the envelope. Without any further delay I ripped it opened.

A sudden rush of panic made my blood pressure drop nearly to the point of collapse when I slid the first item out of the envelope. It was my father's lighter—wrapped in a small plastic bag and covered in coagulated blood. The second item was a stop watch. Along with it was a note:

I hope you realize what this means, Victor. And yes, the blood belongs to her. But don't worry; she's still alive... for now. For how much longer, though, will be entirely up to you.

*I want you to meet me on the rooftop of this hotel in exactly five minutes. And don't worry. I'll know exactly when to start counting. Let's just say I can see your every move from where I'm standing. And if I see you going back to the boat to tell your little princess what's going on, or if I hear any sirens approaching, I **will** pluck the pretty little green eyes of the one you left behind. You may think of this as cowardice. But I assure you, Victor, all I want is to give you the choice you took away from me...*

By the time I'd finished reading, my entire blood supply had drained to my feet. "Oh my God!" the receptionist exclaimed with concern. "Are you okay? You look as if you've just seen a ghost."

"Who gave you this envelope?" I demanded.

"A man," she answered nervously. "He was scarred. He had dark hair and wore sunglasses. I've never seen him before. I doubt he's even staying in the hotel. Why?" she asked. "Is there anything wrong? Should I call for help?"

"No!" I replied curtly. "Just tell me how to get to the roof."

"The roof?" she hesitated, confused. "Well, you can't—"

"How do I get up there?"

The poor girl cringed at my shout and pointed me to the end of the corridor. "The service elevator," she said.

I bolted towards the corridor and pushed the call button for the elevator frantically. As the doors opened I saw the frightened receptionist calling for help, but it was too late. My future was already in motion, and there was nothing that could stop it now. As my hypersenses ignited and reached toward the roof, I realized that they were being damped down somehow, just as they had been late the night before when the dull thud had awakened me. I was desperately worried now, wondering what that had been, but I didn't have time to worry about it. I had to save Sarah. I jumped into the elevator before the doors were quite open and jabbed the button for the top floor—then waited for the future to unfold.

When the doors of the elevator opened again, I was on the roof of the seventeen-story structure. The wind was very strong, but I was in no danger of being blown off the building. Still, it was enough to make my knees quiver as I avoided looking at the miniaturized version of the city below. I stalked over the gravelly surface, looking for the author of the blood-splattered note; but all I could see was tarry gravel and a cooling tower situated in the middle of the wide space.

Soon, I found myself facing south towards the ocean. A myriad of tiny sailboats rested peacefully in the harbor, and the first thing that popped into my mind was Yvette. She was in one of them, waiting for me to come back, waiting for something I was now beginning to think was never going to happen.

A stifled scream caused me to whirl toward the farthest corner of the roof, where what I saw stoked my chest with panic again. Sarah was there, gagged, and chained to a post. A strange metal device, locked to her chains, hung in front of her at chest level. On the ledge not too far from her, a tall, dark-haired man stood in a regal pose, head held high and hands clasped behind his back. And though I couldn't see his face, I could tell he was overseeing the harbor, like a hawk stalking its prey.

"I'm so glad you could join us, Victor," the man on the ledge said casually. And though his eyes had not yet met my stunned glare, his voice was enough to reveal his identity. "Though you barely made it. I hope you're not too out of shape."

I could feel my heart pounding like a trip-hammer as I listened to his voice. "Oh, my God," I whispered in disbelief. "I thought you were—"

"Dead?" he interrupted, looking over his shoulder and allowing me to meet his sulfuric glare. "No," he said contemptuously. "Though a part of me *did* die the moment you let go of that platform… You do remember that, don't you, Victor?" His soft voice dripped with acidic hatred.

He turned to face me then, revealing the horrifying souvenir the warehouse explosion had left him. It was staggering to see the third-degree burns that had permanently scarred the right side of his face—deep, gruesome marks that stretched from his ear down along the side of his neck. It pained me to cast my eyes away.

"Damian." I finally found the strength to say his name. "I'll never be able to take back what happened that night. And only God knows how sorry I am. But you were there. And you know that I did *everything* in my power to save her—"

"But in the end you had to make a choice—and you did, didn't you?"

"Damian, please!"

He hopped from the ledge onto the gravelly roof. Sarah's eyes kept piercing me with panic as blood dripped from her brow. "I wonder," Damian said, with an analytical tone this time. "How did you do it?"

"Do what?" I asked warily.

"*Choose*, of course. Was it an impetuous, last-second decision?" He paused to run his burned fingers through Sara's red curls. "Or did you run your famous numbers in your head?" He waited for my answer, but I gave him nothing. "Tell me!" he pressed, pulling Sarah's hair so violently that her tears began to flow.

"All right!" I conceded desperately. "You're right... I *did* run the numbers. And you know goddamn well I didn't have a choice! Walker killed your wife long before we even got there, Damian! The person we tried to safe that night was no longer your wife! And if you refuse to believe the truth, then there's nothing I can do." I paused for a moment, trying to calm myself down. My next words were as sincere as the guilt I'd been carrying around in my heart. "Not a day goes by that I don't regret what happened to Sonya, Damian... and I *am* sorry. I really am. But she's gone. Now, you can either mourn her or avenge her. It's up to you. And if you've chosen to believe that I am the one responsible for her death... then I accept your grudge. But don't bring any more innocent people into this. Let Sarah go, and deal with me. That *is* what you want, isn't it? To kill me? Well, here I am. Let her go, and let's finish this."

"Well, Victor," Damian chuckled, "I have to admit, that was a pretty impressive speech. But now let me tell you what I think: I think that behind your Boy Scout façade you're nothing but a coward and a hypocrite. And in regards to your decision, I think you knew exactly what you were doing and why. Although I still can't figure out who you were *really* trying to safe that night. Was it your little princess on the boat? Or the martyr who agreed to let you go?" He stroked Sarah's head.

"I don't know what you're talking about."

"No?" he prompted jeeringly. "Well, let me get you up to speed, *Romeo*. These two girls leveled with each other on our way to R.C. Labs, and apparently this one took the higher road." He snorted in disgust. "I have to say, though: what these two girls see in you is beyond me. You're a disgrace to evolution. Look at you! You were offered the gift of unlimited power, and what did you do? You spat on it and neutered it, like it was nothing but a vicious mongrel. Oh, yes… I know what you did, Victor."

I swallowed hard and tried to control the tremor in my voice as I replied, "This power, Damian—it changes who you really are. Don't you see? It's changed you. What happened to you, Damian? What happened to the man who once talked to me with so much faith?"

"*Faith?*" he shouted angrily, his sulfur-yellow eyes glowing. "You took *that* from me too!"

"Then kill me!" I told him. "Kill *me* and get this over and done with! But be a *man*, Damian. Be a man and let her go. This is between you and me… nobody else." My anger boosted my hypersenses, allowing me to cut through whatever was blocking them to feel Damian at the very reach of my powers. I had agreed for him to have his shot at revenge, but that didn't mean I was going down without a fight—although hurting him was the last thing I wanted. But I guess fate couldn't have cared less about what I wanted. A confrontation had been set, and I couldn't back out now; so I clenched my fists and waited for his move.

Damian looked upon my clenched fists and then raised his eyes with disgust. "I think you're missing the point, Victor. I'm not here to kill you. I'm not even going to fight you. That would be too easy. Too quick... too merciful."

"Then what the hell do you want?" I demanded.

"I've told you. I just want to give you the choice that you took away from me." He stepped away from Sarah and took a small hand device out of his jacket pocket. "I'm going to give you the choice to save the one you *really* love." Then he added, "Although I'm not sure you even know who that person is. But don't worry. I'm going to help you decide the same way you decided to let my wife die. By running your goddamn numbers."

"Damian, what did you do?" I asked, terrified.

"Just like NASA, I doubled up on everything!" He laughed disturbingly. "Now, I want you to pay attention, because I'm not going to repeat myself—and believe me, every single detail counts. Every *variable*, as you call them, may represent the difference between who lives and who dies, you understand?" My silence was proof he had gotten my full attention—that and my angry glare.

"Good!" he crowed. "First off, I want you to know that Dr. Walker's the reason I'm still alive. He saved me from the fire, and he helped me understand that killing him was not in my best interests… But that's another story that I may tell you some other time. The reason I bring him up is because his new friendship has allowed me to get my hands on his rather large cache of military-grade equipment and weaponry. Wonderful toys, really, like the one Ginger here has attached to her chest. I'm sure you've noticed."

I nodded sharply.

"Well, let me tell you what it is. It's a very complicated explosive device, powerful enough to blow the entire roof off this nice, shiny building. Can you imagine what it would do to Miss Carrot-Top here?" He laughed and began to pace as I listened quietly to his words, trying to gather as much information as he'd allow me. "But that's not the best part," he continued. "You see this remote detonator?" He showed me the device in his hand. "This baby is not only linked to this particular bomb, but to yet another of the same explosive charge and blast radius." He looked at me and smiled ominously. "Can you guess where the other explosive is, Victor?"

His words filled my heart with dread, and I couldn't speak.

"You know," he continued, "When Mitch finally got ahold of me and told me about the deal he'd put together to sell my boat…" He trailed off ironically. "I mean, what were the odds, right?" He laughed wistfully, looking upon the detonator. "You know, I almost felt sad when I planted the explosive on the bow—"

"You bastard!" I whispered despairingly, remembering the loud thud that had awakened me in the middle of the night. Now everything made sense: my senses going haywire, Mitch's insistence on leaving Yvette alone in the boat, and even the goddamn nickname he had used for the sale... Mr. B. Or should I say, Mr. Damian *Black*. "If you hurt her, I swear—"

"You'll do what?" he challenged. "Kill me?"

"Give me the detonator, Damian," I demanded.

He laughed. "I'll tell you what... if you manage to take it from my hand, I'll let you have it, all right? Come on, give it your best shot!" he taunted, holding the detonator at arm's length.

I lunged forward with my hand aimed at the detonator, ready to pluck it out of his hand. But a simple wave of his hand stopped me in my tracks. An invisible choker tightened around my neck and lifted me from the ground, my feet dangling as I brought my hands to my throat, gasping desperately for air. Another wave of his hand was enough to toss me away like a crumbled piece of paper. I crashed into the cooling tower, completely defeated by his extraordinary display of power.

"You idiot," he growled. "Did you really think your feeble abilities could ever match mine? I haven't even reached my peak yet. You're more pathetic than I thought! You limited your power when you blocked the absorption of dark energy—you could never be a match for me now." He stood there, watching me twist and groan in pain against the crumbled metal of the cooling tower. "Now, here's what's going to happen." He took a piece of paper out of his pocket and squatted in front of me. "You're going to run the numbers according to *my* design. And whether you like it or not, you *are* going to choose which one of these two lovely ladies is going to die today." He threw the piece of paper in my face. "These are the bomb disarming sequences. Now pay attention, because you're going to need every *variable* to make your final decision.

"It takes ten minutes to complete the disarming sequence. Now, after I press this little button on my detonator, a countdown will start on both explosives—a ten-minute timer on Ginger here, and a seventeen-minute timer on the boat where your little princess awaits. I'll explain the time difference in just a minute... Although perhaps you understand now the reason for the stopwatch I gave you. Anyway, here's the good part. I'm going to take the elevator down, and I'm going to disable it as soon as I reach the lobby. Once I do that, I'll start the timer on both explosives—"

"Damian, please!" I begged.

His face turned to stone then, his eyes piercing me with a smoldering glare. "I'd pay more attention if I were you, Victor. These are probably the last minutes you have to run your precious numbers." He took a deep breath and continued. "If you choose to save your Ginger here, all you need to do is enter the sequence I just gave you into the bomb. The timer will stop and she'll be saved. Unfortunately, that'll leave you with only seven minutes left to reach the boat, which I'm afraid won't be enough. You would have to watch your little princess burn in hell from here." He smiled. "Now, if you choose the little princess over Ginger, you'll need to go down seventeen flights of stairs and run 0.8 miles to get to the boat and get her out. I've taken the liberty of making some calculations of my own, hence the precise timing on the explosives. You see, it takes about ten minutes to reach the lobby, even if you run down the stairs, and about five minutes to run 0.8 miles in a crowded street—which would leave you with exactly two minutes left to get her out. Then again, if you do *that*… Well, you'll see some pretty amazing fireworks going off here."

He laughed. "Anyway, it's going to take me about two minutes to reach the lobby and press this little red button. So I guess that's how long you have to run your numbers, Victor… Or perhaps to say goodbye." He twisted a sardonic smile as he got to his feet. "I suppose you wish I *had* killed you now. But like I said… that would be too quick. Too easy. I want you to suffer *every single day* for whatever decision you choose to make today."

He raised his hand again and, with nothing but a tap, bashed my head against the crushed metal, leaving me dazed but conscious enough to watch him leave. "Goodbye, Victor." He turned away and strutted towards the elevator. "We're even now."

I struggled back to my feet and tried to follow him, but he was gone. Moving quickly, I strapped the stopwatch to my wrist and staggered over to Sarah, with seventeen minutes set on the timer. Swiftly, I pulled the gag off her and tried to remove the chains. But they were secured with a huge lock that imprisoned her arms behind her back—which scrapped my first idea of giving her the sequence code to disarm her bomb while I ran to help Yvette. I looked at the bomb's timer, but it was still on zero, which meant Damian hadn't reached the lobby yet.

"What are you doing?!" Sarah yelped. "Go! Save Yvette. You still have time!"

"I am NOT leaving you here to die, Sarah! So shut up and help me think!" My gaze scrambled over everything: the bomb, the chains, even the position of her hands, while my brain revved like the engine of a racecar. I closed my eyes tightly and ran the numbers in my head. Every scenario, however, gave me the same answer, the same outcome. I just didn't have enough time to save them both.

As I searched for options, a memory popped into mind: the huge metal door I'd wrenched open when I rescued Yvette and the others from R.C. Labs. I remembered how the weight of the door had pushed me back when I used my telekinesis powers to blow it off its hinges. Then it hit me! If I were to use my telekinesis to push against an immovable surface, the force would create enough pressure to push me away—it would make me bounce, even! I'd have to push with all of my energy at exactly at the right time. And although it took me a minute to analyze the variables, I knew I was right—at least in theory. And even if I weren't, it was a risk I was prepared to take. Dying seemed only right if I was to lose the people I loved... But at least I had to try.

I damn sure wasn't going down without a fight.

The loud beep on Sarah's timer made me open my eyes and press the button on the stopwatch on my wrist. The countdown was running, and there was nothing that could stop it now. I got up on my feet and took a few of steps away from Sarah. I'm sure she thought I was leaving—yet that didn't stop her from encouraging me to do so. "You're doing the right thing, Victor," she said, her eyes filled with tears. "Go! Save her." I turned around to implement the plan I had devised. But Sarah, who thought I was leaving, stopped me for one final goodbye: "Victor!" she called, her voice breaking. *I love you.*

Without wasting another second, I spun my body fiercely towards the chains that held her, the palms of my hands wide open, aiming at the lock. A connection immediately linked my mind to the metal, which began to strain at the shaking of my hands. It only took seconds for the lock to burst into pieces and the chains to drop to the ground. Sarah was free, but still in danger. With the bomb now in my hands I commanded Sarah to run. But she adamantly refused, staying right at my side.

With no time to argue I asked her to take cover while I focused on the explosive in my hands. I closed my eyes and began to levitate the bomb in front of me, lifting it higher and higher into the blue sky, until an enormous explosion threw me almost unconscious to the ground, my ears ringing, and my skin burning. But still alive.

"Victor!" Sarah's voice emerged from the piercing ringing in my ears. "Are you all right?" She ran to my aid and helped me off the ground.

Looking up into the sky, I saw a huge cloud of slowly dispersing fire and black smoke. My head was spinning as if it had been hit with a baseball bat. But then I forced my eyes to look upon the stopwatch on my wrist, where I saw ten minutes left on the timer. The bastard had set it to go off earlier than he'd told me, hoping to ensure my failure.

Ten minutes wasn't enough time to take the stairs, but then I knew that wasn't going to be my way down.

Sarah helped back on my feet, oblivious of the second part of my desperate plan. I stroked her head lovingly and turned away before she had a chance to stop me. "What are you doing?" she demanded, watching me gather momentum as I hurried towards the end of the roof.

"If I can concentrate hard enough on the asphalt, I can push against it! I can repel it from me. It'll cushion the impact, and it'll make me bounce off the ground," I explained as I trotted, uncoordinated, towards the ledge.

"Are you out of your mind?" But it was too late to stop me. *'Victor!'* Sarah's anguished call was the last thing I heard before I plunged into the abyss.

It's amazing, all the things you get to contemplate when you know you're about to die. Possibilities: that's what I thought about the most. I thought of the choices I'd never get to make, the mistakes I'd never get to mend. But most of all, I thought of Yvette, and the life I'd never get to live with her. As the asphalt rushed up at me, I realized that I had failed to include one variable in my crazy equation: that of my own fear, which had frozen me into a falling statue. Recognizing my failure, I closed my eyes and readied myself for the end. But then my father's voice began to rumble inside my head, reminding me that the jump I had just taken was none other than the leap of faith he'd always talked about. *'Now, you can be skeptical about this, and reject it. Or you can take a leap of faith—and embrace it."*

I had taken the leap… so now it was time for me to embrace it.

As my body rocketed downward, I steeled myself and aimed my hands at the ground. I instantly felt the connection I needed to stop the fall. But it wasn't enough: I had picked up too much speed and was now too close to the ground. So I pushed toward the fast-approaching Earth with everything I had, giving it one final, powerful shove just a few feet away from my deadly end. The invisible barrier I had created between me and the solid asphalt burst like a giant bubble, flinging me away from the ground and into the huge windows of the hotel lobby in one fast, violent blow. All I heard next was the roaring downpour of the shattering glass as I pierced the windows like a thrown stone, still wrapped in a weak version of the field that had saved me from pancake-hood. People must have believed that another bomb had gone off right outside the door, because they began to scream hysterically and run all over the place. *'It's a terrorist attack!"* I heard someone shout.

I forced myself to regain full consciousness, like a dazed boxer on his last count. But the world kept spinning around me, a merry-go-round on steroids. People kept shouting and screaming frantically...

'Did he just fall off the roof?"

'He bounced!"

'Is he okay?"

'Oh, my God! Is he alive?"

'Someone call 911!"

One of the bystanders knelt right next me and said, "Relax, buddy. You shouldn't move."

"What?" His words snapped me out of my daze, making me realize I was, indeed, still alive. But there was no time to celebrate; my race against time wasn't over yet. I grabbed my wrist and brought the stopwatch to my face, trying to focus my bleary eyes on the countdown I was trying so desperately to beat. Eight minutes and fifty-five-seconds were all I had left to get my Yvee off the boat now, and every second counted. The shards of glass covering my body fell like raindrops on the marble floor as I staggered back to my feet. Once oriented, I darted towards the pier, trying desperately to turn my painful limping into a run. But my seventeen-floor drop, along with my glass-shattering impact, had left me in sad shape. I was cut, bruised, and bleeding profusely. Something was stuck in my leg, too—probably a piece of glass. But that didn't stop me, and neither did the shouting from the security guards, who alternately yelled at me to stop and called for help. My hypersenses were back in order, and I heard one of them talking over his radio, giving my description and location to the LAPD.

I glanced at the stopwatch again, and saw less than five minutes left on the timer. I ignored the excruciating pain and ran faster towards the pier. My anguish and desperation were pushing my body to its limits, but I didn't care. Getting to Yvette was all it mattered. I had to get to that boat—even if it was only to die with her. *Please, God!* I prayed. *If you're going to take her, don't you leave me behind!* Tears of frustration began to run down my face. *Please!* I begged.

A rush of adrenaline hit me then, making me push forward as I reached the entrance for Shoreline Village. I was almost there; I could see the boat rocking gently at the dock. Yvette had raised the sailboat's ensign to full staff and she was waiting for me; I could feel it, and tried to send her a warning through our connection. I could hear the loud sirens of the police cruisers wailing behind me as I elbowed through the crowd.

"There he is!" someone shouted. I didn't turn around; I couldn't afford to waste a second. I looked down at the stopwatch again, just to see three minutes and thirty-two seconds left on the timer. My knees failed me then, and I collapsed on the ground, just thirty feet from the boat. I looked up, and there she was: my angel, my life, standing on the main deck smiling. Her beautiful black hair fluttered in the wind while her eyes scanned the clear, blue skies, as if looking for the perfect spot to give thanks above for the happiness she felt.

"Yvette!" I shouted at the top of my lungs, but my voice was drowned in the uproar of the crowd. "Yvette!" I shouted again, but to no avail.

Though she couldn't hear me, I knew she'd be okay. I knew I still had enough time to get her out. I just needed another minute to get close enough to warn her. Then she would jump out of the boat and we'd both take cover, which we could surely do in less than two minutes—and I still had three and a half left on the clock. *I've made it!* I said to myself. *I've made it! I just need to get a little closer—just a little closer, and I'll be with the one I love again.* So, I forced myself back on my feet and began to limp towards the boat again, with three minutes and twenty-six seconds left on the timer—minutes I was never meant to have.

Because once again, Damian had cheated me.

A powerful blast swatted me into the air, stripping from me heart, mind, and soul. A huge cloud of smoke and fire was all that was left of the pedestal where my angel had once stood. I hated my eyes for what they were making me see, so I refused to believe them. "No," I denied with sentiment. "No, no, no, no…"

But soon my reason overcame my denial.

"NOOOOOOOOOOOOOOOOOOOOOO!!!" A heart-rending bawl ripped from the deepest corners of my soul. "NOOOOOOOOOOOOOOOOOOOOOO!!!" And I continued, until my voice and lungs were forced to give up, "NOOOOO…"

I crawled towards the burning boat, consumed with an unfathomable pain, watching the fire spread beyond containment. The flames that engulfed what was left of the boat were too ferocious to even think of the possibility of survival. Yet I kept crawling towards it with my face soaked in blood and tears, calling my angel's name.

Maybe I was already losing my mind, but I thought that if I got close enough I would be able to find her, and hold her, and tell her that everything was going to be all right. I thought that if I could just find her, I'd bury my face in her hair and entwine my fingers with hers, just as we used to… But my goddamn reason kicked in again, and I was forced to accept the truth.

My Yvee was gone… gone! And no force, power, or ability in the world was going to bring her back. I would never see her face again. I would never smell her hair, kiss her lips, or feel her touch. Her voice would never strike that chord in my heart again, the one she played every time she said *I love you*.

The moment I realized these facts, I stopped dead in my tracks, and something in my heart began to darken.

I remember the next few minutes as the last of Victor Bellator—the last few minutes of the man I once was, and would never again be. An epiphany took up most of this time, enlightening me with a reality that I had always sought to ignore. I came to understand many things in those few moments, things I would otherwise have never even considered. One of them was the reason behind Damian's revenge, and how he had succeeded with his plan, which I now understood was *never* meant to test my resolve over whether or not I'd choose Sarah over Yvette. Apparently, he already knew the answer to that. No, his sadistic plan—other than to watch me sacrifice someone who loved me for someone I loved—was to get me as close and powerless to Yvette as he was to Sonya when he watched her die... and then to watch me mourn them both as I had watched him mourn his beloved wife. And though he didn't get to kill Sarah, I knew he saw his victory as complete, from wherever he was watching.

"*Freeze!*" The voice of a police officer reminded me that I was still alive—in body, that is—and that my presence at the crime scene, looking the way I did, needed to be explained. "*Stay on the ground!*"

Ignoring their commands, I got to my feet and stared blankly at the fire. I heard them order me to surrender, but I wasn't ready for them yet. I wasn't ready to let go of that fire.

Instead, I decided to go back to my epiphany, before making the biggest decision of my life.

As I watch the fire consume all my hopes and dreams, I remembered the words of my counterpart, the one I had chosen to call evil. He'd warned me about this in the cavern of my nightmare—about *me* not being strong enough to protect the people I loved. He gave me the choice to keep them safe, and all I had to do was let him out. All I had to do was give in to the same power Damian had, a power that would not only have made me stronger, but would have helped me keep the person I loved the most out of harm's way. But I didn't want to listen— then. My *"delusional views of morality,"* as he so eloquently put it, got in the way. And now Yvette was dead. All because I chose to believe that *good* always needed to prevail over *evil*.

Good and *evil*, *right* and *wrong*. What the hell are these, if not just words? Wouldn't it have been 'good' to stop Damian? Wouldn't it have been 'good' to save Yvette? Wouldn't it have been 'good' to be powerful enough to avert all these things from happening in the first place? Of course it would have. But I chose a different path; the path I thought to be the right one at the time, the *good* one. Now I could only see 'good' as the perception in which we determine our own reality—and my reality had changed, violently and completely. My reason for existence had been taken from me, and I had been left behind in this cynical world with nothing but pain.

There was only one way for me to make sense of my existence now, and that was that I had been left behind to render justice to the memory of the people who'd fallen in vain. People like Tom, Barbara, Billie, Roger, Denali, Sonya. And of course, my beloved Yvette, for whom I was ready to go to any extremity to avenge. But in order to do this, I needed enough power to defeat my adversaries. And Damian couldn't have been any clearer when he'd beaten me earlier on the roof. *My feeble abilities were no match for his ever-growing power.* And he was now not only my biggest adversary, but my primary target.

I knew what I had to do now… and it pained me.

"Victor!" Sarah's voice made me turn as tears slid down my face. I looked for her among the dozens of police officers who were crowding the street, and found her between two of them. They were holding her back, keeping her from approaching their primary suspect, at whom all their guns were aimed. "Victor!" she called again. "Just do as they say. Please!" Tears glazed her beautiful green eyes.

"She's gone, Sarah," I said, my voice breaking. "She's gone…"

"Don't move! Turn around and put your hands behind your head!" the officer in charge commanded. Yet he kept ordering the squad—through his radio—to hold their fire and restrain from approaching the subject. It was obvious they thought they had their bomber. They probably thought I had another bomb on me, or perhaps a device that could detonate another somewhere else—who knows? But they were definitely reluctant to make a move.

"I should've listened," I told Sarah between sobs. "I should've listened…"

"Victor!" Sarah managed to slip away from the officers' restraint. But she was quickly stopped again and held back. "Look at me!" she cried. "I know you're hurting, but this doesn't have to end like this. You don't have to die, Victor. Please!"

"Die?" I considered that, glancing at the fire. "It's too late for that, Sarah. Victor Bellator is already dead. And soon, all the people who have ever hurt him will be dead too. I wasn't strong enough to save her. But I *swear* that I will be strong enough to avenge her." Certain of my final decision, I turned back to Sarah and softened my eyes for her—almost as if saying *thank you*. A sad smile pulled faintly at the corners of my lips as I said, "Good-bye, Sarah."

Sarah's eyes bulged, as if finally realizing my terrible resolution, and pleaded, "Victor—no!" But it was too late.

I closed my eyes, and began to voluntarily call upon the change I had so desperately tried to escape from before. A vortex of power began to whirl inside my head, rearranging memories as it saw fit—memories that had shaped the man I once was. In vivid flashes I saw my Dad, his hand on the handlebars of my bike as he guided me through a beautiful green field; Mrs. Montgomery, reading me a bedtime story as she stroked my head with motherly hands; Xavier, living with me the moments that only two brothers can share. And I saw Yvette, soothing my heart with a smile, as only an angel would have known how to do.

Soon all these memories began to fade away into the eye of the vortex, as if sucked in to be lost for all eternity. But this wasn't the end. The internal tornado then spun backwards and began to deliver all the painful memories of my past. In vivid flashes, I saw the things that had hurt me the most. I relived my accident, as well as the pain of losing my best friend. I saw Xavier's funeral... I saw my Dad's. I remembered the pain of losing him and the years of agony I'd suffered through with my condition. I tasted Dr. Walker's betrayal as I saw him lie to me over and over again. A sharp feeling of pain knocked on my chest when I saw Denali's blood in my hands, and remembered that last lonely tear that had trickled down his face.

The tornado arranged these images in the forefront of my mind in a collage of pain that I could no longer shake off or ignore, where the background that held it all together was the death of my precious Yvette. The agony was so unbearable I thought that it alone would kill me. But instead, an uncontrollable anger began to take over, soothing away the pain the memory tornado had left behind. The more I felt it, the less I hurt. The more I tasted my desire for vengeance, the more purpose I found to go on.

An addictive feeling of euphoria overwhelmed my senses, allowing me to feel the dark energy flow through my body, saturating my brain with an intoxicating feeling of power—unlimited power.

When I opened my eyes, things were exactly as I'd seen them last; in real-time, Victor's death and my birth had taken place in a split second. Not a thing had changed, yet everything was different. My eyes burned with delicious power; and though I couldn't see them myself, I knew they had changed from their natural dull brown to a puissant silver. I turned to the burning boat one last time and stared, feeling nothing but emptiness. My tears had dried, and my new eyes could no longer cry.

I felt nothing.

And that only increased my rage even further.

"Victor?" Sarah called upon a name that no longer had any meaning for me, yet I turned around all the same. "Victor..." she whispered, tears running down her face. *Poor Sarah*, I thought. *She shouldn't waste her tears on me.* Yet I didn't feel bad; not because I didn't want to, but because I couldn't feel anymore. That capacity had been burned out of me. My humanity, my heart, had died with Yvette.

"Get down on your knees and put your hands behind your head! This is your final warning!" the officer in charge commanded again, aiming his gun directly at my head.

My hypersenses reached out toward the group of officers. *'We have Intel on the subject,'* I heard over the cop's radio. *"Get ready to take him down."*

The officer in charged acknowledged.

"NO!" Sarah shouted. "Don't hurt him!"

"Get her out of here!" the commander ordered the two men restraining Sarah, who spun her around to cuff her.

"Let her go." The growl that came from my mouth was almost unnatural, enough to frighten the two cops to their cores. I could smell their fear, taste it, hear it in their accelerated heartbeats. They stopped and looked at me, dumbfounded. "Let her go," I said again, my voice returned to its natural pitch. Then I began to walk toward them.

"Stop!" the commanding officer shouted, watching me take my first step forward. His finger began to tighten on the trigger of his Police Special...but he stood down the moment I showed him my hands, faintly raised and palms open, aiming directly at him. *Poor fool,* I thought. *He probably thinks I'm surrendering.*

As I stepped forward, a wave of healing energy washed through me. I felt my cuts close, and a faint cool sensation as my bruises faded. The glass dagger popped out of my leg with a faint pulling sensation. Smirking, I told my ripped clothing to be whole again, and the drying blood on my skin to powder and drift away. This happened in an instant—and then I sent a gigantic wave of energy into the group of cops, scattering them like bowling pins. Some were propelled backwards so hard they smashed through buildings; some landed dazed on the ground; while others crashed into cars parked along the boulevard. I lost count of how many of them squirmed on the ground over their injuries, and how many just didn't move anymore. I honestly didn't care. That was the beauty of my new state.

I looked at the street where the police standoff had once been and saw nothing but empty police cruisers, their red and blue flashing lights still whirling. A wave of my hands crushed each of them into cubes no greater than three feet on a side; I vaguely hoped no one was still inside, but again, I couldn't give a damn. Then I turned to the only two cops I hadn't hurled away: the ones holding Sarah, which were standing frozen like statues. In this case it was their own fear holding them in place, not my power. I walked over to them and repeated my command one last time: "I said, let her go."

The two cops let go of Sarah then, with their eyes bulging in fear, fixed on me. Sarah elbowed one of them in the stomach, took his sidearm out of his holster, and pointed the gun at them. "Back off!" she wailed, her hands trembling. The two cops exchanged uneasy looks after they met my eyes. Whatever they saw in them was enough to make them run and take cover behind a pair of the crushed cruisers, which were just barely large enough to offer them illusory protection.

Sarah lowered the weapon and looked at me with frightful eyes.

More sirens wailed at the end of the street, and police cruisers began to corner into the boulevard. One of the survivors had called for reinforcements and they were now on their way. Listening to their radio transmissions, I realized they weren't coming to arrest me… not anymore. They had different orders now, and they were coming from higher levels of government. But I laughed at the idea that any of these ordinary humans could take me down, so I stood in the middle of the street and waited for them to come.

"Please don't kill them, Victor!" Sarah shouted.

I didn't acknowledge her, but as I felt them reach the threshold of my ever-growing power, I raised my hands and took aim, automatically compensating for what was to come by bracing myself against the Earth. I flexed my hands and cruiser after cruiser was crushed to ruin; not entirely, but enough to render them useless while keeping those inside them alive. Needless to say, the drivers lost control and some began to crash into each other; a few flipped and slid over the shiny boulevard. As I watched the injured cops crawl out of their vehicles, I noticed the power line that hung above them. I took aim at it, and with a wave of my hand I yanked it off the pole. The high voltage wire swiped over one of the flipped cruisers, making contact with the gas tank, producing a shower of sparks and then an explosion that spread a sheet of flame across the street.

"Victor!" Sarah called desperately from behind me. "Please, stop!"

I turned around and faced her, eyes smoldering.

She started and raised the gun in her hands. "You're not going to hurt me, are you?" Her question sounded more like a statement. But she shuddered when she saw me raise my hand, my lithium eyes piercing right through her. She realized then I was no longer the Victor she had fallen in love with. "Victor…" she whined, unable to contain her sobs anymore, "Please… don't."

As my hand began to clench with the rage that now defined me, Sarah closed her eyes and put a trembling finger over the trigger. A loud thud made her open her eyes again, just to realize that my rage had been aimed at a cop behind her—a cop who would have shot her had I not interfered. He laid on the ground now, his neck broken.

She took a look at him and gasped.

Her eyes flew right back to me as she heard me approach, her gun still aimed at me. "Do it," I demanded. "You know you have to. It's the only way."

"I can't!" she cried. "Please! Just come back to me! I know you're still in there… I love you! I can't replace Yvette, but I can still save you!"

"The Victor you loved is dead," I said coldly, "and nothing in the world can bring him back." I considered her for a moment as the last spark of humanity fizzled in my cold heart. "If you really loved him," I told her, "then you know what to do."

Her eyes came back to life then, and she refocused her aim at my head. Her eyes looked determined now, and no more tears escaped from them. As she began to pull the trigger, my senses alerted me of the danger, allowing me to slip into the slow motion trance in which I was rendered vulnerable to my surroundings. For I focused on Sarah and on Sarah alone. I wanted to sense her, to feel her one last time before jumping to the Other Side to be with Yvette and my father. Her heart was beating faster than I'd ever sensed it before, and her breathing was rapid; but her hands were steady now, her jaw taut, as if ready to carry out the most difficult decision of her life.

I could sense the gun's mechanism moving now, the hammer pulling back. But I wasn't going to stop it. I *wanted* this; or at least, that last puny grain of humanity left in me did. In a fraction of a second I considered death as fulfilling as my desire for revenge, perhaps even more. But Sarah needed to hurry, because that grain of humanity left was fast disappearing inside my hardening heart.

The bullet was fired, leaving the smoky gun barrel behind. A strange feeling of relief washed over me, yet I wasn't sure what to make of it. I suppose that, deep inside my wretched soul, I really was hoping to be on my way to the netherworld, where, if I was lucky enough, I just might find my Yvee. But as I watched the bullet approach, I realized its trajectory was off. My last tinge of humanity vanished then, and rage took over. Stupid wench, she couldn't even aim worth a damn! My slow-motion trance broke abruptly as the projectile passed me by, missing completely.

Yet I managed to follow its trail, watching the bullet pierce the shoulder of a cop behind me. The gun in his hands suggested he was just seconds away from killing me. The injured man fell on the ground cursing at Sarah, who regarded him with a black look as she finally lowered the gun. I kicked the gun away from the cop's hand and turned to Sarah with angry eyes. "You missed!" I accused.

"I never miss," she corrected flatly.

"You shouldn't have done that," I said. "Now you'll never have that chance again."

"I know." She dropped the gun and ran to me with open arms. She threw her arms around me and buried her head in my chest, as if planning to never let go. But I couldn't hug her back; I was indifferent to her pain now. At the same time, though, I didn't want her to hurt anymore. I doubt I felt compassion, but rather a sense of righteousness. Even with my new personality, I never thought of myself as evil. Surrendering to the force of this dark energy had merely adjusted my perception to the true reality.

I still wanted to do *good*, to do what was right. Only 'good' and 'right' were now based solely on my own point of view. Sarah had suffered enough, and she didn't deserve to be hurt any further. Letting her go was only *right*, just as finding Damian to rip his throat out was *right*. And so was killing every single person involved in the creation and maintenance of R.C. Labs, starting with Dr. Walker. Every person. Anyone who became an obstacle to my plans…well, in my eyes they would become an evil hindrance, trying to stop me from fulfilling my sense of what was *good* and *right*. Therefore they would have to die.

Sensing the rotors of helicopters approaching from miles away made me realize it was time for me to get moving. So I took Sarah by the shoulders and pushed her away from me. "Go home, Sarah. There's nothing more you can do for me. It's time for you to put this behind you. Go, and never look back."

"No! I won't leave you! I'm coming with you."

"There's no redemption or absolution where I'm going, Sarah. Following me will be the biggest mistake you'll ever make in your life, and will only cause you pain." I paused, discovering that my mind was now able to search her feelings, as it had with Yvette before. "I can read you now," I told her, "and what you're feeling is something I'll never be able to feel again... do you understand? I have nothing to give you. Nothing to offer you but pain and misery. The person you want me to be, the man you want to go with, is no longer here."

I felt Sarah's eyes fill with tears of dismay as I turned and began my first steps on the dark path poor Roger had warned me about, a path that had only one end. My future was now a clear equation filled with unknown variables, variables I needed to find and fit into place in order to obtain my desired outcome: a final confrontation with my nemesis. But I knew this wasn't going to be easy, especially considering Damian's alliance with Walker. Finding these variables might just take me some time,

I thought, although I was prepared to spend the rest of my life avenging my angel.

But then one of the variables presented itself as I walked down the burning boulevard, one that in my previous incarnation I wouldn't have allowed myself to use. The rear window of a crashed van in the middle of the street reflected Sarah behind me. She was exactly as my last words had left her: dismayed, speechless, and frozen statue-still. But then a deep breath brought her back to life, and she fiercely wiped the tears off her face. Then she crouched and picked up the gun she had dropped before, along with the one I'd kicked out of the cop's hand.

She got to her feet and began to walk in my direction, tucking both guns into the waist of her jeans, one in the back and one in the front, as if ready to confront all the demons she knew lay ahead. As I watched her pick up her pace, I realized she had made her decision. She was coming with me. In spite of all my efforts to keep her out of harm's way, she was coming with me. I couldn't help but twist a painful smile as I realized the truth: there was nothing I could have said to Sarah that would have kept her away. She was in love... Just like Victor once was. And just like Victor, she would ignore any logic and reason if that prevented her from being close to the one she loved.

It almost made me feel jealous, because I wasn't Victor... not anymore. I was now that dark counterpart he'd dreaded so much. The one who, despite his best efforts, was always meant to govern his mind. There was never an alternative, cure, or escape. I was always meant to be the one to prevail. I understood it then better than ever before. As I walked down the burning road, tightening my fist, I tasted the power overflowing my mind—the darkness ruling my heart, the malevolence glowing in my eyes.

The predominance of evil was finally complete.

Epilogue
The List

AFTER WATCHING WHAT became known as the Shoreline Village Incident from afar, Damian Black returned to Ketchikan, where Dr. Walker had begun working on his latest protocol. According to him, it would endow Damian with the abilities he had expected from Yvette Montgomery, yet never had the chance to harness. That was the bargain Dr. Walker had made with Damian: he wanted to continue to probe into the mysterious energy he had discovered. He had convinced Damian that if they worked together, they'd be able to unravel all its secrets—including the one that would allow them to communicate with the energy that leaves the body after one dies.

Damian, obsessed with the idea of speaking again with his dead wife, agreed to work with Walker. They both had a common interest now, as well as a common enemy. Victor, who had turned to malevolence, was coming for revenge, and they both knew it.

"He will come," Damian said to Walker. "I can assure you of that."

"You should've killed him when you had the chance," Walker snapped.

"That wasn't part of my plan," Damian explained calmly. "I never meant to kill him. I'm afraid I had ulterior motives, Doctor. As long as Victor presents a threat to you, you'll have no choice but to honor the agreement you've made with me."

"What makes you so sure of that?" Walker asked with a taunting smile.

Damian sprang from where he was sitting and walked menacingly towards Walker. "Victor's growing stronger by the minute, and he's no longer the goody-goody Boy Scout he was before. And when he finds you—because believe me, he *will* find you—the only thing standing between his hand and your throat will be me. So I'd suggest you consider your situation before even trying screwing with me."

Walker smiled nervously. "Well, then. If that's the case, you should also remember that I'm the one who can help increase your powers. And knowing what I know about Victor, you're going to need all the help you can get."

Damian considered for a moment and said, "Then I guess we're partners after all," sticking his hand out.

Dr. Walker smiled and shook his hand. "Indeed we are."

Back in California, Victor and Sarah had managed to elude the LAPD, with the judicious application of Victor's new-found powers. After retrieving his belongings from the hotel room he'd once shared with Yvette, he decided to hijack a car and drive two hours south into Mexico. Once in Tijuana, they stopped to take stock of the situation.

Victor sat by the window of a small bar and ordered a drink. While Sarah watched, he set his backpack on the table and began to go through his things. His newly gray eyes narrowed with confusion as he pulled a stack of letters out of his pack—the same stack of letters he'd found in Yvette's room before he'd rescued her from R.C. Labs.

He untied the red ribbon that bound them together and began to read the first one on the pile, which had an envelope marked "Return to Sender."

Dear Dad,

I know I should probably stop writing you letters, since you have never answered any of them. But writing to you makes me feel like I haven't lost you completely. Even with your silence I feel less alone... Anyway, I'm happy to tell you that I've finally completed my intense program at the dance conservatory, and that I'll soon be performing in the city. I'm very excited, because it's the same role Mom performed last on Broadway. I only wish I could be as good as she was. I know it sounds strange because she's gone, but... I really hope I can make her proud. Perhaps one day, you could be proud of me too. I know it's a long shot, but I'd love for you to come and see me on opening night. Perhaps we can use this as an excuse for you to finally come out of hiding and answer the question that's been haunting me for years... Why?

Victor stopped reading, and pondered for a moment as an idea struck him. After a pregnant pause, he pulled a pen and paper out of his backpack and began to write.

"What are you doing?" Sarah asked him, taking a sip from her beer.

"I'm making a little list," Victor said casually.

"A list of what?" she asked.

Victor stopped and leaned over the table, letting out a long sigh, his fingers interlocked. "I just realized that Yvette was hurt by a lot more people than I thought. And if I'm to render justice, I should be thorough—hence the list. These are the names of the people I'm planning on paying a visit to before I die." He smiled ominously.

"I thought your plan was to confront Damian," she said nervously, knowing full well what he meant by *paying a visit*. She took another sip of her beer, trying to cover her dread.

"Don't worry," Victor said, "We'll get there." He ordered another drink and continued with his list. When he was finished, he slid the list across the table and raised his eyes to meet Sarah's. "Now, some of these people may be difficult to find. But I want you to track them down. I'm sure you'll be better at it than I."

Sarah looked at the long list and clenched her jaw, feeling Victor's eyes scrutinizing her for hesitancy. She knew that was what he wanted: he was only waiting for her to show the slightest sign of weakness, so he could leave her behind and disappear on her forever. But Sarah wasn't going to let that happen. She loved him too much. Besides, she had a plan of her own—and she knew that in order to have the slightest shot at it, she needed to gain this...*Dark* Victor's complete trust. She was convinced that there was still good in him somewhere— and that if pain had made him turn away from good, then maybe love could make him turn away from evil. Maybe *her* love.

"Is there a problem?" Victor asked, suspicious yet disturbingly calm.

Sarah's eyes rose from the list and met Victor's, which were studying her every move. "No," she said, her voice hard. "There's no problem."

"I wonder how much I should trust you," Victor said, a dubious smile on his face.

"You said you can read my feelings," Sarah noted. "You tell me."

Victor's smile broadened.

Sarah realized then that she had accomplished the first part of her plan, yet she knew the next part was going to be a lot harder. She needed to make him fall in love with her—strongly enough to make him turn away from evil. But she didn't know how deep his feelings were buried, or how long it was going to take to make them resurface. Of one thing she was absolutely sure, however. She was going to make it happen, or die with him while trying. "So," she began with a brand new demeanor, a flirty smile on her face. "To what should we toast?"

"Vengeance?" Victor proposed.

Sarah frowned. "No. To new beginnings."

Victor smiled, lifted his glass in the air, and drank.

***

Meanwhile, at Long Beach Memorial Hospital, Detective Lawrence Perry of the LAPD was walking down the shiny white corridor with his partner, Detective Juana Pesantes. She was giving him the latest report on what had happened at the Hyatt Regency as well as at Shoreline Village.

"So how many fatalities do we have so far?" Detective Perry interrupted.

"Five," Pesantes answered quickly, gesturing with a folder in her hands. "Including a boat broker named Mitch Goodman, who was found in one of the hotel rooms with his neck twisted so far around it was facing backwards. Forensics is having a hard time determining how that was possible. Same with one of the officers who responded to the Shoreline Village Incident."

"Hmm," Perry considered. "What about injuries?"

"Twenty police officers and ten civilians. Most of them were too close to the second explosion at the pier. Oh, this way." She led the way to the next corridor.

"What do we know about our suspects?"

"They've been identified as Victor Bellator and Sarah Grey. Intel on Bellator was provided by a Captain Black from the DOD during the standoff. Bellator was said to be armed and extremely dangerous. We're still trying to get more information on the woman."

Perry stopped in his tracks and mused. "The DOD? You mean the Department of Defense? Are they giving us any jurisdictional crap about this?"

"No, not at all," Pesantes said, sounding a bit confused herself. "They're actually asking us to remain involved in the investigation."

Perry exhaled heavily. "What do you make of all this?"

"I don't know," she sighed. "I guess we're going to have to wait until one of the injured officers can make a statement about what happened."

"You mean none of them are ready to talk yet?"

"I'm afraid most of them are still in ICU."

Perry scowled at Pesantes. "Then why the hell did you ask me to meet you here?"

"Well, there's something else. Come on." She walked him to a restricted room and stopped at the door. "There."

Perry looked through the grilled window with narrowed eyes. "Who is she?" he asked, looking at a girl sleeping on the bed.

"Exactly," she replied, looking at her folder again. "She's been listed as a Jane Doe: Female Caucasian, early twenties, black over blue, and apparently absolutely no memory of who she is. But if you ask me, I think she may be involved in what happened."

"What makes you think that?" Perry asked, intrigued.

"Well, for one thing, she was holding this when she was pulled out of the water." Pesantes showed Perry a dog-eared picture with a single person in it.

Perry's eyes widened as he took it in his hands. "Is that…?"

"Yep," Pesantes confirmed. "What do you want me to do with her?"

Perry looked through the window again and pondered. "Who else knows about her?" he asked.

"Just you, me, the guards, and the medical staff."

"Let's keep it that way, Pesantes. And move her into protective custody as soon as the doctor gives the okay. Something tells me this girl may be in danger. Look at her," he said, gazing at her with fatherly eyes. "You see a suspect, but I see a target."

Pesantes considered the girl with a troubled look on her face. "Yeah, well… either way, I have a bad feeling about this."